PENGUIN BOOKS

WATER ON THE BRAIN

Compton Mackenzie was born in West Hartlepool in 1883. He was educated at St Paul's School and Magdalen College, Oxford. During the First World War he became a Captain in the Royal Marines, becoming Director of the Aegean Intelligence Service. He wrote more than ninety books – novels, history and biography, essays and criticism, children's stories and verse, and was also an outstanding broadcaster. He founded and edited until 1961 the magazine the *Gramophone*, and was President of the Siamese Cat Club. He lived for many years on the Island of Barra in the Outer Hebrides, but later settled in Edinburgh. He was knighted in 1952. His last book was *My Life and Times: Octave Ten* (1971). Compton Mackenzie died in 1972.

WATER ON THE BRAIN

Compton Mackenzie

PENGUIN BOOKS
in association with Chatto & Windus

Penguin Books Ltd, Harmondsworth, Middlesex, England
Penguin Books, 625 Madison Avenue, New York, New York 10022, U.S.A.
Penguin Books Australia Ltd, Ringwood, Victoria, Australia
Penguin Books Canada Ltd, 2801 John Street, Markham, Ontario, Canada L3R 1B4
Penguin Books (N.Z.) Ltd, 182–190 Wairau Road, Auckland 10, New Zealand

—

First published by Chatto & Windus 1933
Published in Penguin Books 1959
Reprinted 1977

—

Copyright © the Estate of Compton Mackenzie, 1933

—

Made and printed in Great Britain
by Richard Clay (The Chaucer Press), Ltd,
Bungay, Suffolk
Set in Linotype Pilgrim

TO
SIR ROBERT RAIT,
C.B.E., LL.D.

CONTENTS

Preface to the 1954 Edition

Water on the Brain was written immediately after my trial at the Old Bailey under the Official Secrets Act. At the time, the book must have seemed to the average reader a fantastic Marx Brothers affair, but during the Second World War many more people discovered that those responsible for Secret Intelligence do, in very fact, as often as not behave like characters created by the Marx Brothers. *Duck Soup*, for instance, appealed to me as a film of stark realism.

Water on the Brain at one time looked like becoming a serious textbook for neophytes of the Secret Service, and indeed if it had not for a time been so difficult to get hold of, it probably would have become a standard work. People who knew the book were convinced that the Edinburgh police had been studying it before the 'conspiracy' trial of four young Scots was embarked upon in November 1953. It has indeed become impossible for me to devise any ludicrous situation the absurdity of which will not soon be surpassed by officialdom.

The film world is still under the impression that *Water on the Brain* might get them into trouble if it were produced as a film. The project has been mooted many times in the last twenty years, but in the end it always fell through because 'They' might not like it, and if 'They' did not like it that might be disadvantageous to the prospects of the film industry in Britain. Quite a number of people believe that I was prosecuted for writing *Water on the Brain* and revealing the secrets of Pomona Lodge.

In a letter to the late Principal of Glasgow University, to whom *Water on the Brain* is dedicated, I insisted that my book was 'only a grotesque fairy tale'. I have little hope that the public's wider experience of the absurdities of Secret Intelligence will persuade them to accept this disclaimer, but I must insist that the book is intended to be comic, and if it does not succeed in being as comic as Intelligence I must plead the impossibility of painting the lily.

31 Drummond Place,
Edinburgh,
March 1954

Chapter 1

THE CALL OF MAJOR BLENKINSOP

ABOUT ten o'clock on a foggy November morning in the year
193– Major Arthur Blenkinsop was sitting by the electric heater
of a small dining-room in a service flat on the seventh floor of
Jerbury Chambers, Jerbury Street, St James's, and waiting for
his wife to come in to breakfast. It was not entirely conjugal
politeness which kept him from his eggs and bacon. He had
made three attempts within twenty minutes to persuade the
kitchen of Jerbury Chambers to provide him with food; but on
the third occasion when he had called sharply down the
whistling-tube to know why breakfast had not been sent up to
number twenty-eight, the cook, or one of her minions, had
blown the question as sharply back into his mouth with such a
strong flavour of burnt grease added as temporarily to deprive
him of even the beginning of an appetite for eggs and bacon.
Throwing down the *Morning Boast*, he now stepped firmly
across to his wife's door to ask a little less firmly :

'Enid, darling, are you nearly ready?'

'Bunny, I've been ready hours!' came the gently indignant
voice of Mrs Blenkinsop from the bedroom, and a moment
later came Mrs Blenkinsop herself.

'I've tried three times to get them to send up breakfast,' the
Major sighed. 'I wish you'd try, darling.'

Mrs Blenkinsop's voice when she had answered her husband
had possessed an exquisitely soft note of wifely devotion. That
gentle voice now dropped like an icicle down the whistling-
tube.

'This is Mrs Blenkinsop speaking. Breakfast was ordered half
an hour ago. Where is it?'

She put her ear to the tube, and immediately afterwards her
mouth.

'Very well, I hope it will not be necessary to send for the
housekeeper,' she said coldly. Then hanging up the tube Mrs
Blenkinsop turned to her husband, once again as soft as her
own powder-puff.

'Poor Bunny,' she murmured with a healing smile.

The epithet suggests an exterior for Major Blenkinsop which might prevent the reader's recognizing him. He was not in the least like a rabbit. With his large teeth, his gaunt lengthy jaw, and heavy deliberate gait, he suggested in a small room the presence of a horse. In fact when he was in the trenches with the Welch Bays during the war he was almost the only link his brother officers had with the cavalry. Mrs Blenkinsop called him 'Bunny' because she had called her first love that, and had allowed the habit to grow upon her during the series of semi-engagements which had culminated in her marriage to Arthur Blenkinsop. She was now a well-preserved woman trembling on the brink of thirty and still unable to persuade herself to take the plunge. Her hair had kept the honied brown which had been her parents' pride at twelve. Her cheeks, if the texture of rose-leaves was less evident, were still rosy. Like many another woman towards the close of the nineteen-twenties she had plumped out; but that could be regarded as a tribute to fashion, not as a surrender to maturity. Three years ago Enid Madison had accompanied her father, General Sir Charles Madison, to test a legend at the Service clubs that living was cheaper on the Continent than at home, and in the course of the General's wanderings in search of a place where nothing was not English except the coinage and the postage stamps they had discovered the island of Parvo off the coast of Mendacia, one of those small nations for whose rights the General had refused to sheath his sword until they were safe in the bosom of bureaucracy. Here at the Hotel Multum they found an earthly paradise for Englishmen.

Parvo was owned by John Blenkinsop, who, after serving through the war as Deputy-Assistant Controller of Agricultural Implements at one of the new Ministries with the temporary rank of Lieutenant-Colonel, had retired with a C.B.E., the eighth class of the Chinese Order of the Excellent Crop, and a largish sum of money to invest. His younger brother Arthur, who had been sent to Mendacia on a Boundary Commission after the Peace of Versailles, had brought back an enthusiastic account of the prospects of Parvo as a place of retirement and diversion for English people, free from frost, fleas, and income-tax, and endowed with a possibility of marvellous golf, a perfect summer climate, and a medieval castle that could easily be turned into an up-to-date hotel with, it was hoped, unlimited baths and good water for tea. John Blenkinsop had displayed the same vision and the same grasp of essentials which had marked his control of agricultural implements. Four years after the Peace of Versailles, when it had been found impossible to argue any longer about the boundaries of Mendacia, Arthur Blenkinsop retired from the Army with the rank of Major in order to act as his brother's representative at the Hotel Multum.

The enterprise had flourished so well at first that every gossip writer in the Press could always rely on it for two paragraphs at any season of the year. Old Sir Charles Madison had per-suaded two other generals, an admiral, and no fewer than five colonels to take up their residence permanently in the jolly little bungalows which John Blenkinsop and the Multum in Parvo Company (Ltd) had erected on the low cliffs above the emerald Adriatic. Enid Madison, chiefly no doubt under the influence of the Mendacian moon, but a little perhaps with the idea of reigning permanently as Queen of Parvo, had accepted the hand of Arthur Blenkinsop and was married to him by the Anglican Bishop of South-East Europe, who was taking his sun-cure on Parvo that year.

Then the first omen of disaster had befallen. General Madi-son, who had been looking forward to an idyllic old age of golf and bridge, died a violent death, having been struck on the right temple by a golf-ball driven by a young Jugo-Slovakian who had not realized that he could hit a ball yet and to whom unkind fate lent a merciless precision of aim when he was less than thirty yards from the General at that moment addressing, after a bad foozle, his own ball with a brassey. The sensational press of a neighbouring great Power, ever on the look out to make the worst of things in Mendacia, magnified the un-fortunate accident into an attempt to upset the republic and restore King Johannis to the throne from which he had been driven during the deliberations of the Boundary Commission. Rumour buzzed at home like a bluebottle in a lamp-globe. The season at Parvo was ruined, and at that moment the gossip-writers and Miss Elsa Maxwell discovered a new *plage*. Within three years of Enid Madison's marriage the Multum in Parvo Company (Ltd) ceased to pay a dividend; and here she was, living with her husband in a furnished service flat in St James's, he wondering if, should the worst come to the worst, he might get a job at the B.B.C., she moderately amused by the novelty of buying winter clothes again. Not that they were more than relatively poor. They had twelve hundred a year between them, and if only Arthur could get a job in which his social qualities would have scope they would be really comfortable.

During this brief history breakfast had arrived, brought up by one of those crosses between a chimney-sweep and an errand-boy which still survive in service flats under the name of valets. Major Blenkinsop cleverly recognized the mess on his plate as bacon and eggs, and started to eat without a moment's hesitation.

'Bunny,' said his wife, 'one of your letters found its way into my bunch.'

She tossed it across the table. The Major looked at the envelope with a dull resentment. His post that morning had consisted of four bills and two appeals for subscriptions. This long rakish-looking envelope might be either. He opened it wearily, caring not at all that the end of it had landed in the marmalade when his wife had tossed it over to him, because he expected to throw it into the wastepaper-basket almost at once. Inside was neither a bill nor an appeal. but another envelope, buff-coloured, inscribed with the initials of authority, heavily sealed with deep-red expensive sealing-wax, and stamped in the top left-hand corner SECRET. Major Blenkinsop threw a quick nervous glance in the direction of his wife. He was a man of forty-two. When he was a boy the belief that a woman cannot keep a secret was still prevalent in the remoter country districts. Enid was hidden by the *Morning Boast*. He slipped the buff envelope into his pocket and tore up the outer envelope with such elaborate nonchalance that the marmalade on it was transferred to his fingers.

'Damn!'

'Another bill, Bunny?' came sympathetically from behind the *Morning Boast*.

'Yes, darling.'

If Major Blenkinsop had been a student of poetry he might have quoted to his conscience 'I could not love thee, dear, so well, loved I not honour more'; but being ignorant of anything in rhyme except the first verse of *Auld Lang Syne*, an odd line here and there in *God Save the King*, and a few juvenile hymns like *We are but little children weak* which had been as it were tattooed upon his memory by a pious and determined nurse, he merely assured himself sentimentally that this was the first lie he had told his wife since they were married, and made an excuse to retire as soon as possible in order to find out what was inside the buff envelope. It did not surprise Major Blenkinsop to find yet a third envelope. He had served on a Boundary Commission in Mendacia, and who should know better than he the superb prodigality of the War Office in the matter of stationery? The Post Office might send out envelopes which, by reading carefully the directions printed on the gummed-on flap and with the necessary practice in sleight of hand, could be used for the answer. The Inland Revenue might use envelopes with windows by which the grasping officials could spare themselves as much ink as would write your name and address twice. The War Office understood that their right to the respect and admiration of the people of Great Britain was on paper. Inside the third envelope, which in addition to being stamped VERY SECRET was inscribed *Personal and Strictly Confidential* in a neat handwriting, was the following communication:

From the Director of Extraordinary Intelligence
To Major Arthur Blenkinsop, M.C.

You are requested to call at the War Office on 5 November at noon and inquire for Lt-General Sir W. W. Westmacott. It is desired that this communication should be considered absolutely confidential.

W. W. Westmacott
Lt-General,
D.E.I

M.Q. 99 (E)

Blenkinsop's first emotion on reading this communication was one of relief. He had been half afraid that he was going to be told that he had been overpaid last time and must refund the balance to the Paymaster-General of the Forces.

But what could Sir William Westmacott be wanting, Sir William Westmacott whose fame as the Director of the most secret activities of British Intelligence was worldwide?

Chapter 2

EXTRAORDINARY INTELLIGENCE

AT two minutes to twelve next morning Major Blenkinsop walked up the steps of the War Office. He had told his wife before leaving Jerbury Chambers (so rapidly does a mono-syllabic lie engender a habit of romancing on a grand scale) that he was going into the City to discuss a directorate for which his name had been suggested.

'Of what, Bunny?'

He was well away now.

'Oh, a company which is being formed to develop the waste products of the banana.'

'How interesting! What do they do with them?'

'Oh, sort of chop them up with machines and all that sort of thing, you know. It's rather a complicated process, I believe. But of course it's only the financial side that appeals to me.'

'Of course it does, Bunny darling. You're always so practical.'

'Well, that was my old dad's idea when he had us educated. I always remember his giving me bradawls for birthday presents and practical things like that. In some ways he was in advance of his time. Of course, he was always a keen Unionist. He didn't believe in advanced politics. Well, look here, darling, I shall be late if I stay here talking to you. Will you be lunching in the flat?'

'No, I'm meeting Tiny Houldsworth at Harrod's. We've got a very heavy afternoon before us trying on furs.'

Ordinarily such an announcement might have cast a momentary shadow on Blenkinsop's brow, but now his con-science was pricking him for spinning that elaborate yarn to his wife.

'I hope you'll find something you really like, darling.'

'I'll do my best, Bunny.'

'I'm sure you will, darling.'

And he was being guiltily cordial, not in the least sardonic.

By the time Blenkinsop reached the War Office self-reproach

17

for the deception of his wife had been forgotten in the anxiety
he felt to do his duty. He had been a dragoon for too many
years to lose the habit easily. On learning Major Blenkinsop's
business the janitor almost hustled him into a waiting-room,
where he remained until a furtive little man came in and
looked at Blenkinsop as if he expected him to blow up at any
moment.

'Major Blenkinsop?'

'Yes, I have an appointment with Sir William Westmacott at
noon. He wrote to me.'

'Quite. Quite. We always have to be a little careful of
course ...' he lowered his voice ... 'in our work. Will you
follow me, and I'll take you up to Sir William's room.'

No sooner was Major Blenkinsop in the corridor than he and
his guide were surrounded by six very tall orderlies.

'My idea,' said the furtive little man complacently. 'We
shan't be noticed by anybody on the way up.'

Major Blenkinsop felt less confident of inconspicuousness. It
seemed to him that to go tramping along the corridors of the
War Office surrounded by six outsize orderlies partook of the
nature of a public ceremony.

'And you'd better keep your head down,' the furtive little
man advised him. 'Of course, we consider the War Office itself
fairly safe, but these bloody Communists are everywhere now
and we can't afford to deport them.'

'Why not?'

'Why, because when war breaks out we want to arrest them.
We can deal with them much better here than we can deal
with them in Russia.'

'I suppose you are in the...'

'I'm a Civil Assistant at the War Office,' the furtive little man
interrupted quickly. 'And this is Sir William's room.' He
opened the door and after murmuring 'Major Blenkinsop, sir,'
he faded away into the smoke-screen of orderlies.

'Excuse me a minute,' said the General. 'I've three or four
things to sign. Take a chair.'

Blenkinsop saw seated at a desk a spare grizzled man of
middle age, the most conspicuous feature of whose counte-

nance were the large dark horn-rimmed spectacles which made his aquiline nose look absolutely owlish. Before long Blenkinsop was to learn that all senior Intelligence officers wore large dark horn-rimmed spectacles and that the first step to advancement in Intelligence work was a pair of dark horn-rimmed spectacles.

Presently the General pushed aside the heap of papers he had been signing. Putting his elbows on the desk, he balanced his face between his hands and stared long and fixedly at his visitor.

'You've not mentioned a word to anybody about the communication you received from me, Major Blenkinsop?' the Director of Extraordinary Intelligence asked at last.

'Not a word, sir.'

'You realized of course that the matter on which I wished to see you was extremely secret?'

'Yes, sir, I certainly gathered that.'

'Good! I'm glad to see you are not afraid to form your own conclusions. That's what we expect in Intelligence work. We want officers who can think for themselves.'

Blenkinsop shifted on his chair. He was a modest Englishman, and beyond the natural desire for promotion which every officer possesses, be he dragoon, rifleman, or gunner, he had never been in the habit of pushing himself forward when he was still on the active list.

'You served for four years on the Commission for determining the boundaries of Mendacia under the terms of the Treaty of Versailles?'

'I did, sir.'

'And after that you spent over six years looking after the island of Parvo off the coast of Mendacia?'

'I did, sir.'

'And of course you have an extensive acquaintance with the country?'

'I know a little about it, sir, particularly the South. That was our pigeon. I mean to say we had to be rather careful of poking about too much in the North because that was the Venetians' pigeon, and the Burgundians didn't much like our poking about

in the East because that was their pigeon. But I had a good
week's shooting at Gassowitz once.'

'That's on the Czecho-Slavian frontier?'

'Yes, sir. I see you know the country as well as I do.'

'No, no, Blenkinsop,' the General disclaimed. 'But I know my
geography pretty well.'

'By Jove, sir, you certainly do.'

It was idle for the Director of Extraordinary Intelligence to
attempt any longer to conceal his pleasure at the unmistakable
admiration of his visitor. He smiled, and on a sudden impulse of
expansive good-fellowship he removed his spectacles.

'Do you speak the language well, Blenkinsop?' he asked.

Blenkinsop shook his head.

'It was too much for me, sir. Of course I can say "good
morning" and "good night" and a few things like that, but all
the waiters and fellows on Parvo spoke English.'

'What's Mendacian like?'

Blenkinsop felt inclined to say that the language was very
like ducks sneezing; but he feared this would make the General
suppose him flippant.

'I believe it's related to Albanian, sir.'

'Quite,' said Sir William sagely. 'Well, I'm not sure that your
not speaking the language will be a handicap in the work I
have in mind for you. Very few of our fellows in control of
things at home know any languages, except a bit of French and
German. And that brings me to my reason for asking you to
come and see me this morning. Have you ever heard of a
Captain Hubert Chancellor?'

'He wasn't in the cavalry, sir?'

'No, I think he was in the Cambridge Light Infantry.'

Blenkinsop looked vague.

'Well, the point is that he was looking after Mendacia for us,
but he's had to resign. Yes, the silly fellow has written some
damned novel or something, and we've had to make a rule that
nobody who writes novels can be employed by M.Q. 99 (E), and
– er – vice versa, of course, if you follow me.'

'Quite. I should think it was a very good rule, sir.'

'It's a vital rule,' said Sir William Westmacott, hurriedly

putting on his glasses to create an atmosphere of intellectual authority. 'What these writing fellows don't realize is that we may be at war again next week.'

'Rather not!' Blenkinsop agreed enthusiastically, for this was the best news he had heard since, three years after the British Commission for Mendacia had been sitting, the impossibility of finding a satisfactory formula to reconcile Burgundian and Venetian aims in Mendacia had made it certain that the Commission would have to sit for at least another year and possibly for two.

'N was rather anxious at first to give Chancellor another chance. No joke intended,' the General interposed quickly, with a suspicious glance at Blenkinsop, who murmured, 'Oh, rather not.' 'But I told N that E.I. wouldn't hear of it.'

Blenkinsop's face began to wear the same strained expression it had worn when, in the first flush of pleasure at being appointed to the Mendacian Boundary Commission, he had engaged a native to give him an hour's daily instruction in the language.

'E.I. Extraordinary Intelligence,' the General explained.

'Quite, quite,' Blenkinsop hastily acknowledged. He had smelt a job in the offing. He must not appear dull. He was relieved when the General said that of course he did not know who N was, and when by admitting his ignorance he could evidently please him.

'Ever hear of Henry Nutting?' asked Sir William, with a piercing look.

'Henry Nutting of the 13th Lancers?'

'That's the man. Know what he's doing now?'

'I know he commanded the 13th before he retired. He was with them in Cologne. I've played polo with him.'

'You don't know what he's doing now?'

'No idea, sir.'

'And that,' said Sir William triumphantly, 'is the answer to those fellows in the S.R.D.M.'

'S.R.D.M.?'

'Safety of the Realm Division (Military). That's a recent development. We found there was a certain amount of friction between Scotland Yard and the War Office. So we formed S.R.D. (Military) and S.R.D. (Civil) and put them both under P—,* which taught the Admiralty a lesson. Yes, we showed our friends there that coordination of Intelligence activities could be achieved without them if they wouldn't cooperate with us. They'll be sorry they didn't come in with us when hostilities break out, for between you and me, Blenkinsop, I've absolutely no opinion of Naval Intelligence. Absolutely none at all. You'd think Nelson was still stumping about on his wooden leg to hear some of them. Prehistoric, that's my opinion of Naval Intelligence.'

Blenkinsop, who when he had nothing better to do sometimes read a book that his wife had taken out from the library, wondered if he ought to correct Sir William's idea of Nelson's appearance, but decided it was not his business.

'I haven't a word to say against the S.R.D. people,' the General continued. 'I believe that the coordination, for which, between ourselves, I was largely responsible, is working well. I don't believe that we shall have any repetition in Scotland of that dismal mismanagement of the Irish business. But in some ways P is an alarmist. He told me the other day he was convinced a large number of people knew that Nutting was the head of M.Q. 99 (E). He said it was dangerous to print Nutting's name in the *War Office Guide*, because it can be bought by anybody for seven shillings and sixpence.'

'Oh, but people never buy books,' Blenkinsop put in hopefully. 'They get them out of lending libraries.'

'Exactly,' said the General. 'I pointed that out to P. I said that the *War Office Guide* was an absolute necessity for the people in the War Office. Otherwise we should be wasting all our time – and I reminded him that our time was the nation's time – wasting all our time in finding out where everybody was. After all, the War Office is a very big building. "So long as nobody knows what M.Q. 99 (E) is," I said, "M.Q. 99 (E) is a convenient cover." You don't know what M.Q. 99 (E) is, Blenkinsop?'

* Although Sir William Westmacott mentioned the name and rank of this officer it was decided to withhold it from the public in a work which will certainly be eagerly read by foreign agents.

'Not in the least, sir.'

'Exactly! P's a splendid chap, but he *is* a bit of an alarmist. I think these flying people often get like that when they give up flying. They don't realize they're on terra firma again. Well, to get back to our particular business, Blenkinsop, how would you like to tackle Mendacia again?'

'Well, frankly, sir, I think the unfortunate rumours that have gone round about the disturbed state of the country have for the time being spoilt our chances. People feel safer on the Riviera, in spite of the exchange.'

To Blenkinsop's immense surprise Sir William rose from his chair, walked rapidly round his desk, and patted him on the back. He was not accustomed to seeing generals a prey to cordial and benevolent emotions.

'You're the very man we want,' Sir William declared. 'You're discreet. You knew I was offering you the charge of Mendacian espionage, but you never batted an eyelid. By gad, Blenkinsop, you've got an instinct for this work. I thought a good deal of Chancellor until he broke out as a confounded novel writer, but you'll go further than Chancellor. Well, what's your answer now to my question?'

'I should like to have a shot at it, sir. I had a little practice when I was running the Hotel Multum for my brother. I mean to say, I had to find out more or less what was going on in the hotel, but of course I don't know what I could do on a larger scale. The political situation in Mendacia is very tricky just now.'

'It's an absolute powder-magazine. It may go off at any moment. I believe war's more likely to come from there than anywhere else. Well, the next thing is for you to see N. I suppose Paris is the place.'

'Paris?'

'Yes. N makes a great point of all preliminaries being settled as far away as convenient from his headquarters, which naturally are in London. You'd better disguise yourself of course. Nothing much. Say an imperial. You've got the type of chin for an imperial. Only be sure you fix it firmly. One of our fellows put on a false moustache to meet a foreign agent in Seville, and not having allowed for the heat in Spain it fell off in the soup on the first night at dinner in the hotel.'

'A bit awkward that, sir.'

'It might have been, but he had the presence of mind to call the waiter and say "Take this soup away, waiter, there are a lot of hairs in it", and he did it so well that the waiter apologized. You want to think quickly in our work, Blenkinsop, and act at once in even the most trifling emergency. So if you do stick on an imperial, stick it on firmly, though of course the climate of Paris is much the same as ours. You'd better go to the Plonplon. We always find it less conspicuous to do our work in the better-class hotels. When N goes abroad he's usually known as Captain W. S. Churchill. A rumour goes round that Winston has arrived. Other guests all stare. Realize at once it isn't Winston. Take no more interest in him. That's what we call a convenient cover. Nobody asks who he is. He's not Winston, and that's enough.'

'Shall I call myself Captain Chamberlain?'

'No, I don't think you'd better start an alias right away. I think that's a matter that should be decided between you and N. I think he might resent your going ahead quite so fast.'

'Shall I go back on the active list, sir?'

'Not apparently,' said the General, his eyes glittering with what might be called an expression of diabolical cunning. 'Not openly. You will receive full pay, but for the sake of a convenient cover you will remain to the world at large apparently on the retired list. Besides your pay you will receive a generous allowance for incidental expenses. We're finding it a little easier to get money nowadays. There's so much of this bloody communism about. The people at the top are frightened. They think that we're the only thing that stands between them and the first lamp-post. I will say this for P: he may be an alarmist, but he knows how to put the fear of God into those dam' politicians. In fact, one of the fellows at the Foreign Office said to me the other day that in his opinion P was either a lunatic or a criminal and probably both. That shows they're beginning to realize that P means business. It's a pity he wasted his talents in the Flying Corps during the war. He didn't take up Intelligence work till fairly recently, and since the S.R.D. was organized we've doubled the Secret Vote. You can't do this kind of work without money.'

'Of course you can't, sir,' Blenkinsop agreed fervidly, for there are few things which arouse so much enthusiasm in the human breast as the prospect of spending other people's money.

'And now you mustn't keep me any longer, Blenkinsop. I've got three or four things to sign and a long report to read through about a steel wall which the Poles are said to be building right along the top of the Carpathians. It sounds almost incredible when you read it, but the agent from whom we have received the information is very highly paid and he ought to be reliable.'

'When shall I hear where I am to meet Colonel Nutting, sir?'

Sir William Westmacott took off his spectacles and shook his head reproachfully at Blenkinsop.

'N, Blenkinsop, N. We never allude to N by his name.'

'I'm sorry, sir.'

'I know you won't do it again. Of course, in one way it doesn't matter in my room at the War Office. But it's against the principles of the Secret Service. You do it once in private, and then before you know where you are you'll go and do it in the middle of Piccadilly. After all, the whole point of the Secret Service is that it should be secret.'

'Quite, quite, sir, I'm very sorry.'

'Of course I wouldn't go so far as to say that the secrecy was *more* important than the service, but it's every bit *as* important. Well, it stands to reason that if the Secret Service was no longer secret it would cease to be the Secret Service. After all, we're not cabinet ministers. We can't afford to talk. Now, let me see, you were asking where you were to meet N. Look here, on second thoughts, I think you'd better not wear an imperial. If it happened to come off, N mightn't recognize you. How would it be if you wore a white malmaison in your buttonhole?'

'I should think that could be managed, sir, and anyway I daresay Colonel – I daresay N will recognize me. We played polo together quite a lot. Besides, I shall certainly recognize him.'

'Ah, but will you?' said the D.E.I. 'Don't you be too sure, Blenkinsop. Some time ago N went over to Paris disguised as an opera singer, and he looked the part so well that the agent whom he was to meet thought he really was an opera singer and never went near him for a week. In fact, it turned out a little awkwardly, because one evening this agent saw a member of the French Cabinet dining at the Ritz and he looked so much like somebody disguised as an opera singer that this dam' fool of an agent went up and spoke to him. He was at once arrested by the French secret police, and there was very nearly a most unpleasant scandal. However, I'll warn N not to disguise himself too elaborately this time. In fact I think he'd better go as Captain Churchill, and you can just meet as brother officers who have not seen each other for some time. You could say, "Hullo, Churchill, I haven't seen you since we met in that German pillbox in the summer of 'eighteen." Yes, that's it. We'll arrange that definitely. You won't forget, will you, because N is a tremendously cautious chap and if we arranged for you to have met him in a pillbox and you said you'd met him last at a forward observation-post he'd be off like an arrow and you'd have to meet him all over again. And don't forget 'eighteen. He won't answer to any other year. German pillbox 'eighteen. G.P.E. Ever do Pelmanism? If you think of G.P.O., General Post Office, or G.P.I., General Paralysis of the Insane, you won't forget G.P.E. G for German, P for pillbox, E for eighteen.'

'I won't forget, sir.'

'Now the only thing left to arrange is where you are to meet N. I can't say that until I know when N can manage to run over to Paris. You're on the telephone?'

'Yes, sir. Double five double seven double eight Whitehall.'

'I must make a note of that. When I was younger I used to be able to remember telephone numbers by Pelmanism, but I have such a lot to remember nowadays that I find it safer to write them down. Double five double seven double eight, you said? Good. Then you'll get a message. "Please tell Major Blenkinsop if he's not in that the appointment is on such and such an afternoon or evening at such and such a time." I'll arrange with N that the place is to be the Palm Court at the Hôtel Plonplon. You know the Palm Court at the Plonplon, I suppose?'

'No, but I can easily find it, sir.'

'Well, there's only one thing you want to watch. Up till six the women are perfectly respectable. In fact it's the fashionable place for tea. But after six the fashionable women all go away, and it becomes a little – er – lively. I thought I'd just warn you, because personally I find it very difficult nowadays to distinguish one kind of woman from another. Post-war. You know the sort of thing I mean? And now, Blenkinsop, I really must get on with my work. Just walk out of my room quite naturally, and if you call a taxi outside the War Office don't give your address to the driver right off. I don't suppose anybody will be looking out for you, but you can never be absolutely sure. From now on you want to remember that "secrecy and caution" is your motto. I never go either to N's headquarters or P's headquarters without changing taxis at least twice on the way. Don't be afraid of the expense. We never question anybody's expenses if he can satisfy us they were incurred on behalf of secrecy. Well, good-bye, Blenkinsop. We may meet some time at an Intelligence Conference. But not here. So long as you are in the Secret Service I would rather you did not even walk past the War Office. And of course in no circumstances must you ever go inside it. We've spent several months now in perfecting a system of communication between M.Q. 99 (E) and the S.R.D. and by both of them with the War Office and Scotland Yard which is regarded even by P as absolutely impenetrable by foreign agents. However, N will explain lots of things that I haven't time to explain. I really must sign three or four letters before I go to lunch. I'm glad you've made up your mind to join us, Blenkinsop. You'll find the work fascinating even in peace time, and after all there's a jolly good chance of another war soon. A jolly good chance! All our information points that way.'

With these cheering words the Director of Extraordinary Intelligence sped Major Blenkinsop on his way.

Chapter 3

PARIS

'BUNNY, darling,' said Mrs Blenkinsop, an evening or two after the interview at the War Office, 'there was a telephone message for you this afternoon when Tiny Houldsworth was having tea with me. You are to meet somebody or other at the place arranged at five o'clock next Tuesday.'

Blenkinsop's usually impassive face took on that expression of passionate stealth which is to be seen on the countenances of secret service agents in novels, of publishers trying to secure an option on a writer's next three books in real life, and on foxes in the fables of Aesop, and Lafontaine.

'Thanks very much, darling,' he muttered.

'The voice sounded rather mysterious,' his wife went on.

'Did it?'

Blenkinsop tried to make the question sound quite casual; but the consciousness that her blue eyes were fixed upon him shook his self-control and he fancied that there was a guilty tremor in his speech.

'Very mysterious in fact. So mysterious, Bunny darling, that if it hadn't been a man's voice Bunny would have been awful jealous.'

Blenkinsop's heart sank. When Enid called herself Bunny and began to put on that baby voice it meant business. Soon after they were married she had with that voice wheedled a diamond wrist-watch out of him as if she were asking for a rubber teat. He liked her to call him Bunny, but when she called herself Bunny the hutch of matrimony closed in upon him.

'Well, luckily it was a man's voice, darling.'

'Who was it?'

'Oh, it's a man I have to meet over that banana business I was telling you about. It's one of the directors. After I've seen him I shall know whether I'm going to get the job.'

'What's his name?'

'His name?'

'Yes, Bunny.'

'Oh, his name! His name's Godley. Mr Godley.'

'But where are you going to meet him on Tuesday?'

'Where am I going to meet him? Oh yes, at – er – Godalming. And as a matter of fact I think I'll probably have to spend the night with him.'

'Oh, you think you will?'

'Yes, I think so. You've no idea what a lot there is to talk about.'

'About bananas?'

'Exactly. The subject is a much wider one than you might fancy from just eating them at odd times.'

'And I suppose this Mr Godley is a great expert on bananas?'

'Oh, rather! I could almost say that what Godley doesn't know about bananas isn't worth knowing. They tell me he has devoted his whole life to them.'

'I see,' said Mrs Blenkinsop.

Was it fancy or did he detect in the tone of her comment a menacing pensiveness, even a suggestion of absolute incredulity? He decided to be optimistic.

'If I get this job, darling, I'll be able to run to a car.'

The Greeks are feared when they bring gifts: husbands are often suspected. There was a hint of steel in the heart of Mrs Blenkinsop's wide-open blue eyes.

'Oh, by the way, darling,' said her husband on Sunday night. 'I forgot to tell you that Godley wants me to go to Paris with him tomorrow.'

'To Paris?' his wife repeated in amazement.

Even she, well versed in the ways of masculine evasiveness before she married Arthur, was not prepared for such a crude excuse as this.

'Yes, apparently the man who invented the process lives in Paris.'

'Inventing?'

'Yes.'

'I expect you'll find his company very congenial.'

'Well, of course we shall be talking business all the time.'

'In French?'

'Oh, I don't think he's a Frenchman.'

'No, I don't think so either.'

Blenkinsop looked at his wife with what he hoped was an expression of stern and dignified reproachfulness.

'You're not suggesting, darling, are you, that I am going to Paris for any reason except business?'

'No, Arthur, all I'm suggesting is that you shall take me to Paris with you tomorrow. While you're discussing bananas, I can look at the new models.'

'Not this time, darling,' said Arthur desperately. 'If I get this job I shall probably have to run over to Paris again, and then we might run over together.'

'Oh, Arthur, how have you the heart to treat me like this? What has happened to you since we came home from Parvo? You've got such a horrible sly look now, and you seem quite a different person from my innocent old Bunny.'

Mrs Blenkinsop flung herself down into an armchair, which, with the unnaturally tight springs of all armchairs in furnished service-flats, bounced her two or three times up in the air before she could collapse in the appropriate attitude of the misused wife. It says much for her husband's patriotism that he did not make up his mind to telephone to the War Office next day and decline General Westmacott's offer. It was only the consciousness that his country needed him coupled with the prospect of adding a decent sum to his income which gave him the strength to resist the appeal of his wife's tears.

'Enid,' he pleaded earnestly. 'I must ask you to trust me. I cannot explain now why it is absolutely impossible for me to take you to Paris tomorrow. One day my lips will be unsealed, and then you will bitterly regret the wrong you have done me by your suspicions.'

'Don't talk such damned rot,' Enid sobbed, and the convulsive shudder of repugnance she gave in that tight-springed armchair nearly bounced her off on the hearthrug.

Blenkinsop was a dragoon. He had simple old-world ideas about the womanliness of women. During the sordid aftermath of the Great War he had passed through the period of disil-

lusionment unscathed, happily occupied at first with the mani-
fold problems of the Mendacian Boundary Commission and
later with the creation of a Britannic Eden on the island of
Parvo.

'I wish you wouldn't swear, Enid,' he said.

'My God, Arthur,' she retorted furiously, 'you'd make Queen
Victoria swear.'

'I say, I rather wish you wouldn't talk like that, Enid dear. I
know you don't really mean it, but it does sound sort of
blasphemous.'

Enid sat upright in the armchair.

'How old are you, Arthur?'

'Forty-two.'

'To hear you talk one would think you'd ridden in the charge
of the Light Brigade.'

They wrangled for a while about Arthur's prehistoric out-
look, and simple though he might seem he was clever enough
to keep the argument going, because the more old-fashioned he
made himself out to be, the more innocuous he hoped his trip
to Paris would appear.

In the end Enid seemed to surrender abruptly to the inevitable.

'All right, Arthur, we'll say no more about it now,' she told
him. 'But if you *don't* get this job I'll never again believe a
word you say.'

'That depends, that must depend on Godley,' Arthur replied
firmly. 'Are you coming down to see me off at Victoria?'

'Is Mr Godley going to be there?'

'No, I rather gather he is meeting me in Paris.'

'Yes, I rather gathered that too,' she murmured.

So Enid did not accompany her husband to the station next
morning, and he with a couple of novels about the Secret
Service to keep him amused on the way to Paris settled himself
down in a first-class carriage to enjoy the consciousness of his
own position. It gave him a sharp pleasure, this thought that
none of the other occupants of the compartment could be
guessing what his mission was and that if any of them did
guess with what respectful curiosity they would have regarded

him. Presently he picked up one of the novels and began to read. Strangely enough, the story opened in the boat-train from Victoria with a King's Messenger who was carrying dispatches, the contents of which would if known have plunged all the chancelleries of Europe into consternation, yet who with an imprudent gallantry that Blenkinsop felt reflected gravely upon his sense of responsibility allowed himself to listen to what was obviously a cock-and-bull story by a dazzlingly beautiful Russian princess who declared she had had her passport stolen. The train (in the story) had just entered a tunnel, and the King's Messenger's last effort of consciousness had been to note the green eyes of the Russian princess fixed on his own, when Blenkinsop became aware that a pair of eyes (not in the story) were fixed intently on him, the eyes not belonging to a lovely woman but to a little man with thin sandy hair, wrapped in a heavy overcoat, the colour and texture of which approximated in outward appearance to stewed tripe.

'Looks as if we're going to have a rough crossing,' said the sandy-haired man.

Now Blenkinsop when talking to his wife might seem almost eagerly apologetic, but he could be very crushing when addressed by strangers in a train.

'I haven't looked,' he said coldly, and held the novel he was reading high enough to exclude the whole of the sandy-haired man's objectionable face from his own.

'I was going by the washing in the back-gardens. Blowing about like anything, it is,' the stranger continued.

'It may be,' said Blenkinsop in a tone of icy non-committal from behind his novel, making up his mind that if this bounder addressed another remark to him he should ignore it. He reckoned without the next remark.

'I see you're interested in spies,' was what the bounder said.

If the sandy-haired man had offered him the loan of the gold toothpick with which at this moment he was playing upon his teeth as on a dulcimer, Blenkinsop would not have jumped more perceptibly. He experienced in one blinding moment enough physical sensations to last all the characters in a 'thriller' from cover to cover. Beads of perspiration stood out upon his forehead. His tongue clove to his palate. His heart went into his mouth. His hair stood on end. His flesh was goose.

No wonder General Westmacott had impressed upon him the necessity for extreme caution. Evidently foreign agents were even more indefatigable than the D.E.I. supposed. The old soldier in him rescued Blenkinsop from the momentary consternation produced by the stranger's remark.

'Not at all interested,' he said with that British sangfroid which is the envy of the world.

'I deserved that,' said the stranger. 'But I couldn't help letting myself in for it. You see I'm Yorke Lankester!'

'What of it?' Blenkinsop asked in a tone of chill contempt.

'Well, I wrote that book you're reading.'

Blenkinsop turned to the title-page and read *The Green-Eyed Spy. By Yorke Lankester.* He looked at the sandy-haired stranger with a glimmer of interest. He had never seen an author before. Indeed, it had never really occurred to him that such people actually existed.

'How do you write a book?' he asked.

'How does a hen lay an egg?' Mr Lankester laughed.

Blenkinsop threw a nervous glance across the compartment to the far corner where a well-dressed woman was turning over the pages of an illustrated weekly. Women who travelled by themselves in smoking-carriages had only themselves to blame if the conversation was definitely masculine, but . . .

'Quite,' he said to Mr Lankester to show that he perfectly understood the process and did not require any further examples from natural history.

'As a matter of fact,' Mr Lankester went on, 'that's my first novel, and it gave me a very queer sensation when I saw you reading it. It's been out over six months and I've never seen anybody reading it till I saw you. So that must be my excuse for butting in upon you as I did.'

'Oh, that's quite all right,' said Blenkinsop kindly. Now that this writer fellow had grasped it was not the thing to address remarks to people sitting opposite to him in a railway-carriage he was prepared to stretch a point in his favour. In some way the reading of a book might be considered a kind of introduction to the author.

'Much must be forgiven to a fond parent,' Mr Lankester added.

'Quite, quite,' said Blenkinsop; but he wished that his new acquaintance would avoid these reproductive similes in public.

'Naturally, I don't consider myself a professional,' Mr Lankester went on, 'I mean to say I just took up writing novels as a hobby. I've always been a great novel reader all my life, and one evening in my office when I was waiting for a cable from Jamaica I suddenly took up my pen and started writing *The Green-Eyed Spy*. Of course, I don't pretend it's literature. I really wrote it to amuse myself. But I've had two reviews already, though the book has only been out six months, and I'm told that if a first novel gets two reviews in the first six months it's pretty good. I mean it's lucky for the author. One of the reviews was in the *Dimes Literary Supplement*, but that just told the story, and I couldn't make out whether the critic thought it was good or not. The way he told the story made it sound rather improbable. The other review was awfully enthusiastic; but to be quite candid that was written by a business friend in our trade journal *The Banana World*.'

'*The Banana World?*' Blenkinsop repeated. 'Oh, then you are interested in bananas?'

'Well, they are my real business,' Mr Lankester admitted. 'And this is my real name.'

He handed Blenkinsop a card:

MR WILLIAM HUDSON
HUDSON BROTHERS,
BANANA IMPORTERS,
210 KING STREET,
COVENT GARDEN.

Blenkinsop put out his hand.

'How d'ye do, Mr Hudson?'

The depth of his grateful emotion may be gauged by the fact that he only just managed to restrain himself from adding: 'I'm very glad to meet you.'

Mr Hudson's emotions were nearer to the surface than the

dragoon's, for when Blenkinsop offered his own card he had no hesitation in saying:

'I'm awfully glad to make your acquaintance, Major.'

'Some time when you're feeling in the mood, Mr Hudson, I should very much like you to tell me a little about bananas. It's a subject which has always had a great fascination for me. After all, when you come to think of it, what does the ordinary man like myself know about bananas?'

Mr Hudson looked a shade rueful. He did not really want to talk about bananas. He wanted to talk about his book, or at any rate to sit back in his seat and watch Blenkinsop read his book and then spend the rest of the journey talking to him about it and about his next one, the proofs of which he had not so long ago passed for press. It hurt his pride that this new acquaintance should thaw to him as a banana importer after being so gelid to him as a novelist. He wished that he had never mentioned *The Banana World* or revealed his real name. However, perhaps if he talked about bananas now later on he should be able to talk about books. So much to Blenkinsop's gratification he talked about bananas and was rewarded by an invitation to dine with him at the Hôtel Plonplon.

As for Blenkinsop himself the first thing he did when he reached Paris was to write the following letter to his wife:

My darling Wife,

I have arrived safely in Paris and shall telegraph to you when I am returning. I am sorry to say that poor Mr Godley, the man I was to meet about this banana business, has died quite suddenly, but another director, Mr William Hudson, is to decide about everything tomorrow, and I have every reason to suppose that the business will go through satisfactorily. Mr Hudson belongs to the well-known firm of Hudson Brothers of 210 King Street, Covent Garden. You can look them up in the telephone book. I wish you were here with me, but we shall enjoy it better when this banana business is definitely settled. No time to tell you anything more.

Always your loving
Bunny

PS. Mr Hudson tells me that there are some bananas in Africa over two feet long and as thick as a man's arm. What an opening for waste products!

Chapter 4

THE PALM COURT

WHEN Blenkinsop went up to bed that night and when, as had been his custom since he was a small boy, he reviewed the events of the day, a mental exercise to which he attributed whatever success had come to him in the contest with existence, he looked back on this particular day with a measure of satisfaction. It might be considered his first day of activity as an officer in the Secret Service, and he could flatter himself that a veteran of secret activities could hardly have improved upon the technique he had displayed in making the most of his opportunities. He had had, to be sure, a stroke of luck in meeting Hudson like that, but he had taken the fullest advantage of such a fortunate encounter. When he returned to London and found himself exposed to the fire of Enid's questions he should now be able to give her an unusually wide survey of bananas. He now possessed that convenient cover of which General Westmacott had spoken. There need be no more stumblings over Godleys and Godalmings. Not even Enid's blue eyes would be able to X-ray that convenient cover and recognize the secret agent serving his country under the guise of a banana expert. He had treated Hudson himself like a banana. He had peeled him and extracted from him every morsel of nourishment, remaining himself as impenetrably innutritious to Hudson as a brazil nut to a toothless man. Hudson, who as Yorke Lankester would have exchanged whole cargoes of bananas for the information he could have given him about the Secret Service, had gone off at the end of the evening with that flashy-looking cocotte, utterly unaware what his companion of the journey really was. And there was a Mrs Hudson. That meant Hudson possessed a guilty secret, and Hudson as the possessor of a guilty secret himself would have to support his story with Enid. 'Oh, by the way Hudson, my wife was a little inquisitive about my reasons for going to Paris the other day. You know what women are? Well, just to keep her quiet I told her you had asked me to join you in a development of your ordinary banana business. So if she says anything about it, forewarned is forearmed, you know.' Hudson would have to support him because he in turn would be requiring support for the account he would have to give his wife of the way he had spent the evenings in Paris. Blenkinsop recognized that conspiracy with people like Hudson was not dignified; but nobody in the Secret Service could afford to be squeamish. On this thought he sank happily and confidently into the profundities of sleep.

The next morning Blenkinsop was standing at the bookstall of the Hôtel Plonplon, apparently preoccupied with the purchase of a *Continental Daily Tale*, but actually trying to muster up courage to tell the young woman that he wanted one of those French publications, in which no scenic background is too inappropriate and no climate too severe to deter young women from spending the whole of their existence in underclothes, in which indeed any young woman not in underclothes appears as a vulgar intrusion upon an idyll. Thus engaged as discreetly as he could manage it, Blenkinsop noticed a pile of luggage in the lobby on every piece of which was printed in thick white letters the name W. S. CHURCHILL. So Nutting – so N – he *must* remember to say N even to himself – had arrived. Ah-ha! Presently he heard the Deputy Vice-Head Porter of the Plonplon ask a thickset clean-shaven man in a suit of tweeds, on which any game could have been played from backgammon to reversé, if he had registered yet. This then was N himself. He had broadened out considerably in the fifteen years since they had played polo together. Blenkinsop could not resist the fascination of staring at the chief of the Secret Service above a young woman who was tripping through the snow with nothing on but a crimson muff and a pair of crimson garters. Presently the owner of the luggage turned round and stared hard at Blenkinsop who was astonished by the perfection of N's disguise. If he had not known who it really was he would never have dreamt that this stocky individual, who looked as if his chin had been pulled out with a winch and his nose pushed back with a beetle, was the debonair lancer of fifteen years ago. Evidently N recognized him, and Blenkinsop wondered if in the circumstances he ought not to anticipate the rendezvous arranged in the Palm Court for that afternoon at five o'clock. However, military training came to his aid. So long as he obeyed the letter of his instructions he knew he was safe. If N recognized him, it was for N to make the signal. Instead of doing so he turned away and said to the Deputy Vice-Head Porter in a voice which Blenkinsop thought was the best imitation of an American accent he had ever heard.

'Say, who is that guy?'

The porter murmured something.

'Well, tell him that I'm not Mr Winston Churchill, and that I don't care to be stared at by suckers like him.'

With this the pseudo-American threw his chin out even another half-inch and chewing on a large cigar went off with the obsequious head porter in the direction of the reception desk.

Blenkinsop had been invited to lunch with Mr Hudson in his hotel, so he was spared the embarrassment of running into N again before the appointed hour.

'What a night!' Hudson sighed. 'After we left you we went the round of Montmartre.' He clicked his tongue. 'Well, they say Paris isn't what it was, but in my opinion, Major, it's more so. We went to a place called *Les Abeilles*, where I give you my word the girls served the drinks with nothing on except a pair of wings. But they didn't forget to sting us. Two hundred and fifty francs for a bottle of champagne! I couldn't help laughing when I thought what the wife would have said. I remember she once said to me she thought the waitresses at the Corner House wore their skirts too short. Still, what the eyes don't see the heart doesn't grieve for, eh, Major? And after all if a man's going to write books he wants to see a bit of life.'

'Where did you end up?' Blenkinsop asked.

'Ah, that's telling. But it was all very jolly. And I put through a very nice little bit of business this morning.'

'In bananas, I take it?'

'That's right.'

'I suppose you find bananas very useful on trips like this?'

'Meaning?'

'Well, I suppose Mrs Hudson might object to your running over to Paris if she did not know you were called there for business reasons?'

'Yes, I suppose she might.'

'I mean you wouldn't like her to know what you were doing last night?'

'No, it's a fact I shouldn't! Mrs Hudson's father was a Wesleyan minister, and she was very strictly brought up.'

'Oh, she was?' Blenkinsop observed, a note of cunning in his voice. 'Oh, well, I hope very much that when we're back in London you and Mrs Hudson will dine with my wife and myself at the Olympic one evening.'

And they parted after lunch with warm mutual assurances of meeting again soon.

Blenkinsop entered the Palm Court of the Hôtel Plonplon half an hour before the time he was due. The tinkle of numerous teacups mingled with the bleating of well-bred conversation in a pastoral symphony, and lounge-lizards darted in and out among the foliage to attend upon their patronesses. Blenkinsop, remembering General Westmacott's warning that at this hour the Palm Court was the resort of fashion, did not look twice at any woman, but took his seat where, sheltered against the glare of the electric light by the arching fronds of a great Phoenix Canariensis palm, he could watch the pleasurable scene and mark the exits and the entrances. At the nearest table to him a woman with cropped hair, a monocle, and a stiff collar was talking in a deep reproachful voice to a slim young feminine creature with plucked eyebrows and a sulky mouth. Blenkinsop could not help hearing what the older woman was saying in English:

'Look here, my darling, I simply will not go on being treated as you are treating me. You promised faithfully to meet me at the Salle Rouge yesterday to hear that new piano quintet. There I stood like a dummy in the lobby, waiting and watching for you to arrive, and in the end I had to sit right through the concert with an empty fauteuil on one side of me and an odious man on the other who leered at me continuously. If you no longer love me, say so, but don't try to sneak out of things like a man. It's not worthy of you, darling.'

Blenkinsop stared in astonishment at this extraordinary couple. He had never in his life heard one woman talk in such a way to another.

'Move your chair, sweetest,' the woman with the monocle went on. 'That horrible satyr at the next table is gloating over you, darling.'

Blenkinsop flushed under the imputation of such ungentlemanly behaviour, and turned sharply in the other direction. At the table now in his line of vision and hearing a woman between forty and eighty, whose bediamonded hands flashed heliographically, was scolding in raucous American a slim young masculine creature with plucked eyebrows and a sulky mouth.

'Now, see here, Dick, I'm not going to stand for it any longer. I may have been fool enough to let myself get crazy over you, but I'm not fool enough to share you with other women – I didn't bring you to Parrus to have you trail around after Mrs Schweppes-Perrier. You may think you'll get more out of her, but I gave up knowing Angela Schweppes-Perrier before you were out of the cradle, and she'll plackay you between lunch and dinner. Why, only last year when she was in Italy she caused so much trouble among the young men that the Fascisti told her to leave the country. Besides, Dick, I'm fond of you, and a boy like you can't afford to throw away real affection like mine.'

Blenkinsop was now staring with a combination of astonishment and disgust at the unspeakable subject of this passionate address, only to hear the speaker say sharply :

'Dick, move your chair around. There's a nasty old homo at the next table trying to catch your eye. And that I won't stand for.'

It took Blenkinsop all the self-control he had learnt as a dragoon not to summon the waiter and make a scene. To be accused of trying to catch the eye of that wretched little barber's apprentice! Blenkinsop of the Welch Bays! Fortunately for his outraged feelings he caught sight a few minutes later of N's stocky figure at the far end of the Court. He at once rose from the table at which he had been sitting and after blasting in turn the woman with the monocle and the woman with the diamonds with a glance of indignant disgust he strode off to keep his appointment. Nor did he like Lot's wife when leaving a similar milieu turn round and look back.

Blenkinsop had rehearsed over and over again the very words and the very tone with which he intended to announce his presence to the Chief of the Secret Service. So now when he saw N walking slowly round the cement pond in the middle of the Court where about twenty flaccid goldfish spent their lives in ignoring the various food flung to them by the frequenters, Blenkinsop came quickly up behind and said without a moment's hesitation:

'By gad, Churchill, I haven't seen you since we met in that German pillbox in 'eighteen.'

Blenkinsop had never bothered to imagine in detail what would be N's reply to this greeting; but he had taken for granted either a friendly exclamation of surprise or the silent grip with which two strong men salute when they meet on India's coral strand. It came therefore as an unpleasant shock when the old acquaintance he had accosted swung round to show a countenance distorted by rage and a chin which seemed to be rushing towards him like a cow-catcher of a locomotive.

'Say, who in hell *are* you?' snarled the chinny man.

Blenkinsop did not give ground, which was just as well, for if his soldierly instincts had betrayed him he would probably have tripped backwards over the raised edge of the pond and brought a little excitement into the lives of the goldfish.

'You are not Captain Churchill of the Bluffs?' he inquired with dignity.

'No, by gard, I'm not, and you know derned well I'm not, what's more.'

'I'm sorry,' said Blenkinsop with superb sarcasm. 'I owe an apology to my friend.'

'If you trail around after me any more,' the angry American

snarled, 'I'll complain to the management of this hotel and have you put out. I saw through your little game this morning.'

'And that,' thought Blenkinsop bitterly as he threaded his way through the crowded Court towards a chair as far as possible from the exhibitors of decadent vice he had recently been compelled to overhear and at the same time as far as possible from Mr W. S. Churchill, 'that is the kind of bounder who is responsible for sixpence on my income-tax.'

Blenkinsop recovered himself from the shock of his mistake with a double whisky and a large soda, the price of which was enough to send down the value of the pound another twopence all over France. Presently the waiter placed on the table an envelope addressed to Major Blenkinsop. He tore it open and read on a slip of paper inside: *Shall be glad to see you as soon as possible in Room 256.*

Blenkinsop wasted no more time in the Palm Court, but hastened to the lift, and a minute or two later really was in the presence of the Chief of the Secret Service, who was sitting at one of those flimsy writing-desks which are provided all the world over in the private sitting-rooms of luxury hotels. Taking off the horn-rimmed spectacles he was wearing, an even larger and darker pair than those worn by General Westmacott, Colonel Henry Nutting rose from his chair and came half-way across the room to greet his old comrade-in-arms with a cordiality that was far removed indeed from the snarl of that cantankerous bounder in the Palm Court.

'Hullo, Blenkinsop, how are you?' was the exact phrase employed by Colonel Nutting, and if Major Blenkinsop had not been on the verge of entering the Secret Service himself he would have replied, 'How are you, Nutting?' for the dragoon immediately recognized this tall narrow-headed man with grizzled hair and grizzled toothbrush moustache as the lancer with whom in days gone by he had often played polo. He decided, however, that it was his duty to obey General Westmacott's instructions to the letter, especially after the mistake he had made in the Court, and he replied:

'By gad, Churchill, I haven't seen you since we met in that German pillbox in 'eighteen.'

'Good man!' the authentic N said enthusiastically. 'That's just what we're looking for in our work. You can't be too careful. Of course, I remembered you at once, and you remembered me. Still, that was the agreed recognition signal, and you were quite right to give it. Absolutely right. I see already that you're just the man we want.'

'Well, as a matter of fact – er . . .'

'Nutting,' said the Chief, 'I'm staying here as myself this time. It's a splendid way of confusing foreign agents to be oneself occasionally.'

'I'm afraid that's how the mistake happened,' said Blenkinsop. 'I hope I've not done any harm, but the D.E.I. told me you would be staying here as Captain W. S. Churchill, and having seen that name this morning on a lot of luggage I went up to the owner of it just now in the Palm Court and gave him the recognition signal.'

'What was this man like?' Nutting asked anxiously.

'He was an American with such a prominent chin that I thought it must be false, and having heard about your wonderful disguises I stupidly made up my mind it must be you.'

'Katzenschlosser!' exclaimed Nutting. 'Katzenschlosser, the smartest agent in the American service! But this time he's overstepped himself. They've found out that I've been using the name Churchill as a convenient cover, and Katzenschlosser is evidently in hopes of piercing our organization by pretending to be me.'

'But this man didn't seem to relish it at all when I addressed him as Churchill,' Blenkinsop pointed out. 'In fact he was confoundedly offensive. In fact if I could have been perfectly sure his chin wasn't false I should have slogged him in the jaw. Only I thought it might have been a bit awkward if his chin had shot off into the goldfish.'

'He thought you were a British agent,' said Nutting decidedly. 'I tell you, Blenkinsop, there's nobody in this job for whose ability I have a greater respect. By Jove, it's lucky you spotted him, and doubly lucky I happened to be here as myself just when he arrived here as me. Now, let me see, what's the best thing to do?'

The Chief of the Secret Service put on his spectacles and stared before him into space in a long pregnant silence. Blenkinsop marvelled at the man's iron nerve. Here he was faced with what might mean the ruin of the whole organization he had been laboriously building up through the long weary years of peace. Yet he could sit there, looking as unmoved as one of those goldfish in the Palm Court pond when another piece of cake was thrown into it.

'I must telephone to London,' he decided at last.

While he was waiting for the call to be put through to the number in Hampstead he had asked for, Nutting gave Blenkinsop a few examples of Katzenschlosser's diabolical cunning.

'It was his idea to transfer all the Bolshies from the United States to England.'

'Well, you can't blame him for that.'

'Ah, but do you see the idea?'

'I suppose he wants to get rid of them. Everybody does.'

Colonel Nutting drummed impatiently with his fingers.

'You've got a lot to learn yet, Blenkinsop.'

'Oh, of course,' the neophyte agreed modestly.

'Don't you see that the Yanks will score either way? If we find ourselves at war with them they will have a vast organization for blowing up things like the Houses of Parliament and . . .'

'But wouldn't it be rather a good thing to blow up Parliament as soon as war began? We had too many dam' politicians poking about in the last war.'

'Don't be too ready to sneer at politicians, Blenkinsop. Don't forget the House of Commons voted four hundred million pounds to carry on the war whenever they were asked to do so, without even discussing it. No, I'm not one of those unimaginative soldiers who sneer at politicians. But the beauty of Katzenschlosser's plan is that, if on the other hand America is fighting on the same side as ourselves in the next war, the expense of interning all these Bolshies will fall on us. Neat, isn't it?'

'Very neat.'

Further tales about the redoubtable Katzenschlosser were interrupted by the telephone bell.

'Hullo!' said Colonel Nutting, lifting the receiver. 'Hullo, is that 10,000 Hampstead? Is Miss Glidden there? Ask her to speak to the head plumber ... Hullo, hullo, is that you, Miss Glidden? This is the head plumber speaking. Miss Glidden, I'm sorry to say the cistern in Captain Churchill's Paris flat shows signs of leaking badly. It is advisable to tell all his friends not to call upon him for the present. Will you take the necessary steps immediately? Is that fully understood? Everything all right at The Elms? Good! Will you tell Major H. H. that Captain Churchill is returning tomorrow? Thank you.'

Colonel Nutting replaced the receiver.

'I have done everything possible to check Mr Katzenschlosser,' he said with simple pride. 'And now let us talk about your pigeon, Blenkinsop.'

Chapter 5

THE MENDACIAN SITUATION

COLONEL NUTTING offered Blenkinsop a cigar and after lighting one for himself took his seat at the desk.

'Pull up that armchair, Blenkinsop,' he said, 'and make yourself comfortable. You don't mind if I sit at my desk? I find my ideas are clearer when I'm sitting at my desk.'

With this he put on his dark horn-rimmed spectacles and stared fixedly at his brother officer for the space of fully a minute.

'First and foremost,' he began at last, 'let me say I believe you are going to be the ideal man to succeed Hubert Chancellor. I believe the D.E.I. told you about that unfortunate business?'

'About his writing a novel?'

'Exactly. He wrote a novel called *The Foreign Agent* which might have smashed up the whole of the Secret Service.'

'Surely he didn't give away any of the secrets?' Blenkinsop exclaimed in horror.

'He did what was almost as bad,' said Colonel Nutting. 'He wrote what he honestly thought was a completely misleading picture of the Secret Service as it really is. The consequence is that any foreign agent who reads Chancellor's novel knows perfectly well now what the British Secret Service is not, and to know what it is not is half-way to knowing what it is.'

'Quite,' Blenkinsop agreed. 'But then don't lots of novelists write stories about the Secret Service? I was reading one coming over. It was called *The Green-Eyed Spy*.'

'But the author of that isn't in the Secret Service himself,' Colonel Nutting pointed out.

'Quite, quite,' said Blenkinsop. 'But would a foreign agent know that?'

'Ah, but Hubert Chancellor's name is printed in the *War Office Guide* under M.Q. 99 (E).'

'Isn't that a bit risky?'

46

'Not at all. Nobody knows what M.Q. 99 (E) means. You see, if Chancellor was still on the active list and if he told people he was working in the War Office they would ask him what he was doing, and he would be able to say that he was working in M.Q. 99 (E). It offers what we call a convenient cover.'

'But suppose people tried to find out what working in M.Q. 99 (E) meant?'

'That's where the Safety of the Realm Division comes in. Old P who is the D.S.R.D. has a special set of sleuths who devote the whole of their time to preventing people from finding out what M.Q. 99 (E) means. Of course, now that Chancellor has published this novel we shan't be able to use M.Q. 99 (E) any longer, and in the next *War Office Guide* we shall have to find another convenient method of reference.'

'Is your name in the *War Office Guide*?'

'No, because I'm on the retired list and people don't ask an officer on the retired list what he's doing. They take it for granted that he's playing golf.'

'Quite, quite.'

'That's why I'm glad you're on the retired list, Blenkinsop. It means we can keep your name out of the *War Office Guide*.'

'But I don't think golf will be enough cover for me,' Blenkinsop objected. 'I mean to say my wife knows I'm not at all keen on golf and ...'

'Oh, you're married, are you?' said Colonel Nutting in what Blenkinsop feared was a disappointed voice. 'Oh well, it can't be helped, and I dare say you'll be getting divorced quite soon,' he added cheerily.

'Still, I've already arranged for a convenient cover,' Blenkinsop explained.

'Ah, what's that? It must be impenetrable. If your wife finds out you're in the Secret Service you might as well go and announce it over the wireless. By gad! By gad, yes! Why didn't I ever think of that before? Oh, it's a great idea!'

'What?'

'Why, we've never used the B.B.C. for espionage yet. Oh, it's terrific. By Jove, what a development it suggests! Look here, Blenkinsop, I don't care if you're married or not. You're going to join us. You've given me the finest idea I ever had for espionage.'

'Oh, but it was your idea,' Blenkinsop disclaimed modestly.

'Yes, but if you hadn't been married I should never have thought of it.'

'But to return to the question of a convenient cover,' Blenkinsop ventured. 'I have more or less arranged for one, sir.'

Now that Blenkinsop felt sure of his engagement in the Secret Service he called his superior officer 'sir' by reflex action. His tongue formed the word automatically as the salivary glands of a dog respond to the sight of a bone.

Colonel Nutting held up a warning hand.

'N, not sir, Blenkinsop. We avoid any suggestion of rank in our work. One of the important things about it is not to let any foreign agent guess who is the head of the Secret Service. After all, war may break out any moment, and if the head of the Secret Service is known what chance do we stand against the enemy?'

'All right, N, I won't forget,' Blenkinsop promised, with a hint of self-consciousness in his tone.

'That's it,' N encouraged, 'you'll soon get used to calling people by their initials. But you were saying something about a convenient cover when I interrupted you.'

'Of course, I don't know how the notion will appear to you, but it would be quite easy for me to be the director of a company for exploiting the waste products of the banana. In fact I've already tried that on my wife. And she seemed to think it was quite a natural occupation for me.'

'Capital!' N declared enthusiastically. 'Couldn't be better. That's one of the most convenient covers I've ever come across. Look here, Blenkinsop, you're going to be invaluable to us. I ought to warn you, though, that our work doesn't consist entirely of meeting mysterious Polish countesses in old castles. Of course, we have our little dramas, but the greater part of the work is routine stuff. Card-indexing, filing, making out lists, putting agents' reports into proper English. We have a house in Hampstead. Do you know the Spaniards Road? Well, on the left-hand side going down towards the Bull and Bush, there's a large house which we call The Elms among ourselves, but which is really called Pomona Lodge. It stands back from the road in its own grounds. Absolutely secluded. We might be in the depths of the country. That's our headquarters. And do be careful when you come there. If you have to come by taxi never take fewer than two taxis, and always give a false address in a loud voice to the first taxi-driver. However, come by tube or by train and tube fairly often. And if you've reason to suppose you're being followed get out at some station like Goodge Street which is pretty empty. And if you notice somebody else getting out with you and hanging about, leave the station and find some excuse for having got out at Goodge Street.'

'That will be a bit difficult,' said Blenkinsop.

'Oh, I don't know, you can always go and buy a bit of furniture in Tottenham Court Road. You can always charge up anything like that if you can show it was bought for cover. Don't do it too often of course, because we can never get as much money as we want. I put up a scheme the other day for constructing a secret passage under the Heath from a house in Golders Green to The Elms, but it was turned down on the score of expense. A pity, because it does take up time getting our people to The Elms without being spotted by foreign agents. However, luckily the S.R.D. sleuths under P are regular tigers. And now let's talk about Mendacia. I don't have to tell you that Mendacia is the danger spot to European peace. You see, everybody wants it.'

'Yes, we found that when we were working on the boundaries after Versailles,' Blenkinsop agreed.

'So you see the main problem is to keep ourselves informed what other people are doing in Mendacia. We don't want to go blundering into the next war at the last minute as we blundered into the last one. As Chief of the Secret Service I want to be in a position to tell the Government that war will break out at least six months before it really does.'

'Yes, but will the Government believe it?' Blenkinsop questioned. 'I know when we were working on the Boundary Commission, the Government never believed anything we told them. And if the Government in power is a Labour Government they'll do anything to avoid a war.'

'That's taking rather a pessimistic view. There may not be a Labour Government. I think the patriotism of the country was thoroughly roused when the pound fell. And you must remember that all the cleverest politicians joined the National Government. That seems to me a tremendous sign of confidence in its stability. No, I think we can count on a Government that will envisage the possibility of war. Now, Clavering our Minister in Gadaro is, as you probably know, very much against the restoration of King Johannis to the throne of Mendacia. The Venetians accuse him of being pro-Burgundian. I don't believe that myself. I think he's one of these sentimental radicals who think any republic is better than a monarchy. Clavering has always pooh-poohed the chances of a royal restoration. Our job is to find out if Clavering is right. Personally, I don't believe he is. In my opinion the Mendacians themselves are waiting to see if Clavering's point of view is really the point of view of the British Government. So you see what your job is?'

Blenkinsop did not in the least see what his job was; but he nodded gravely and looked as wise as he could without the help of a pair of dark horn-rimmed spectacles.

'Now first of all about your organization. I don't want you to feel bound to take on Chancellor's organization, lock, stock, and barrel. I suppose there's no chance of opening that hotel again on the island of Parvo?'

Blenkinsop shook his head.

'Not without a good deal more capital. My brother made up his mind to cut his losses.'

'What was it losing a week roughly at the end?'

'About nine thousand bubas a week.'

'What's that in pounds?'

'Well, at the rate of exchange then, about ninety pounds a week.'

'No, I don't think we could run to that,' said N. 'I'd been wondering if we could finance the business out of the funds at my disposal just to keep it afloat. But I couldn't run to that. It's a pity, because it would have made such a very convenient cover. Suppose all the hotel staff were agents? We could save a bit that way.'

'Yes, but they couldn't very well do their hotel work and go spying about all over Mendacia at the same time,' Blenkinsop objected.

'I say, don't use that word, if you don't mind, when you're talking about our own people. We only use it of foreign agents. It may not seem to you important, but it's just these little things that make the wheels of the show go round smoothly. There's always a slight stigma attached to that word, and since the war we've really worked up a rather jolly pull-together spirit in the Secret Service. Some of the fellows who were in it during the war were apt to think that because they were in the Secret Service they could forget they were once gentlemen. Well, of course, they let in a lot of confounded amateurs, who had no traditions, no discipline, no anything. As a matter of fact, in ordinary conversation, we always call the work "plumbing" and in writing reports we say that an agent ascertained. We have three grades of agents – very reliable, reliable, and usually reliable.'

'What about an agent who isn't reliable at all?'

'Well, he would cease to be employed; but we count on the various fellows in charge of the various countries – who are all pukka soldiers now – not to employ unreliable agents. Of course, that doesn't say an odd agent might not make a few mistakes now and then, but he'd have to be pretty bad not to be "usually reliable". I see your point of view about the difficulty of running an hotel with even usually reliable agents, and equally your difficulty in running an efficient subsection of information with what you would consider even usually reliable hotel servants. Mendacia by the way is a subsection of the South-East Europe Section, which is under Claudie Hunter-Hunt. Did you ever meet him? He was in the Rutland Fusiliers.'

Blenkinsop shook his head.

'Well, you'll find H. H. a great man,' N declared. 'He'll be disappointed to hear that it isn't practical to start that hotel again on Parvo. But what *are* you doing with the place?'

'Oh, there's just a caretaker and his family living in the castle. People occasionally make excursions there from Gadaro, and he's allowed to sell them refreshments.'

'So that in case of need we *could* use it as a cistern.'

'As a what?'

'A cistern is a centre of information.'

'Oh, I think that could be arranged.'

'You see, we might want you to go out to Mendacia, and with the hotel you've always got a capital cover. However, that will depend on developments. The important matter is to establish contact at once with Madame Tekta.'

'With Madame Tekta?' Blenkinsop repeated. 'You don't mean *the* Madame Tekta?'

'The wife of the last Prime Minister of Mendacia under the Royalists. I see you know something about her?' N said, his light-blue eyes flashing through the horn-rimmed spectacles with a power of penetration that revealed him as an Intelligence officer of the very front rank.

'I've never actually met her,' Blenkinsop explained. 'But her name was a byword in Mendacia.'

'She is said to possess a fatal charm,' said N gravely, 'to have been the cause of six suicides, innumerable duels, and her husband's banishment.'

'There certainly was a lot of unpleasant gossip about her,' Blenkinsop agreed. 'In fact when old Tekta threw himself overboard from the Mendacian cruiser that was taking him to Trieste after he was booted out, everybody was saying that his wife pushed him into the Adriatic with the help of one of the junior officers who was in love with her.'

'That was never confirmed, but undoubtedly she is a very remarkable woman. She has more ways of finding out what is really going on in Mendacia than anybody, and she knows what King Johannis means to do. We approached her very carefully to find out if she would work for us, and at last it was fixed up for Chancellor to establish contact with her this evening. In the ordinary course of events I am absolutely against employing women in our work. For counter-espionage a woman may be useful. In espionage she is always a source of potential weakness. Mademoiselle quarrels with her lover, a foreign aviator, engineer, clerk in a government office, anything you like. She meets an agent on the look out for useful information. Anxious to be revenged on her lover she tells him all the gossip she has heard. The agent thinks he has tumbled on a good thing. Next day Mademoiselle makes it up with her lover and to show her goodwill gives away the agent. Result? Arrest of agent, possible trial for espionage, a stink in the newspapers, and general unpleasantness all round. On the other hand if Mademoiselle's lover is himself a foreign agent and is foolish enough to quarrel with her she gives him away to the police and it's too late then to make up the quarrel. So keep off women, Blenkinsop, in your work. I'll back you up whatever other mistakes you make, but if you start employing women I'll not put out a hand to get you out of any mess you get yourself into.'

'But is it wise to use Madame Tekta?' Blenkinsop asked nervously. It was going to be difficult enough to keep Enid quiet even with the help of the banana directorship; if she were to suspect another woman all the bananas in the world would not avail to cover him.

'I've thought over it a lot,' said N. 'I've given the proposal a great deal of anxious thought, and if I have decided to make an exception in this case it is only because I feel the situation in Mendacia justifies a risk I would not ordinarily authorize. Madame Tekta is herself the storm-centre.'

The Chief of the Secret Service stopped and took another long look at his new officer.

'Look here, Blenkinsop,' he said at last, 'I don't believe in letting a man in for a job of this sort wearing blinkers. If King Johannis makes an attempt to regain the throne, and we stand on one side it may easily mean another European war. But if we satisfy ourselves that the people of Mendacia really want their king back we can give him moral support, in which case the Burgundians will realize that it isn't just a matter of quarrelling with the Venetians. I'm going to give you a piece of absolutely confidential secret information. The other day the Foreign Secretary himself sent for me just before he started off for the Eighty-Ninth Disarmament Conference at Geneva and said: "Colonel, it's vital for me to know what the situation in Mendacia really is." Now the Foreign Secretary usually pretends he doesn't know there is such a person as the Chief of the Secret Service, and his sending for me like that shows that Sir Thomas Freshcote is the best Foreign Secretary our country has had for years. And he knows which side his own bread is buttered. I respect him for that. We want practical men at Geneva, not idealists. After all, Blenkinsop, we are still on earth.'

'Quite,' the dragoon agreed.

'So when we've got a practical man on the job we want to take advantage of it, and for that reason I'm going to take a sporting chance with Madame Tekta. The immediate problem is whether to let the lady know who you are or whether to let her think you're Chancellor.'

'I don't see much point in letting her think I'm somebody else,' said Blenkinsop. If he had to make his wife think he was a banana director and at the same time to delude Madame Tekta into supposing that he was his predecessor, Blenkinsop began to feel doubtful of his ability to do anything else in the near future.

'Well, it might be useful,' N said. 'If Madame T ... Look here we must find another name for her. Juno will do. We'll call her Juno. If Juno ...'

'Is she a very large woman then?' Blenkinsop inquired apprehensively.

'I've never seen her in the flesh; but her photographs don't give that impression.'

'That's what I was thinking, and Juno suggests a largish woman to me.'

'Well, I don't mind what we call her,' said N agreeably. 'We'll call her Venus if you prefer it. She's your pigeon.'

'No, no, don't call her Venus,' said Blenkinsop quickly. 'Let's call her Joan of Arc. I think that's less suggestive.'

'Suggestive of what?'

'Oh, nothing, nothing. We'll call her Juno. I'm sorry I interrupted.'

'What I was going to say was that if Juno double-crossed us and there was any kind of scandal . . .'

'Of scandal?' Blenkinsop asked with the hint of a quaver in his usually unemotional voice.

'We have to face such an eventuality,' said N firmly. 'If there is any kind of scandal Hubert Chancellor can be disowned absolutely.'

'Yes, but what will Chancellor's wife . . . I mean, what will Chancellor say?'

'Chancellor has made his bed by writing that confounded novel, though indirectly it has not been without its uses. Juno is very interested in literature. Women often are, of course.'

'Well, they have a lot of time on their hands,' said Blenkinsop, who was always chivalrous. 'My wife's a tremendous reader.'

'And when Juno agreed to meet Chancellor this evening she mentioned how much she looked forward to discussing his novel.'

'But I can't go to Madame Tekta as . . .'

'Juno. Juno! You *must* remember never to call her Madame Tekta when you're talking about her.'

'I can't go to Juno and start spouting a lot of rot about books. I've only met one novelist in my life, and I was pumping him about bananas all the time. So I didn't get much idea of the way that kind of fellow talks when he's spouting about books.'

'I've met one or two,' said N reassuringly. 'You know, at week-ends and that sort of thing. They're getting quite common nowadays. You see them everywhere since the war. It didn't change Chancellor a bit outwardly, writing this novel of his. Of course, it may begin to tell on him after he's written one or two more.'

'Look here, N, unless you're absolutely set on my meeting Juno as Chancellor I'd much rather meet her as myself,' Blenkinsop urged.

'No, you simply must not be yourself. She expects Chancellor to dine with her tonight in her flat, and if at the last moment I send a friend – by the way don't forget that in our work a friend always means a confidential agent – if I send a friend to tell her that somebody called Blenkinsop is coming instead she might call the whole deal off. I've just signalled all friends in Paris to keep away from me on account of Katzen-schlosser. Oh, from every point of view, you'd better be Chancellor. It's really the greatest bit of luck that you should be able to take advantage of such a convenient cover.'

'Well, I'll do my best,' Blenkinsop promised gloomily. 'But I'd like to know exactly what you want me to say at this interview.'

'I just want you to establish contact. Get on good terms with the lady. I gather that isn't too difficult, though you'll want to keep a cool head. I'm told she's a real scorcher. Dandle her along. You know the sort of thing. She'll probably ask for a larger regular salary. We're paying her a thousand francs a week as a start. Tell her that if she gives us what we want we shall never be ungrateful. Impress on her that we only want the real goods. No nonsense about guns and aeroplanes. We can find out all that sort of stuff without her help. And now you'll want to go off and think out a plan of campaign while you're dressing. Dinner is at eight. Here's her address – 44 bis Avenue Delacour. That's somewhere up by the Parc Monceau. Take the usual precautions. Three taxis. Drive the first one to the Louvre. Then take another and drive to the Folies Bergère. Then take a third, and just for an added precaution give him the wrong number. I'm travelling back to London tonight by Havre. This Katzenschlosser business has made it impossible for me to do anything in Paris this time. Which way did you cross?'

'By Folkestone and Boulogne.'

'You'd better go back by Newhaven and Dieppe.'

'But I've got a return ticket.'

'And that's the very reason for your going back by another route. You may think us over-cautious, Blenkinsop. But when you've been with us for a little while and have been stalked all over the place by foreign agents you'll get into the swing of it. It's great fun really, this matching your wits against the keenest wits in Europe and America. Only last summer George Spicer who's in charge of Western Europe spent two weeks in Seville disguised as a retired matador.'

'Great Scott! He must speak Spanish awfully well,' Blenkinsop exclaimed.

'Oh, like a native. But he was brought up there as a child. His people are in sherry. I'm great on disguises myself. My last effort was to travel right across Poland establishing contacts, disguised as a Liberal M.P. I'm pretty good at disguises. One of the chief C.I.D. men said it was lucky for Scotland Yard I went into the Secret Service instead of taking up crime. Well, so long, Blenkinsop. You'd better turn up at The Elms the day after tomorrow. You remember the real name of the house? Pomona Lodge. It's printed in white letters on a black gate. If one of P's sleuths slips out from the shrubbery and asks you what you want, tell him you've come to see about the drains. He'll pass you along at once. Ring four times and tell the orderly who opens the door that you want to see Miss Glidden. She's my secretary and will take you up to my room right away. Now is that all clear?'

'Yes, I think so.'

'Well, so long, Blenkinsop, and get busy with Juno right away.'

Blenkinsop walked out of that room on the second floor of the Hôtel Plonplon not exactly with a profounder sense of his own importance, for he was innately diffident; but he felt within himself the first stirrings of a richer personality, and as he walked along the corridor towards the lift there was already in his gait a suggestion of stealth, in his glance a hint of preternatural acumen. He looked at his watch. Was there time to go and buy himself a pair of dark horn-rimmed spectacles? No, it would be wiser to wait until he got back to London. He doubted if his French was fluent enough to explain that he wanted plain glasses which, though they would add something to the size of the subject, would add nothing to the size of the object.

When he reached his own room Blenkinsop threw himself down in an armchair, and spent a quarter of an hour in awed contemplation of himself. He was an officer in the Secret Service entrusted with a mission of European significance.

Chapter 6

JUNO

No officer in the Secret Service with a single drop of patriotic blood in his veins desires that the world at large should guess that he is an officer in the Secret Service. At the same time no officer in the Secret Service likes to be mistaken for an ignorant tourist. So when at half past seven that evening Blenkinsop told the first taximan to drive him to the Louvre he was not a little annoyed when the Deputy-Assistant Night Porter who had escorted him to the taxi informed him on hearing of his destination that the Louvre was shut at this hour.

'I know that,' said Blenkinsop haughtily. 'But I've changed my mind. Tell the driver to go to the Folies Bergère.'

'Oh yes, sare, ollright,' said the Deputy-Assistant Night Porter, 'and he can arrange good guide for you. Oh yes, sare, ollright.'

At this moment to his dismay Blenkinsop saw a sinister chin protruding from the revolving door of the Hotel, followed a second later by the rest of Katzenschlosser's stocky form. Blenkinsop drew back into the darkness of the taxi. At all costs he must avoid being seen by the famous American agent. Then he noticed that Katzenschlosser was being escorted to a rich-looking car by the Head Porter himself. Blenkinsop was not vain, but as a patriotic Briton he did resent that the agent of a power which did not enter the war until 1917 should be escorted to a rich-looking car by the Head Porter in person whereas a mere Deputy-Assistant was considered good enough for the taxi of himself. He made up his mind to spoil Katzenschlosser's little game, at any rate in the Hôtel Plonplon.

'Porter,' he called.

The Deputy-Assistant checked the taxi-driver who was by now pawing impatiently at the steering-wheel and leaned obsequiously through the window.

'You see that gentleman getting into the large car? Do you know who he is?' Blenkinsop asked.

'Yes, sare. That is Mr Churchill, the great American banker. He goes for dinner with Monsieur le Président.'

'The President of what?'

'*Le Président de la République Française,*' the Deputy-Assistant gravely announced, so gravely that if the driver had struck up the *Marseillaise* on the horn of the taxi it would not have sounded obtrusive.

'But are you sure that is Mr Churchill the banker?'

'Oh yes, sare. He come to the Plonplon perhaps twenty years.'

'Merci bocoo,' said Blenkinsop. He spoke in French to conceal the emotion he felt at the Deputy-Assistant's fallibility. Then he signed to drive on.

The taxi-driver after being kept waiting for at least two minutes was by now in one of those overwrought moods which turn Parisian taxi-drivers into demon huntsmen. Blowing his horn madly he set out to kill as many foot-passengers as possible before reaching the Folies Bergère; but, though helped by the fog, he had bad luck, and when he drew up at the Folies Bergère his game-bag was empty. To console himself he had an argument with Blenkinsop about the fare, which Blenkinsop lost, partly from lack of fluency in French and partly because all the other taxi-drivers were shouting out at his taxi-driver to get on and leave the way clear to the entrance of the theatre. Blenkinsop was rid of him at last, but the experience had shaken him and when he took another taxi he did not feel he could sustain in an argument his desire to go to the Louvre after closing time. The only other place he could think of on the spur of the moment was the Eiffel Tower, but when he was half-way there he began to get nervous about the time and decided so far to disobey N's instructions as to stop the taxi and tell the driver to go to the Avenue Delacour instead. The driver was so much disturbed by Blenkinsop's change of plans that he unstrapped himself and came round to the door of the taxi to find out if his ears had deceived him.

'*Alors, vous ne voulez pas aller au Tour Eiffel?*'

'*Non.*'

'*Mais vous m'avez dit le Tour Eiffel?*'

'*Oui.*'

The driver looked at the taximeter and shook his head. By his gesture he conveyed to Blenkinsop that people who told taxis to go to the Eiffel Tower and when half-way there changed their minds and indicated a street in the neighbourhood of the Parc Monceau as their destination must not grumble if such indecision cost them money.

'*Ça ne fait rien*,' said Blenkinsop.

The driver shrugged his shoulders, remounted his seat, strapped himself in again, turned the taxi, and shot off in the direction of the Parc Monceau like a shell from a gun.

'*Avenue Delacour!*' the driver shouted at last. '*Quel numéro?*'

'*Ça ne fait rien*,' Blenkinsop shouted back through the swirling fog of the wretched November night.

'*Comment ça ne fait rien?*' the driver shouted indignantly. '*Quel numéro?*'

'*Quatorze*,' shouted Blenkinsop in desperation.

The driver peered through the murk, and then with shrieks of protest from the gears turned the taxi round in order to deposit his fare at the number he wanted. He pulled up, and after unstrapping himself again, got down to open the door.

'*Voilà numéro quatorze.*'

Blenkinsop paid him generously with what he thought was a fifty-franc note, so generously that the driver expressed his gratitude by hastily preceding his fare to the door and ringing the concierge's bell.

'*Angliche*, yes,' he observed to Blenkinsop with a benevolent smile while they waited for the concierge to open the door. '*I no spik Angliche very good.*'

'*Non*,' Blenkinsop agreed, wishing the officious fellow would take himself off and leave him to explain to the concierge in his own way that he must have come to the wrong house. In his confusion the only French name he could think of when the concierge opened the door was Front de Bœuf. He had read *Ivanhoe* at school.

'*Qui?*' repeated the concierge. '*Madame Front de Bœuf? Je ne connais pas ce nom.*'

'*Ah, evidentement j'ai fait un erreur,*' observed Blenkinsop.

The concierge looked at Blenkinsop with that expression of ferocious misanthropy which Parisian concierges share with the mandril and slammed the door.

'*Type infecte!*' the taxi-driver commented. '*Mais n'ayez pas peur. Nous trouverons cette Madame Front de Bœuf.*'

And no French that Blenkinsop could command availed to discourage the driver's benevolence. He was not the foul type to leave a stranger at the mercy of such uncivil beasts as that concierge. Front de Bœuf was not a common name. Somebody in the quarter would certainly have heard of her and be able to give her correct address. Front de Bœuf? A very droll name. Was Madame a friend of Monsieur? Monsieur had given fourteen as her number. Well, why not try twenty-four? And if not twenty-four, thirty-four? *Courage!* There were plenty of other numbers in this street, and only one had been tried so far.

At last the moment came to try number forty-four itself, and Blenkinsop, despair lending his French a lucidity that amazed him, suggested that his companion should try the number of forty-one while he inquired at number forty-four. The taxi-driver thought this was a good idea, and now everything depended on whether the concierge opened the door in time to deny the presence of Madame Front de Bœuf before the concierge opened the door of number forty-four to admit that of Madame Tekta.

Blenkinsop won the stratagem by a short head, for just as the taxi-driver was coming disappointed away from number forty-one he slipped inside number forty-four and to his profound relief heard the door close behind him. On his way upstairs, for his hostess occupied the top half of the house, Blenkinsop began to consider the taxi-driver's friendly behaviour extremely suspicious. He should have to be careful when he left Juno tonight. A smart French maid of the type familiar to British playgoers over many years, but rarely seen in actuality, admitted Blenkinsop to Madame Tekta's maisonette. In the hall an ormolu clock chimed a reproach for being a quarter of an hour late. He entered the presence of his hostess full of apologies. As she rose from the couch to greet him, Blenkinsop tripped over the head of a bearskin and as nearly as possible dived past her to land head foremost on the couch from which she had just risen.

'Oh, I am so sorry,' murmured a voice melodious and low like the sound of water in sea caves. 'My silly old bear must always behave so badly.'

'My fault entirely for being so clumsy,' said Blenkinsop. 'I'm afraid I'm disgracefully late.'

'No, no, you are in very good time,' his hostess reassured him. 'But I think you are ready for a cocktail, yes?'

Blenkinsop accepted the glass from her slim hand and for the first time took a proper look at the widow of the late Prime Minister of Mendacia.

She was dark and tiny, dressed in some black material that was shot with amber. Her lips were full, her eyes a deep glittering impenetrable brown, her complexion lily white. She wore no jewellery except a platinum ring on the forefinger of her left hand in which was set a large solitary pearl faintly sheened with blue. That this exquisite miniature of womanhood who could hardly yet be much over thirty should have been alluded to as Juno revolted Blenkinsop's sense of fitness.

'You see I read your book, Monsieur Chancellor,' she was saying, and sure enough there beside her on the emerald-green satin of the couch was *The Foreign Agent*. 'How can you be so clever to think of so much?'

'Well, really, I don't know,' said the putative author.

'Ah, that is because you are so modest like all Englishmen.'

'That's very kind of you, Madame,' Blenkinsop muttered uncomfortably.

'Ah, but I am not supposed to be at all kind,' she avowed. 'My enemies, and I have so many many enemies, call me the most cruel woman in Europe.'

'Oh, enemies will say anything,' Blenkinsop reassured her.

Madame Tekta sighed deeply.

'You are so right, Monsieur Chancellor. Yes, indeed, you are so right.'

Blenkinsop's whole being went out to this lovely victim of

slander. He felt an almost overwhelming desire to interpose himself between her and the javelins of scandal. She roused in him the noblest instinct of the male – the instinct to protect a woman with her back to the wall. And what a back …

'No, I won't have another cocktail, thanks,' he said quickly.

'It must be so wonderful to write a book, Monsieur Chancellor.'

'Look here, don't let's talk any more about backs – books, I should say.'

It struck Blenkinsop as an almost intolerable thought that when at last fate did introduce him to the ideal woman the introduction should be effected under a name and a profession that were not his own.

'You will forgive me, Monsieur Chancellor, if I say something that is most terribly frank?'

'Of course.'

'You do not look to me at all like a man who writes books.'

'I'm delighted to hear it,' Blenkinsop declared.

'Once, before I have been married to my husband,' Madame Tekta said dreamily, 'a young poet of my own country was so much in love with me; but for me it was impossible to give back that love he was wanting.'

'Why should you?' Blenkinsop demanded indignantly.

'And he has thrown himself into the sea and become drowned. *It was a great tragedy*. People were saying that I was guilty of his death. Oh, it was quite terrible. Once I have gone to put flowers on his grave, and his mother has tossed them on me so injuriously.'

'Very bad form on her part,' Blenkinsop declared. 'My sympathies are entirely with you over this business.'

Madame Tekta turned and gazed full into Blenkinsop's eyes. He felt a shock go through him.

'Ah, you are so full of sympathy, Monsieur Chancellor,' she murmured. 'You encourage me to talk outside myself.'

'Do I?' Blenkinsop gulped.

'But here is Antoinette to say dinner is served,' she interposed quickly with a seductive coolness. 'Forgive me, my friend, if I cannot offer you such dinners as once upon a time I could offer you in my own land. I think you have never been in Mendacia. I wish it might be my pleasure to show it to you for the first time.'

'I wish that too,' Blenkinsop declared fervidly as they passed from the salon into the dining-room. 'But as a matter of fact I have been in Mendacia. I was working on the Boundary Commission.'

'So you know my beloved country!' Madame Tekta exclaimed in a rapture.

'Yes, and afterwards I was responsible for the development of the island of Parvo as a tourist resort.'

Madame Tekta looked puzzled.

'But, pardon, monsieur, I think Blenkinsoup was the name of that gentleman.'

'Sop not soup – Blenkinsop. And that is my real name.'

It was out now. It might be a violation of that eccentric code of honour which governs the Secret Service. It might involve him in resigning from his job as soon as he returned to London. No matter! Better be a stillborn officer of the Secret Service than creep into a woman's affection with another man's name.

'Then you did not write that beautiful novel?' Madame Tekta sighed in evident disappointment.

It might be a nice point to decide whether Blenkinsop answered as he did for fear of disappointing his chief or the lady. Anyway, he regarded his answer as a masterpiece of evasion.

'Hubert Chancellor is an assumed name,' he declared. 'There is nobody actually of that name working on behalf of British Intelligence. My chief considered it advisable to approach the matter on which I have come to see you with a certain amount of caution. Hence the advantage we took of the name Hubert Chancellor. But as soon as I saw you, madame, I realized that I must give you my fullest confidence. My real name is Arthur Blenkinsop – Major Arthur Blenkinsop.'

'Arthur,' she murmured. 'Oh, I have read such beautiful things about King Arthur. I am so glad you are called Arthur. And I am called Renata.'

'Renata,' Blenkinsop repeated, rolling the sweet syllables over and over until they acquired an 'r' at the end of them.

Madame Tekta put a hand to her heart.

'What's the matter? You not feeling ill?' he asked anxiously.

'No, no, it is quite a little nothing. But when you have whispered "Renata" like that it has made me so *émotionée*.'

'You know, it's a most extraordinary thing, but you have the most extraordinary effect on me,' Blenkinsop declared, with an emphasis that was by no means Nordic.

'Yes? How is that?'

'Well, usually I'm rather shy with women, but I don't feel at all shy with you. I feel I could say anything to you. I mean to say you seem to understand me so frightfully well.'

'It may be there can be an affinity between us, my friend,' Madame Tekta murmured. 'I am so very mystic. I believe so much that a soul can speak to a soul.'

'Oh, there's no doubt about it,' Blenkinsop agreed enthusiastically. 'Now if I were a musical sort of chap I could imagine myself inspired by you to play the violin or the piano like anything.'

And as if to show what he could do with a piano Blenkinsop pressed the soft pedal of her foot, for the table at which they were dining was as small and intimate as one of those tables which a head waiter reserves for lovers who look able to reward his solicitude.

'But I shall inspire you to write a wonnderful book,' Madame Tekta promised.

Blenkinsop looked less capable of responding to her afflatus as a writer than with his foot on that soft pedal he felt capable of responding as a pianist.

'*Alors, soyez sage*,' she warned him. 'And let Antoinette put you more champagne.'

The rest of the dinner was carried through in an atmosphere of discretion which made Blenkinsop long for the moment when he and his hostess should be left alone together to discuss the business which had brought him here tonight. His behaviour may suggest that he was too volatile for the important mission which had been entrusted to him. It is true that Madame

Tekta's personality had made a deep impression upon him. It is true that he hoped his own personality had made at any rate a slight impression upon her. Yet he was an officer of the Secret Service first and a human being second all the time. Madame Tekta's help was wanted. In that case it was plainly his duty to use whatever measures seemed most likely to secure it. In fact so far was Blenkinsop from any idea of taking advantage of the position in which he found himself in regard to Madame Tekta that in the course of talking at dinner about the lighter side of Mendacian life he did not hesitate to let her know that he was married.

'And you have been married long?'

'Three years last June.'

'And what is Madame Blenkinsob like? She is certainly beautiful?'

'Oh, yes, she's considered very pretty.'

'Blonde? Brunette?'

'She's fair.'

'And of course you admire that so much?'

'Oh, I don't think I admire fair women any more than dark women as a whole.'

'And of course she loves you *à la folie*?'

'I think we're very fond of one another.'

'What a beautiful idyll,' Madame Tekta sighed deeply. 'For me it is like paradise to hear of two people who love one another and are so happy together. I have always been unhappy in love ... *mais n'en parlons plus*. I find it so selfish for the unhappy to intrude upon happiness. I wish so much I could have met Madame. She sounds *ravissante* as you describe her with such eloquence.'

For a moment Blenkinsop thought his hostess was taking advantage of his foot's touching hers under the table to pull his leg; but there was no sparkle of malice in those great brown pools that were her eyes. They gazed into his own with the unmistakable expression of a much misjudged and very unhappy woman.

'I hope that one day we shall meet in Mendacia. Something is bound to happen there very soon,' Blenkinsop said.

'Indeed you are right, my friend. But we shall talk of that presently.'

Yet when at last Blenkinsop found himself alone with Madame Tekta in that dim salon the conversation did not veer round to Mendacian politics as rapidly as might have been expected.

'You were saying just now, Madame Tekta . . .' Blenkinsop had begun, when with a shudder which made him long to steady her between his arms Madame Tekta herself rejected the name.

'Ah, do not call me that. For me it is bound up with too much wretchedness. I have told to you my name. Call me by that. We are friends, are we not?'

'I hope so . . . I hope so indeed,' Blenkinsop replied. Then he swallowed at one gulp the glass of green chartreuse beside him. 'The best of friends, Renata,' he added boldly. 'Isn't that a pearl in your ring?'

'Yes, it is a pearl, Arthur. It is beautiful. Yes?'

'Very beautiful indeed,' Blenkinsop assented, crossing over from the armchair, seating himself beside her on the couch, and taking up her hand to look at the pearl with that immense interest it is occasionally so easy to bestow on inanimate objects. 'But look what a beautiful hand it has to set it off.'

She snatched away the prize it had cost such a fight against self-consciousness to seize.

'Oh, you are like every man, my friend Arthur. I have to be for you a *joujou* which you will play with for a few sweet moments and then fling away.'

'No, no, Renata,' Blenkinsop declared with a passion that surprised himself. 'You're a million times more to me than any jujube. You may think me a rotter, but . . .'

'What is rotter?'

'Well, a cad.'

'But what is cad?'

'Well, you may despise me, Renata. But I can't help it. You fascinate me. They say you've driven six men into committing suicide for love of you. I suppose that young fool of a poet was one of them. Well, you can make a fool of me if you want to. You'll find me an easy victim.'

Renata's eyes filled with tears.

'So that is what you have heard about me, my friend? And because you have heard so much you think that you must be cruel first.'

'How can I possibly be cruel to you? The idea's ridiculous.'

'Why must it be ridiculous?'

'As if you cared two straws about me!'

'You are so sure of that?' she asked gently.

'But what is there about me that could possibly attract a woman like you? I'm not good-looking. I'm not clever. I'm not anything that a woman like you would expect a man to be.'

'You are so sure of that?' she repeated. 'Let me tell you, my friend, that I do not look for – oh, how can I say what I mean in your language? Did I not say to you that *au fond* I am a mystic? To me you are the expression of my poor country's will to be free. When you have said to me your name is Arthur, my heart has beatened. "This is the saviour of my country, the saviour of my King," I have told to myself. What does beauty mean to me when I behold strength? What does cleverness mean to me when I behold loyalty? But when you have made love like so many others my heart has become a stone because I have perceived that for you I am a piece of feminine flesh . . .'

'Look here, I wish you wouldn't talk like that,' Blenkinsop interrupted. 'All I know is that you've absolutely bowled me over, and I suppose I behaved as most men would behave under the circumstances. I apologize for my brutality.'

'No, no, it is my *faiblesse* for which I must ask your pardon, Arthur. Perhaps when my poor country shall be free to choose her own destiny and give her loyalty to her King we can ask ourselves where this wonderful mystic love can take us. Let us remember, my friend, that our duty is not first to ourselves.'

'You're absolutely right, Renata,' Blenkinsop declared, 'You've got your King and country to think about and I've got the Service.'

'The Service,' she whispered to herself. 'The Secret Service!

What a grand *roman* there is in those two words! And do you think it is really so secret, *mon cher ami?*'

'Good lord, yes,' Blenkinsop replied hurriedly. 'Why, the whole point of the Secret Service is the secrecy. You've no idea what precautions I took even just to come and dine here tonight.'

'You are armed, yes.'

'No, I'm not armed. As a matter of fact we rather discourage arms in our country. Even the police are only allowed to carry truncheons.'

'What is truncheon? That word is new for me.'

'A truncheon is a sort of short thick stick with which you hit a man on the head if necessary.'

'And you have a truncheon with you tonight?'

'No. I haven't one.'

'Oh, please always to bring your truncheon when you come to visit me,' she begged.

'That's all right, Renata. I can look after myself without any kind of defensive weapon.'

'I hope so,' she said anxiously. 'But since I can read your book and am knowing now what perils there can be in the Secret Service, I am afraid for you.'

'You must remember that's only a book.'

She put a hand on his.

'You are very brave, Arthur.'

'Oh no, not particularly.'

'Ah, but I know better. Feel my heart how much it can beaten.'

With an impulsive gesture she had clasped his hand to her breast. Blenkinsop tried as hard as he could to feel like a doctor, but he was not successful in suppressing entirely a most unprofessional thrill.

'Yes, it is beating, isn't it?'

'You know why?' she murmured huskily. 'It is beatening for your safety.'

Blenkinsop put his disengaged arm round her and was just bringing himself to the point of leaning over to kiss her when a bell shrilled through the quiet of the dim salon, at the sound of which Blenkinsop whose conscience cannot have been perfectly clear sprang up from the couch and seated himself in the armchair opposite.

'Who can it be?' Madame Tekta exclaimed.

'The bell sounded as if it was in the room,' said Blenkinsop.

'No, no, it must be somebody who has called to see me. *Écoutez!*'

Blenkinsop listened with all his might, but nothing was to be heard.

'Antoinette will say that I am not at home,' his hostess reassured him. 'But that is a little lesson that we must be serious. We have our business to arrange, *n'est-ce pas*? Now first of all for the money – oh, how I hate to talk of money! You have really no idea how it abases my spirit to talk about such a dirty thing as money. Yet if I must do the work your Government requires from me it is sure I must have quite a little amount of money.'

'It was arranged that you should receive a thousand francs a week,' Blenkinsop reminded her.

'And you think that can be altogether quite enough for what I must do?' she asked.

'My chief has authorized me to say that if you are able to give us what we want you will not find us ungrateful.'

'But it is you who will judge what you want. Listen, my friend, I find all this talk about money extremely disgustful. But it is better that I am frank now so that we need not always mortify ourselves with these abominable discussions when we are meeting again. You concur?'

'I think you're absolutely right. I think it's vital to have a clear understanding beforehand about these matters.'

'You are so excessively intelligent, *cher ami*. I declare to you that it is one of the greatest pleasures of my life to find that you are so easily able to understand the difficulties of my position. Thank you a thousand thousand times for your tender consideration. It makes business a thing of beauty when I talk of business with you. Thank you, oh thank you, my dear dear friend, for your agreement that I must have – wait now for me to think in English. To speak of money abases me so much that

I must be translating from my own language very hardly. One thousand five hundreds? Yes, one thousand five hundreds of francs every week. That is settled, yes? Oh, what a *soulagement*!'

'Look here,' said Blenkinsop, who by this time was feeling a little bewildered by the rapidity with which Madame Tekta's weekly salary had soared to half as much again as that agreed upon, 'look here, I mustn't promise too much. I shall have to put your point of view before my chief, and I hope that he will see the matter from your point of view. I am returning to London tomorrow, and you may rely on my doing everything I can to secure you the additional five hundred francs.'

'Oh yes, please, Arthur, please, because an intelligent man like you must see that it is entirely impossible for me to contrive anything with one thousand francs. If I shall work for the British Government I must show to my countrymen that I am not a nothing. I can assure you that the whole of Mendacia is waiting to throw away President Grandako and bring back the good King Johannis. The Venetians will put themselves beside him. And perhaps Burgundy will fight with Venetia, and that is what England is wanting, yes?'

'No, no,' Blenkinsop exclaimed. 'England never wants a war. You must not put ideas like that into the heads of the people of Mendacia. All we want to know is whether there is going to be a war in spite of all we can do to stop it.'

'Yes, yes, I have perfectly understood,' she said impatiently. 'What I say is quite the same to what you say.'

'Not exactly,' he argued. 'It would not do at all to give the people against the republic the least idea that England was backing them up.'

'What strange business is backing up?'

'Supporting them, encouraging them. If Sir John Clavering, our Minister in Gadaro, heard that the Secret Service was interfering in the internal politics of Mendacia there would be trouble at once. I assure you there would be. Of course, if the people of Mendacia bring back the King of their own accord, that's another matter. What we want to know is whether they will bring him back.'

'But I will have one thousand five hundreds of francs every week?' Madame Tekta pressed.

'I'll do my best to get it for you,' he promised. 'But the great thing is to start off with plenty of really interesting information. However, I expect I shall be seeing you again very soon with fuller instructions. This visit is only what we call to establish contact.'

'To establish contact,' she echoed with a sigh. 'How beautiful that can sound with somebody for whom one has a profound sympathy; but how brutal, how terrible, how ignoble it could be with others. *Enfin*, I discover myself to be a very fortunate woman. You cannot imagine how much I was afraid for meeting you before you came. Oh, I was entirely *assommée*. Figure, please, that my greatest enemy in Mendacia was Colonel Cokolambra, the Chief of our Secret Police, who has betrayed King Johannis and my poor husband. And I was thinking always that you would be a second Cokolambra. Figure then my joy when instead of that black poisonous traitor always without shavings and with a face like a *congre*.'

'Like a what?'

'*Comme une anguille de mer*. How you say it in English? It is a sea-monster.'

'A whale?'

'No, no, a whale is a *baleine*. Not at all that.'

'A shark?'

'No, no. Eel – eel. That is the word I lost. An eel of the sea, the *congre*.'

'Oh, a conger-eel,' Blenkinsop guessed.

'*Oui, oui, c'est ça!* Cokolambra had a face like a conger-eel. But you are so different, Arthur. You are so entirely a gentleman. And of all things the good God has made, for me an English gentleman is His *chef d'œuvre*. How you say it? His misterpiece?'

'Masterpiece,' Blenkinsop corrected.

'It is when I agitate myself that I forget all my English.'

'I think you speak English marvellously. I only wish I could speak French a twentieth as well.'

'I will teach you all the languages I know, *cher ami*,' she murmured tenderly. 'Now that we are contacting with each other.'

Blenkinsop's eyes gleamed like a sheep's in the motor lamps of her bright onrush.

'What languages do you know?' he asked, his voice sounding as if his mouth was full of cracknel biscuits.

'I speak Mendacian, French, Italian, German, a little English, a little Hungarian, a little Serbian, and a few words of Ruritanian.'

'I think you're marvellous, Renata,' Blenkinsop avowed. 'And which is the best language for love?'

'In my country,' she replied, 'we have a proverb which says, "To look love an Italian woman, to speak love a French man, but to make love all the whole people of Mendacia." '

'By gad, I believe that!' Blenkinsop declared with conviction. 'So you have many little Mendacian sweethearts, yes?'

'No, no, oh no, I give you my word, Renata. If a fellow is on a Boundary Commission he hasn't the time for that sort of thing. Why, some days it was all I could do to get any exercise. And when I was looking after Parvo for my brother I was kept busy the whole time.'

Madame Tekta leaned back on the couch and murmured from a pile of cushions:

'I see you are quite a Saint Anthony, my friend. I am so much afraid that I have entirely shocked you.'

Blenkinsop noticed that there was just room to seat himself on the couch where one of the cushions was embayed by the curve of Renata's waist and her negligently outspread left arm. He rose deliberately from his own chair, walked deliberately across the space that separated him from his lovely creature, and sat deliberately upon that embayed cushion, in which position at nothing worse than the risk of a cricked neck he could gaze down into the sparkling depths of her dark eyes.

'So you are not quite so shocked at all?' she said softly.

'Renata! Do I looked shocked?' he reproached her.

'No, but let me tell you that you look excessively tragic for the beautiful situation in which you find yourself.'

'That's because I can't make you out.'

'The fortress of a woman is her mystery. But you who are a soldier cannot be afraid of such a poor little fortress.'

'Renata, may I kiss you?'

'*Mais, mon dieu, quelle politesse!*'

Blenkinsop accepted the raillery in her tone as evidence that he would not ruin himself for ever in her eyes by adopting the bold course. He turned round to seize her in his arms. At that moment the bell again shrilled through the salon, and Blenkinsop again leaped back into his armchair.

'Antoinette will say that I am not receiving visitors,' the hostess declared confidently. 'But it is always a warning that we must be prudent. What is the time? Already nearly eleven o'clock!'

'That's not very late,' Blenkinsop pointed out.

'It is late for me, my friend. When one is past thirty it is time to think of tomorrow morning.'

Blenkinsop could not help comparing in his own mind Enid's unwillingness to face the fact of thirty with this frank acceptation of it. A moment later he was ashamed of his disloyalty and trying to make up for it (as he supposed) by saying to himself that Renata's awareness of the hour coincided oddly with the noise of that confounded bell.

'It's not too late,' he said suspiciously, 'for a visitor to think you will probably be at home.'

'How quickly we have become so intimate, *cher ami*, that already you give to yourself entirely an air of being the only man in the world.'

There was an edge to her tongue as she said this, and Blenkinsop remembering how important her services might be to his country controlled his jealousy.

'I beg your pardon, Renata. I had no right to say that. No right at all, I apologize.'

'You are already quite forgiven,' she assured him. 'But yet, my dear friend, you have hurted me a small bit by what you have said. It is for you perhaps a little nothing, but I am in a very *triste* situation, and in you I was finding some person who would be a friend.'

'Look here,' Blenkinsop declared fervidly. 'You can count on me absolutely. There was no excuse for talking like that. Will you forget I ever said what I did?'

'I will try to forget,' she promised, with a tremor in her voice that made Blenkinsop wish bitterly he could demonstrate to this much-wronged woman that all men were not the cynical brutes she evidently through sad experience had come to believe them.

'I shall leave you now,' he went on, 'and the day after tomorrow I shall report to my chief that you feel you can give us the information we want for six thousand francs a month.'

'Let me see – I am so foolish with money – that is one thousand five hundreds of francs every week?'

'That's right.'

'And I am quite sure that he will agree because you are so clever for explaining those material matters.'

'I shall certainly do my best,' Blenkinsop promised.

'*Alors, au revoir, mon cher ami,*' she said, offering him that lilywhite hand. 'I can never tell to you what this contact – yes, that is right? – what this contact has been for me. Oh, I must tell to you it has been one of the true pleasures of my life. *Enfin, vous êtes romancier,* and for that you have a grand understandingness of woman. I assure you that for us to meet again will be for me such a sweet dream.'

Blenkinsop bent over the lilywhite hand and brushed it tenderly with his toothbrush moustache.

'Ah, one can see that you are a true cosmopolitan, for I think that in England you do not salute a woman so. *Alors, à bientôt, n'est-ce pas?*'

'*Oh, oui, oui, oui, oui!*' Blenkinsop replied, breaking into fluent French under the stress of his emotion.

It was only when the concierge was going to let him out that Blenkinsop remembered he ought to have asked Renata to telephone for a taxi, and he turned to the man in an attempt to inquire in less eloquent French where he would find one quickly. To his surprise he was informed that the taxi was already waiting for him, and sure enough on walking down the steps of number forty-four he was greeted by the very same driver who had brought him here with such a display of ciceronage.

'*Et voilà,*' the man cried, '*Où allez-vous, monsieur?*'

'*Aux Folies Bergère,*' said Blenkinsop, determined to throw this foreign agent off his trail.

'*Mais non,*' said the driver. '*Fineesh les Folies Bergère! Trop tard!* You like nice girl? I take.'

'*Non, non,*' said Blenkinsop fretfully. Let this man be a foreign agent. He could not cope with him. '*Allez à l'hôtel Plonplon.*'

'*Bien, monsieur, tout de suite!*'

Blenkinsop entered the taxi which started off at the usual furious pace, the driver adding to the eccentricity of his course by beating his chest with one arm, presumably in order to impress on his fare that he had been waiting a long time for him in the cold.

At the Plonplon Blenkinsop gave him a hundred-franc note. He did not want an argument with the man which would let the porters of the hotel know where he had been.

'*Merci, monsieur,*' said the driver. '*Vive Madame Front de Bœuf!*' he added with a wink that would have dislocated a more sensitive eyelid. '*Je viens demain, oui?*'

'*Non, non, non, non,*' Blenkinsop almost groaned as he hurried into the hotel.

On looking through his notecase he found that he was without a five-hundred-franc note which had certainly been there when he started out this evening. He must have given it to the taxi-driver the first time he paid him.

'Oh well,' Blenkinsop said to himself, 'if he's a foreign agent I don't suppose he's the first one we've overpaid by mistake.'

Chapter 7

THE ELMS

LITTLE did the author and composer of the celebrated song *Down by the Old Bull and Bush* think when they were in the throes of inspiration that one day in a not so distant future the Secret Service would respond to their melodious invitation and come down within a mile of the famous hostelry to Pomona Lodge. Do not tremble, reader, for the safety of the realm. Pomona Lodge is no longer the headquarters of the Secret Service for reasons which this tale will horribly reveal.

Pomona Lodge is now an asylum for the servants of bureaucracy who have been driven mad in the service of their country. Only the other day the chronicler was privileged to be shown over it by one of the most distinguished alienists of the day, and it will be long before he forgets the experience. There he saw distracted typists typing away feverishly at reports which would never be read even in eternity. There he saw worn-out servants of the Inland Revenue assessing their own nurses' incomes at fabulous amounts. There cheek by jowl sat the squander-maniac and the suicidal junior clerk – the one writing out cheques for trillions of pounds, the other collecting the odd bits of red tape of which he hoped one day to weave a rope to hang himself. There moped ex-inspectors of food who had to be forcibly fed because the meals provided at the asylum appeared to them not up to the standard of purity required.

However, at the time of this tale, Pomona Lodge was not yet officially a lunatic asylum. It was still the headquarters of the Secret Service which had bought it soon after the war when the boom of the guns had just been succeeded by the boom of big business. The late owner had been Lord Cairngorm, one of those super-patriotic Scots who, free from any petty spirit of national pride, believed that by making his money in Scotland and spending it in England he was a living example of the benefits of the Union between the two countries. When a few parochially minded fellow-countrymen dared to sneer at Lord

77

Cairngorm's super-patriotism his answer was devastating. No sooner had he sold Pomona Lodge to the Government for three times the price he had paid for it than he bought a deer-forest in Ross-shire where local legend relates that he has been seen in the flesh on at least two occasions during the last decade. Pomona Lodge at the time of this tale was a large Georgian house standing well back from the road in its own grounds of five acres. As a habitation for the organizers of the Secret Service it was, not to use too precious an epithet, ideal. Behind it stretched Hampstead Heath, the rolling greenery of which was white in spring with daisies and even whiter in summer with paperbags and empty cigarette packets. On either side were the gardens and shrubberies of Golders Grange and Eagle Hall, its neighbours. In front, shielding the front door from the inquisitive listener, was what was generally believed to be the oldest and thickest grove of Portuguese laurels in Great Britain, through which the drive wound mysteriously.

The interior of Pomona Lodge was replete with every convenience for secret service. Lord Cairngorm had added a frigidarium, a magnificent sight when it was well stocked on the eve of one of those great banquets he used to give to members of the Coalition Government on putting through a big deal in the interests of national economy. This frigidarium had been converted into a dark-room where four expert developers worked continuously at the photographs which had been taken by British agents all over the world of foreign weapons and fortifications; but it would be an indiscretion that might cause the proclamation of a state of national emergency if any details were given of these photographs, which were only shown to influential members of parliament just before the Army Estimates were being discussed.

Lord Cairngorm's swimming-bath had been emptied and turned into a laboratory when the Government bought it. Here a staff of chemists worked on the enigmas offered by secret inks and analysed the specimens of poison-gas which other countries intended to use in the next war. One of the most deadly of these, according to the agent's report, would if dropped on gasometers in two-ounce packets by hostile aero-

planes turn every living creature within a radius of two
hundred miles a vivid pea-green and afflict many with demen-
tia praecox. A pamphlet on this gas was published by the
League of Nations and gave a great impetus to peace.

The wireless equipment was of course a feature of Pomona
Lodge. The whole of the top floor was fitted out for a staff of
confidential Russian scholars who sat in two-hour watches
listening to the propaganda from Moscow which they dictated
to stenographers in English. This arduous work won many an
M.B.E. for the devoted employees engaged upon it. Two or
three of them, alas, are still in Pomona Lodge though the wireless is now only used to amuse the patients with vaudeville
from the B.B.C. It would take too long to enumerate all the
little luxuries which once the war was over made the less
active side of the Secret Service such an enviable billet. It has
long been the boast of Great Britain that she possesses the finest
Secret Service in the world, and it was the delight of the
romantic enthusiasts at Pomona Lodge to ensure that such a
fine service was better housed, better equipped, and more
mysterious than any rival organization.

The counter-espionage measures taken by P and the Safety of
the Realm Division were worthy of the perfection with which
N had housed his organization. Half a dozen free-lance
shadowers haunted the stretch between the tube-stations at
Hampstead and Golders Green. They were given what might be
described as a roving commission to follow anybody whose
movements or appearance struck them as suspicious. There
were a few 'incidents' with the local police, and on one
occasion the shadower was actually run in by the constable on
point duty for persistently following a lady to whose cook the
constable was engaged to be married. Thanks to P's energetic
intervention the case was heard in camera, and the public
interest was not endangered by the revelation of the existence
of a military organization to look after the safety of the realm.
Moreover, as the case was held in camera, only the friends and
acquaintances of government officials knew all the details.

Indoors the arrangements for protecting the archives in
charge of the various sections were left to N himself who

would not have trusted even P's picked men for such a responsible position. N had begun by employing muscular deaf-mutes,
but he had given this up after the manhandling of a high
official in the Home Office who had not taken the precaution to
arrange beforehand with N that he was going to call and who
in consequence had been suspected of being a foreign agent by
these worthy fellows. After trying various other people N had
by now come to rely entirely upon army gymnasium-instructors
under a regimental sergeant-major.

The Chief's own room was in the very heart of Pomona
Lodge and had been built inside another room, the space
between the walls being filled with a special composition called
Smotherite which deprived even walls of their notorious ears
and was also fireproof and noxious to rats. The room was
furnished with a simplicity that well expressed the character
of the Chief himself. There was a large writing-table on which
were three pairs of dark horn-rimmed spectacles, a magnifying-
glass, an instrument for slitting open sealed envelopes, the
necessary stationery, and a bottle of that green ink which is
reserved for the correspondence of high officials in the Secret
Service. There were three or four armchairs, any one of
which could be floodlighted by pressing a button under the
table. Floodlighting is now considered the finest laxative for the
tongue that exists, and some of the results achieved by the
sudden application of it to untrustworthy agents were remarkable. He was indeed an exceptional human being who could for
long endure the strain of sitting in the middle of a fiercer light
than ever beat upon a throne while the Chief's horn-rimmed
spectacles gleamed at him from the shadow opposite and the
Chief's quiet remorseless questions gradually pierced his duplicity. On the walls hung large maps into which were stuck
little green flags. As no reader will ever see those flags with his
own eyes there is no harm in revealing that they stood for the
agents which the Chief had scattered over the whole world as
thick as missionaries in Polynesia. Two large safes in one
corner, a shelf of reference books, a couple of electric heaters,
a brazier for burning at the end of the day the blotting-paper
used by the Chief in the course of it, and a telephone that

connected him directly with the desks of all his section-chiefs, with Sir William Westmacott the Director of Extraordinary Intelligence, and with P completed the equipment with which N was forearming his country for the next war with fore-warnings.

It was in this room that on the morning after his return from Paris the Chief of the Secret Service was sitting with Major Claude Hunter-Hunt of the Rutland Fusiliers. H.H. as he signed himself on the reports of the South-East Europe Section, or 'our Claudie' as he was called by the stenographers and card-indexers when they were chatting lightly among themselves in their own tea-room, was a small man tending all over to globularity who in the full-dress uniform of his regiment must have looked like a red china teapot peeping from beneath a tea-cosy. However, he had by now been seconded to M.Q. 99 (E) for so long that he had probably forgotten what he did look like in uniform. In his globular head were set a pair of globular eyes the convexity of which was accentuated by the lenses of his horn-rimmed spectacles, behind which you could fancy that you saw his thoughts swimming about like minnows in a jar.

'Claudie is slow, but he's devilish sure,' his Chief had once declared. 'And above all he's genuinely cautious.'

Of that there was no doubt. And he was equally polite. In fact, he would probably have apologized to his own shadow for being afraid of it. No officer under N's orders was so jealous for the secrecy of The Elms. On one occasion an elderly aunt of his had greeted him just as he was emerging from Hampstead Tube Station with more caution than a badger from its earth, and he had run the risk of being disinherited rather than stop and speak to her at a spot so near to Pomona Lodge. His caution was indeed heroic, and it was believed that he had remained single all these years solely because he dreaded talk-ing in his dreams. In fact even on his narrow bachelor's bed he always tied a respirator round his mouth before going to sleep. Major Claude Hunter-Hunt lived in the Secret Service by the Secret Service for the Secret Service. Let us hope that in the new generation we shall find officers with a devotion equal to his: otherwise the old country will be in a bad way.

'Well, H. H.,' said his Chief, 'I think I've found the right man for Mendacia.'

Hunter-Hunt looked nervously over his shoulder. He had a dog-like trust in N's infallibility, but he did wish that he would not let out the names of countries in his section quite so casually.

'You think he's all right, Chief?' he asked in a low voice.

'Cavalry,' said N.

Hunter-Hunt did not seem perfectly reassured. It was true that N himself had been a lancer, but for the South-East Europe Section of M.Q. 99 (E) Hunter-Hunt would have preferred a man who had never galloped anywhere in his life.

'Blenkinsop of the Welch Bays,' N continued. 'Ever heard of him? He used to have some good ponies.'

Hunter-Hunt performed the negative gesture which when performed by the average person is called shaking the head. Shake, however, is not a word that can be applied to the testudinal deliberation of his neck's motion.

'It was Westy who dug him up,' N continued. 'He heard of him from General Cumberbatch who spent a winter at an hotel on the island of Parvo which Blenkinsop ran for his brother after the Mendacian Boundary Commission broke up. I gave him a rough idea of what we wanted, and I told him he would have the benefit of a consultation with you before he got really going.'

Hunter-Hunt's chin sank very slowly, touched bottom upon his tie, rested there a moment, and then rose again with equal slowness to signify a nod of assent.

'Meanwhile, I left him in Paris to establish contact with Madame T, who by the way, I think, had better be known as Juno in future.'

'Juno,' Hunter-Hunt repeated in a voice of hushed approval.

'Of course, it's an experiment using her,' N continued, 'but the circumstances justify it, I think. Military information is another matter. I will never sanction the employment of female agents for that.'

Hunter-Hunt trembled all over with agreement.

'However, Blenkinsop himself should be back tomorrow, and

I shall hear from him what are the prospects of a successful experiment. And now I have a serious bit of news, H. H. There's a leakage somewhere.'

'A leakage?' Hunter-Hunt echoed with a horrified break in his voice. 'You appal me, Chief. Not from The Elms?'

'I hope not, indeed,' said N. 'I hope it's only one of Spicer's people. I didn't like to fetch him back from Madrid until he's settled up things there. Nor did I like to cable over to America and fetch back Gossington; but it's confoundedly awkward that both of them should be away just when Katzenschlosser is impersonating me in Paris.'

'My God, Chief! This is dreadful news,' Hunter-Hunt gasped.

'Yes, it's pretty bad, though I can't help admiring the dam' fellow. One can't deny his smartness. Blenkinsop only had this one interview with Westy at the War Office when it was arranged he was to meet me in Paris. Yet Katzenschlosser got wind of it and was at the Plonplon with luggage actually printed W. S. CHURCHILL when Blenkinsop arrived, and what is more tried to get into touch with him in the Palm Court. Fortunately I had a kind of inkling that something was wrong. So instead of going down to the Palm Court myself I sent a note telling Blenkinsop to come up to my room.'

'By gad, Chief, you've got an absolutely uncanny instinct for things going wrong,' Hunter-Hunt declared, his voice throbbing with admiration.

'We must give Blenkinsop a good deal of credit for keeping his head too,' N continued. 'He seemed to scent somehow that it wasn't me as soon as he'd spoken to Katzenschlosser, and said quickly that he'd mistaken him for a Captain Churchill of the Bluffs. He's a cool hand, that fellow. You're going to find him a great help, H. H. Apparently Katzenschlosser was rabid when he realized that Blenkinsop had spotted his game. And now we've got to find out where the leakage is.'

'At the War Office,' said Hunter-Hunt with a promptitude so remarkable for him that his Chief could not help being impressed.

'Oh, you think it is at the War Office?'

'Well, who knew here that you were going to meet Blenkinsop in Paris?'

'Nobody. Only Miss Glidden knew I was even going to Paris, and you don't suggest...'

'Indeed, I do not,' Hunter-Hunt interrupted warmly. 'You know my opinion of Miss Glidden's discretion. If nobody except yourself and Miss Glidden knew that you were going to Paris that is the equivalent of saying that nobody at all knew. Yet Katzenschlosser's arrival before you shows that he knew beforehand you were going.'

The Chief of the Secret Service pondered this problem for a minute or two.

'Yes,' he admitted at last, 'it certainly looks as if he must have known. No, I don't see any alternative explanation.'

'Very well then, we have eliminated every possible channel for the leakage except the War Office.'

'Or Blenkinsop himself?' N suggested.

'You cannot expect me to give an opinion on that, Chief. In the first place it would put me in a very painful position to suggest that an officer in my own section had been indiscreet, and in the second place I have never met Blenkinsop. Do you consider him capable of such a gross irregularity?'

The Chief paused.

'No, H. H., frankly I do not. Had I thought so I would never have suggested him to you for Mendacia. You have always said that I was an infallible judge of a man's character.'

'And I still say so, Chief.'

'Of course, after this wretched Chancellor business...'

'But that was beyond anything that any of us could have imagined. Reading novels is bad enough, but writing them ... well, the kindest thing is to believe that poor Chancellor went off his head. We must remember he had shell-shock early in the war.'

'Did he? Do you know, I never knew that. I thought he had a staff job all the way through. Oh well, of course that accounts for it. But to come back to Blenkinsop. I must say I was tremendously impressed by his caution.'

'Then it must be the War Office,' Hunter-Hunt declared with positive finality.

'Do you think Westy talked?'

'Not necessarily, but I think it's extraordinarily indiscreet of him to interview people at the War Office. The last time I was there was at the Conference which merged M.Q. 44 (X) and all E.I. in M.Q. 99 (E) under the D.E.I. for general direction. Well, I never liked the idea of going to the War Office. I thought at the time and I still think that the Conference should have been held here. Anyway, as I was coming out, a stranger stopped me and asked which was the way to the pictures. It gave me a great shock. Luckily I had a handkerchief up to my face. So I don't think he'll recognize me anywhere. I warned one of P's people, and apparently the explanation the fellow gave was that he thought he was visiting the War Museum. Of course, the fellow may have made a genuine mistake, but you never know.'

'You never told me about this, H. H.'

'Well, you have such a weight of responsibility upon you, Chief. I didn't want to add to your worries. Still, I hope after this Katzenschlosser business you'll persuade the D.E.I. not to interview anybody at the War Office in future.'

'You don't think P's system of surrounding a visitor with tall orderlies and rushing him along to Westy's room is a sufficiently watertight precaution?'

'No, I do not.'

'I dare say you're right. I'll take the matter up with Westy. And we shall have to get busy about changing M.Q. 99 to M.Q. 88 for the next *War Office Guide*. Westy suggested we should be shown under E.I., but I think that's risky. Westy himself is all right, but a new D.E.I. might think it entitled him to interfere, and after the fight we've had to establish our independent status we don't want to throw away by a false move all the ground we've won.'

'Indeed, we do not, Chief,' Hunter-Hunt quickly agreed. 'Is there anything more you want to tell me?'

'No, that's all. I'm working out an important new scheme in my head, but it's too soon yet to say anything about it.'

'Then I'll get back to my room,' said Hunter-Hunt. 'We've just received O. K. 202's final instalment of the Ruritanian mobilization plan, and I want to get really down to it.'

N nodded encouragingly, and Major Hunter-Hunt departed to wrestle in solitude with the military ambitions of one of the States in his section.

When he was gone the Chief of the Secret Service pressed a blue button beside his table. A moment or two afterwards there slid into the room as stealthily as a spectre in an old-fashioned ghost story the tenuous form of his secretary. If Miss Glidden had not found her ideal occupation in working for the Chief of the Secret Service she might have been engaged by a showman as the world's thinnest woman. Yet she was not bony. She was as smooth and as supple as an eel, as light as a daddy-longlegs, and as swift as a dragon-fly. Her slim hands when they were not engaged upon the task of dictation floated upon the air like thistledown, and in repose she seemed to sway like weeds on the bed of a stream. Her voice was as the susurration of aspen leaves, and her face was perpetually tense with mental alertness, nostrils quivering, ears as nearly as possible pricked as human ears can be, lips parted, and eyes screwed up with concentration. As for secrets she carried them as multitudinously, as easily, as safely, and as neatly packed away as the female herring carries her roe.

'Take down this letter to the D.E.I., Miss Glidden,' said her chief.

Miss Glidden's finger coiled itself round a pencil as a young anaconda might seize its prey, and upon what one was bound by the elementary principles of anatomy to suppose were two knees in spite of the little space they occupied she poised her writing-block.

'My dear General,' N dictated, 'you will no doubt be as much disturbed as I was to hear that the news of Major B's departure to Paris was signalled to the American S.S. almost before he left the War Office. I do not want to take the matter up personally with P, for reasons which you will be the first to appreciate. The least appearance of criticism from our side of the show is always apt to put his back up. Still, it's no use blinking unpleasant facts, and the unpleasant fact remains that it is not safe.' N broke off the thread for a moment to ask Miss Glidden to underline 'safe' twice in green ink. 'It is not safe,' he continued, 'for members of M.Q. 99 (E) to go within a mile of the War Office. I am therefore writing to propose subject to your approval that in future any interview of the kind that you had with Major B should be held here. I've talked the matter over very carefully with H. H. and he agrees with me that it is vital for the security of our organization to avoid in future the chance of what might – underline "might" twice, Miss Glidden – what might have been a fatal check to all our plans.

'It would be a very great relief to me if I could hear from you as soon as possible that you concur with me in this proposal and will take the necessary steps to have it made an absolute rule at the earliest possible moment.

'I was delighted with Major B, and am most – underline "most" once, Miss Glidden – most grateful to you for putting us on to him. I value your judgement so much that I hope you will arrange matters from your end without telling P about this unfortunate business.

'You yourself put the thing in a nutshell the other day when you said that after all the whole point of the Secret Service was that it should be secret. Yours sincerely.'

When he had finished N looked at his secretary.

'I don't think there's anything to add to that, Miss Glidden?'

'It seems to me that you've said everything that can be said . . .' she paused '. . . usefully.'

'Before you type that out, Miss Glidden, I want to consult you about a stenographer for Major Blenkinsop.'

'What about Miss Harker?'

'Could you spare Miss Harker?'

'Well, of course I shall miss her. But it's hardly fair to let my own convenience stand in the way of her advancement. She's an exceptionally bright and intelligent girl. And I believe I can honestly say that I have trained her to be most discreet.'

'I'm sure you have, Miss Glidden. But what will you do if Miss Harker goes to Major Blenkinsop?'

'I was wondering if you would agree to let me have Miss Beddoes from the card-index, Colonel N? I think it's always a good thing to train girls along so that when war breaks out we shall have a body of highly trained and really dependable girls ready for anything.'

'Quite,' the Chief agreed. 'Well, I have complete confidence in your ability to pick out the best material. Of course, this means we shall want another girl for the card-index. Will you make the necessary discreet inquiries on the usual lines? By the way, what are we going to do about Captain Chancellor's stenographer?'

'Miss Camberly?' Miss Glidden pursed her lips and sighed. 'I'm afraid she's going to be a rather a problem. Major Hunter-Hunt gave her some work to do when Captain Chancellor left us. But the day before yesterday he heard that she had typed out Captain Chancellor's novel for him in her spare time, and since then I can see that her presence in the South-East Europe Section makes him rather jumpy. What do you suggest we had better do with her, Colonel N?'

'You don't think she might be transferred to Major Blenkinsop? That would leave Miss Harker with you, and Major Blenkinsop might find Miss Camberly's experience useful.'

Miss Glidden shook her head.

'I'm afraid Miss Camberly won't be a great deal of use to Major Blenkinsop. You won't misunderstand me, Colonel N, if I say she was rather fond of Captain Chancellor?'

'Really? I'd no idea of that, at all,' the Chief exclaimed.

'Oh, I'm sure it was nothing in the least serious. Still, I think she feels Captain Chancellor's novel didn't do so much harm as the rest of us thought. So I don't think it would be fair to give Major Blenkinsop somebody who might be inclined to resent his taking Captain Chancellor's place.'

'But this is all very irregular,' the Chief said severely. 'Surely Miss Camberly has been with us long enough to learn that "resentment" is a word that cannot exist in the same diction-ary as "discipline"? It seems to me that if Miss Camberly is going to surrender to these inappropriate emotions we had better dispense with her services altogether.'

'Well, of course, that is a point of view which must be considered, Colonel N.'

'In my opinion, Miss Glidden, we're only at the beginning of the harm that confounded novel has done. Resentment, indeed! You'd better send Miss Camberly to me at once. I shall have to make it clear to that young woman that if she wants to enjoy luxuries like resentment she will have to enjoy them somewhere else than in M.Q. 99 (E).'

'I'm so distressed, Colonel N, that I should have to worry you like this on top of all your anxiety over this leakage from the War Office.'

'Do not blame yourself at all, Miss Glidden. I should have resented ... I mean, I should have been extremely displeased if you had tried to hide this business from me.'

Miss Glidden smiled sadly. She suggested with her smile the mingled pathos and humour of the notion that anybody could hide anything from her Chief.

'You'd like me to send Miss Camberly to you now?' she asked.

'Immediately,' the Chief snapped.

Miss Glidden opened the door about ten inches and slid out of the room.

While he was waiting for the culprit to reach the presence the Chief of the Secret Service took off the horn-rimmed spectacles he was wearing and wiped carefully the lenses of that pair with which he was wont to pierce the inmost being of a doubtful agent. Then after putting them on he sat back in his chair, and fixed the door with an expression that a crouching jaguar would have envied.

Presently the door opened and his prey entered in the shape of a young woman with light brown hair, a pretty complexion, and wide blue eyes.

'You wished to speak to me, Colonel N?' she asked in a voice that sounded to the Chief astonishingly self-possessed.

'I did,' he replied grimly. 'Sit down.'

Miss Camberly sat down, and for two minutes and eleven seconds the Chief of the Secret Service gazed through her.

'Well?' he asked sternly when at the end of this ordeal she was still apparently solid flesh.

'Perfectly well, thank you,' she replied.

'You understand why I have sent for you, Miss Camberly?'

'No, Colonel N. Miss Glidden merely said that you wished to speak to me.'

'Never mind what Miss Glidden did or did not say. You must have some idea in your own mind of the reason for this interview?'

'None whatever, Colonel N,' said Miss Camberly, opening still a little wider her wide blue eyes.

'I sent for you, Miss Camberly, because I hear that you have ventured to criticize my action in dispensing with the services of Captain Chancellor. Criticism by one of the very subordinate members of my staff is a form of disloyalty to the Service.'

'But even the lower forms of staff life must have opinions of their own, Colonel N,' the reckless young woman enunciated as coolly as if she was stating a fact of natural history.

'In other words,' said N, 'you admit your disloyalty?'

'Loyalty to Captain Chancellor does not necessarily imply disloyalty to the Service,' Miss Camberly argued calmly; and her calmness roused the Chief to fury.

'If that is your opinion,' he growled, 'you are not fit to remain any longer in the Service. You are dismissed. Possibly Captain Chancellor will find you further work typing out his novels for him in your spare time.'

'He's sure to,' said Miss Camberly.

'Oh,' said her Chief with fierce sarcasm, 'and what makes you so confident of that, may I ask?'

'Well, we're going to be married next week, and you don't suppose I should be so silly as to let him get another woman to type his novels for him?'

'Married?' N gasped. 'Do you seriously mean to tell me that you were intending to remain on in the Service, although married to an officer who had forfeited our confidence?'

'Certainly not. I intended to tell Major Hardwick that I was giving up my job. And I strongly resent your saying that Bertie has forfeited the confidence of the Service. I'm ashamed of you,

Colonel N. I thought you were at heart a friend of Bertie's. I never thought you allowed him to be treated like this except to save your own face with busy old bumble-bees like General Westmacott.'

'Do you know, Miss Camberly,' asked the Chief, 'that your action in concealing from me your intention to marry Captain Chancellor renders you liable to a prosecution under the Official Secrets Act? Do you realize that your action might present itself to a jury in a very unpleasant light?'

'Ha-ha, twice,' said Miss Camberly, with a scornful little laugh that Colonel N thought was the most unpleasant sound he had ever heard in the throat of a woman.

'Your brazen attitude,' he said deliberately, 'does not impress me. You say now that you intended to notify Major Hardwick of your desire to resign from the Service? What proof have we of that? It looks very much as if you intended to remain on with the sole purpose of revenging a fancied injury by keeping your husband in touch with what was going on here so that he could write about it in novels.'

'What good would that be to Bertie? The reading public is getting sick of improbable rubbish. And anyway he's got a job as an announcer at the B.B.C. So he'll have no time to do much writing at present. You must think again, Colonel N,' she advised, and to give him an opportunity to do so she took out a pocket-mirror and dabbed her nose with powder.

As the Chief of the Secret Service did not reply Miss Camberly went on talking without noticing, so deeply engaged was she with her prenuptial appearance, that the reason why the Chief did not reply was a condition of speechless rage.

'Of course, I know you've all got to pretend that what you're doing is secret. You're like film stars the other way round. They live by publicity, and you live by secrecy. When I was a kiddie I used to hide behind the door and when my father had looked everywhere round the room in the most absurd places I used to jump out and say "Bo!" and he used to pretend to be frightened. Well, isn't that just the way you all behave? Good-bye, Colonel N, and sleep well. There are no naughty bears or lions or tigers under the bed. I've enjoyed my time at The Elms.

You're the Peter Pans of officialdom, and I love you very much really.'

The Chief of the Secret Service could stand no more. He pressed, as he thought, the yellow button which summoned Major Hardwick, who was the controller of his household, to pay this outrageous young woman off and eject her for ever from The Elms; but blinded with rage he pressed instead the orange button which sounded the fire-alarm, and instead of Major Hardwick four of the ex-gymnasium-instructors rushed into his room with buckets of water followed by the Sergeant-Major with a patent extinguisher.

'What the devil do *you* want?' the Chief shouted.

'The fire-alarm sounded, sir, from your room,' the Sergeant-Major explained.

'It's Colonel N who is on fire,' said Miss Camberly quickly.

'Put her out! Put that woman out!' the Colonel shouted.

Fortunately Miss Glidden came into the room before the amateur firemen confused by their instructions had actually emptied their pails over both Miss Camberly and Colonel N. A born secretary, she guessed at once that her Chief had pressed the wrong button.

'You are satisfied with the test, Colonel N?' she asked. 'That is quite all right, Sergeant-Major. The Chief was giving you a test alarm.'

When the Sergeant-Major and the gymnasium-instructors had retired Miss Glidden slipped across to her desk.

'I think you meant to ring for Major Hardwick,' she suggested.

'I wish Major Hardwick to pay Miss Camberly off,' said the Chief of the Secret Service. 'And in future if Miss Camberly comes into The Elms on any excuse whatever, she is to be put under instant arrest. I have nothing more to say to you, Miss Camberly, except to warn you that the Public Prosecutor may take a very grave view of your behaviour.'

'Well, that's what he's paid to take about everybody's behaviour, poor dear,' said the dismissed stenographer. 'Isn't he, Colonel Nutting?'

The average reader unversed in the ways of the Secret

Service with a secret may not be suitably horrified by the deadly venom with which Miss Camberly's Parthian arrow had been smeared. To such a reader the consternation caused by hearing a stenographer at Pomona Lodge address the Chief of the Secret Service by his own name cannot be conveyed without making him suspect the writer of exaggeration. Under the shock even Miss Glidden, whose presence of mind was a byword at The Elms, reeled. If the Lord Mayor had walked down Cheapside with nothing on except his cocked hat he would not have felt so improperly exposed as the Chief of the Secret Service when he heard his own name uttered aloud in his own room. He turned red, white, and blue, made strange atavistic noises through his nose, and with one last desperate effort to be the captain of his soul he made a sign that Miss Glidden should remove Miss Camberly from his presence.

And to this day she is never spoken of in the Secret Service except as 'that woman'.

Chapter 8

OF EUROPEAN IMPORTANCE

IT was not until Blenkinsop actually gave the address of his furnished flat to a taxi-driver at Victoria Station that he began to worry himself seriously about his wife's attitude. All the way from Paris to Dieppe the wheels of the train had sung steadily to him the name 'Renata', and even when the engine-driver followed the habit of French engine-drivers by taking the points at about seventy miles an hour the irregular rhythm only added 'Tekta' to 'Renata'. All the way across to Newhaven the myriad noises of a cross-channel steamer were merged to utter the one word 'Renata'. He nearly declared his love for her to the Customs officer when he was asked if he had any aero-plane parts, musical instruments, or spirits in his suitcase. All the way up to London the wheels of the train still sang her name to his bemused fancy, and it was only when he heard himself as in a dream saying 'Jerbury Chambers, Jerbury Street', that he woke up to the grim realities of married life.

Enid was sitting beside the electric-heater in the furnished service flat when he arrived, and when he leant over to kiss her it seemed to her husband that she was older than when he had said 'good-bye' to her the day before yesterday. There was about her cheek a roughness he had hardly noticed before, and when he had noticed it he had accepted it as the natural penalty for playing golf in all weathers. Now as he kissed that cheek he noticed lurking beneath the powder several little purple veins which like worms seemed to be eating away her roses. Her hair, the fairness of which he had always accepted as a survival of girlish tresses, now seemed less like hair than ... he thrust aside the comparison as an anchorite the tempter, and took refuge in the traditional fatigue of the business man.

'By Jove, Enid, these business deals take it out of one,' he declared with a sort of enthusiastic weariness.

'Yes, Paris can be very tiring,' she observed, with that in her tone which made him reach instinctively for the sugar. It was not there. He had forgotten to bring her back even the most trivial contribution from the capital of femininity.

'It wasn't so much Paris,' he said, 'it was having to talk all the time about bananas. However, I've got the job.'

'How much a year will it mean?'

'Oh, about a thousand with expenses.'

'Expenses? Expenses for what?'

'Well, little trips like this one, for instance. I shall have to explore new avenues and open up new markets if I can.'

'New what?'

'New markets, darling,' he said in a wounded voice.

It was not that he wanted Enid to call him Bunny, but he would have felt more at ease if she did. These short sharp questions were unpleasantly reminiscent of machine-gun fire.

'Markets for what?'

She was at it again.

'For bananas, darling,' he explained, with gentle patience. 'And that reminds me. I want you to invite Mr and Mrs Hudson to dinner with us at the Olympic some night soon. Hudson was extremely considerate, and I want to show a little appreciation. Why do you look at me like that, darling? Anybody would think you doubted the existence of Mr and Mrs Hudson.'

'I do.'

Blenkinsop rose from his chair and walked across the room for the telephone directory. There was in his gait the solid dignity of an unjustly suspected man who is about to triumph over his accusers.

'There you are, Enid,' he said in a tone that strove to rise superior to the suggestion that his wife deserved to be put across his knee and smacked with the directory for her suspicions. 'There you are! Hudson Brothers, Banana Importers, 210 King Street, Covent Garden.'

'What has that got to do with Mrs Hudson?' his wife demanded coldly.

'Really, Enid, I don't want to get angry. But I shall get angry in a moment if you adopt this unreasonable attitude. Mrs Hudson is the wife of Mr William Hudson, the senior partner of this firm of banana importers. They are extending the field of their operations and have formed a company to utilize the waste products of bananas and banana trees.'

'Bananas aren't trees.'

'Well, banana bushes.'

'Bananas aren't bushes.'

'Dash it, to hear you talk you might know more about bananas than I do after spending the better part of three days discussing nothing else.'

'And I spent several hours yesterday with Tiny Houldsworth reading up all there is to know about bananas. There are no waste products.'

'Aren't there? What about the skins?'

Mrs Blenkinsop uttered a contemptuous exclamation.

'Are you going to pretend to me that this visit to Paris was made to look for banana skins?'

'No, not to look for them, but to discuss their commercial value. We intend to utilize them for making a special polish for brown boots.'

'Indeed?'

'It's all very well for you to say "indeed" in that offensive voice.'

'Oh, my voice is offensive now, is it? I remember the time when you told me it reminded you of mermaids singing. That was when we were walking along the beach at Parvo, in case you have forgotten.'

'I wish you wouldn't talk like that about Parvo when I'm trying to tell you what you can do with banana skins. You may think you have read all there is to read about bananas, but you don't seem to have found out that one of the best ways to darken the leather of new brown boots is to rub them with the skin of the common or garden banana. Now perhaps you can understand what a chance there is for our scheme?'

Blenkinsop was out of breath after what for him was a long speech. His wife took advantage of his exhaustion to ask:

'And what has Mrs Hudson got to do with brown boots?'

'Nothing at all.'

'Exactly.'

'I haven't met Mrs Hudson.'

'But you propose to introduce her to me as Mrs Hudson.'

'Really, Enid, your suggestion is monstrous. You don't seriously believe that I would introduce another woman to you as Mrs Hudson?'

'I believe that men are capable of anything,' Mrs Blenkinsop declared. 'Anything,' she repeated with a bitter emphasis that shocked her husband.

'Perhaps you believe that this extra thousand a year on our income is imaginary?'

'I haven't seen it yet.'

'You can't see income. Even income-tax inspectors don't expect to do that. But what is the use of continuing this discussion? You are not in the mood to be reasonable, and I am tired with...'

'Paris,' said his wife quickly. 'That does not surprise me at all as I told you just now.'

'Well, if you won't invite the Hudsons to dinner, I shall invite them and leave it to your better feelings to realize that you have misjudged me. Where shall we dine tonight?'

'Somewhere economical. I expect dining with Mrs Hudson in Paris has been expensive, hasn't it?'

'Damn it, Enid, I tell you Mrs Hudson is no more than a name to me.'

'I've no doubt of that. Like Mr Godley.'

'Who's Mr Godley?'

Mrs Blenkinsop tinkled like a struck chandelier with mirthless laughter.

'Mr Godley of Godalming whom you were going to meet in Paris ... till you thought of a better cover.'

Blenkinsop started. What had inspired Enid to use that word of such significance in the Secret Service? Could she have followed him to Paris? Could she have found out about Renata? But of course not. It was merely a coincidence.

'I told you that Mr Godley died suddenly,' he said. 'I shouldn't have thought that his death was a matter for amusement.'

'Oh, you've remembered who he was now? My dear Arthur, the best liars never require prompting by their dupes.'

'I refuse to argue any more with you in this mood,' said Blenkinsop, who felt on less suitable banana soil with Godley than he had felt with Hudson Brothers. 'I suggest we dine somewhere and go to a film this evening.'

'Won't that be rather dull for you after the delights of Paris?'

'Look here, let's drop the subject of Paris. In due course you will meet Mr and Mrs Hudson, and then you'll be sorry that you've treated me like this. Until then I shall not mention the subject of bananas again.'

Yet this was a rash announcement, for the following morning before Blenkinsop set out to his appointment at The Elms, his wife asked him where he was going, and he told her that he was going to Croydon on business for the new company.

'Banana business?' she pressed.

'Certainly. My whole time now will be taken up with bananas.'

As Blenkinsop walked up St James's Street he could not help thinking that N had been right to look a little disappointed when he had told him that he was married. He consoled himself with the reflection that as soon as Enid had met the Hudsons and as soon as, thanks to his personal influence over Hudson, he had obtained his direct testimony to the truth of the banana story she would forget her unworthy suspicions. That dinner must be arranged as soon as possible.

The new broom sweeps clean, and Blenkinsop naturally took the maximum of precaution in making his first visit to the headquarters of the Secret Service. At the top of St James's Street he hailed a taxi and told the driver in a voice loud enough to make several passers-by turn round and stare to go to Madame Tussaud's. As he entered the taxi he had the mixed satisfaction of hearing a sandwich-man call out over his shoulder to the sandwich-man behind him:

'Latest addition to the Chamber of Horrors. You'll be carrying round that bloke's head on your board next week, Bill.'

Some hostile star must have been aspecting Blenkinsop's taxis, for just as this one reached Marylebone Road it ran into the two minutes' silence of Armistice Day, and the driver omitted to shut off his engine. It is difficult to imagine a more unpleasant publicity for an officer of the Secret Service than to find himself during the two minutes' silence seated in a taxi, the engine of which is the only sound for miles in any direction that breaks the silence. The passers-by standing hatless glared angrily at Blenkinsop as if he were responsible for the sacrilegious noise. Instead of slipping quietly out of the taxi as he had intended and a minute or two later inconspicuously finding another taxi, he had to sit here for two minutes while everybody within range stared at him with an expression of fierce disapproval. Somewhere among them might be standing a foreign agent on whose memory his features thus beheld must make an indelible impression. As the first minute dragged out its solemn length the engine chugged even more loudly, and when at the end of the second minute the silence lifted there was a rush from the outraged passers-by whose commemoration had been profaned by the engine of Blenkinsop's taxi.

'Pull them out and smash up the blurry boneshaker,' shouted one.

'Duck 'em in Regent's Park,' advised the self-righteous driver of a motor-omnibus which had behaved itself with decorum.

'They're a couple of Bolshevists,' screamed a well-dressed middle-aged woman. 'I'm a member of the British Fascisti and they ought to be lynched.'

The driver of the taxi alighted very deliberately and flinging his hat in the road challenged anybody to cut off his engine.

'And anybody who does,' he shouted, 'can drive the blurry old tin-rattle back to my guvnor's because once it's stopped it takes two blurry hours to start it again.'

'Well, what did you want to come out for on Armistice Day if you knew you couldn't stop your blurry engine?' queried a passer-by. 'You ought to be ashamed of yourself. Where was you in the war?'

'Yuss,' breathed another indignant passer-by, 'you was a blurry conchie. Others could do their fighting for you then, you dirty tyke.'

'Oh, go and boil your blurry head, you,' the driver advised

contemptuously. 'I killed more blurry Germans than you said you killed, mate.'

'Boil my blurry head?' repeated the indignant victim of the accusation.

'Yes, boil your blurry head.'

'I'll boil *your* blurry head.'

'Who will?'

'I will.'

'You will, will yer?' demanded the taxi-driver. 'Well, why don't you blurry well start in with your blurry boiling? You'd give anyone the sick, you would.'

This debate occupied the attention of the onlookers sufficiently to allow Blenkinsop to slip away comparatively unnoticed and enter another taxi which drove him without further mishap to Golders Green Station, whence he cautiously made his way on foot to The Elms.

With the talisman of N's instructions he passed through the defences, and he had not been a minute in the waiting-room before Miss Glidden joined him.

'Will you come along with me, Major Blenkinsop, and I'll show you the way to Major Hunter-Hunt's room. The Chief will see you presently. At the moment,' she threw a quick apprehensive glance back over her shoulder, and her voice sank to a tense whisper, 'at the moment he has a V.I.P. with him.'

Blenkinsop trying to solve the problem of these initials could only think of Volunteer Indian Police, Veterinary Inspector of ... but Pigs sounded improbable, and he tried Volunteer Intelligence Patrol before finally giving it up.

Miss Glidden seemed to divine his perplexity, for just as they reached the threshold of Major Hunter-Hunt's room she turned round and whispered through a pursed-up mouth, 'Very Important Personage', her eyes flashing with the excitement of inside information.

Hunter-Hunt rose from his desk and greeted his new colleague with that outward cordiality which is such a pleasant feature of Secret Service relationships and which so ably conceals the faint anxiety that every officer feels over being superseded by the newcomer. Miss Glidden, having handed over Blenkinsop to the good will of Major Hunter-Hunt retired, her expression resembling that of the stork, in illustrated tales for the young, who has just brought another baby to some steep-roofed Nordic house.

'When the V.I.P. has gone the Chief will let you know, Major H. H.'; she paused in the doorway to murmur in a voice arch with mystery.

Hunter-Hunt goggled at her sagely.

'Quite, quite, Miss Glidden.' Then he turned to Blenkinsop. 'The Chief and I are most anxious to hear the result of your first interview with Juno. I may tell you in absolute and strictest confidence that immensely important developments have taken place since yesterday. At this very moment the P.U.S. is discussing the situation with N.'

'The P.U.S.?'

'The Permanent Under-Secretary,' Hunter-Hunt explained with such a gust of warm breath that he had to take off his horn-rimmed spectacles and wipe away the traces of it. 'He drove straight here from the Foreign Office about half an hour ago.'

'Straight here?' repeated Blenkinsop, with a hint of censure in the question.

Hunter-Hunt waggled his head gravely.

'Only the present emergency would justify doing that,' he agreed. 'But it was safer to let him do that than for N to go to the F.O. That might have been fatal. Of course, now we know why Katzenschlosser was trying to impersonate N in Paris.'

'Oh, I ought to explain,' Blenkinsop put in. 'Further inquiries showed that the man with the chin was not Katzenschlosser at all. It really *was* Churchill the famous American banker.'

'Where did you get that information?'

'From the porter at the Plonplon.'

Major Hunter-Hunt smiled the sad compassionate smile of experience.

'It is almost an axiom in our work, my dear fellow, that no hotel porter is reliable.'

'Oh, but I feel pretty sure the fellow at the Plonplon was speaking the truth.'

'It is possible,' said Hunter-Hunt gently, 'that the porter at the Plonplon genuinely believed that Katzenschlosser was Churchill the American banker; but those who have had practical experience of Katzenschlosser's almost miraculous skill in disguising himself will know that it was not the real Churchill.'

Blenkinsop still looked sceptical, and the more experienced Intelligence officer went on earnestly :

'I know you'll understand that I'm not trying to be offensive, my dear fellow, when I say that after you have been in the Service a little longer you'll realize like the rest of us that there is nothing of which Katzenschlosser is not capable. In my opinion, apart from N himself, Katzenschlosser is the greatest brain now working on Intelligence, for he combines the thoroughness of the German with the quickness of the Yankee.'

'Well, of course, I haven't had your experience,' Blenkinsop admitted.

'I know, I know. And in dealing with people like Katzenschlosser it is experience which counts first and last every time.'

Even yet Blenkinsop did not feel convinced that the bounder with the chin was in very fact Katzenschlosser; but his modesty kept him from arguing with a man of so much longer experience in this kind of work than himself, and he learnt what is the most valuable early lesson that a Secret Service officer can learn, which is to believe because it is impossible. Moreover, in retrospect of what had happened at the Plonplon Hotel he began to feel how much more important his mission had been if it really had been Katzenschlosser. The rewards of simple faith are the richest bestowed upon human nature.

'Then of course if it was Katzenschlosser . . .'

'It was, it was, my dear fellow,' Hunter-Hunt interposed with the serene assurance of Tertullian himself.

'In that case,' Blenkinsop continued, 'I was right to suspect the taxi-driver.'

'The taxi-driver?' Hunter-Hunt asked quickly.

Blenkinsop related his adventure with the persistent taxi-driver who had waited for him outside Juno's house. By the time he had finished Hunter-Hunt was in a state of almost painful agitation.

'By George,' he ejaculated, 'it's my candid opinion that you were lucky to get back to the Plonplon alive. You took a tremendous risk, and it came off. But don't do it again. You should never have entered that taxi a second time, my dear B! You were, to use a vulgar phrase, asking for it.'

Any lingering doubts Blenkinsop may have retained about the desperate nature of his Parisian mission were dispelled by being addressed as B by his colleague. He too was now an initial. He felt proud indeed of that simple B, for it betokened a companionship more intimate than that of the Bath.

'And now tell me about Juno,' said Major Hunter-Hunt.

'I think she's a remarkable woman; in fact, I think she's a very remarkable woman,' Blenkinsop replied emphatically.

'I'm so glad to hear you say that,' the other declared, 'because everything indicates that at any moment she may become – well, it's no exaggeration to say that she may become an important factor in the general European situation. Indeed, not to mince matters, B, I may as well anticipate what the Chief himself will tell you by warning you that the peace of the world may depend on your ability to handle Juno in the right way.'

'I say, that's rather a responsibility,' Blenkinsop commented solemnly. At the back of his mind was a slightly uneasy feeling that in handling Renata he was going to be handling a bit of a handful.

'Well, the moment you joined us you assumed a tremendous responsibility.'

'Quite.'

'We don't want another war,' Major Hunter-Hunt declared.

'No, rather not.'

'We do *not* want another war,' Major Hunter-Hunt repeated.

'No, no.'

'But if war comes there's one thing nobody at the top will be able to say. Nobody will be able to say that we haven't warned them time after time for the last ten years that war is inevitable.

And though of course we do not *want* another war we all feel that if war is inevitable the sooner it comes the better. I tell you, B, that M.Q. 99 (E) was never so fighting fit in all its history as it is now.'

Blenkinsop's normally dull eyes were fanned to a glow by that enthusiasm with which globular little Hunter-Hunt knew how to inspire all those who worked with him.

'One great point that Madame ... Madame Juno made was that a thousand francs a week would hardly be enough for her to carry through the work we want from her. She suggested to me – and though of course I didn't give her the least encouragement to suppose that she'd get it, I can't help seeing the force of her argument – she suggested to me that fifteen hundred francs would help her.'

'That's a matter for N to decide,' said Hunter-Hunt. 'But I don't think you need be in the least afraid he will not see the force of your argument. N is always generous if he believes the money will be usefully spent. So don't be afraid to ask him, B. He can only say "no". Nothing is gained by not asking. Personally I've always advocated the spending of money. The only snag is the Treasury. They've been sticky lately. I know it's their job to be sticky. Still ...'

Major Hunter-Hunt let his emotion over the stickiness of the Treasury evaporate in a deep sigh.

'Of course, these fellows who aren't in the Service never can understand Service ways,' said Blenkinsop.

'Never,' Hunter-Hunt agreed fervidly. 'And what's more they never will.'

'It's the civilian mind,' Blenkinsop argued. 'Damned awful thing, when you come to think of it, the civilian mind.'

'Well, of course, what it'll end in is rank Bolshevism,' said Hunter-Hunt gloomily.

'Absolutely. Nothing else.'

'Still, *we* must carry on.'

'Oh, rather! All the time,' Blenkinsop agreed.

Further discussion of ways and means was closed by the entrance of Miss Glidden.

'The Chief would like to see Major Blenkinsop,' she revealed.

'Does he want me too?' Hunter-Hunt asked, it might have seemed a little anxiously.

'He didn't say so, Major H. H.'

'Oh, well, I expect he'll send for me if he wants me. You might tell him, will you, Miss Glidden, that I've worked out that Ruritanian mobilization plan he was asking for.'

'I will certainly, Major H. H.'

Blenkinsop, although a newcomer to the Secret Service, had been long enough in the Army to understand that Hunter-Hunt was a little huffed by not being invited to be present at the interview. Nominally of the same rank as himself Hunter-Hunt was yet a year senior to him. He should have to be tactful. If his success with Juno led N to push him along, that would not be his fault. At the same time, it might cause trouble if Hunter-Hunt got it into his head that he either wanted to be pushed along or expected it. That was the worst of a Line regiment. Always suspicious of Cavalry. Well, poor devils, perhaps it was only natural.

'Ah, Blenkinsop, sit down. You've arrived just at the right moment,' said the Chief when his latest recruit entered the room. 'Now tell me all about Jumbo – I mean Juno.'

'You won't be wanting me, Colonel N?' Miss Glidden asked a little wistfully.

The Chief shook his head brusquely, and she squeezed her way out with noiseless efficiency.

Blenkinsop gave an account of his established contact, spoke in the highest terms of Madame Tekta's intelligence, laid due stress on the advantage of treating her generously in the way of money, and expressed his positive opinion that she would prove invaluable.

'Capital,' the Chief approved. 'Now listen carefully. Perhaps H. H. has already told you that the Mendacian situation has developed rapidly since I saw you in Paris?'

'He did, but of course without giving me any details.'

'It has developed in a way that even I did not expect, Blenkinsop. I'll be quite candid with you and admit that if I had known a week ago what I know now I should have hesitated before I entrusted you with what is likely to be the most important job that any of my officers has had for a very long time. However, beginner's luck, and now that you've made such a promising start I'm going all out on you. You remember our discussion of the Mendacian situation in Paris and what I said about Sir John Clavering, our Minister out there?'

'Perfectly.'

'Well, when I tell you that Sir Wilfred Camden has just driven down from the F.O. to tell me that it has been decided to recall Sir John Clavering you will understand what it means.'

Blenkinsop had no more idea what it meant than a child of nature confronted with an income-tax form, and he made up his mind that never again would he interview N without a pair of horn-rimmed spectacles. For lack of them he corrugated his forehead and ejaculated darkly:

'Do I not!'

Fortunately for Blenkinsop N, wrapped up in his own exposition of the Mendacian situation, went on to explain what it did mean.

'Clavering has been steadily opposed to giving the supporters of King Johannis the very slightest encouragement. He will be succeeded by Giles Ballantyne, who is a great personal friend of King Johannis. In other words it has been decided for reasons of state, which of course do not concern us, to encourage a restoration. Naturally, Sir Wilfred did not admit so much even to me; but he is anxious to be kept in the closest touch with Mendacian opinion, and it's up to us to give him what he wants.'

'I'll do my best,' Blenkinsop promised. 'I suppose I ought to go over to Paris again as soon as possible and fix things with – er – Juno.'

'I don't know. Frankly I'm inclined to give Paris a wide berth. It won't do for the Yanks to get into their heads that we're encouraging a royal restoration. They cannot bear the idea of our doing anything except pay off their confounded debt. And if Katzenschlosser is on the track of this business we must look out for squalls.'

'But surely it will be necessary for me to see Juno again?' Blenkinsop asked a little anxiously.

'Of course, of course. But where? That's the problem. Look here, I think you'd better keep away from The Elms for the present. I'll telegraph you where I want you to meet Juno. You don't think anybody saw you coming here this morning?'

'I don't think so. I came by a roundabout route, and all the way from Golders Green I kept looking back to see if anybody was following me.'

'And nobody was?'

'No, I'm sure of that.'

'Good! Then you'd better get back home right away. My own man will drive you. Wait a minute, I'll lend you a mask.'

The Chief opened a drawer in his desk and presently chose for Blenkinsop's disguise what looked like the face of a comic Frenchman in late Victorian farce.

'Keep it on till the car reaches a quiet stretch in Regent's Park. My man will drop you at Oxford Circus.'

'But when I meet Juno what do you want me to arrange with her?' Blenkinsop asked.

'I can't tell you that just yet. I shall have to think everything out. We don't know yet where the King is. As soon as Spicer gets back from Madrid, I'll communicate with Juno through him.'

'Who's Spicer?' Blenkinsop asked, with a noticeable coldness in his tone.

'George Spicer of the 27th Hussars. He's in charge of Western Europe.'

'But wouldn't it be risky for him to – er – establish contact with Juno?'

'He won't do it himself. He'll use one of his best agents. We'll pay her a certain amount of money in advance, and after that you had better pay her. I'll see that £500 is paid into your bank. You'll be wanting money for yourself probably. Hardwick expects an account every quarter of how it is spent. Now there's only one thing more to settle, and that is the name you will go by when you are on hush-hush work. Blenkinsop is a bit conspicuous.'

'Perhaps you remember my telling you that for a convenient

cover I was going to use bananas?' Blenkinsop reminded his Chief.

'Yes, and I thought it couldn't be bettered.'

'The business as a matter of fact is a real one called Hudson Brothers. One of the partners is William Hudson. Suppose I were to call myself Arthur Hudson? That's a very ordinary sort of name.'

'Good! We'll fix on that. You've got a splendid natural instinct for this work, Blenkinsop. That's understood then, when we wish to communicate with you anywhere except at your own address we shall use "Arthur Hudson". Well, I'll ring now for my man to bring the car round to the side door. Don't forget your mask. And just keep on quietly building up the banana business until we tell you where to meet Juno. It's exciting work, isn't it?'

'Oh, tremendously,' the recruit assented.

'And it get's more and more exciting,' said the Chief of the Secret Service, with the simple pride of a best-seller telling an editor about a new serial.

Chapter 9

MRS HUDSON

It had been Blenkinsop's intention at first to ask Mr and Mrs Hudson to dinner without warning his train acquaintance of the extent to which his own future was supposed to be linked with the banana trade. However, Enid's attitude was so sceptical that he decided it would be more prudent to warn Hudson in advance that his support was expected for anything his host might say.

Blenkinsop was disappointed on arriving at 210 King Street two or three days later to find so little evidence of the business which presumably occupied Hudson Brothers in Covent Garden.

'But this is only the office,' Mr William Hudson explained. 'Our stuff is all at the docks.'

'Well, what I really looked in for was to ask if you and Mrs Hudson would come and dine with us at the Olympic – say the Wednesday of next week.'

'Speaking for myself, Major,' said Mr Hudson, 'we shall be delighted. Only the wife's a little shy. You may remember my telling you that her father was a clergyman, and that meant she didn't get about a lot when she was a girl.'

'Quite. But I hope all the same she'll make an exception in our favour,' said Blenkinsop. 'My wife will be awfully disappointed if she doesn't meet her.'

'Oh, well, I'll jolly her along. At the Olympic, eh? Bong! How did you get on in Paree, after we parted?'

'Quite all right, thanks.'

'Run across anything winsome in the way of fluff?'

'What? Oh, I see what you mean. No, nothing particular.'

'But there's a twinkle in your eye, Major. Naughty, naughty!' Mr Hudson rallied with a jocose manner which Blenkinsop found distasteful and which in ordinary circumstances he would not have tolerated. However, his country was calling to him, and with an effort he conquered his pride.

109

'Look here, Hudson, I wonder if you'd ... if you'd help me out over a little difficulty? You're a married man yourself ...'

'Very much so.'

'And of course I dare say your wife sometimes wonders what you do when you run over to the continent?'

'It's the riddle of her existence, Major,' Hudson confessed solemnly.

'Quite. Well, just to ... just lightly when I got back I told my wife I'd been discussing a business proposition with a friend.'

'And that just about expresses it, Major. In fact, the only thing I've got against French girls is the way they argue about the money part of it. Outside that, it's my belief that a French girl can leave any English girl at the bedpost.'

'I'm not talking about girls,' Blenkinsop insisted. 'The business proposition to which I was referring was with you.'

'Oh, was it?'

'I mean to say that's what I said it was. You'll remember you told me a good deal about bananas? Well, I told my wife, to cut short a rather silly argument, that I was going into a business with you for utilizing the waste products of the banana.'

'And she believed you, of course?' said Mr Hudson with a smile that was evidently cynical.

'No, to be frank, I'm not perfectly sure that she did.'

'No, and I'm not perfectly sure either. You ought to have thought of something better than bananas, Major. I really have been going over to Paris on business about bananas, but my missus never has believed that was the reason I went, and she never will. If you'd asked my advice beforehand, I'd have given you something better than bananas. Take it from me, so far as excuses go, bananas are lemons. No thank you, I've got something better than bananas now.'

'Yes, but in this case you can support my story and I can support yours.'

'Major, Major, for a man of the world you're as innocent as a baby. Haven't you ever observed that the more men support one another the less women believe them?'

Blenkinsop would have liked to say frigidly that he was not accustomed to lying in concert with his men friends; but for the sake of the Secret Service he steeled himself to endure being dragged down to the level of William Hudson's social habits.

'Yes, but surely if I say something like this, "This is Mr Hudson whom I was telling you about" you could say something like this, "Yes, we're very glad to have your husband with us." '

'Well, I don't know Mrs Blenkinsop, Major, but I know my own missus, and that would have no more effect on her than water on a duck's back.'

'Still, it will put me in an awkward position if you don't back me up, Hudson. I mean to say, you really must. I've gone all out on this banana business. And even if my wife doesn't believe you, she'll have to pretend to believe you.'

'I'm not the one to let a pal down, Major.' Blenkinsop winced at this. 'And if you're bent on it,' Hudson continued, 'I'll play my part for all it's worth; but if you want my frank opinion, your story is crude. It's not original.'

'Not to you,' Blenkinsop agreed. 'But that's because bananas are so familiar to you. To an old soldier like myself they seem quite different. After all, there's no doubt that you *are* in the banana business. I could bring my wife round to your office to prove it to her.'

'All right, old man. I'm not the one to spoil anybody's sport. If it's going to help you with your missus I'll stand by.'

'I'm very much obliged to you, Hudson. Of course, I should never have suggested anything like this if it had to involve you in any way; but it can't do you any harm with Mrs Hudson, and in fact I can't help thinking it may do you a bit of good.'

'You haven't met Mrs Hudson yet, Major.'

'No, that's a pleasure to come.'

'If I were to tell my wife the story you want me to tell *your* wife she'd never let me over the Channel again, or at any rate not without two first-class returns.'

'You mean she'd insist on going and coming back with you?'

'Going and coming back wouldn't be the end of it. She wouldn't lose sight of me from the moment we left Victoria till we were inside our front hall again. No, I've had to think of something better than bananas, and this is where you'll be able to help me, Major.'

'Delighted, of course,' the dragoon murmured.

'You remember the way we chin-chinned first in the boat-train?'

'Over your book, which I was reading?'

'I didn't know you so well then as I know you now, and I never told you the real reason how I came to write *The Green-Eyed Spy*. Before I ever took to writing novels I'd been spinning spy yarns to the wife. That's how I found out I was a born storyteller. Yes, when she began to grumble at me for not taking her with me when I went to the continent I told her I was in the Secret Service.'

'I beg your pardon?' Blenkinsop gasped. 'But surely she didn't believe that?'

'Didn't she? You haven't heard me yarning about the Secret Service in our home, Major, I tell you I've had my old lady quaking in her chair till the dog had only to turn round in his basket to make her think the Bolsheviks were on us.'

'I thought you said Mrs Hudson was so incredulous?'

'Not about the Secret Service. But who is? Look at yourself. Look at the way you were swallowing *The Green-Eyed Spy* the morning I met you. No, if you'd wanted a cast-iron yarn for your good lady, Major, you ought to have told her you were in the Secret Service. And as a matter of fact you are.'

'What?' Blenkinsop gasped, turning as nearly pale as a dragoon can.

'There you are! What did I tell you? Look at the way you jumped when I said that. No, but joking apart, I did tell my missus you were the Chief of the Secret Service. That's why she's so scared at the idea of meeting you. That's why I hummed and hawed a bit about her coming to dinner at the Olympic. But she'll come all right. Curiosity will win. Only, if she looks at you a bit hard, you'll know the reason. Why don't you go back on the banana yarn, Major, and let's give the ladies a treat on Wednesday, swapping experiences?'

'No, no,' said Blenkinsop. 'My wife would never believe that I'd suddenly become the Chief of the Secret Service.'

'She'll believe it just as quickly as your banana story. However, fair exchange is no robbery. You see me through and I'll do my best to see you through, old man. Of course, I'll make it clear to my missus that she's not supposed to know what you are. Official Secrets Act, eh? I'll tell her they'll have me in the Tower if she doesn't look out. Lord, you would laugh if you could see her poking about with a stick under the bed every night for Bolsheviks. I wonder what it's really like to be in the Secret Service?'

'Yes, I wonder,' Blenkinsop echoed.

'A friend of mine knows a fellow who's got a cousin that's pretty high up in the C.I.D., and he gets the inside dope on some of these big murders; but I must say I would like to meet a real Secret Service man. What a life they must lead!'

'Terrific!' said Blenkinsop.

'And yet some people say romance is dead.'

'Some people say anything,' Blenkinsop opined. 'Well, so long, Hudson. We'll meet on Wednesday. Eight o'clock in the lobby, just above the dining-room.'

As Blenkinsop walked along the Strand searching for an optician he decided that Hudson's choice of a convenient cover was really a tribute to the success with which he himself had avoided conveying the very slightest suggestion of his actual occupation.

'I want a pair of large horn-rimmed spectacles, please,' he told the young man in the optician's.

'Certainly, sir. Have you the prescription?'

'The what?'

'For the lenses.'

'Oh, I just want plain glass. They're for amateur theatricals.'

'I see, sir. Try this frame, will you?'

Blenkinsop was astonished at the effect on his appearance. He had hardly dared to hope for such a superb expression of sagacity.

'Makes you look quite a philosopher, sir,' said the optician's assistant, who felt that a mild joke would not be in bad taste as the customer intended to use the spectacles for theatricals.

'And they'll look even better with glasses in them?' Blenkin-sop suggested.

'Oh, certainly, sir,' the assistant agreed. 'I'll have the glasses fitted by this afternoon. Can we send them anywhere for you, sir?'

Blenkinsop gave the address of his club. He had not yet prepared Enid for the weakening of his eyesight and in her present mood the least thing seemed to make her suspicious.

'The Hudson's are coming to dinner with us at the Olympic on next Wednesday, darling,' he announced, and he could not bring himself to believe that the monosyllabic 'Oh' represented as much eager desire in Enid to display hospitality as he would have liked.

'Hudson is very anxious to show you round their warehouse down at the docks,' he went on.

'Is he?'

'Yes, he was telling me what astounding things they some-times find among the bananas when they arrive. Fancy, only the other day they found a young boa-constrictor in a con-signment from Honduras.'

'So I read in the paper yesterday.'

'Oh, did you?'

Blenkinsop decided to be careful what items of news he served up as his own in future. It had never struck him before that Enid's rearrangement of the daily paper implied the least attention to any news that was in it.

'I hope you won't bring back any boa-constrictors here as a proof that you are interested in bananas,' Enid said. 'This flat is quite uncomfortable enough as it is.'

'Should I be likely to do anything like that, darling?'

'I really don't know. You've changed so completely of late that I believe you capable of anything.'

'Changed in what way?'

'This horrible surreptitious ... but don't let's talk about it. I suppose every married woman has to suffer sooner or later. Still, even if you are deceiving me, Arthur,' she burst out passionately, 'I don't see why you should go walking about the flat on tiptoe all the time.'

'I didn't know I was.'

'Deceitfulness soon becomes second nature,' she observed bitterly.

'I'm not going to argue with you about this, Enid, because when you meet the Hudsons you will realize how much you have wronged me. Time will tell.'

'You brute!'

'What on earth have I said now?'

'Oh, nothing, nothing. You've only sneered at me because I shall be thirty in a few months. I begin to think that my dear old Dad was the only sahib I ever knew. He never reminded me of my age.'

Stung beyond endurance by this taunt, Blenkinsop allowed himself to overstep the bounds of a dragoon's decency.

'If I had reminded you of your age,' he said, 'you'd have been thirty, three years ago.' And it was all he could do to resist adding, 'And perhaps more.'

'Tiny Houldsworth said that underneath she always suspected you of being cruel,' Enid wept. 'And I used to defend you.'

'I don't care a damn about Tiny Houldsworth. I loathe the woman.'

'Yes, just because she's too loyal to me to let you make eyes at her.'

'Make eyes at Tiny Houldsworth?' he echoed in dismay. 'You'll accuse me next of making eyes at the hippopotamus in the Zoo.'

'Now be coarse.'

'It was you who started being coarse when you suggested I could make eyes at Tiny Houldsworth.'

'Arthur, be careful,' his wife said in a cold voice of warning. 'Do not try me too hard. There is a limit to what I can stand.'

'Yes, and to what I can stand. And Tiny Houldsworth stretches well beyond the limit.'

'She's coming here to tea this afternoon.'

'Is she? Then there won't be room for me in the flat as well.'

'Arthur, I would never have believed you capable of sneering at a woman because her figure is a little developed. Tiny is a loyal friend to me, and I shall soon want all the loyal friends I can find. That's perfectly evident.'

With this Enid sank as far as it was possible for anybody to sink into one of those well-sprung armchairs and wept softly to herself.

'Look here, Enid,' her husband said, gentleness returning to his voice and bearing. 'I'm sorry I spoke like that about your friend. But you stung me rather on the raw.'

Enid wept less softly now that he was penitent.

'Leave me,' she besought; 'I'll try to forget all the ghastly things you've said to me this morning, but I want to be alone. You'd better go and lunch at your club. I shan't be able to eat anything. I suppose when a man falls in love with another woman he hardly knows what he is saying to his wife. Leave me now, Arthur, please.'

'You'll soon get over this,' Blenkinsop prophesied hopefully.

'Oh, you needn't be afraid that I shall break down when I meet this Mrs Hudson. I have plenty of pride.'

'When you see Mrs Hudson,' he answered with perfect confidence in his tone, 'you'll realize the absurdity of your suspicions.'

And this Blenkinsop genuinely believed. He had formed a picture in his own mind of Mrs Hudson which was based partly on the insignificant appearance of her husband and partly on what that insignificant husband had told him about his wife. He imagined a dowdy timid little woman, between forty and fifty, somewhat bewildered by the luxury of the Hotel Olympic, who would bear upon her the hall-mark of Norbiton (wherever that might be) and who would perhaps speak with a slight Cockney accent.

Therefore when, some days after this discourse with Enid, Blenkinsop caught sight of Hudson entering the lobby of the Olympic in the company of a beautiful young woman in the grand style of feminine beauty which was fashionable in classic days and admired by the Prince of Wales while Queen Victoria still reigned he was considerably surprised. In fact the only detail in which his prefiguration of Mrs Hudson coincided with the reality was in her possession of a slight Cockney accent. Hers was not the kind of beauty that thrilled Blenkinsop. He wanted a feminine type towards which he could feel protective. Still, he felt inclined to judge Hudson more harshly for his behaviour in Paris. That girl in the Montmartre Café could not compare with his own wife, whereas Renata ... Blenkinsop pulled himself up. He had an idea, though he did not look directly at her, that Enid's eyes were fixed upon him. When it came to the greetings the shyness of which her husband had spoken was more apparent in Mrs Hudson. She was evidently not used to dining in great palaces of luxury like the Olympic, and when the waiters darted round the table with menus and what not she looked as apprehensive as a small child before the bars of a monkey-cage.

Blenkinsop decided to carry the preliminaries with a rush.

'My wife's very much impressed by my becoming a director of your new company, Hudson,' he said, with a quick glance at Enid, who was looking like some sceptical and unwilling member of a conjuror's audience that has been invited to step up on the platform and observe his sleight of hand at close quarters.

'We think we're very lucky to have got hold of the Major, Mrs Blenkinsop,' Hudson declared enthusiastically.

'I only hope you'll find him as useful to you as he has found you useful to him,' she replied.

It was Hudson's turn now to throw a quick glance at Blenkinsop, a glance that said plainly, 'I told you so.'

Blenkinsop patted his moustache as one pats the family terrier when conversation flags.

'Oh, we shall, we shall, Mrs Blenkinsop,' Hudson assured her. 'What was I saying to you, dear, eh?'

Mrs Hudson was at that moment recovering from the shock of seeing a waiter strew a plate of purple soup with cream, and could not recover her breath in time to make a suitable reply.

'It's Russian soup, dear,' her husband informed her.

'Russian?' she echoed in alarm.

'It's all right, Azzie, it won't blow up. The wife's a bit nervous of all this Bolshevism, aren't you, dear?' he explained.

'Well, I mean to say,' Mrs Hudson testified in a genteel Cockney drawl, 'it is dreadful, isn't it? I mean to say you don't know what's going to happen next, do you?'

With this she looked round at the waiter as if he might follow up the cream by dropping a new-laid egg in her soup.

'Yes, I was saying to the Major, Mrs Blenkinsop,' Hudson continued gallantly, 'that he ought to bring you down to our warehouse one day.'

'You'd like that, wouldn't you, Enid?' the new director put in. 'We might take Tiny Houldsworth with us.'

Since that dispute over Enid's friend her husband had made a point of pushing her into the picture at the slightest excuse.

'Oh, I think it's always better not to bring wives into business,' said Enid discouragingly. 'Don't you, Mrs Hudson?'

Mrs Hudson had just at that moment come to the conclusion that if the soup reminded her of anything it reminded her of raspberry vinegar. She pulled herself together to say:

'Well, business is business, isn't it? I mean to say it's what men are really for, isn't it? When Mr Hudson and I were first married I used to ask him all sorts of questions, didn't I, Willie?'

'That's right,' Willie confirmed. 'I used to say sometimes in joke that she'd inherited the catechism habit from her dad. Mrs Hudson's father was a Wesleyan minister,' he informed his hostess.

Enid was not bigoted on most points of Christian doctrine, but if there was one article of the creed in which she did fervidly believe it was that Nonconformists were not gentlemen. So in the 'Oh, indeed', of her reply there was more charitable condescension than reverent acknowledgement.

'Yes, but I don't ask so many questions now, Willie,' Mrs Hudson protested. 'Not since I knew ...' Here she stopped abruptly, looking quickly across at her host, and then blushed to nearly as deep a hue as the bortsch in her plate.

'Knew what?' Mrs Blenkinsop asked with a smile that was more remote from the tone of her voice than the peak of Everest from Darjeeling.

'Knew I'd taken to writing novels,' Hudson put in quickly.

'Writing novels?' Mrs Blenkinsop exclaimed.

Mrs Hudson's early training led her to meet disapproval in the exclamation, and she said:

'Under another name. Well, it wouldn't do, would it, for a business man to write novels under his own name? Customers might think he wasn't really serious about his business.'

'What is Mr Hudson's pen name?' Enid asked. 'Godley?'

Blenkinsop wished now that he had mentioned Hudson's book to her. Evidently she had reduced herself to a state of not believing anything, even if it was true.

'No, I call myself Yorke Lankester.'

'I don't remember any novels by that name,' Enid said.

'Well, I've only published one so far. It's called *The Green-Eyed Spy*. But I've got another coming out before Christmas.'

'Sensational, I suppose?' observed Enid loftily.

'Oh, yes, Mrs Blenkinsop, it is indeed,' Mrs Hudson avowed with eagerness. 'Well, really, I don't know how he thought of it all.' Then Puritan prejudice against fiction intervened. 'Well, of course, in one way he didn't. Only except just to write it down. Still even that was wonderful really. The paper he used! You'd be surprised what a lot of paper it takes to write a novel. Oo!' she squeaked suddenly.

The waiter had just put before her a red mullet.

'What's the matter, Azzie?' her husband asked.

'Nothing. Only for a moment I thought it was alive, and it made me jump. Isn't it pretty?'

'Red mullet,' said Blenkinsop.

'It is pretty,' she murmured. 'It seems quite a shame to eat anything so pretty.'

'Our friends will think you rather an innocent abroad,' said Hudson, who as a novelist felt that she should display a greater sophistication than might be expected from the wife of a banana importer.

'Not so innocent as all that,' retorted Mrs Hudson, who now that the first embarrassment of this grand dinner was beginning to wear off was not prepared to be snubbed. 'Don't husbands give themselves airs, Mrs Blenkinsop? I mean to say they do, don't they?'

And the longer dinner went on, the more Mrs Hudson chattered, for in the excitement of the Olympic surroundings she allowed herself to be persuaded into drinking a glass of champagne, although, as she protested, she considered herself a strict T.T. The champagne lent her classic features the animation they needed for perfect beauty, and eyes from many surrounding tables were turned upon her.

'Well, it's been a grand evening, old man,' Hudson declared warmly when the moment came to say good-bye. 'Thank you very much indeed, Mrs Blenkinsop, for your hospitality. Mrs Hudson and I hope very much you'll dine with us soon. And any time you want to give the bananas a call, I'll only be too happy to show you our warehouses.'

'Good-bye, Mrs Blenkinsop,' said Mrs Hudson. 'And thanks so much for such a nice time. And good-bye, Major, and you won't let Mr Hudson run into too many dangers, will you?'

'From boa-constrictors, I suppose?' Enid inquired in a voice that to her husband seemed to come from some chill vault.

'Oh, it was Bolsheviks I really meant,' said Mrs Hudson. 'Well, I mean to say they are dreadful, aren't they? I shall be thinking about them all the way home.'

'Come along, Azzie,' said her husband, 'we mustn't outstay our welcome.'

With this the insignificant little man with thin sandy hair led his lovely wife towards the entrance, her exit watched by everybody in sight.

'So that,' said Enid, 'is Mrs Hudson or Mrs Lankester or even Mrs Godley. Quite a Juno!'

'Quite a – quite a what?' Blenkinsop stammered.

'I don't wonder your voice is shaky. The whole evening must have been a severe strain for you.'

'Not at all, I thought it went off splendidly.'

'And what may Azzie be short for?' Enid asked abruptly.

'I haven't the least idea. Perhaps it isn't short for anything. Anyway, I hope you're satisfied now that this banana business is genuine?'

'Satisfied? I was never less satisfied in my life,' Enid declared. 'I'd no idea Mrs Hudson was such a good-looking woman.'

'I, on the other hand, my dear Arthur, was quite convinced of it. Though, mind you, Junos like that don't wear. They soon become blowsy.'

After this Enid did not speak again until in the taxi on the way home her husband tried to take hold of her hand.

'We are not still at dinner,' she said as she withdrew it from his clasp.

The next day, when after an uncomfortable breakfast Blenkinsop returned from his club to see if his wife was in a more yielding temper, he found a telegram waiting for him in the flat.

Opening it he read:

Meet juno urgently at glenmore hydro stop she has full instructions how to proceed with the business stop telegraph me when leaving stop remember name we agreed upon for you stop inadvisable to visit the elms

bananas

'If Enid had opened this!' Blenkinsop groaned aloud. At The Elms they did not know his private difficulties. It would not have struck N that such a telegram, however little it might compromise the Mendacian situation, might compromise the matrimonial situation beyond recovery. What a mercy Enid had been out when it came!

Chapter 10

PRIVATE INQUIRIES

But Enid had not been out when that telegram arrived. She had just finished giving Miss Tiny Houldsworth a full account of the dinner-party at the Olympic, and at the moment the telegram was delivered she was saying to her friend:

'I suppose some people would call her handsome, and if you like the Juno type she *is* handsome.'

It has been suggested already that Enid was beginning to fill out, and of Miss Houldsworth it might be said that she was beginning to brim over. Hence on the feminine principle of admiring a woman of the same type as yourself but an obviously less successful replica of it both Enid and her confidante regarded Junos without the least admiration.

'A telegram for Arthur,' observed his wife.

'For Arthur personally?' asked Miss Houldsworth.

'Major Arthur Blenkinsop,' his wife read.

'Odd,' murmured Miss Houldsworth.

'You think so?'

'Well, it's not usual to spend twopence extra on a name unless . . .'

'Unless the person who sends it . . .'

'Exactly, dear.'

'I've a very good mind to open it,' declared Enid.

'If you do that you may find out all you want to know, but Arthur will know what you do know,' her friend warned her.

'Anything would be better than this gnawing anxiety,' said Enid.

'Of course, dear, of course; but I was going to suggest that if you *could* open it and seal it up again, *you* would know, but Arthur wouldn't.'

'Steam it open?' Enid murmured, half aghast at such a daring notion. 'Wouldn't he notice if it had been steamed open and closed again?'

'In that case you'd be where you were by tearing it open.'

'What an awful thing it is, Tiny darling, when a man drives a woman to this sort of thing,' Enid exclaimed tragically.

'Awful,' her friend agreed. 'But what can you do?'

'And after all,' Enid went on, 'perhaps it's not anything he'd be ashamed of, in which case I should feel so glad I had opened it.'

'Of course you would,' Miss Houldsworth urged.

So Enid lighted her spirit lamp, and when the little kettle began to boil she steamed open the telegram.

'It's worse than I thought,' she moaned. 'Oh, Tiny, darling, it's – it's conclusive. And the vile creature actually calls herself Juno. The conceit of it! Oh, wait till Arthur comes home. I'll ... I'll ...'

Under the weight of future action poor Enid broke down utterly.

'There's only one practical step you can take,' said her friend. 'If you tax him with this telegram he'll only find another excuse. He'll swear it's something to do with bananas.'

'And to think of him calling her Juno! The deceit of it! Why, when I said she was a Juno you'd have thought by his face he didn't know what a Juno was. And only the other day when I suggested we should go to the Glenmore Hydro for the winter sports he said we couldn't afford it!'

During this tirade Miss Houldsworth had taken a copy of the telegram, sealed it up again, and put it on the table.

'Be brave, darling,' she now urged her friend. 'You must, you *must* have him shadowed.'

'What for?'

'What for? Why, for proof. You must divorce him after this.'

'But her husband might divorce her and then Arthur would marry this great lump of a creature,' Enid demurred.

'In my opinion that's exactly what her husband hopes. In my opinion the contemptible creature is throwing his wife into another man's arms.'

Enid beat a tattoo upon the floor with her heels.

'I won't let her have him. Why should I?' she half screamed.

'Well, you must decide what you'll do when you know all,'

said Miss Houldsworth. She had just heard of a small villa at Alassio which would be perfect if she could find a friend to share it, and she therefore felt convinced that Enid who had six hundred a year of her own must leave her husband. 'When Connie Butterwick had trouble with her husband,' she continued persuasively, 'I went with her to Pinches and Pinches. We'll put them on Arthur's tracks. Come along, darling. Do pull yourself together. The only thing to do when one is up against it is to do something. Come along, pop on that dinky hat we bought yesterday, and we'll go straight off to Pinches now without wasting any more time.'

So when Blenkinsop was blessing his good fortune that Enid had not opened his telegram she and Tiny Houldsworth were actually on their way to the offices of Pinches and Pinches, Private Inquiry Agents, 600 Chancery Lane.

The ceremonies and equipment of the offices of Messrs Pinches and Pinches not being financed by the taxpayer could not compete outwardly with the ceremonies and equipment of the headquarters of the Secret Service. Nevertheless they were not unimpressive, and Mr Pinches himself (the second Pinches was a mere name) was definitely a more monumental figure of secrecy, silence, sagacity, and discretion than even the great Colonel N. He was rotund, large, and pallid. Seated at his desk in that dusty room with Enid and her friend, he looked like a turnip communing with two pink radishes.

'I fear I must ask you a few somewhat intimate questions, Mrs Blenkinsop,' he said gravely, when he had noted down the external characteristics of her husband. 'I shall endeavour to make them as little unpleasant as possible.'

Enid braced herself in the way in which a thwarted intellectual suffering from a lack of psycho-analysis goes to have an inhibition removed or a complex stopped.

'I realize that you must ask them, Mr Pinches,' she murmured.

The edge of the desk cut into the midriff of Mr Pinches as a knife cuts into cheese. He had bowed an acknowledgement of his client's courage.

'You have been married, how long, Mrs Blenkinsop?'

'Four years next May.'

'Have you had any reason to suspect your husband's fidelity before now?'

'None at all. That's what has made this business such a fearful shock.'

'Poor precious,' Miss Houldsworth commiserated in a whisper.

Mr Pinches made a note of the answer before proceeding.

'And before marriage had you any reason to suspect your future husband of – ah – fickleness?'

'None at all. He always seemed devoted. I think I could fairly say that he was never happy away from me.'

'In fact you are convinced that this is the first occasion his attention has wandered from yourself?'

'Well, of course, Mr Pinches, the revelation of this intrigue shakes one's whole faith in human nature. I really feel it is tempting providence to answer that last question.'

Mr Pinches nodded compassionately.

'I appreciate your attitude, Mrs Blenkinsop,' he said. 'We will not press that point for the moment. And now about this Mrs Hudson. Is she a particularly handsome woman?'

'I suppose some people might describe her like that,' Enid admitted unwillingly.

'Some people,' Miss Houldsworth echoed.

'What type is she? Blonde? Brunette? Petite?'

'A large woman,' said Enid.

'A very large woman indeed,' Miss Houldsworth added quickly. 'You can see by the telegram that he evidently calls her Juno as a term of endearment.'

'And you have never before noticed, Mrs Blenkinsop, that your husband's interest has been – ah – mildly aroused by – ah – large women?'

'Never!' Enid declared.

'Would you consider that this Mrs Hudson possesses in any marked degree what we call sex appeal?'

'Personally, I thought her common, stupid, and – er . . .'

'Cowlike,' Miss Houldsworth suggested when Enid hesitated for an epithet.

'Yes, cowlike describes her perfectly,' Enid agreed, 'But it is difficult to answer your question about sex appeal, Mr Pinches. Men have such different standards from women in matters like that.'

'Well, let us leave that – ah – topic for the moment,' said Mr Pinches, uplifting a large hand the flabbiness of which was itself a sedative. 'You suspect your husband of planning to spend the next few days in Mrs Hudson's company at the Glenmore Hydro?'

'Surely that is what the telegram indicates?'

Mr Pinches studied profoundly the copy which Miss Houldsworth had made.

'I'm a little puzzled by the signature,' he said at last. 'If Juno is the name by which he calls her, why is the telegram signed "Bananas"? No doubt, that may be another pet name, though I do not recall its being used in any previous case I have had the privilege of investigating.'

Enid explained the way in which her husband had tried to pass himself off as the director of a banana company.

'But I am still puzzled by the precise significance of the word in this communication,' said Mr Pinches. 'The Elms of course would be the home address of this Mrs Hudson, or it might be a house of assignation. However, that we can investigate. Bananas? I think when we come to go into it further that we shall find a peculiar significance attached to the use of "bananas" in this telegram. Bananas? Bananas? Wait a minute. Perhaps "bananas" is a code word used to designate Mr Hudson. "Inadvisable to visit the elms bananas." In other words, do not come to the house, because my husband is suspicious. You see my point, Mrs Blenkinsop? We want to know how far Hudson himself is flinging his wife into the arms of another man. That, I understand, was your first reaction to the position of affairs. It may be so, of course, but I'm bound to say that the use of "bananas" in such close juxtaposition to The Elms looks to me as if this Mrs Hudson was – ah – deceiving her husband in the same way as Major Blenkinsop is – ah – deceiving you. Anyway, I am clear that the next step is to ascertain whether they are staying together at the . . .'

Enid gasped out an ejaculation of repugnance and despair.

'Be brave, my darling, be brave,' begged her friend, with an encouraging squeeze.

'It is indeed extremely painful,' Mr Pinches agreed. 'But the – ah – grim facts of life must be faced and in my office I am continually being brought right up against them so hard that I am – ah – bruised. I have described myself as – ah – mentally black and blue from my contact with the hard facts of life. So, as I was saying, the next step is to ascertain whether they are staying together in the Hydro as Mr and Mrs Hudson or as Major and Mrs Blenkinsop.'

'Not that, not that,' Enid moaned, 'It would kill me if that monster called herself Mrs Blenkinsop.'

'Yet it would simplify the whole investigation if she did,' Mr Pinches pointed out. 'However, they may not be staying to-gether – ah – openly at the Hydro, and if they are not the position will demand the services of a trained investigator. Fortunately I can entrust the job to the best man on my staff.'

He rang the bell.

'Ask Mr Doggett to come into my room,' he told the clerk who answered his summons.

A moment later there entered the dusty office a small man with shiny apple-cheeks, a waxed moustache, carefully over-strung hair, and a bright deferential manner.

'Doggett, I have a case for you,' Mr Pinches announced with a portentous scowl that John Knox might have envied.

'Thank you, Mr Pinches,' said Mr Doggett. 'I shall be glad to be on active service again. Things have been very sedentary lately, very sedentary indeed. I only passed the remark to Mr Wigmore yesterday, "Mr Wigmore," I said, "people are getting pre-war again."'

'This is a very delicate case, Mr Doggett.'

'Blackmail or divorce?'

'Bananas!' exclaimed Mr Pinches.

'Bananas?' echoed Mr Doggett. 'I'm afraid I don't quite fol-low ...'

'Don't talk, Mr Doggett. Can't you see I'm wrapped up in a problem?'

After meditating for some time Mr Pinches announced that he had returned to his original theory.

'And which was exactly?' the subordinate sleuth asked.

Mr Pinches with a fine tact declined to harrow his client's feeling by repeating all the details in front of her.

'I will give you your instructions presently, Mr Doggett. I do not think we need detain you now, Mrs Blenkinsop. It would be helpful if you could either telephone (number 11111 Holborn) or telegraph (telegraphic address Bloodhounds, Cent. London) just when Major Blenkinsop intends to leave. It is not absolutely material, but it might help Mr Doggett's inquiries if he could get into touch with him on the journey up. At the same time, dear madam, let me warn you to be most careful not to let your husband suspect that you know his destination. Good morning, Mrs Blenkinsop. Good morning, Miss Houldsworth. I am so glad to hear that Mrs Butterwick has found life easier since we were able to – ah – elucidate matters for her. Rely upon me to do all I can to help you, Mrs Blenkinsop, as I would help my own daughter.'

When his client had been ushered out of the office, Mr Pinches turned to his lieutenant.

'Another galloping major, Doggett. Ever noticed that for one captain who jumps the rails over a skirt there's three majors? How do you explain it?'

'Forty.'

'Eh?'

'The roaring forties, Mr Pinches.'

'Eh?'

'A few more years shall roll. Put it that way.'

'Yes. I reckon you're about right, Doggett. Well, come on, let's get down to this Major who's galloping like a three-year-old after his – ah – Juno.'

'Of course I know,' said Mr Doggett. 'What else would he be galloping after?'

'J-U-N-O. Juno. A goddess on the large side. An outsize good-looker.'

When Blenkinsop greeted his wife on her return from Chan-

cery Lane with the news that he had been called away to
Scotland for a few days on urgent business connected with the
new company, he was surprised and pleased to find that she
accepted the news with apparent equanimity.

'I shall be rushing around a good deal, darling,' he began.

'Rushing around what?'

'Why, the North. I've a number of business men to interview
up there. And what I was going to say was you had better not
forward any letters till I can give you an address. I shall be in
touch with Hudson.'

'Oh, you will?'

'And I was thinking that perhaps it would be a friendly act
to ring up Hudson and suggest a visit to the banana warehouses. You might imply that it would add to the pleasure if
Mrs Hudson came too.'

Enid could not help a twinge of admiration for her husband's
audacity. He was counting on her behaviour the previous night
at dinner and felt sure that she would scoff at the idea of
having any communication with the Hudsons. She made up her
mind to give him a shock.

'What a good idea! I'll ring up Mr Hudson tomorrow.'

'I wish you would,' said Arthur. 'I'm sure you'll get to like
them if you see more of them.'

Enid was staggered by his coolness. It was all she could do to
obey the instructions she had received from Mr Pinches and
not quote the telegram word for word.

'What train are you going by?' she asked.

'The 11.12 from King's Cross, darling. The Nocturnal Scot.'

'Are you travelling up first?'

'Oh, yes. The company is paying my expenses.'

Chapter 11

NORTHWARD BOUND

BLENKINSOP'S plan to travel up to Glenmore in a first-class sleeper booked in the name of Mr A. Hudson looked like being frustrated by his wife, who announced an hour or so before he left Jerbury Chambers that she was going to see him off.

It was not that he minded the expense of paying for a first-class fare and sleeper to Glasgow in addition to the first-class fare and sleeper to Glenmore which he had paid for and booked in the name of Mr A. Hudson. That the country would pay for. What he regretted was the bore of changing and then arriving at Glenmore by a later train, for with the prospect of seeing Renata again he grudged the extra time involved. However, with Enid in her present mood, he did not venture to discourage her from the display of wifely affection on which she seemed set.

'I see you've bought yourself a lot of new luggage this afternoon,' she had observed. 'You look as if you were going on your honeymoon.'

Blenkinsop had smiled feebly.

'I thought my suitcases were looking a bit the worse for wear, and it's important to impress these business people in small ways,' he had explained.

'You've not had your name put on your latest purchases,' Enid had pointed out.

'No, there wasn't time. Besides, I won't want to advertise my name wherever I go.'

'I can well understand that,' she had replied with a bitterness in her voice that would have added a flavour even to the Dead Sea.

Enid's reason for accompanying her husband to King's Cross was to make sure that Mr Doggett would identify him. It had been Tiny Houldsworth's advice not to run the faintest risk of the inquiry agent's making any mistake. She did not suppose for a moment that Arthur would meet Mrs Hudson on the platform. As soon as she caught sight of Mr Doggett's apple cheeks and waxed moustache and perceived that he had turned his eye on his quarry, she told Arthur that it was unlucky to see anybody's train leave the station and left him to fall a victim to the inquiry agent's remorseless pursuit.

Blenkinsop looked at the clock. There was still another ten minutes before the Nocturnal Scot was due to dash northward through the night. He decided to rescue his luggage from the Glasgow sleeper and transfer it to the original sleeper he had booked in the Glenmore coach. He made no attempt to cancel the extra ticket, for he reflected that as the country was paying for that ticket it would not be fair to imperil the future of the country by calling attention to himself any more than he had done already by what must appear to the porter at the least a curious vagueness about his destination.

No sooner did Doggett perceive that his quarry was changing his sleeper than he changed his, for he reflected that as his client would pay for the other sleeper it would not be fair to imperil the future of her divorce by false economy. When he saw his quarry enter sleeping berth Number 10 and on referring to the number on the pasted up list of passengers read that it had been booked in the name of Mr A. Hudson, Doggett emitted a low chuckle which sounded like the chatter of a ferret as it disappears into a burrow where the scent of rabbit is unusually strong. A minute or two later he and his bags were in Number 11, which by that fortune which favours the brave and the detective of fiction was vacant.

Blenkinsop had just congratulated himself upon the ease with which he had circumvented the vigilance of his wife and was bending over to push his new suitcases beneath the bed when he experienced once again all the horrific emotions of one upon a secret errand, for on looking under the bed to see what prevented the smooth disappearance of his luggage he discovered that the entire space was occupied by the form of a man.

'It's quite all right, Major B,' the intruder whispered raucously. 'I've got a letter for you from The Elms. Only I won't come out till the train starts. Somebody might hear us talking and I think you're being followed.'

Blenkinsop rose and sat down upon the bed, his heart beating as it had never beaten on the field of battle. Most people who have been severely frightened feel angry when their nerves begin to recover, and Blenkinsop could not help feeling angry with the heads of the Secret Service. It would have been perfectly easy for him to visit The Elms and receive from the mouth of N himself the instructions for his meeting with Juno. There was surely no need to communicate with him like this. And it might have led to a great deal of awkwardness. It was pure luck that Enid had retired from King's Cross in time to give him an opportunity to transfer from the Glasgow coach to the Glenmore coach. This messenger might have missed him altogether. A European crisis might have been precipitated. For the first time Blenkinsop was inclined to think that the importance of secrecy compared with service had been exaggerated.

Presently from beneath the bed he heard his name being growled, and in a thoroughly irritable whisper he asked what was the matter now.

'Could you kindly turn off the heater, sir?' the messenger whispered. 'It's really like an oven under here. The pipes are just against my back.'

'The handle is at "off",' Blenkinsop whispered sharply.

'Could you try it at "on", sir? Sometimes these gadgets don't work quite according.'

Blenkinsop turned the handle controlling the heat to 'on'.

Presently the messenger rolled out from underneath the bed. After puffing and blowing for a while stretched out at full length, he sat up and said he was very sorry but flesh and blood couldn't stand such heat. Then the whistle sounded, and the train began to rumble northward. The messenger rose from the floor, foraged in the pockets of his greatcoat, and handed Blenkinsop a heavily sealed envelope.

'Sorry to cause you so much trouble, sir,' he panted respectfully. 'But Colonel N and Major H. H. made a very big point of nobody seeing me hand you this letter. You was to read it, and give me a verbal message that you understood what you had to do.'

'But are you going to spend the rest of the night in my sleeper?' Blenkinsop asked with a hint of displeasure.

'No, sir. I shall slip off the train at Grantham. Colonel N wants to hear you've received this letter as soon as possible. I've got my own sleeper further along, but I thought it was better not to come knocking at the door of yours. In my opinion the fellow next door to you isn't up to no good. He followed you along from that other carriage you went into like a cat follows a mouse. That's why I nipped under your bed the way I did.'

'You're one of The Elms staff, I suppose?'

'That's right, sir, Sergeant-Instructor Flack.'

Blenkinsop's shaken nerves were by now calm again.

'Sit down, Sergeant,' he said, indicating the far end of the bed.

'That's quite all right, sir, I won't disturb you. It was only the hot pipes I was beginning to feel a bit.'

Blenkinsop opened the outer envelope and saw in green ink on the inside envelope a large B, and opening this he drew forth a letter written entirely in N's own hand:

Thursday, 20 November

The Elms.

Dear B: Here are your instructions which please destroy immediately you have mastered them. Juno is staying at the Glenmore Hydro in rooms Number 27 and 28 under the name of Señora Miranda, a wealthy native of the Canary Islands, who will let it be generally known that she has come to this country to dispose of a large banana plantation while taking the cure at Glenmore. S booked the rooms for her from Paris. We booked a room for you as Mr Arthur Hudson of Hudson Brothers, Banana Importers, King Street, Covent Garden. So your cover is perfect, and you can establish contact with Juno without rousing any suspicion of your real business. H.M. King Johannis of Mendacia is staying with his friend the MacAdam of MacAdam at Drumroy Castle which is about twenty miles from Glenmore.

I am arranging for you to give a talk next week on Mendacia over the wireless. In this talk which you will prepare with the help of H.M. (whom in future communications we shall allude to as Mr

Johnson) you will convey to the King's agents in Mendacia the date when the King will sail from Scotland with the idea of a restoration. You must arrange how this is to be done without upsetting the B.B.C. In other words only those in the secret over here and in Mendacia will understand. Officially, of course, the British Government will not apparently have anything to do with Mr Johnson's restoration; but as there is no doubt that his restoration is most desirable in the present state of affairs in South-East Europe, we are sailing as near to the wind as we can in the interests of peace. We consider that if it were generally known in Mendacia that we favoured a royal restoration a number of adherents secretly in favour of Mr Johnson would declare themselves openly. The fact of the news of his coming being announced through the B.B.C. is thought a sufficient indication of our sympathies, especially on top of the change of Ministers. It is undesirable to run any risk of upsetting Burgundian opinion; but we are acting in concord with the Venetian Government, which favours a Royalist reaction. Therefore the main thing is absolute secrecy, and you should exercise the greatest caution in any meetings you may find it necessary to have with Mr Johnson.

By the way, you need not worry about Juno's money. We had no difficulty in providing all she wanted, and a little more. £250 for your own current expenses has been paid into your bank. I wish I could have a chance to talk things over with you again, but it is so vital to prevent the slightest suspicion that we are in any way connected with this restoration getting about that I did not dare risk another meeting with you. I'm particularly anxious that not a word of what we are doing reaches P and the S.R.D. people who never quite understand the importance of something which isn't their pigeon. Of course, you realize that if anything does get out we shall completely disown you. On no account go to Drumroy. You must arrange to meet Mr Johnson elsewhere.

I don't think there's anything more to say except to wish you the best of luck in this tricky business. Give the bearer of this the following verbal message, and then I shall know that you have received my letter safely, noted its contents, and *destroyed* it. 'Tell Colonel N that Mr Hudson has eaten his banana.'

Yours,
N

Blenkinsop read through his Chief's letter three times. Then he lowered the wash-basin, put the letter inside, lighted it, and watched it burn to ashes.

'Tell Colonel B, Sergeant,' he said gravely, 'that Mr Hudson has eaten his banana.'

'I beg pardon, sir?' the Sergeant-Instructor muttered in evident surprise. He seemed to think that the fumes of burning paper had gone to Blenkinsop's head.

'I wish you to tell Colonel N as soon as you get back that Mr Hudson has eaten his banana.'

'Oh, you want me to say, "Mr Hudson has eaten his banana" just like that, sir?'

'Exactly.'

'Yes, sir. Beg pardon, sir. Only I just wanted to be sure. Colonel N gets a bit rorty with us sometimes, and I don't want to make a mistake. Hudson was the name, sir?'

'That's right.'

'And banana the fruit he ate?'

'*His* banana.'

'I see, sir. Not Colonel N's banana? I mean to say I wouldn't like him to turn on me if I said "Mr Hudson's eaten *your* banana."'

Blenkinsop was worried. He had burnt the letter now. Which had N meant? He had not expressed himself at all clearly.

'I think you'd better say "Mr Hudson has eaten *his* banana." If Colonel N says, "Do you mean my banana?" you could say "yes, your banana." I'm sure it will be all right, Sergeant.'

'Yes, sir, I'm sure it will too, sir. I wouldn't have bothered you over such a detail. Only you know what it is in our work. But Colonel N's not as nervous as what Major H. H. is, sir. I remember once I gave four knocks on his door instead of five, and which is our regulation for him, and absent-minded like I walked in without waiting for the signal, and which is a double ring on his handbell. Gawd, sir – excuse the rough language – if I'd have been the hangman come in to take him for execution he couldn't have looked more scared. Something gashly, sir. Well, it gave me a funny kind of feeling, just to look at him. And he didn't half give me a dressing down after he collected himself. "What you done just now, Sergeant Flack," he says to me, "what you done just now might have broken up the whole Secret Service," he said. So you'll excuse me, sir, for being just a bit over anxious, as you might say, about just whose banana it was.'

'That's all right, Sergeant.'

'And now, sir, if you've no further need for me I'll go along and have a bit of a lay down till we make Grantham. I've never travelled in a first-class sleeper before. So it's what you might call a bit of an experience for me, sir. Good night, sir.'

'Good night, Sergeant. When do you expect to be back in London?'

'Oh, I reckon I'll get in with the milk, sir. "Mr Hudson has eaten his banana." That's right, isn't it, sir?'

'That's right.'

Sergeant-Instructor Flack touched his cap, opened the door of the sleeper, and took a quick glance up and down the dim corridor. Then he slipped out, not unobserved, however, by Mr Doggett, who made the following note:

Major B reached King's X at 10.15 p.m. 20 Nov. accompanied by Mrs B. Booked first-class sleeper to Glasgow, but on Mrs B's departure removed himself and belongings to a first-class sleeper in Glenmore coach in name of A. Hudson. Secured sleeper next him. Observed through slit in door of my sleeper heavily muffled figure emerge from Major B's sleeper. Unknown figure seemed anxious to avoid being seen and proceeded surreptitiously to sleeping-berth further along coach. Query. Is this the real Hudson, or Mrs H disguised as a man?

The inquiry agent lay back on his bed and concentrated the whole of his mental forces upon the problem. At the end of half an hour's intensive ratiocination he decided that it was insoluble.

'Not enough data,' Mr Doggett muttered to himself.

There are few places on this earth which lend themselves with less facility to social intercourse than the first-class sleeping-cars of British railways. Mr Doggett itched to pay a pleasant little call on his next-door neighbour; but even his ingenious fancy could think of no satisfactory excuse for doing so.

An obvious excuse would certainly awake suspicion. It would be more prudent to wait until tomorrow morning and make an attempt to get acquainted over the breakfast-table.

Mr Doggett decided to sleep on it.

Chapter 12

GLENMORE

> O Caledonia! Stern and wild,
> Meet nurse for a poetic child!
> Land of brown heath and shaggy wood,
> Land of the mountain and the flood,
> Land of my sires!

With these stirring words the Wizard of the North apostrophized in glowing poesie his native land; but as the Roman poet said 'Times change and we change with them'. It is in this spirit that the Management of the Glenmore Hydro ventures to urge the claim of a great hotel which, while it offers to its patrons all those glories which Caledonia has made peculiarly her own, has neglected nothing which could possibly minister to the comfort of their sojourn in the land of glens and bens and heroes.

Glenmore Castle, the ancestral home of the mighty Earls of Glenmore whose proud motto ...

Blenkinsop had read as far as this in a booklet which was lying beside his plate at breakfast next morning when to his annoyance a horrid little bounder with shiny apple cheeks, a waxed moustache, and overstrung hair took the seat opposite to him.

'Good morning,' said this horrid little bounder.

Blenkinsop grunted.

'We're well up to time,' the intruder persisted, looking out of the window at the station through which the train was passing and then at his watch. 'We reach Glenmore at eleven, I think.'

'I don't know,' said Blenkinsop.

'You expecting to get any of what they call these winter sports?'

'No.'

'Going for the waters perhaps?'

'No.'

'Ah, just for the scenery, I suppose?'

'Excuse me, but I happen to be reading,' said Blenkinsop sternly.

'Yes, I read that book through last night. It sounds all right, eh? Well, of course, they've got to do something to get people so far from good old London. Are you Scotch?'

'I may be.'

The bounder laughed loudly.

'That's a good one! Well, that's one of the best I ever heard. I really must remember that. You couldn't have put it neater. Are you Scotch? I may be!'

Blenkinsop scowled and buried himself again in the booklet.

Everything is done to give the guests a real Highland welcome. The characteristic Highland atmosphere has been carefully preserved, but at the same time the Glenmore Hydro can justly claim to be the last word in modern hotel comfort ... unsurpassable views of noble Ben Buidhe (pron. Booey) and wild Ben Uaine (pron. Oðana) from every bedroom ... foaming torrent of the famous Fluich (pron. Flooch) and the majestic waters of divine Loch Fluich, the fishing of which is renowned even in a country so renowned for the splendour of its fishing ...

'The country's getting a bit prettier as we go along,' observed Mr Doggett, gazing from the window at one of the latest excesses of the Forestry Commission in the way of reafforestation.

Blenkinsop, after cramming his mouth with toast and that curious synthetic secretion which is known as marmalade in the dining-cars of British railways, buried himself deeper in the booklet.

Winter sports are a feature of life at Glenmore Hydro, the higher slopes of Ben Buidhe providing some of the finest ski runs in Europe ... the electro-therapeutic equipment is second to none in the world, and the most recent developments of hydrotherapy are at the disposal of guests ... pine baths, mud baths, peat baths, sea-weed baths, sulphur baths, radium baths ... a superbly equipped Turkish bath ... a swimming pool of generous dimensions and a large covered swimming bath add to the amenities of life at Glenmore, and the final touch to the luxurious indulgence of hydrotherapy is provided by a magnificent glass-domed siesta-lounge irradiated by artificial sunlight.

Blenkinsop laid down the booklet for a moment and gazed pensively in the other direction from the face of the bounder opposite. There had turned out to be a lack of water at the Hotel Multum in the island of Parvo. Perhaps it had been as much the rationing of the baths there as the unsettled politics of the country which had led to failure.

'I see you're reading about these baths at Glenmore,' said Mr Doggett, glancing at the open booklet on the table in front of Blenkinsop. 'They don't mean us to come away from Scotland dirty, that's a sure thing.'

Blenkinsop could stand no more. He rose from the remains of his breakfast and returned, with as much dignity as the down gradient allowed him, to his sleeper.

Mr Doggett took out his pocket-book and noted:

Engaged Major B in conversation at breakfast. Found him a nasty subject. Nothing free and easy about him at all. Query. Worried about the future?

'Glenmore! Glenmore! Glenmore!' called the porters. And nearly all the passengers emerged from what was left of the Nocturnal Scot. The station was not a large one, but a pleasing touch of colour was given to the muggy November morning by the brilliant posters advertising (it might be thought a little superfluously) the glories of the Glenmore Hydro. 'A Highland welcome awaits you at glorious Glenmore,' they all cried out in unshaded reds and blues and greens. 'Come to stay at the Glenmore Hydro and experience real Highland hospitality.' Where anybody would have gone from that remote platform if he had not been prepared to accept this invitation might have been difficult to say. Only two posters struck a false note. One asked in black, yellow, and amber, 'Why not Bruges this year?' The other observed reproachfully in red, white, and blue, 'See England First. Bridlington for Brine and Breeze. Bracing Bridlington the Empress of the East Coast.'

Outside the station were waiting two bulging green motor-buses, both surrounded by several gentlemen in uniform who eyed the new arrivals as admirals might eye midshipmen. The arrivals were not many. There was a party of young people in winter sports attire, looking as brightly coloured as the posters along the platform and all carrying virgin skis. There was a pair of elderly maiden ladies anxious about the comfort of their dog, a West Highland terrier who had told a fox-terrier belonging to the young people that the fox-terrier was a wretched Sasunnach and therefore had no business at Glenmore. There was a sharp encounter before they were dragged apart, each uttering threats of what he would do to the other when they met again. Finally there was a pair of rich people whose appearance kindled a light in the eyes of the uniformed officials round the motor-buses, one of whom relieved the rich lady of her gold handbag and deposited it on the seat of the bus he commanded.

Blenkinsop tried to guess which of the two buses the objectionable bounder with the waxed moustache would enter, in order that he might travel by the other; but in the end the men in uniform managed to put all the passengers in one bus and all the luggage in the other, thus complicating to the utmost of their ability the problem of tipping. However, he did manage to avoid sitting next him.

On leaving the station the bus swept at a rapid speed up a wide main road until it came to the village of Glenmore, which consisted of a row of grey cottages, a quantity of villas empty at the moment but in summer gay with tenants, an Established Church, a United Free Church, a Free Presbyterian Church, an Episcopalian Church closed for the winter, and the Glenmore Arms, a pleasant-looking little hotel surrounded by a platoon of petrol-pumps in the gay uniforms of the various combines to which they belonged.

At the end of the village the bus stopped on a bridge over a tumbling river, and one of the admirals looked in to warn visitors that on the right they could see the ancient burial-ground of the Macadams. The two maiden ladies, who were Macadams themselves and were beginning to hear ancestral voices, both got out and stared at the sombre reliquary of their forefathers' bones, the lure of which had brought them here all the way from Worthing. The fox-terrier who answered to the name of Lousy, resented the West Highland terrier's ancestral bumptiousness on re-entering the bus and went for him.

'Fingal, you naughty little dog,' exclaimed one mistress.

'Fingal, lie down, sir, will you?' exclaimed the other.

'Lousy, lie down, damn you? Do catch hold of him, Peanut,' begged one of the girls.

The youth called Peanut contrived to seize Lousy. The two maiden ladies clung to Fingal. To the accompaniment of low growls the bus turned off the main road and entered dark Glenmore, the natural savagery of which had roused in the hearts of the Forestry Commissioners a desire to tame it. With this end in view they had nearly finished ringing the birch-trees after some years of arduous labour, and by next autumn they might hope that the last of them would scatter with gold the mossy crags of dark Glenmore and break green again with another spring. To take the place of the uneconomical birches the Forestry Commission had planted row after row of Douglas firs and notice-board after notice-board warning people not to burn their handiwork. Dark Glenmore would spend the next ten years looking like a vast seedsman's nursery and the next thirty or more beneath a quantity of huge monotonous dark-green rugs, and not even frayed rugs at that.

Further up the Glen the scene became more wild and beyond the efforts of the Forestry Commission to tame it. The two maiden ladies were wrought up to a state of ancestral frenzy.

'It must be about here, Flora, that the Macadams massacred the Mackillops,' the elder of the two gloated. 'Oh, could we stop just a moment?'

'Excuse me,' said Miss Flora to one of the admirals. 'Do you think the bus could stop here? My sister wants to verify an historical spot. Quiet, Fingal! Quiet, bad dog!'

The two maiden ladies dragged Fingal away from an attempt to massacre Lousy, and alighted. Then they stood poring over *Through Wild West Alba in Kilt and Plaid* and trying to extract from the flowers of its prose the hard roots of their clan history.

'It says "About two miles up Glenmore on the south side a

large cairn marks the site of the Battle of the Brogue between the Clan Macadam and the Clan Mackillop in 1410, so called because when the Chief of the Mackillops lay dying one of the Macadams thrust his brogue into his mouth and put an end to his agony." Oh, Caroline, doesn't it all seem like only yesterday?'

'But where's the cairn, Flora?' asked her sister.

'There it is! There it is!' cried Flora, pointing to a neat-looking monument.

'No, madam,' one of the admirals explained, 'that's the memorial erected by the last Lord Glenmore's father to a favourite retriever which was accidentally shot by one of the shooting party. I don't quite know where this battle-place is you're looking for, but it may interest you to know that the last wolf killed in Scotland was killed where you see that old cottage.'

'When was that?' asked Miss Flora eagerly.

'I don't know, madam, but some time ago now.'

'Thank you very much. That's most interesting. My sister and I are Macadams, you know.'

'Oh, indeed, madam?' said the admiral who, since he came to the Glenmore Hydro from the Savoy some four years ago, had been told this by at least a hundred elderly maiden ladies.

'And this is our first visit to the land of our forefathers,' Miss Flora went on.

And the admiral had heard that before too.

'There doesn't look much chance of ski-ing,' observed the young man known as Peanut.

'No, sir, the snow seems to be hanging back. But the greens on the golf course are in lovely condition.'

'Aren't they a bit wet?'

'Well, perhaps a bit on the wet side, sir. We've had a lot of rain lately.'

As the admiral spoke the rain began again, and by the time the bus stopped before the Glenmore Hydro it was a downpour. Any depression that the arriving guests might have felt was dispelled by the sounds of a bagpipe. The Highland wel-

come less conspicuous at the railway-station was here bounte-
ous. While the pipe marched up and down in the rain, half a
dozen field-marshals and the A.D.C.s appeared in the great
Gothic entrance, and a moment later the central heating of the
interior enfolded the guests.

Glenmore Castle was one of the most majestic fruits of the
Gothic revival that began on Strawberry Hill and reached the
peak of its architectural achievement with the Albert Memorial. The fortunes of the Glenmores never recovered from the
expense of such an extravagance of romantic decoration, and
when soon after the war the earldom became extinct Glenmore
Castle had not been inhabited by the family for the last twenty
years. The company which bought it with the idea of convert-
ing it into a Hydro bought it as it stood with its Gothic tables,
chairs, curtains, coverlets, bookshelves, books, and saucepans.
Such additions as they were compelled to make in order that
the outward appearance of antiquity should be combined with
a comfortable and up-to-date present were made as far as
possible in harmony with the Gothic splendours of a century
ago. The open-air swimming-pool, the indoor swimming-bath,
the siesta-lounge, the gymnasium, all were outwardly medieval.
And to the picturesque externals of the Middle Ages were
added the equally picturesque externals of Highland life in its
most romantic and improbable aspects. Each bedroom was
dedicated to a different clan or division of a clan, and in these
the perpendicular four-posters and decorated Norman toilet-
tables and Early English washstands were given a national
setting by hangings of the particular clan tartan demanded by
the room's dedication. In some bedrooms even the carpets were
woven in tartan, and wherever possible pictures to illustrate
clan history had been hung upon the walls.

The hydro-therapeutic fame of Glenmore was based upon the
curative qualities of the water in St Ninian's Well which since
the earliest times had been regarded as a panacea. The Glenmore Hydropathic Hotel Company succeeded in making the
famous water of St Ninian more conveniently available than by
the time-honoured method of drinking it by being held by the
heels over the source, from which according to local super-

stition it was necessary to lap like a dog in order to obtain one's wish and be healed of one's ills. The Glenmore Hydropathic Company had lost no time in putting St Ninian's water on tap, though younger visitors were encouraged to perform the time-honoured gymnastic feat at the original well, the successful achievement of which was a feature of a stay at Glenmore.

For some years it had been the custom to close the hotel between the end of September and Easter, but when the fall of the pound made winter sports in Switzerland a more expensive prospect than usual it was resolved to open Glenmore in winter, a patriotic move which the weather did its best to block by remaining obstinately mild. Consequently when Blenkinsop arrived towards the end of this November he found the rooms occupied by very few winter sportsmen. Those that had come in answer to the posters were consoled during the day by golf and during the evening by the Glenmore Golliwogs, a dance band whose hot rhythm compensated for the delay of the expected cold spell. The remainder of the guests was an extension of those who had travelled up with Blenkinsop, that is a certain number of elderly maiden ladies, a widow or two, and half a dozen lonely bachelors trying to feel that they were not home on leave. Besides these there were the usual valetudinarians of both sexes whose life was regulated by the irregularity of their internal machinery.

But what did the other guests matter to Blenkinsop when he read in the hotel register *Señora Miranda, nationality Spanish, place of domicile Canary Islands, rooms 27 and 28*. The young winter sportswoman on the Glenmore poster who sailed on her skis across the azure vault of heaven from snowy peak to snowy peak was not so light as Blenkinsop's heart.

'We have reserved for you the Macmillan room, Mr Hudson. That's number 32. It is full south,' said the reception clerk in an exquisitely languid voice.

'That should be all right,' said Blenkinsop.

The reception clerk told the porters where to take the luggage, and turned to Mr Doggett who was just behind Blenkinsop.

'Let me see, did you book a room?' she asked.

Mr Doggett shook his head.

'We can give you Campbell of Cawdor,' she suggested.

'I beg your pardon?'

'Unless you'd prefer Hunting Macpherson?'

'Why should I want to hunt anybody?' Mr Doggett asked, indignantly. 'What I want is a good room.'

'Hunting Macpherson is a very good room. Number 30. It is full south.'

'That'll do me,' said Doggett. 'But what did you call it Hunting Macpherson for?'

'It is one of the clan tartans. All our rooms are called after clan tartans. Will you register, please?'

When half an hour later Blenkinsop emerged in plus-fours from his room papered and hung with the red and yellow of Macmillan he was annoyed to perceive the shiny-cheeked bounder who had pestered him at breakfast emerging from a room papered and hung with the grey, black, and crimson of Hunting Macpherson. He disliked extremely the notion that this objectionable fellow should be occupying a room between him and Renata.

'Ah, there you are!' Mr Doggett exclaimed. 'Comfortable and cosy?'

'Perfectly comfortable,' Blenkinsop replied frigidly.

'Here's the lift,' said Doggett. 'You're going past it.'

'Thanks, I'm walking down,' said Blenkinsop icily.

'Winter sports, eh?' the inquiry agent muttered to himself as Blenkinsop disappeared round the bend of the staircase. 'Well if that la-di-da Blenkinsop thinks he's going to start skying over John Doggett he's thinking very wrong. Walking down, eh? Yes, and walking down a bit faster than he thinks.'

Doggett from the lift reached the entrance hall just as Blenkinsop was inquiring at the desk for Señora Miranda.

'Let me see, Mr Hudson, isn't it? I think the lady in Number 28 was expecting you,' said the reception clerk. 'This note was to be handed to you on arrival.' She gave him the envelope which Blenkinsop carried off to read in the library. The emotion of receiving his first communication from Renata was too acute for the entrance hall to share it. Doggett, however, was without decent feelings. No sooner had Blenkinsop sat down in a deep leather armchair stamped all over with gilt wyverns than to his disgust Doggett sat down at his elbow in a deep leather armchair stamped all over with gilt cockatrices.

Blenkinsop thrust Renata's note unopened into his pocket.

'Are you following me about, or what?' he asked angrily.

'That's all right, Mr Hudson,' the inquiry agent replied. 'This is a public smoking-room.'

'Who the hell are you calling – who the hell told you to accost me in this offensive manner?' Blenkinsop demanded with a truculence in his tone that made the persistent Doggett push his chair back a couple of feet.

'Now there's no need for unpleasantness, Mr Hudson,' he said. 'This is a free country, and a cat may look at a king. I don't want to force my company on anybody where it's not welcome. If you want to read your correspondence don't bother about me.'

Blenkinsop rose and moved to the other end of the great Gothic library on the heavily carved shelves of which the books of the Earls of Glenmore still brooded unread. Here in a deep leather armchair stamped all over with gilt unicorns he took Renata's note out of his pocket and opened it. From the other end of the library came the sound of a detestably sibilant whistle. It was Doggett expressing indifference to the snub he had received.

'Little bounder!' scoffed Blenkinsop as he eyed fondly the fine sloping hand of the woman for whose sake he would have suffered the contamination from a thousand Doggetts.

Just as Blenkinsop read the opening words of Renata's note, a sudden apprehensiveness was visible upon his countenance. What was that tune being whistled at the other end of the room? Was it not *Down by the Old Bull and Bush*? And if it was that tune, was there not something sinister in its being whistled on an occasion like this? Perhaps Sergeant Flack had been right in supposing that he was followed at King's Cross. He had ascribed his fancy at the time to nervousness over the importance of the message he had had to deliver. Perhaps this horrid little brute with the waxed moustache was the agent of a foreign power.

With a perturbed shake of the head Blenkinsop turned to the letter he had not yet read:

Cher ami:

I am so content that you are here. Please to take your dinner with me in my private room at eight o'clock tonight. I have so much things to tell you. This morning I must go to lunch at Drumroy Castle.

Bien à vous,
Renata

Blenkinsop looked gloomily at the clock which at the moment struck twelve, a procedure which was startling to those who witnessed it for the first time, for at every hour the portcullis of a Gothic archway above the dial was raised and a knight in armour emerged on a platform where he struck the strokes of the hour upon a bell.

'Goolor!' ejaculated Doggett. 'That 'ud be a nice thing to see sudden after anyone had had one or two. When knights were bold, eh? Well, they don't mean you to forget the time in this hotel, Mr Hudson. I wonder if St George and the Dragon pops out like that at every quarter.'

'You'd better ask him. You seem to like asking questions,' said Blenkinsop sarcastically as he strode from the library.

The inquiry agent took out his notebook.

B seems nervous [he wrote]. He doesn't like being addressed as Mr H. Nearly bit my head off when I did so this morning. A woman calling herself Señora Miranda from the Canary Islands sent a note down to him when he arrived. I reckon it's Mrs H under an assumed name. The whole business is very hoky-poky, but it ought to be easy going unless they want flagrant delight. That may not be so easy. He's a hefty blighter in spite of being so la-di-da. Petty expenses: tips to porters on arrival £1 5s. Two large whiskies and soda for information, and various disbursements £2 17s.

Mr Doggett rang the bell.
'Bring me a large whisky and soda,' he told the waiter.
'Yes, sir.'

WATER ON THE BRAIN

'Oh, and waiter, what's this St Ninian's water?'

'It's considered very good, sir.'

'Does it taste funny?'

'That rather depends on one's sense of humour, sir.'

'Oh, you're a wag too, are you?' said the inquiry agent. 'So help me, this hotel's full of funny turns. Well, bring me a glass of it. What's it good for?'

'It's considered good for everything, sir.'

'Will it cure corns?'

'I don't know about that, sir.'

Presently the waiter returned with a tray.

Mr Doggett sniffed the healing water suspiciously.

'It smells a bit like the day before yesterday,' he observed.

'Yes, sir.'

Mr Doggett took a gulp.

'Oh, my god, what's been cooked in this?' he exclaimed.

'It's the natural spring, sir.'

'Natural? My god, I never tasted anything so unnatural in my life. If you call bad eggs and old bicycle tyres natural spring ... here, have you ever tasted any of this stuff yourself?'

The waiter shuddered.

'No, sir.'

'Well, go and get me another large whisky.'

'Very good, sir.'

'And bring me a bottle of this St Ninian's water done up in a parcel. What time does the London post go?'

'Two o'clock, sir.'

While the waiter was fetching the bottle the inquiry agent wrote to his employer:

Mr Pinches
Dear Sir:

Everything looks like going all according. Herewith I am sending you a bottle of the famous St Ninian's water. You may think it tastes a bit funny at first.

Yours faithfully,
J. Doggett

'I reckon that squares up any old scores between me and the

governor,' Doggett murmured to himself as he addressed the envelope. 'If he starts investigating that he'll want to call in a sanitary engineer.'

At this moment swathed in tartan tweed the two Miss Macadams, who had been wandering about in a romantic haze ever since they had arrived at Glenmore, entered the library.

'Oh, Caroline, what a divine room!' exclaimed the younger.

'Not quite divine, Flora,' the elder reproved. 'But truly majestic. This must have been the late Lord Glenmore's library.'

'Have you ladies drunk any of this St Ninian's water yet?' Mr Doggett inquired.

'No, my sister and I have not as yet indulged in that beverage,' Miss Caroline replied with stately good humour.

'Oh, you ought to. You really ought to,' Doggett urged.

'We were going to drink some at St Ninian's Well after lunch,' said Miss Flora, 'and wish.'

'Yes, it does make you wish,' he agreed fervidly.

'They say if you drink it and turn round three times,' Miss Flora went on dreamily, 'that next morning if you go out at dawn you'll see the fairies.'

'I wouldn't put anything beyond such a water,' Doggett declared. 'But I shouldn't turn round too much. I should let the water settle first if I was you.'

'Are you Scottish?' Miss Caroline asked.

'Not guilty, m'lud,' said Doggett.

'My sister and I are standing upon our native heath for the first time,' Miss Caroline announced proudly.

'My own native heath is Blackheath,' said Doggett.

'We are Macadams,' Miss Flora explained.

'Pleased to meet you, Miss Macadam. My name is Doggett.'

The waiter came back with the second whisky and the bottle of St Ninian's water ready packed.

'I'm sending off a bottle of this exquisite sherbet to an old friend,' Doggett explained.

'Oh, what a delightful notion, Caroline,' Miss Flora gushed. 'Do let us send a bottle to Mr Leslie. Mr Leslie is our minister at Worthing where we live. He preaches such a strong sermon.'

'Does he?' said Doggett. 'Well, I reckon after he's drunk a bottle of St Ninian's water he'll preach the strongest sermon he ever has preached.'

'Look, Flora, I do believe the sun is coming out,' said the elder Miss Macadam. 'Should we not take a short turn in the grounds before lunch? We mustn't forget poor little Fingal. Fingal is our little West Highland terrier,' she explained to Doggett.

'Yes, I saw the little love in the bus,' he said.

Miss Macadam smiled graciously at this, and made a stately exit followed by her younger sister.

Presently Doggett left the library and found a place for himself in the siesta-lounge where, attracted by the artificial sunlight, most of the hotel guests were sitting about in wicker chairs. The siesta-lounge commanded a view of woodland, moor, and loch, of noble Ben Buidhe and wild Ben Uaine, and of the Glenmore Hydro golf-course in the foreground; but the view that at this moment was attracting all the attention was MacAdam of MacAdam alighting from his car at the door of the hotel. Several of the guests claimed to have caught sight of stags during their rambles: one or two had asserted they had seen an eagle; one had even sworn that a wild cat had spat at him from the top of a boulder on the lower slopes of Ben Buidhe: none had seen or even ventured to claim that he had seen a Highland chieftain in a kilt. The excitement in the siesta-lounge was intense. Perhaps for the first time the guests in the Glenmore Hydro would have admitted that the scenes on the posters were less exaggerated than they were beginning to consider them.

The rich man who had arrived that morning hurried across to fetch his wife from the drawing-room to see the spectacle.

'Emmie, Emmie!' the others heard him shouting. 'Come on here. There's a native outside. In kilts. Come on! You can finish those picture postcards later. Hurry up, or you'll miss him, and then you'll be asking me whatever I brought you all the way up here for.'

The rich man's wife came waddling into the siesta-lounge to stare with the rest. She might have been too late if the Misses

Macadam had not availed themselves of the privilege of clans-women to engage their chief in conversation for a minute or two while they paid their respects to him.

'He's talking to them,' one guest observed with awe in his tones.

'Fine figure of a man, I will say,' said another, with a con-temptuous glance at the youth called Peanut who in a rose-pink pullover and a beret was telling his young companions that he had a jolly good mind to go to the Chelsea Arts Ball next year in a rig-out like that.

MacAdam, who was tall with a weather-beaten complexion, a large nose, and reddish hair, touched his bonnet to his two clanswomen and passed into the hotel. A few minutes later the Misses Macadam reached the siesta-lounge, and there was a general eagerness to engage them in conversation, an experi-ence which few elderly ladies enjoy in large hotels.

'You saw the fairies a bit sooner than you reckoned,' observed Mr Doggett.

'But we had just drunk at the Well,' said Miss Flora. 'My sister and I both drank and wished, and lo and behold we had the honour of meeting MacAdam.'

Some of the guests thought that even if Miss Flora had met her chief she need not put on airs about it by referring to him with a familiarity that grated on polite ears.

'How wonderful these old legends are!' sighed a permanently fair, thin, and elderly young woman with hair like a forsaken nest. 'I haven't a drop of Scottish blood in my veins, but I adore Scotland. I feel so psychic up here.'

'I had a Scotch great-grandmother on my mother's side,' a woman with convex tartan cheeks looked up from her knitting to announce complacently.

'What was she?' asked Miss Caroline.

'I don't think she was anything. Women weren't free then,' said the woman with the tartan cheeks, a gloomy sympathy in her voice for the wrongs of her sex.

'What clan, I mean?' Miss Caroline pressed haughtily.

'Her name was Janet Fletcher.'

'Oh, not Highland,' said Miss Caroline coldly.

'She came from Aberdeen. That's Highland enough for any-body.'

The Misses Macadam looked at one another.

'You are not a Scottish Nationalist?' Miss Caroline inquired severely.

'No, I couldn't call myself that with just a Scotch great-grandmother,' admitted the lady with the tartan cheeks, 'if by Scottish Nationalist you mean a proper Scotch-woman.'

'A Scottish Nationalist,' said Miss Flora in a voice that would have rung out like Helen Macgregor's, had excitement not imparted a tremolo, 'A Scottish Nationalist is a patriot who believes that Scotland should rule itself.'

'But surely the Scotch rule the Empire already?' declared a man in plus-fours with a melancholy oval face. 'I know that out in Nigeria we think they do.'

'Let me speak, Flora,' said Miss Caroline, and there is no doubt that if at that moment Fingal had not tried to teach Lousy what Scottish Nationalism meant Mr Oliver Woodburn, the oval-faced man, would have been annihilated in a political argument. As it was the Misses Macadam had to retreat with their dog, and presently politics were forgotten in the spectacle of MacAdam of MacAdam escorting Señora Miranda to his car.

'What ho! the monarch of the glen got off,' Mr Doggett observed to his neighbour, as Madame Tekta in a dark brown tailor-made of the most beguiling austerity passed in full view of her fellow-guests.

'Who's the little lady?' he asked.

'That's Señora Miranda,' replied the neighbour, a hearty man, with a florid face and white hair and whiskers who in the vivid check suit he was wearing looked like a trainer of race-horses.

'Oh, that's Her Nibs, is it?' said Mr Doggett. 'And a very hotsy-totsy piece of goods, too, which nobody can deny.'

'Spanish,' remarked the neighbour. 'From the Canary Islands.'

'Yes, that's what they say in the bird-shops when they've just painted a sparrow yellow.'

'Oh, she's Spanish right enough,' the neighbour insisted. 'She's selling a big banana property to a man called Hudson. I know Hudson well. I'm at Covent Garden myself. Lobbins is my name. I'm up here for the water. And I'm feeling much better already.'

'I'll lay a fiver you are. One sip cured me half an hour ago.'

'Dr Maclaren, the resident physician, tells me that when he gets me up to six glasses a day, with a judicious course of peat baths, there won't be a trace of uric acid left in my system till next year.'

'Six glasses a day?'

'Six. And a course of strict dieting. He says I'll walk out of here next week a new man.'

'Walk out? It would surprise me if you didn't fly out. I'm proud to have met you, Mr Lobbins. Doggett is my name. So you know Mr Hudson, do you?'

'I know him well.'

'Know his wife?'

'No, we've only met in business. He's one of the big men in Covent Garden. I'll point him out to you if he comes in to lunch.'

'You needn't bother to do that. He's sitting over in a corner of the lounge.'

The inquiry agent pointed out Blenkinsop who had just been gloomily watching Renata driving off with MacAdam. No doubt the King had wanted to see her, but it was galling not to have been allowed even a brief greeting.

'That's not Hudson,' said Mr Lobbins.

'That's the name he's registered under. Room 32.'

'That's not Hudson,' Mr Lobbins repeated firmly.

Doggett was congratulating himself inwardly. This man might be a valuable witness if he survived the water of St Ninian's. Nevertheless it would not do to frighten Blenkinsop prematurely.

'Perhaps it's another Hudson,' he suggested.

'There's only one Hudson in the banana business,' Mr Lobbins affirmed. 'It's called Hudson Brothers, but Hudson's brother Alf died four or five years back. I smell a rat.'

'No, no, it's the water on that table,' said Doggett.

'There's something fishy going on,' Mr Lobbins insisted.

'It's the water, I tell you.'

'I think I ought to warn Señora Miranda. It looks to me as if an impostor has got hold of her.'

'Go on, don't tell me that little lady can't look after herself. She's the hardest nut to crack in Barceloner I'll lay. Little lady? That's funny. Here, do you know what a Juno is?'

'A large handsome woman.'

'That's right. Now you wouldn't call Her Nibs large, would you?'

'The Señora? Certainly not.'

'St Ninian's water must have shrunk her,' declared the inquiry agent.

'You're talking very mysteriously, Mr Doggett.'

'Don't worry. I get like that on holiday. I think I've got a touch of the artificial sunlight. Here, throw that water of yours away and have a whisky, old man.'

'I wish I could,' said Mr Lobbins. 'But I'm only allowed one small whisky after dinner.'

Mr Doggett found this statement so depressing that he felt impelled to seek the American Bar. Here he observed half a dozen young winter sportsmen and sportswomen perched on high chairs and drinking cocktails as brightly tinted as their pullovers and lips and hair. When one of the young men reached his twentieth 'too marvellous' in relating a story Doggett took his whisky away to a corner and wrote in his notebook:

Had first glimpse of Mrs H about 12.30. She drove off with Harry Lauder the Second to lunch. B sat in a corner looking like a dog with distemper. Mrs H no more a Juno than what I am. More like a pocket Venus. Looks as if she and B don't intend to be seen about together much in *daylight*. Chinned for a bit with a fellow called Lobbins who knows H in Covent Garden. Useful witness that B was masquerading here as H. I'll do a bit of work among the staff this afternoon. The sooner I can get away from here with a bit of evidence the better. St Ninian's Well, but nobody else in this b. place. It turns uric acid into sulphuric acid. N.B. Jokes for the next meeting of the Jolly-fellows Club.

The longer Mr Lobbins of Covent Garden thought about it, the less he liked the notion of allowing the pseudo-Hudson to carry through the fraud he was evidently planning. Having ascertained from a waiter that Blenkinsop, who was listlessly turning over the pages of *Scottish Country Life*, really was supposed to be Mr Hudson, he determined to probe the matter more deeply. With this end in view he accosted him after lunch with a blunt question.

'Excuse me, but I understand you are interested in bananas, sir?'

Normally, Blenkinsop would have put a damper on such inquisitiveness; but he had his cover to preserve, and therefore he admitted that he was interested in bananas.

'I'm not a banana man myself, but I know Mr William Hudson very well in business, and when I saw the address in the hotel book I quite expected to meet my old business friend.'

'I am Mr Arthur Hudson,' said Blenkinsop.

'I knew Alfred Hudson, Will's brother. Poor chap, his early death was a sad loss to the firm.'

Blenkinsop picked up a glass of water on the table near him in order to find inspiration for the next lie. Unluckily it was St Ninian's water, and the shock made him lose his head.

'Yes, we were very cut up about Alfred's death. I say, I don't think they ought to leave water like this standing about everywhere,' he complained peevishly.

Mr Lobbins in his determination to get at the truth resisted the temptation to brag that he was already up to four glasses a day, and would be on six tomorrow.

'Are you a relation of Will Hudson?' he asked.

'Yes, yes, I'm a cousin.'

'I knew old John Hudson well. I didn't think he had a brother.'

'I'm a grandson of John Hudson's father.'

Mr Lobbins looked puzzled.

'But that ...' he began.

'No, I mean to say my father was a son of John Hudson's father's brother's son.'

Mr Lobbins tried another approach.

'I've never seen you in Covent Garden.'

'No, I've been abroad ever since the War.'

'In the banana business?'

'Oh, yes, very much so.'

'Were you buying for the firm?'

'Yes, that was my job. That's why I'm up here. Señora Miranda is selling a banana plantation to us. And Will asked me to come up and put the matter through. Señora Miranda is taking the cure here.'

And then Mr Lobbins plied Blenkinsop with technicalities about the banana trade, which left Blenkinsop determined to find a more convenient cover as soon as he possibly could and sent Mr Lobbins, now positive that Blenkinsop knew less about the banana than Adam did about the apple before he ate it, off to write a letter to his friend Hudson:

21 Nov.

Dear Hudson:

I'm up here at Glenmore doing a cure, and you may imagine my pleasure when I heard that you were expected up to meet a certain Señora Miranda in connection with a banana deal. Judge my surprise then when an individual calling himself Mr A. Hudson turned up and gave your address in the hotel book. He claims to be your cousin, but I soon discovered that he knows nothing about bananas, nothing about Covent Garden, nothing about anything that would justify him in claiming to be a cousin of yours and a member of your firm. I think you ought to take the first opportunity to travel up here and go into the matter. I suspect a swindle. You could combine business with pleasure by taking a course of the water. I am up to four glasses a day, with strict dieting and peat baths. I start six tomorrow, and I hope to be back in the Garden next week without a trace of acid in my system.

Yours sincerely,

C. Carton Lobbins

Chapter 13

DOGGETT'S DAY

THE clouds which had broken for a brief hour in order to give the Misses Macadam an opportunity to perform the gymnastic feat of drinking from St Ninian's original source gathered more densely than ever after lunch, and the rain poured down in a steady drench which increased in volume as the dusk of the dreich November day descended upon dark Glenmore. Even the manager of the Hydro was driven into admitting that the weather was definitely wet. No amount of tapping on the glass tubes of Admiral Fitzroy's barometer hanging in the hall could persuade the turbid liquids they contained to show any more vivacity than a forgotten gasogene in the attic of a lifelong teetotaller. The only revenge that the guests of the Glenmore Hydro could take upon the weather was to defy it by drenching themselves in the various baths provided by the management.

Blenkinsop was almost alone in not taking advantage of the hydro-therapeutics at his disposal. He spent the wet afternoon in wandering from Gothic room to Gothic room, remaining in each one merely long enough to turn listlessly over the pages of the illustrated papers and the various trade periodicals which lie upon the tables of the public rooms in luxury hotels. About five o'clock he had discovered a Glastonbury chair in Lady Glenmore's private oratory, now a supplementary smoking-room, a pile of old *Tatlers* and *Sketches*, and for a while he was able to assuage the dull ache of longing for Renata's return by studying society at various summery functions: Lady This at Ascot, Lady That at Goodwood, Mrs Thing at Henley, Miss Pamela Hownow at Le Touquet, and Lord Whatnot at Cowes. They appeared like figures of a golden age in a legendary sunlight, these snapshots which had given the originals the sweetness of publicity made bitter by the unfortunate expressions on their faces at the moment of being snapped. These heliotropes of outlived amusement lasted Blenkinsop till nearly six o'clock, and in despair he had just picked up *The Gas World*, which was now the only periodical in the hotel he had not examined, when the sound of a car's arrival fetched him out into the entrance hall in time to see Renata come in with MacAdam in attendance. Blenkinsop could not help thinking that it was an exaggeration of Highland hospitality which amounted to ostentatiousness for MacAdam himself to accompany Renata back from Drumroy when he had already displayed all that was necessary by calling for her in the morning.

Nor did Blenkinsop like the condescension with which MacAdam allowed Renata to present Mr Hudson to him. After all, he was Blenkinsop of the Welch Bays, and though this long-nosed Territorial might not know that he must know that he was not really Mr Hudson of Covent Garden.

'I am so very content to see you, Monsieur Hudson,' Renata was saying. 'I have enjoyed such a wonderful day in this land of poesy. I was never thinking that England could be so beautiful.'

'Scotland, dear lady, Scotland,' MacAdam corrected with a benevolent, an almost fond growl.

'Oh, I am so sorry,' she said, with a warmth of penitence that Blenkinsop found excessive, 'but it is only now that I am learning there can be any difference. And now I must go to my room and repose myself and dream of so much. You I shall see for dinner, Monsieur Hudson. You,' she added, with a smile for her escort that made Blenkinsop's legs in his ample plus-fours feel like captive birds beating their wings against a cage, 'you I shall see so soon again. *Au revoir, et mille remerciements!*'

Then she turned to Blenkinsop, this time with a smile so bright that he was under the impression that the artificial sunlight had suddenly been turned on. '*A tout à l'heure, cher ami.*'

The dragoon disguised as a banana importer and the Highland chieftain upon his native heath stood in the hall watching what her enemies called the hidden hand of Mendacia disappear from sight in the lift.

'A wonderful little woman, Hudson,' MacAdam sighed. 'God send that all goes well with her in this business!'

Although Blenkinsop felt it was MacAdam's duty to concern himself with the business so far as it affected the King of Mendacia rather than with the business so far as it affected the future of Madame Tekta, he could not but acknowledge that in making that last remark the Highland chief was recognizing that he was not really a banana importer.

'Won't you have a drink before you start back?' he asked.

'That's very good of you, thanks. But it must be a quick one, for I've got twenty miles to drive, and the road between here and Drumroy is like a swamp.'

But it was not quite such a rapid drink as MacAdam intended, for when Blenkinsop led the way to the library Miss Caroline and Miss Flora Macadam rose from the leather armchairs in which they had been sitting and said solemnly and simultaneously:

'Good evening, MacAdam!'

Their chief looked as startled as Macbeth must have looked when the three witches suddenly greeted him upon that blasted heath near Forres.

The Misses Macadam had spent the afternoon in nationalistic meditation, Miss Caroline's angularities packed away in peat, Miss Flora's curves wallowing in a pine-bath. On top of this they had each drunk a large glass of St Ninian's water, and they were now in a condition of acute Scottish ecstasy. They were therefore both in a mood to testify to the faith that this visit to Glenmore had kindled to a fervid glow; and the reappearance of their chief acted like a bellows to fan the fervid glow to a white heat of patriotism.

'Feasgair math, 'ic Adhamh,' said Miss Caroline.

Blenkinsop jumped. How was he to know that Miss Caroline, intoxicated by the fumes of St Ninian's water, had ventured to wish her chief good evening in Gaelic? To him the strange words sounded very like Mendacian. In a moment of exquisite apprehension he asked himself if the whole plot had been discovered and if these two apparently harmless maiden ladies were agents of the Mendacian Republic uttering a grim warning of assassination. Fortunately for MacAdam he had enough Gaelic to recognize that his clanswoman was trying to talk to

him in that language, but fortunately for his clanswoman, who
had been struggling for two years with the first few pages of
Gaelic for Beginners, he had not enough of his ancestral
language to carry the conversation any further without the
help of English.

'Ah, you – ah – have the Gaelic,' he observed.

'Only a few words to my shame,' Miss Caroline confessed.
'But my sister and I devote a great deal of time to learning it.'

'You of course speak it fluently, MacAdam?' Miss Flora
asked.

'No, no, just a word here and there. I – ah – wish I did,' their
chief replied apologetically.

'Shame on you, MacAdam!' Miss Caroline exclaimed.

'Shame on you!' Miss Flora echoed.

'Bring two large whiskies as soon as you can,' Blenkinsop
told the waiter who had answered the bell. He was beginning
to feel embarrassed. 'Soda?' he asked MacAdam.

'Soda, please.'

Miss Caroline and Miss Flora looked at one another in
dismay. Had they reached at last the land of their forefathers
to see their chief drinking soda with his whisky like somebody
at Worthing?

'Drink water with it, drink water,' Miss Caroline adjured
him.

Blenkinsop uttered a horrified exclamation.

'No, no, the water here has a most appalling taste.'

'Oh, I know it well,' said MacAdam. 'I had to drink some at
the lunch they gave when they opened this place. I've never
forgotten it.'

'When are you going to put yourself at the head of the Clan,
and lead us to recover our freedom?' Miss Caroline now
demanded.

'Yes, when are you going to set the heather on fire?' Miss
Flora asked fiercely.

Blenkinsop gave his guest a cautionary prod. He might not
understand the wiles of foreign agents. And he evidently did
not, for with deplorable lack of prudence he at once turned
round and asked Blenkinsop what he wanted.

Blenkinsop scowled at him and shook his head.

'The people of Scotland look to their hereditary leaders to come forward in the van,' Miss Caroline proclaimed.

'And drive the Sasunnach from our beloved Alba,' Miss Flora added viciously.

The waiter came back with the whisky. MacAdam swallowed it at a gulp and mopping his weather-flamed forehead with a bandanna handkerchief muttered that he really must be driving back to Drumroy.

'Remember the ancient prophecy of the Glenmore Seer,' Miss Caroline boomed. *'When the red sails of MacAdam are seen on Loch Roy the blood of the Saxon shall flow faster than Fliuch when the snow melts on Ben Buidhe in spring.'*

'And remember what was foretold by the fairy woman who appeared to the young chief when he was sleeping on Inchbeg,' said Miss Flora with the faintest hint of self-consciousness in her tones. *'When a brown-eyed woman shall come from the South and bid MacAdam strike, he shall gather his men and his arms and drive the Saxon forth for ever.'*

'Look here,' said MacAdam to Blenkinsop, 'I really must be driving back now, or I shall be keeping a certain August Personage waiting for his dinner.'

Blenkinsop, aghast at the indiscretion of this remark, almost hustled him out of the library.

'Remember, MacAdam,' his two clanswomen called after him, 'Scotland is determined to have Home Rule!'

'I don't know what the Highlands are coming to,' MacAdam observed angrily to Blenkinsop as he walked to the door of the hotel. 'They're infested nowadays by hikers and nationalists. Those two old frumps are typical of this infernal agitation for Home Rule. I've no patience with it.'

'You are sure they weren't' – Blenkinsop lowered his voice – 'Mendacian agents?'

'Mendacian fiddlesticks! I never enter this damned Hydro without being pestered by lunatics or nationalists, though why I say lunatics or nationalists I don't know. It's a distinction without a difference.'

'Still, I think you should be careful not to allude to you

know who like that in front of anybody not in our confidence. I know there's one foreign agent in the hotel already and there may be more.'

'Perhaps you're right, Hudson. Well, I envy you your tête-à-tête with that wonderful little woman tonight. I said to the . . .'

'To Mr Johnson,' Blenkinsop interrupted in an agony of prudence.

'Eh?'

'That's what we call him as a convenient cover,' Blenkinsop whispered hoarsely.

'Call who?'

'The K.'

'Oh, I see what you mean. Well, as I was telling you, I said to him, "Sir, that's a woman in a million", and he said to me, "MacAdam, she's a woman in ten million". Well, good night, Hudson. By the way, you're in bananas, aren't you? Tell me, do they offer any opportunity to a young man? My third boy is looking out for a job, and – oh – but of course I forgot, I suppose you've nothing more to do with bananas than she has . . .'

'Good night, good night,' said Blenkinsop, hurriedly pushing the Highland chief out into his native element.

As Blenkinsop passed the door of the smoking-room he saw with an emotion of grave insecurity that the Misses Macadam were in confabulation with Doggett. The suspicions about them which MacAdam had dispersed clouded as thickly round him once again as the mists round the head of noble Ben Buidhe.

The inquiry agent had been snoozing in one of the deep armchairs after a busy afternoon among the staff, in the course of which he had found out that Blenkinsop was going to dine with Señora Miranda in her private sitting-room at eight o'clock. He had discovered that champagne had been ordered. He had discovered various other things which led him to hope for a successful evening. While snoozing in the armchair he had been wakened by the sound of Miss Caroline Macadam's ancestral voice prophesying war, and when Blenkinsop had retired with MacAdam he chaffed them lightly about their bloodthirsty sentiments.

'Here, you want to look out with that St Ninian's water. What's poor old England done to you?'

'England is our hereditary foe,' Miss Caroline declared.

'Come off it,' Doggett advised. 'That's talking like an Irishman who's had one over the eight in Mooney's on a Saturday night. What would they say in Worthing if you started in talking like that?'

'We are not returning to Worthing. We feel that we are needed in Scotland,' Miss Caroline announced.

'We have been exiles too long from our beloved land,' said Miss Flora.

'If the country rises we must do our bit,' said Miss Caroline.

'Ah, if it does,' said Doggett. 'But no country's going to rise in weather like this. Only really if I were you I wouldn't drink any more of that water. I only had one sip, and it soured my whole nature for a while. If you've been laying into it all day long, I'm not surprised you feel like a couple of Crippens.'

'We can't expect you to understand our emotions,' said Miss Flora. 'You are a Sasunnach.'

'I'm a what?'

'A Sasunnach.'

'Well, I may be, but if anybody except a perfect lady had told me that I'd have said "you're another and a bit more besides".'

'We mustn't jeer at Mr Doggett, Flora,' said the elder sister. 'He can't help being English.'

'But I don't want to help it,' Doggett declared indignantly.

The first gong sounded through the hotel, drowning the argument in waves of hideous sound.

'If that gong doesn't make Scotland rise for freedom nothing will,' said Doggett as the two ladies retired to dress.

'We shall have the piper at dinner,' Miss Caroline gloated. 'Come along, Flora.'

When they had gone Mr Doggett rang the bell.

'Is this true that they have the bagpipes at dinner?' he asked the waiter.

'Yes, sir.'

'Well, bring me a large double whisky.'

While he was waiting for it the inquiry agent recorded progress in his notebook:

Worked the waiter upstairs. Worked the head waiter. Worked the chambermaid. Total expenditure on tips £7. Casual disbursements including drinks in exchange for information £2 4s. 6d. All in order. Tonight's the night for flagrant delight. Mrs H turned up again with Auld Lang Syne in tow. She's h.s. all right.

Upstairs in the Macmillan room Blenkinsop was tying his sixth tie while from below, in the great Gothic dining-hall hung with heraldic banners and equestrian portraits, the faint skirling of the pipes ascended like an unwelcome reminder of MacAdam. Then he emerged into the corridor just as the floorwaiter marshalled his aides for the dinner to which he had been looking forward all day.

Blenkinsop could not pretend to himself that the background of Renata at Glenmore became her as well as the tempered and intimate light of her salon in the Avenue Delacour. There are few combinations of colour so difficult to carry off as the Buchanan tartan when new, and it happened that Renata's sitting-room had recently been repapered. Nor did the clumsy Gothic furniture of a century's antiquity provide the right frame for such a miniature of delicate beauty. Yet when she came across the room to greet him, murmuring as she offered him her hand to kiss: 'Arthur! This is for me a great, great joy,' the prismatic network of the Buchanan tartan turned into an iridescent nimbus in which she swam towards him like a seraph.

'*Alors, cher ami*, I perceive that you also are content.'

'Bo-coo! Bo-coo!' Blenkinsop lowed, as he tenderly nuzzled the hand he had just saluted.

'*Soyez sage! Voilà le garçon!*' she warned him sharply. 'You will drink a cocktail, yes?'

When Blenkinsop had first entered the room he had been blinded by a mixture of emotion and Buchanan tartan, but he was now able to discern that Renata was wearing a severely cut frock of black chiffon velvet, on the corsage of which was pinned a sprig of Scots fir held by an ancient brooch.

Blenkinsop looked darkly at this. It did not require the acumen of an experienced Intelligence officer to divine that this vegetable addition to her dress was connected with her visit to Drumroy.

'You are looking at the brooch which Monsieur ... no, no, I must not say Monsieur ... which MacAdam has given to me with the budge of his family.'

'I should have thought a fig-leaf would have been his badge, not budge,' Blenkinsop growled.

Renata shook her head at him.

'You must please to be wise, Monsieur Hudson, because MacAdam is being so much a friend for somebody to whose success we shall very soon drink a good glass of champagne. *N'est-ce pas?*'

'I'm afraid all this Highland grandeur has made me look a very ordinary sort of person in your eyes,' he muttered.

'Now that is to be quite a bear when you talk so. If you give to me your budge – no, badge – I shall with pleasure wear it.'

'In England we don't go about wearing badges,' Blenkinsop said contemptuously. 'Except a few people, on boat-race day.'

By the time Blenkinsop had managed to explain the mysteries of the Oxford and Cambridge boat-race the soup was on the table, and he felt that it was his duty to play up to his cover for a while in order to lull any suspicion that might have entered the waiter's heart about the real object of this meeting.

'We are very glad, Señora, that you are giving us this opportunity to acquire your banana plantations. I hope you won't miss them. I mean to say, I hope you don't mind parting with them.'

'Ah, but it is always a sorrow to part with anything.'

'Yes, I can understand that. Still, it isn't as if the bananas were alive. They won't feel anything.'

'Who knows?' she sighed. 'With my mystic emotions I am often thinking that perhaps a flower or a fruit can suffer like us. We pluck a rose for our pleasure; we do not ask the rose what it may feel.'

'That's a little too imaginative for me, I'm afraid,' said Blenkinsop. 'I can't really believe that a rose bothers whether it's picked or not.'

'Do not be too sure.'

'Anyway, you can't compare a rose with a banana, though I don't want to run down the banana, because, mind you, the banana is my pigeon.'

'*Eh, voilà,*' Renata interrupted. 'For you a banana can be a pigeon. Surely that is to express what I am saying?'

'You rather misunderstand me, Señora. We say in English that anything is our pigeon when we want to express that it is our business. The banana is my business.'

'But the English are very fond of business. Big business, *n'est-ce pas*? So the banana is your big business?'

'The banana is my livelihood, yes. But I can't afford to be sentimental over it. It's a pretty fancy to wonder what the rose feels. But if I started pitying every banana we imported my life would be a misery.'

'Perhaps you are right. But I cannot help my mystic emotions.'

'I mean to say, think where you'd get yourself if you started being sorry for bananas. Look what happens to them. Packed while they're green and hung up in warehouses to turn yellow and then skinned ...'

'Ah, do not speak no more of it, Monsieur Hudson. If I would think about it I would never sell a banana again. And you see it is necessary to sell my bananas.'

'That is the common-sense attitude,' Blenkinsop said in a relieved voice. 'After dinner we'll go into the matter more fully. You have all the necessary papers with you?'

'Oh yes, I have everything we can want.'

'When are you thinking of returning to the Canary Islands?'

'Very very very soon,' said Renata with a glance of tremendous meaning. 'My friend who I am meeting in Scotland can hardly wait one minute.'

'Oh well, we'll have everything settled, I hope, this evening. At least, in some ways I hope so. In others,' he broke off emotionally before risking the next question. 'Have you drunk any of this water in this hotel? St Ninian's water they call it.'

'I have drunk two or three drips, but I did not find it very agreeable.'

'I shouldn't think you did! But they say it cures a lot of complaints, and I notice a lot of people in the hotel do drink it somehow. Now, there's a well on the Island of Parvo – one of the Canary Islands that is.'

'Ah yes, I know it.'

'And the water from this well is even nastier than the water here. I think I'll have it analysed. You know, if all goes as we hope it will go, I think I'll talk to my brother about the possibility of reopening the hotel.'

'In the Canary Islands?' she asked, with what to a third person might have seemed like a twinkle in her eyes.

'Would it please you, Re – Señora?' Blenkinsop gulped.

'What will please me is to make first what we desire to make,' she replied, it seemed to him remotely.

And after dinner, when the crudity of the Buchanan tartan and the hideousness of that Gothic furniture had been softened by pieces of silk hung over the electric lamps by Madame Tekta herself, she proceeded to demonstrate this.

'*Enfin*, we are alone and now we can talk for our affairs,' she announced with a sigh of relief. But when Blenkinsop picked up the lilywhite hand that rested on the table the other lilywhite hand offered him a small writing-block and a pencil.

'I think you will have to be writing sometimes what I can tell you,' she said in a matter-of-fact voice that made Blenkinsop feel he had been drinking St Ninian's water at dinner instead of champagne.

'The evening is before us,' he said gloomily.

'Surely the evening is before us,' she agreed. 'But when Arthur Blenkinsop becomes Captain Chancellor for writing his wonnderful books he thinks only of what he must do. Is that not true, my friend Arthur? I am excessively grateful for your good help to me, because you have made it easy for me to have the money for which most injuriously to my soul I have had to ask. Now you must make me excessively grateful by your help to gain a country's freedom.'

'In other words,' said Blenkinsop, 'I only interest you as a pawn in this game of politics.'

'In a little while we will talk of that,' she said impatiently. 'Please listen to what I can tell you. With MacAdam now is the King, General Bandamilo, Gandina, who was Minister of Foreign Affairs in the last Royalist Government, Admiral Cabalomaka, and some more exiled officers of the King. Everything has been prepared. We hope your new Minister will arrive this week to Gadaro. The Venetian Ambassador has been informed and is so very sympathetic. Tomorrow comes to Drumroy Heisswasser with his yacht.'

'Who on earth is Heisswasser?'

'Ah, my friend Arthur, please do not pretend to me,' she said with a sharpness that mortified poor Blenkinsop. 'I give you confidence. I must have your confidence. Is it not to know when Heisswasser comes that we are playing this game with bananas?'

'Oh, quite,' said Blenkinsop, sinking deeper every moment into a slough of bewilderment, lovesickness, and depression.

'*Enfin*, I have told you everything. What have you to tell me?'

'I am going down to London to give a talk at the B.B.C. about Mendacia. And I am authorized to add a message at the end of this talk to say that the King is leaving when the King is ready to leave. Frankly, I don't see how this is going to be done without upsetting listeners over here, but that's not my business. My business is to obey orders from above. Still, this message oughtn't to be too obvious.'

'I think you must see the King and Heisswasser.'

'It won't do for me to go to Drumroy. Secrecy is absolutely essential in this affair.'

'*Bien entendu*. What do you propose?'

'Well, I don't know if this will appeal to his Majesty, but I thought if we could arrange to meet by accident in the hotel here ...'

'Yes, that can certainly be arranged, and of course Heisswasser could be in the hotel.'

'Undoubtedly ... but look here, Renata. I've not received any instructions about Heisswasser. What is he?'

She looked at him reproachfully.

'You know, I find it quite a disillusion that you must pretend to me like this, Arthur.'

'I'm not pretending at all. In our service we are given dangerous and difficult tasks, but we are not always told why. For instance, when I was instructed to give a talk on Mendacia at the B.B.C. I did not flinch. I don't mind admitting that when I think about it I tremble all over. I admit that. Call me a coward if you like. But I shall go through with it somehow.'

'I will not call you at all a coward,' she said softly. 'Forgive me, my friend, I fear I have wounded your splendid soul.'

'That's all right, Renata,' he murmured in a voice broken with self-pity. 'But the idea that this man Heisswasser could come between us upset me rather. Perhaps I oughtn't to reveal these secrets, but I cannot pretend to you. I haven't the slightest idea who Heisswasser is, why he's coming here, or what he's going to do. And that's the solemn truth. Do you or do you not believe me?'

'You compel me to believe you. But it seems so strange that you would not hear of the man who is so rich that he can buy half of Europe. It is he who will give the ship, the arms, and the money for our King to save his poor country from these dirty republicans. I think the British Government knows very well who is Heisswasser.'

Blenkinsop was not satisfied with the progress of the evening. It seemed to him that between himself and Renata stretched the shadow of MacAdam, of which the tartan wall-paper and hangings of this room ruthlessly reminded him all the time. He recognized that it was her first duty and his first duty to put the preparations for the King's restoration on a practical basis; but in Paris there had been Renata's own future to be put on a practical basis, and that operation had been effected with an abundance of romantic emotion, not sitting at a table like this with a block of notepaper and a couple of pencils as if they were both solving a cross-word puzzle. Even the damned table-cloth was tartan.

'I'm afraid that since you've met MacAdam I seem to you a hopelessly ordinary sort of chap,' Blenkinsop repeated in an effort to bring the conversation back to the point it had reached before she had been able to sidetrack it to the lines of political intrigue.

Renata rose from the table in a fit of petulance, which was exactly what Blenkinsop hoped she would do.

'Oh, but you make me a little impatient, Arthur, when you talk like that. Must I treat the friend of my country without politeness because it can ...' she hesitated.

'Because it makes somebody else jealous?' he supplied. 'Finish your sentence.'

'But listen, *cher ami*, are you not being a small bit rapid to be speaking of jealousy already? I am quite thinking that you are.'

'You mean that I'm presuming on our friendship?'

Renata sat down on the sofa and shook her head reproachfully.

'Please, please, let us not make a drama. For me the grand pleasure of Englishmen is that they do not make dramas. I have given you too much of my confidence in Paris. I must blame myself. I see now that I have been imprudent.'

'Since you met MacAdam in fact,' said Blenkinsop bitterly.

'Please, enough of that,' she begged.

Blenkinsop was seized with remorse. He plunged down on the sofa beside her in an access of penitence. A bell shrilled.

'What does that mean?' Blenkinsop hissed in a tense whisper.

The noise of the bell was followed by the sound of a low shuddering moan from the next room.

'Is that your bedroom in there?' Blenkinsop asked, and when she nodded he threw open the door between the two rooms just in time to see the figure of that bounder with the waxed moustache stealing out into the passage.

'Come back, you!' he shouted. 'I know who you are.'

But Doggett had had too long an experience as an inquiry agent to be caught like this. He ran. Blenkinsop was on the point of running after him when he remembered that the mission with which he had been entrusted was too important to endanger. He allowed Doggett to escape and returned to Renata's room.

'A spy,' he said curtly. 'Probably a republican agent.'

The prospect of danger brought out all that was best in Blenkinsop. His jealousy of MacAdam and his anxiety to be sentimental with Renata were at once put aside. His country needed him. And he answered the call.

'I hope that bell doesn't mean there's an infernal machine in this room,' he said with a deadly calm.

And with this he began to search for it with as little appearance of nervousness as if he were searching for Renata's cigarette-case.

'Look here,' he said to her, 'do you mind leaving me to it? There's no sense in the two of us getting blown up.'

'I think you are most awfully wonnderful, Arthur,' she declared.

'Not more wonderful than you are, little woman,' he said with a grave smile. 'If every woman were as calm as you in an emergency like this...' he broke off to resume his search for the bomb; but as Renata had put the bell inside a drawer and locked it up while Blenkinsop was out of the room the search discovered nothing.

'However, it's a serious enough business, bomb or no bomb. Fortunately we did not make any definite date or time for...' he paused, and wrote on the notepaper: *I shall refer to His Majesty as Mr Johnson in conversation and to Heisswasser as Mr Johnson's friend. Walls have ears.*

Renata nodded her comprehension.

'Fortunately we did not arrange a meeting with Mr Johnson and his friend,' Blenkinsop went on aloud. 'And I think that until I can get instructions from my Chief no meeting must take place. Meanwhile I'll write out my talk for the B.B.C. And now I must leave you.'

'So soon?' she murmured.

'Yes, I must deal with this spy.'

'You will be careful, Arthur? Remember how much depends on your *sang froid*.'

'You no longer trust me,' he said sadly. 'You think because I showed a momentary weakness over you I am going to be weak in everything.'

'No, no, Arthur. I trust you absolutely. Forgive me if I seemed not to understand. I cannot tell you everything now; but one day you will know all, and you will forgive Renata.'

Blenkinsop had never read a Ruritanian novel. If he had he might have prolonged his parting with Renata that night. As it was, he could only mutter:

'Well, I think I'll buzz along. Shall I see you tomorrow at lunch?'

'No, tomorrow MacAdam comes to drive me to Drumroy.'

'All right. Then I'll get on with my talk. I brought up some of the reports I wrote when I was working on the Boundary Commission, and I've also got the prospectus of the Hotel Multum.'

His voice was calm. Nobody who heard him would have supposed that he was tormented by a romantic passion and certainly not that a few minutes ago he had narrowly escaped being blown up by the bomb of a republican agent.

'You are quite wonnderful, Arthur,' Renata murmured.

'If you understand, Renata, that's all I care,' he said, and then abruptly he turned away and left her, thinking to himself that for the rest of his life the picture of her standing there in a mist of Buchanan tartan would remain in his memory.

Blenkinsop found Doggett alone in the library. He wasted no time in preliminaries, but strode across the room and stood menacingly over the little assassin who was sitting back in a leather armchair stamped all over with gilded lions rampant and lapping up a whisky and soda as dark in hue as one of the burns that furrow the steep sides of noble Ben Buidhe.

'Give me that bomb,' he said.

'Bomb?' repeated the inquiry agent. 'What d'ye mean bomb? It's whisky.'

'Don't try to bluff me. I know who you are and who sent you up here to spy on Señora Miranda,' said Blenkinsop fiercely.

Doggett had been an inquiry agent too long to let himself be caught like this. Tempting though it was to retort that he knew

equally well who Blenkinsop and Señora Miranda were, he
restrained himself.

'If you're one of the Knowits of Knowall Park,' he retorted, 'you ought to know a glass of whisky when you see
one.'

'What do you mean by stealing into Señora Miranda's bedroom and ringing bells and groaning like that?'

'Now, look here, Mr Hudson, wait a minute, and listen to
me. I went into Seenorer Mirander's bedroom by mistake for
my own.'

'A likely story!' Blenkinsop scoffed.

'And I was just thinking it was the wrong room,' Doggett
continued, 'when all of a sudden a bell went off like a fire-
alarm and gave me such a shocking turn that I swallowed a
gulp of water by the bed, forgetting it wasn't my night-cap.
The noise you heard me make was when I found out I'd swallowed – mark you, *swallowed* – a mouthful of that liquid
disaster they call St Ninian's water. Any man with less control
than what I have would have made as much noise as those
bagpipes at dinner.'

Blenkinsop fixed the inquiry agent with a cold eye.

'For various reasons I cannot deal with you here as you
ought to be dealt with. But I warn you that the sooner you
leave this hotel the safer you will be. Do you understand?'

'No man could put it plainer than what you have,' Doggett
admitted. 'And I'm sure I'm very much obliged. Will you have
a drink?'

'I do not drink with hired spies.'

With this rebuke Blenkinsop strode from the library just as
the Misses Macadam came into it.

'Well, ladies,' said Doggett cordially, 'I heard a bit of news
tonight that'll cheer you up.'

The two ladies awaited the news graciously.

'From what I can make out you've properly stirred up the
monarch of the glen.'

'I don't think I quite understand you, Mr Doggett,' said Miss
Caroline.

'From what I can make out, after you tackled him this afternoon he went straight off back home and started a revolution. All the English are to be massacred this week, and the monarch of the glen's going to land at Westminster and become the monarch of Buckingham Palace.'

'MacAdam is going to rise?' exclaimed his clanswomen in an ecstasy.

'No going to about it. He's risen already. Yeast isn't in it with him,' said Doggett. 'He's all of a froth.'

'I felt it in the air, Flora,' declared her sister. 'I felt something was astir when the piper was playing at dinner.'

'So did I,' said Doggett. 'I was expecting to see the butter turn into gorgonzola before my eyes.'

'I could hardly sit still,' Miss Flora exclaimed.

'Nor could I,' said Doggett. 'I was all of a shake. And in fact he did drive me out of the dining-room before the sweet.'

'Now's the time and now's the hour,' Miss Caroline intoned solemnly.

'Yes, that's all right,' said Doggett. 'But you'll want to keep an eye on that fellow Hudson. He's out to do the monarch of the glen down. He's one of the most ferocious Englishmen you ever met.'

'We'll watch him like eagles,' Miss Caroline promised. 'We will do something for our beloved country.'

'I feel a little overawed by what we have done already, Caroline,' her sister said. 'Oh, how glad I am that we drank at the Well properly and wished. You know when that nice gillie was holding on to my – on to me, I very nearly told him I didn't think I could lean over quite so far.'

'Do you know when the rising will start?' Miss Caroline asked of Doggett.

'No, that I couldn't say within an hour or two. But I'm leaving for London myself by the morning train to avoid being massacred.'

Miss Flora turned to her sister.

'Caroline, I think we ought to warn Mr Woodburn, that nice man from Nigeria we were talking to after dinner about Home Rule. He was pig-headed, but he was very kind and pleasant, and I don't quite like the idea of his getting into trouble,' said Miss Flora.

'Come, Flora, we will do so,' said the elder sister. 'Good night, Mr Doggett.'

'Good night, ladies. And pleasant dreams.'

'We shall dream of our country's freedom,' Miss Caroline proclaimed. '*When the red sails of MacAdam are seen on Loch Roy the blood of the Saxon shall flow faster than Fliuch when the snow melts on Ben Buidhe in Spring.*'

Doggett shook his head when the sisters were gone. Then he took out his notebook and made the following entry:

> Friday night 10.45 p.m.
> What an evening! I reached Mrs H's bedroom by arrangements with the chambermaid about a quarter of an hour after Mrs H and B had started dinner. Something's up beside flagrant delight. Confidence trick? Blackmail? There's some German in it with a name like a gas escape, and a whole lot of Italians. There's some fellow they call the King, and there's the monarch of the glen. I reckon it's a case for the police. After dinner just when I thought they were coming to the flagrant delight a bell went off and gave me such a shock I drank the Señora's water. Then I bolted. But B saw me and warned me to get out of this hotel if I don't want trouble. I reckon it's an international gang of crooks. That B is a deep one. Well, the Governor will have to settle whether it pays him most to put the police on to him or count on getting it out of Mrs B. There are two old crows staying here and I told them there was going to be a massacre of the English. They've been swallowing water all day. So this went down like syrup. And meantime I've put them on to shadowing B.
> Laugh? Well, after what I went through waiting for that flagrant delight I wanted a good laugh.

When he had finished these jottings Doggett drank the rest of his whisky and started for bed. On the way he looked into the drawing-room and saw the Misses Macadam in lively conversation with Woodburn, the oval-faced man home on leave from Nigeria. He chuckled to himself, and after leaving word with the night-porter that he intended to go back to London next morning he entered the lift.

TO ALL WHOM IT MAY CONCERN

The first part of Chapter 14 was originally written in invisible ink; but when it was pointed out to the author that such a manuscript offered almost insuperable difficulties to the printers he decided to redouble his precautions in order that what the *Daily Herald* in the month of March 1933 called 'a group of famous Secret Service men in mufti' should not run the slightest risk of the unpleasant experience that the Emperor underwent in Hans Andersen's tale, in which, it will be remembered, a small child among the spectators called out that the Emperor so far from wearing a beautiful new suit was walking in the procession with nothing on at all.

Chapter 14

SAFETY AND SECRECY

THE Safety of the Realm Division was housed in Z— Terrace, a row of three solid and dignified mid-Victorian dwelling-houses, the gardens of which at the back sloped down to the Y— Canal where it passed through the district of Q— in the great metropolis of X—. Only the central house Number Two was actually occupied by the offices of the S.R.D., but Number One and Number Three were both used as convenient covers, Number One being apparently the headquarters of the Society for the Protection of Indigent Gentlewomen and Number Three being apparently the headquarters of the Poor Aliens Bureau. By means of 'Sprig', as it was playfully called by the stenographers and card-indexers, the female agents of the S.R.D. were inconspicuously interviewed and instructed in their duties, and by means of 'Pab' the foreign counter-espionage agents employed by the S.R.D. were able to communicate unnoticed even with the great P himself. By a flash of that happy wit which helps to lighten sometimes the grim routine of counter-espionage the business of Pab was known as 'pabulum'.

'P has a lot of pabulum this morning,' you might hear some clear-eyed young stenographer murmur to one of her colleagues at Number Two, and you would feel as safe and comfortable as a frightened child whose mother is watching by its bedside. The secrecy of P himself was so impressive that in comparison even N seemed as conspicuous as a popular actor. He did not allow an allusion to be made to his rank. He would not be referred to as the Director or addressed as 'Sir'. He was P whether he was being consulted by the Chief of the Imperial General staff or given a good morning by the charwoman who scrubbed out Number Two under the supervision of confidential Staff-Sergeants with impeccable military histories.

Tempting though it is to allow a reader a peep into the arcana of Number Two, it is not safe. At The Elms secrecy might sometimes appear to take precedence of service. At Number Two secrecy marched hand in hand with safety. When it is revealed that foreign counter-espionage agents were sometimes met at G—d by an S.R.D. motor-launch, transferred to a barge at G—h, transferred again to a Y— Canal barge at C—a, and landed on a moonless midnight at the bottom of the gardens of Z— Terrace it will be enough to show the thoroughness of P's precautions. Perhaps the 'margin of safety' – a favourite phrase at Number Two – has already been overstepped in an anxiety to give credit where credit is due. No more risks shall be taken.

On the Monday after the events related in the preceding chapter, P sat in his own room at Number Two reading through his dark horn-rimmed spectacles* a letter, at the head of which was stamped the address of the Glenmore Hydro.

Here is the text of the letter:

22 Nov.

Dear Grimshaw:

Knowing you are in some way in touch with the Intelligence people, I think you ought to be told of what appear on the surface to be some queer happenings up here. There may be nothing in it of course, but I give you my information for what it is worth and leave it to you to throw this letter into the waste-paper basket if you think it is nothing but a mare's-nest.

I came up here to put in a bit of my leave doing a cure and found to my surprise that since I was home there has been an astonishing development of something apparently called 'Scottish Nationalism'.

I thought at first that the whole business was a lot of hot air, but apparently from information received from two ladies staying in this hotel there is at the present moment a projected rising. The headquarters of the plot seem to be at Drumroy, the seat of MacAdam of MacAdam. Perhaps it may be more talk than anything else, but I was at the 'Castle' in Dublin for a while before the war and I learnt not to laugh too easily at talk. I think it might be

---

* Although the slightest suggestion of P's personal appearance and room has been deliberately omitted in order not to endanger the safety of the realm, it was not considered that the margin of safety would be overstepped by revealing that he did wear dark horn-rimmed glasses.

worth your while to put the matter before the proper people, for I am not able to investigate matters myself as this water cure keeps me pretty well a prisoner in the Hydro. I've just reached eight glasses a day, which the doctor seems to think rather remarkable. Very few people get beyond six, and apparently to reach eight glasses within a fortnight is a record.

I hope you will not think me too much of a credulous duffer if on investigation you find that I have started you off on a wild-goose chase. Perhaps my present job in Nigeria makes me too apt to think that the rest of the world is like Nigeria. Still, I should never forgive myself if any kind of Sinn Fein business started up here and I had said nothing about it for fear of being wrong. I would have tried to do a little first-hand spy work, but eight glasses of St Ninian's water a day really does keep one a close prisoner as the water has a rather rapid effect.

Remember me most kindly to the Memsahib.

Yours sincerely,
Oliver Woodburn

P stroked his chin for a while meditatively when he had finished the melancholy oval-faced man's letter. Then he picked up the telephone receiver on his desk.

'Tell Major Grimshaw I wish to speak to him at once,' he said.

Presently a tall button-headed man came in.

'This letter, Grim, what do *you* think about it?' P asked, still stroking his chin.* Is this man Woodburn a reliable source of information?'

'I've known him for a long time, P,' said Grimshaw, 'and I should consider him far from being an alarmist.'

'How does he know that you are connected with S.R.D.?' P asked sharply. 'I didn't like that. I hope he's not a Paul Pry.'

'We were in communication over one of our cases.'

'I see. Colonial Office, I suppose?'

'Yes.'

*It would not be fair to suggest that P did nothing else except stroke his chin; but to preserve the margin of safety it was not felt prudent to mention any mannerism that could possibly help the many foreign agents who will everywhere be reading this book to identify P.

'And this letter was sent to you "care of The War Office" without apparently being sealed?'

'It was not sealed, no,' Major Grimshaw admitted.

'And not put inside a second envelope?'

'No, I'm afraid it wasn't.'

'Good God!' P burst out contemptuously. 'Still, even if this Colonial Office fellow doesn't know the most elementary rules of discretion I am impressed by his information.'

'From my knowledge of Woodburn, P, I think he's the last man to go mare's-nesting.'

'Well, they may call me an alarmist,' P declared sardonically, 'but I have been saying for some time now that the state of Scotland is far from satisfactory, very far from satisfactory. You remember that report we had about rifles being hidden on some island on the West Coast?'

'Rather! We never found the rifles actually.'

'No, because we entrusted the job to the police. Wait a minute, I'll ring through now to Canonbury at the Yard. He may have some information which will fit in with ours.'

P picked up the telephone.

'Put me through to Inspector Canonbury. The confidential line, of course. Hullo? Hullo? Is that you, Inspector Canonbury? This is P speaking. Have you had any information lately about anything that sounds at all unusual in the West of Scotland? ... An international gang of crooks? ... Really? ... How did you hear all that? ... I see ... Well, please don't take any steps ... You weren't going to? Oh! ... Between you and me, Inspector, we have had some rather curious information from Scotland which may be of political importance ... we shall want to make a few quiet inquiries ourselves, so if you hear of anything more we should appreciate it very much if you'd communicate with us ... What's that? ... You don't expect to hear any more about it? ... Well, we shall see ... What's that, Inspector? I don't remember anything about any Pole. Oh, you were looking after him for us? Very well, if you can't find anything in the least suspicious about his movements, don't bother about him any more. We don't want the C.I.D. officers to waste their time. And it's understood that you'll leave the

Scottish business for us to deal with? All right, that's understood. Good-bye.'

P hung up the receiver.

'Extraordinary people the police,' he observed with a compassionate shake of the head. 'Really, you know, to hear
Canonbury you'd think we were a lot of children in S.R.D.
Fussing away about some Pole whom we apparently asked him
to make a few inquiries about. Gloriously oblivious of the fact
that at this moment we may be on the verge of having to deal
with another Easter Rising. It's a lucky thing for the people of
this country that they have us to look after them. If matters
were left entirely to the police, the whole of England would be
Bolshie by now.'

'Absolutely, P,' his second-in-command agreed.

'Well, that was a singularly interesting conversation with
Inspector Canonbury, Grim. I fancy your friend Wood – what
is it? – has got right on to it in one. Yesterday, it appears, some
private inquiry agent called Pinches sent word to Scotland Yard
that one of his men in the course of his duty had got word of
what he thought might be some blackmailing plot being
hatched in Drumroy Castle by a gang of international crooks. I
asked him not to take any steps, and he said they had no
intention of taking any steps. The information was too vague
for Canonbury, if you please. I nearly asked him how he
expected information to be anything except vague unless he
took steps to clarify it. But it's no use chaffing them at Scotland
Yard. I suppose one day somebody will wake up to the fact
that point duty at Hyde Park Corner and a beat in Whitechapel
do not provide the ideal training for a detective. But really,
Grim, can you understand the political ignorance of a fellow
like Canonbury? It never strikes him for a moment that this
information about a supposed gang of international crooks
may be information of the most vital political importance. It
never enters his head that this information about a gang of
crooks, which doesn't happen to fit in with his particular
knowledge of crooks, might be looked at from a more imaginative angle. However, even friend Canonbury has not been able
to hide from us that there is something on foot in Scotland. It's

now up to us to find out what exactly it is. We shall have to move very cautiously, and not a word must get out that we even know that such a place as Scotland exists. I shall only take one other person outside yourself into my confidence. That is Mackillop, whom I shall send up to this Glenmore place.'

'The very man!' Grimshaw exclaimed.

'Mackillop can go up tonight in a kilt, disguised as a Scottish Nationalist. It oughtn't to take him very long to find out what is going on.'

'It oughtn't to take him half an hour,' declared Major Grimshaw enthusiastically.

'I shan't see him here, of course,' said P. 'You will arrange for him to meet me over the river at the usual place this afternoon.'

'That shall be done,' said Major Grimshaw.

'Oh, by the way, Grim, I've just thought of a special disguise for one or two of our sleuths. Salvation Army uniforms.'

'Oh, splendid!'

'The beauty of it is that if a fellow we were interested in noticed he was being followed by somebody in the Salvation Army uniform he'd only think he was going to be touched for a subscription or converted.'

'I call that one of the best ideas, P, that even you have ever had,' declared his button-headed second-in-command.

'Yes, I must say I was rather pleased with it myself. Well, you might see about getting a couple of uniforms ordered.'

'I will, P.'

'And make out a list of religious catch phrases.'

While at Number Two P and his second-in-command were discussing the steps to take for the safety of the realm, over at The Elms the head of M.Q. 99 (E) was mastering the contents of a letter from Blenkinsop.

Saturday, November 22

My dear N:

I successfully established contact with Juno on the evening of my arrival here, and so far as making arrangements about the broadcast message from Mr Johnson to the people of M. all is well. I am working at my talk now, and have provisionally arranged to meet

Mr Johnson and a friend of Mr Johnson called Heisswasser who is to arrive in Loch Roy with an armed yacht, a supply of ammunition and arms, and as I understand financial backing for the enterprise. I was a little shy at first of meeting Heisswasser as I had no instructions from you about him. Perhaps you would let me know before I go any further if he can be trusted. He is *apparently* the big international financier, but after our experience with Katzenschlosser in Paris I want to be perfectly sure that this is not another ruse of K's. If Katzenschlosser can persuade the staff of the Hôtel Plonplon that he is Churchill the great American banker, I see no reason why he should not be able to impose himself upon Mr Johnson, Juno, and the rest of them at Drumroy as Heisswasser.

I have certainly been followed up here by *some* agent, but whether an agent of the M. Republic, or the American S.S., or of some other S.S. I do not know. I began to be suspicious in the train on the way up when an offensive little Cockney calling himself Doggett persistently tried to engage me in conversation at breakfast. Sergeant Flack may have mentioned to you that he observed me being followed from one sleeping-coach to another. I found this fellow Doggett very difficult to shake off.

Then while I was at dinner with Juno in her private room at the Hydro, Doggett managed to conceal himself in her bedroom, and as far as I can make out made an attempt to blow us up with an infernal machine. Fortunately, some kind of alarum went off prematurely – I fancy it was a clock bomb – and I nearly managed to catch him. I could have caught him in the corridor, but I was afraid to make a scene in the hotel on account of the publicity. So I took the bull by the horns and warned the little brute that if he did not clear out of the hotel it would be the worse for him. He left for London next morning. I thought of telegraphing to warn you to have him met and followed at King's Cross on arrival, but decided that as you had particularly warned me not to do anything which would possibly let even the S.R.D. people know what was going on it would be better to use my discretion and let this fellow Doggett go. It seemed to me that you would hardly be able to prevent his communicating with the M. Government if he meant business. He has apparently left his two female agents behind. They call themselves Macadam and pretend to be Scottish Nationalists. They follow me about like leeches, but I do not think they are actually dangerous. I shall now wait for instructions. Please let me know when Sir John Clavering leaves and when Sir Wilfred Camden arrives in Gadaro. This is important for Mr Johnson's plans. Also, please let me know the exact date and time of the broadcast, As soon as I hear from you about these matters and about Heisswasser, I propose to meet Mr Johnson and his friend. After a good deal of thought I have come to the conclusion that the best place would be in the Turkish bath at this hotel. I have inspected it. The very hot room is absolutely secluded, and indeed the bath is not often used owing to there being so many other baths more out of the usual which the hotel visitors like trying. Would you be good enough to approve this suggestion?

Yours sincerely,

B

The Chief of the Secret Service leant back in his chair and sought inspiration from the ceiling. He received it.

'Is that you, H. H.?' he asked through the telephone. 'Come along to my room, will you? I want to discuss an important letter with you.'

Major Hunter-Hunt came along, quivering in anticipation of what was the greatest treat his Chief could have promised him. He sat down on the other side of N's table as if he were sitting down in a bath much hotter than anything at Glenmore, and when his Chief tossed Blenkinsop's letter across to him he picked it up as carefully as a lepidopterist picks up a new butterfly.

'I say, this is really tremendously interesting, Chief,' he gloated, when he had read through the letter twice, putting his forefinger from time to time on some word or name that might otherwise have leapt out of the text and hidden itself where it would never be found again.

'I think we can congratulate ourselves on the way Blenkinsop has handled this business so far,' said N.

'I think we can indeed,' Hunter-Hunt agreed warmly.

'At first I was a little inclined to think he made a mistake in not notifying us of the departure of this agent who calls himself Doggett.'

'Yes, I was inclined to think that too.'

'But on consideration I decided that he was right. You know my opinion of P; but it's no use blinking the fact that he *is* apt to think it is more important to catch out somebody who is spying on us than for us to succeed in ascertaining what is happening elsewhere.'

'I know what you mean, Chief.'

'And P is jealous – not personally jealous of course, but jealous for the status of S.R.D. He would have resented our trying to shadow this so-called Doggett ourselves. He would have considered Doggett his pigeon, and that would have meant letting P know about this Mendacian business, which would have upset the P.U.S. It's a pity, of course, that Doggett should have got away, but to have arrested him would have been out of the question.'

'Absolutely out of the question. It would have meant that the whole world would know we are interested in Mendacia,' Hunter-Hunt declared.

'I thought you'd agree with me, H. H. Let sleeping Doggetts lie, eh?'

Hunter-Hunt laughed gustily.

'I say, that's very good, Chief. That's really very good indeed.'

'Oh, it was a pretty obvious joke, really,' said N modestly.

Hunter-Hunt was not going to let his Chief make light of his gifts in this way.

'Yes, but true wit consists in saying the obvious thing first,' he pointed out.

They laughed again with reminiscent pleasure in the fine flavour of the joke and then N suddenly turned grave.

'But this Heisswasser scare is more serious,' he said. 'Do you think it is Katzenschlosser?'

'It's exactly the sort of thing Katzenschlosser would delight in doing,' Hunter-Hunt pointed out.

'Blenkinsop seems nervous. Of course he may have been shaken by that bomb.'

'But it didn't actually go off, did it?' Hunter-Hunt exclaimed as he reached over to read again that portion of Blenkinsop's letter of which he seemed to have missed the meaning.

'No, no, I mean the idea of the bomb. He would be in a mood to suspect Katzenschlosser.'

'Quite, quite,' Hunter-Hunt agreed.

'What about my going up to investigate?' N suggested. 'I've never disguised myself yet in a kilt.'

'In a kilt?' exclaimed Hunter-Hunt. 'But what would be the exact cover? I mean to say, I think you might find the Harry Lauder accent and all that a bit of a job to manage. And suppose you were spotted? Wouldn't it involve us rather with the P.U.S.?'

'Do you mean our funds?'

'Well, yes, you know what a horror the Foreign Office has of being mixed up with plumbing.'

'Perhaps I'd better not go up myself,' said N regretfully, for the notion of a kilt had been appealing to him. 'Now that Blenkinsop has started with the job, he'd better see it through. And after all it may not be Katzenschlosser.'

'As you say, it may not be.'

'Have we got any good descriptions of Katzenschlosser?'

'We have a dozen at least on the files. The only thing is that superficially they sound like descriptions of a dozen different people. I'm glad you're not going near Glenmore yourself. For the King of Mendacia to regain his throne would be a poor exchange for compromising you. After all, what is M.Q. 99 (E)? The answer is you, every time.'

'And Blenkinsop seems to be handling the business with the right kind of caution.'

'I quite agree.'

'And he doesn't ask for anything more than instructions.'

'For nothing.'

'And he seems to have guts.'

'I thought his account of the attempt on his life with an infernal machine was written without any unpleasant sensationalism,' said Hunter-Hunt.

'And he has to come down here next week to do that broadcast business at the B.B.C.'

'Exactly. You can have a consultation then if necessary, though personally I think he should keep away from M.Q. 99 (E) till the King is safely back in Mendacia.'

'I don't like the idea of writing him instructions by post,' said N.

'Nor do I.'

'We might send them up by Sergeant Flack. He carried through that other business in the train very efficiently, and we've never used him on any other occasion for outside work, have we?'

'Never.'

'All right, H. H., then that's settled. Your advice has been very helpful. Will you see to putting together a description of Katzenschlosser as far as it is possible to do so from the files? I'll write to Blenkinsop, and then I'll give Sergeant Flack his instructions.'

'I'll get busy with the description of Katzenschlosser at once, Chief. Nothing more you want from me now?'

'Nothing more, thanks, H. H.'

When Major Hunter-Hunt had retired N refilled his fountain-pen with green ink and wrote the following letter to Blenkinsop:

Monday, 24 November

Dear B:

Your letter was very helpful, and we all congratulate you on dodging that infernal machine. I wish you had managed to find it, as it sounds an interesting new type of clock bomb. But no doubt this fellow Doggett took it away with him. You were right not to signal him to us, and in the circumstances I think you were probably right to frighten him out of the Hydro. You should be careful that neither of these female agents he left behind has any bombs, and also that they really are females. We have no information about Katzenschlosser's present whereabouts, but I am sending you with this a description based on the reports of various reliable agents, and you should be able with this to check Heisswasser's bona fides. My own belief is that it probably *is* Heisswasser. It was reported last year that he and Mr Johnson had had one or two secret meetings. As he holds a controlling share in several armament firms, it is very likely that he is interested from a practical point of view in Mr Johnson's restoration.

The B.B.C. talk is next Thursday. I have arranged for it to be given at 9.45 p.m. which will allow you to return immediately to Glenmore the same night, and by travelling down that same day you can be at the B.B.C. comfortably by nine o'clock. Your idea of establishing contact with Mr Johnson in the Turkish bath at the Hydro is approved. I hope that everything at Drumroy is ready. Please impress on Mr Johnson that the moment will never be more favourable.

You ask when Sir Wilfred Camden is going to replace Sir John Clavering at Gadaro. This must be a mistake. There has never been any intention of sending the Permanent Under-Secretary to Mendacia as a Minister. It is Mr Giles Ballantyne who is succeeding Sir John Clavering. I heard this morning from the F.O. that he has already left for Gadaro. I impressed on Sir Wilfred Camden at a second interview I had with him that all our information from Mendacia pointed to an overwhelming feeling in favour of the monarchy. He seemed pleased, but naturally he is most nervous of Burgundian opinion, and I decided not to say anything to him about the message at the end of the B.B.C. talk.

The B.B.C. have been a little difficult. In fact they simply will not allow this talk to be broadcast without being censored. I think between ourselves that General Westmacott did not handle them quite as tactfully as he might have done. I have therefore had the talk written out here so that it can be approved by the B.B.C. people. I am sending you a copy of this, which you might read through to Mr Johnson at your meeting. You will then add the message at the end. Something like this: 'Finally I would say to the people of Mendacia that there is no country to which British commercial enterprise may look with greater confidence in the near future, especially if the happy event planned for (whatever date Mr Johnson decides) should receive the welcome it deserves from the people of Mendacia.' I'm sorry to say that your predecessor Chancellor has been taken on at the B.B.C. as an announcer. Of course, he won't know who you are, but I'm a little afraid that as Mendacia was his pigeon he may be announcing for you, and once a fellow gets in with these so-called artistic people you can never absolutely trust him again. Still, I think people are beginning to realize that there is such a thing as the Official Secrets Act, and I don't suppose he really has been talking. However, I thought it wiser for you to broadcast under your present cover as Mr Arthur Hudson. When you have done your broadcast I want you to go back to Glenmore, keep in touch with Juno, and as soon as the yacht sails from Scotland telegraph the time and date of sailing. Then leave Glenmore at once, and report here. I may decide to send you out to Mendacia.

I am sending this letter by Sergeant Flack. He will leave here tonight disguised as a hiker and has instructions to get out the station

before Glenmore and walk to the Hydro. You could establish contact with him in a spirit of friendly curiosity about his walk. However, you're getting an old hand at this sort of thing now, and I
needn't overload you with instructions. Flack will telegraph us in
a safe code to a safe address that he has handed you this letter.
You can keep him with you till the business is finished or use him
as a messenger in case of necessity. He can go hiking about the
country apparently and let you know what's happening at Mac-
Adam's place.

You were quite right to send your letter to me c/o the D.E.I. at
the War Office, but I'm always nervous of local post-offices, and if
you have anything urgent and secret to communicate it will be
wiser to use Flack in future.

Yours sincerely,

N

By the time this long letter was written Major Hunter-Hunt
had produced a synthetic description of Katzenschlosser from
the files.

'Oh, and, H. H.,' said N, 'I think I'd better send up the talk on
Mendacia for the B.B.C. Will you have a copy of it made, so
that Blenkinsop can study it beforehand?'

Major Hunter-Hunt went off again, and the Chief took up the
receiver.

'Put me through to Sergeant-Major Garnett. Is that you,
Sergeant-Major? Send Sergeant Flack up to me.'

The ex-gymnasium-instructor appeared.

'Sergeant Flack, I have an important confidential mission for
you,' the Chief announced.

The trusty fellow stood rigidly at attention.

'I wish you to deliver an extremely important packet of
papers into the hands of Major Blenkinsop.'

'Yes, sir.'

'Major Blenkinsop is now staying at the Glenmore Hydro
under the name of Mr A. Hudson.'

'Yes, sir.'

'It is of course vitally important that nobody should suspect
for a moment that either of you is connected with The Elms'

'Very good, sir.'

'Have you ever done any hiking, Sergeant?'

'No, sir.'

'But you're still in good training?'

'Oh yes, sir. I've always kept up with my physical exercises so far as my present duties permitted.'

'I want you to go up to Glenmore tonight as a hiker.'

'Very good, sir.'

'You will want to get yourself a pair of shorts, some stout nailed boots and puttees, a rucksack, and a beret.'

'I beg pardon, sir? Exactly what kind of a berry was you meaning?'

'A b-e-r-e-t – a kind of cap which hikers wear when they wear any kind of headgear at all.'

'Oh, I beg pardon, sir. A berett. I misunderstood your meaning, sir, at first.'

'You should alight at the station before Glenmore and hike on foot from there to the Hydro so as to give the impression of having walked some distance.'

'Yes, sir. About how far would it be, sir?'

'Oh, I don't know. I should think about ten miles. You can manage that?'

'Oh yes, sir, I think I can manage ten miles, sir,' said Sergeant Flack, with the faint beginnings of a respectful smile at the notion that he might not be able to manage such a paltry distance.

'You will place yourself at Major Blenkinsop's disposal and consider yourself under his direct orders. You will of course put up at the same hotel.'

'Very good, sir.'

'You will leave King's Cross tonight by the same train as that in which you travelled to Grantham with Major Blenkinsop, and you should be with Major Blenkinsop – don't forget he's Mr Hudson up there – about lunchtime.'

'Yes, sir.'

'I suppose you don't speak Scotch?'

'Beg pardon, sir? I don't think I quite take your meaning.'

'Why, I was thinking that it would add a natural touch if you hiked up in a kilt instead of shorts. Only you'd want to speak Scotch in that case.'

'Yes, sir, I think sir, if I might make the suggestion, I'd feel easier in shorts, sir. I only once had kilts on, sir, and that was some time ago now when we was lying next to the Blue Watch, sir, soon after I joined the Colours. Me and one of the Jocks exchanged from the belt downwards, sir. Well, we'd had what you call a lively evening, sir, but even though I was feeling very merry and bright at the time I couldn't somehow keep those kilts on properly, and if it's all the same to you, sir, I'd feel more confidential, sir, in shorts.'

'All right, Sergeant. I don't want to embarrass you unnecessarily.'

'No, sir. Thank you, sir. I'm much obliged. Beg pardon, sir, while we're on the subject of equipment, I have a sports coat at home, sir. Would that be in order?'

'Perfectly. And of course you'd better take a greatcoat. It may be raining in Scotland.'

'Yes, sir. Then I leave tonight, sir?'

'That's right. I'll give you the papers presently. You'd better go right off now and get your kit together. Major Hardwick will provide you with the necessary funds. I'll tell him to give you twenty-five pounds, for which of course you will account to me.'

'Yes, sir. Thank you, sir.'

'When you have delivered the packet safely to Major Blenkinsop, telegraph as follows :

'Smith, 42 Western Road, Balham.
Arrived safe. Writing. Joe.'

'Would it be in order for me to make a note of that, sir?'

'All right, but don't leave the address lying about. It's very secret.'

'No, sir, I'll be specially careful, sir. Any further instructions, sir?'

'No, that's all. I rely on your discretion, Sergeant.'

The ex-gymnasium-instructor clicked his heels and smartly retired.

The Chief of the Secret Service lit a cigarette and pressed the white button which summoned Miss Glidden. The restoration

Chapter 15

ENID

DOGGETT'S report on his investigation of Blenkinsop's behaviour at the Glenmore Hydro did not satisfy Mrs Blenkinsop.

'It's all very well for you to be so sure of Arthur's guilt, Tiny,' she told her friend with a trace of irritation in her voice when after a visit to the office of Mr Pinches in Chancery Lane they were discussing what Mr Pinches called the 'data' of the case.

'But is there any room for doubt?' Miss Houldsworth asked.

'A great deal of room. For one thing I'm not satisfied that this woman Miranda with whom Arthur is reported to have ... to have dined is Mrs Hudson at all. You haven't seen Mrs Hudson. If you had you would realize how utterly different she is from this woman Miranda as described by this Doggett person.'

'But men are always very bad at describing women,' Miss Houldsworth argued. 'For instance, this Doggett person would probably describe me as rather well filled out, whereas a woman would know at once how to allow for the present fashion.'

'Yes, but Mrs Hudson is definitely a very large woman. It's not just a question of fat.'

Miss Houldsworth frowned. Fat was a word she never used even of bacon.

'Mrs Hudson,' Enid went on, 'is at least five feet ten, and fair enough to use a camomile shampoo powder. She has great stupid blue eyes and could not possibly pass herself off as a Spaniard. The Doggett person was absolutely positive that this Miranda woman was small, slim, and dark.'

'But if Arthur was chasing another woman at Glenmore, why did he call himself Hudson?' Miss Houldsworth asked. 'Doggett was quite clear on that point anyway. And he couldn't have made a mistake about Arthur, because you yourself pointed Arthur out to him at King's Cross.'

'And then all this mystery about the business perhaps being

graver than I suspected, which Pinches talked about. What can be graver than one's husband making love to another man's wife? Yet when I pressed Doggett about that, all he could do was to tell some ridiculous story about a bell going off and his having to escape from this Miranda woman's bedroom. No, Tiny, I wasn't satisfied. And look at the bill of costs already! Forty-six pounds eleven shillings and fivepence-halfpenny!'

Enid flung the account across the table to her friend.

'It is a good deal,' Miss Houldsworth admitted.

'A good deal? I should think it was a good deal. And so far as any positive evidence against Arthur goes, it is forty-six pounds eleven shillings and fivepence-halfpenny thrown away. What's the halfpenny for I should like to know?'

'Darling Enid, if you're going to query the account I should start at the other end,' her friend suggested. 'The halfpenny is comparatively unimportant.'

'Well, Tiny, you recommended this Pinches creature.'

'He was very helpful to Connie Butterwick.'

'He may have been helpful to Connie Butterwick; but he hasn't been at all helpful to me. At this rate it will cost me a small fortune, and I've no security that by the end of it I shall know any better what Arthur is up to than I know now.'

'I think that's taking rather a pessimistic view,' said Miss Houldsworth.

'I began to take a pessimistic view the moment the Doggett person started talking.'

'I'm not so pessimistic as you,' declared Miss Houldsworth, who still had hopes of settling into that villa at Alassio with her friend.

'No, it's not your husband and it's not your money,' Enid reminded her tartly.

'Darling, if you're going to take up that position . . .'

'It's a very natural position to take up,' Enid interrupted.

'Of course it is, darling,' Miss Houldsworth hastily assented. 'But what I was going to say was that you could hardly expect to go through an ordeal like this without a good deal of pain. You must admit that to remain in a state of uncertainty about Arthur's behaviour was unthinkable.'

'But aren't I in the same state of uncertainty now, after spending forty-six pounds eleven shillings and fivepence-half-penny?'

'I think you ought to give Pinches another chance...' Miss Houldsworth began.

'Not at forty-six pounds eleven shillings and fivepence-half-penny a time,' said Enid with determination. 'That beastly halfpenny is beginning to get on my nerves.'

'I've found it,' Miss Houldsworth exclaimed gleefully. 'There's a charge of three halfpence for a letter to Pinches from the Hydro notifying him of Doggett's arrival.'

'Why should I pay for that?' Enid indignantly demanded. 'He didn't notify *me* of his arrival. If he didn't arrive, that was his employer's funeral. Pinches shouldn't employ people who don't arrive at their destinations.'

'Why not query the halfpenny if it worries you?' Miss Houldsworth suggested. 'Or just deduct it when you send Pinches your cheque? He can hardly argue about a halfpenny.'

'A man like that will argue about anything. All he does is argue. And I pay forty-six pounds eleven shillings and five-pence-halfpenny for the privilege of listening to his arguments. Tiny, I'm going to get at the facts.'

'Of course, Enid, darling,' said her friend soothingly. 'You must not suffer any more of this gnawing suspense. Shall I go and talk the matter over with Pinches and spare you any...'

'I'm not going to have anything more to do with Pinches,' Enid declared passionately. 'I'm going straight to King Street, Covent Garden.'

'To Covent Garden? Why to Covent Garden?'

'To see Mr Hudson's bananas,' declared Enid, laughing shrilly, so shrilly that her friend fancied she detected in her tone the high note of hysteria.

'Would you like me to come with you?'

Enid thought it would be a good snub for Tiny if she visited Mr Hudson's offices alone.

'No, thank you,' she said coldly.

'Very well, darling.' Tiny accepted the snub with meekness. She was anxious to do nothing that might suggest she was not the ideal person with whom one of matrimony's martyrs might one day share a villa in Alassio.

The next morning Enid set out alone to Covent Garden. Not being sure where King Street was she drove there in a taxi. On inquiring for Mr Hudson she was told that he was away. Something in the expression of disappointment on her face must have touched the heart of an elderly clerk, whom a lifelong occupation with the affairs of bananas had not succeeded in depriving entirely of human sympathy.

'Was there any message I could give Mr Hudson, ma'am?' he inquired.

'I was anxious to see him on a private matter. Perhaps if I could ring up Mrs Hudson I could explain what I wanted,' she suggested.

'I'm sorry, ma'am, but Mrs Hudson is away with Mr Hudson.'

'Oh dear,' Enid sighed. 'Then I'm afraid there's nothing to be done.'

The elderly clerk's human sympathy was harrowed by the visitor's evident distress.

'Well, ma'am, I happen to know that Mr Hudson will be back in London either tomorrow or at the latest on Friday. His intention was to leave Mrs Hudson up in Scotland.'

'In Scotland?' Enid repeated. 'Not at the Glenmore Hydro?'

'Well, ma'am,' said the elderly clerk with a smile, 'I don't know if I am exceeding my duty, but as a matter of fact it is to the Glenmore Hydro that Mr and Mrs Hudson have gone. Mr Hudson thought that it would be a nice change for Mrs Hudson.'

'Thank you,' Enid managed to choke out. 'I'm much obliged to you. I'll write to ... or perhaps I'll call when Mr Hudson returns.'

'Shall I give him your name, ma'am?'

'Mrs Blenkinsop.'

'I didn't quite catch the name, I'm afraid.'

'B-l-e-n-k-i-n-S-O-P.'

The elderly clerk wrote the name down, and Enid walked out of the office, her brain swirling with the shock of the news she had received. When she had sat in the office of Pinches and

Pinches yesterday, listening to Doggett's description of Mrs Hudson and the account of the interview between her and Arthur she had begun to ask herself if she had misjudged her husband, if indeed he had been on banana business seriously bent. She did not know that before Pinches communicated with her he had already communicated with the police on the strength of his subordinate's report. Now with her own ears she had heard the damning evidence of his duplicity. Tiny had been right. She had snubbed her best friend. She must hasten back to her and make amends.

In her hurry to apologize to Tiny Houldsworth for her irritability Enid did not notice that she had taken the wrong direction from the office of Hudson Brothers and plunged blindly into the noise and bustle that surrounds Covent Garden Market. She found herself being jostled by excitable red-faced men in shirt-sleeves who kept rushing out on the pavement to shout hoarse orders to men with still redder faces perched high up on the box-seats of drays made mountainous by piles of empty baskets. Small boys dived beneath her legs to save muddy apples from rolling into the gutter. Taxis hooted despairingly in the jam of wagons, lorries, and vans. Young men in dark-blue aprons with pencils behind their ears darted out from one entrance of the glass-covered market and in again by another. The air was heavy with the odour of vegetables and fruit unripe, ripe, overripe, and rotting. The faster Enid tried to walk in order to escape from this sweating, swearing confusion the less speed she seemed to make.

At last in the direction of Bow Street she thought she saw an avenue in the jam of traffic which would allow her to attain the comparative calm of Kingsway's hinterland. She dived down from the pavement, landed on (of all fruits) a squashed banana, slid forward with velocity, and struck full in the stomach a porter who was carrying a pile of at least a dozen empty baskets on his head. Half of them shot over the roof of a waiting taxi and laid out several pedestrians on the pavement, one of whom was carrying another dozen similar baskets. Three more baskets from the original pile landed on top of the taxi. Of the other three one landed on Enid herself.

'Gorblimy, lady,' exclaimed the porter into whom Enid had cannoned, 'next time you wants to throw your arms round a poor blurry porter, wait till he's put his blurry baskets down.'

Fortunately for Enid's embarrassment the traffic jam was released at this moment. She and the porter had to leap aside in different directions, he to pick up the baskets that still strewed the road, she to find that peace for which she craved on the opposite pavement. Enid fancied that her forehead was grazed and on putting up a hand to ascertain the damage she was horrified to see what looked like a large clot of blood adhering to her gloves. Then she looked again and found to her relief that it was a piece of red cabbage.

'Taxi! Taxi!' she called faintly.

Inside Enid examined her appearance in the glass. Bits of red cabbage were all over her face and hat and shoulders. But when she had picked them off there was left a nasty bruise on her forehead.

Back at Jerbury Chambers Enid rang up Tiny.

'Come round to me, darling! I've had the most awful time,' she wailed into the telephone.

'My precious, I'll come at once,' Tiny called back.

Enid sat in the tight-springed armchair of the service flat, bruised inside and out. Twenty minutes later she heard the agitated knock of her friend.

'My dear, what's happened?' Tiny exclaimed. 'My darling, you've been assaulted! That monster of a woman has attacked you! Oh, Enid, Enid, why didn't you let me go with you? I may be small, but I would have protected you.'

Enid was too grateful for such a spontaneous flow of affectionate solicitude to criticize Tiny's estimate of herself, to think that 'short' would have been a better epithet than 'small'.

'It wasn't Mrs Hudson,' said Enid, 'it was a basket.'

'A basket?'

'In Covent Garden. It fell on me. But that's nothing. It's Arthur, Tiny. You were right!'

'He's not run off with Mrs Hudson?'

'He's as good as run off with her. Her husband took her up to Glenmore and is leaving her there with Arthur.' Enid broke down into sobs. 'He told his clerk it would be a nice change for her. Did you ever hear anything so brutally cynical in all your life?'

'Well, really, men!' declared Tiny. 'I sometimes ask myself if men are really human beings at all.'

'But they needn't think I'm going to be made a fool of any longer,' Enid burst out.

'What will you do?'

'What will I do? I shall go to Glenmore and confront them,' the injured wife proclaimed.

'Oh, darling, how splendidly brave of you!' Tiny exulted. 'You might have been a glorious Brunnhilda when you said that,' and in her enthusiasm she began to hum the Ride of the Valkyries.

'You're very cheerful about it,' said Enid, with a touch of resentment in her voice, for she thought that her friend was humming 'We won't go home till morning'.

'No, Enid, it's not cheerfulness. It's a kind of intoxication I feel at your courage.'

'I'll go to Glenmore,' Enid went on, 'and I'll take Pinches and Pinches' bill, and I'll throw it at Arthur and I'll tell him it's the first item in the expenses of my divorce.'

'I think you're too marvellous,' Tiny cried, clapping her fat little hands in an ecstasy.

'And you shall come with me to Glenmore,' declared Enid, who was feeling that she must have a sympathetic audience for the histrionic displays she was planning.

'My dear, I'd love to. But can you afford it?'

Enid had not really intended to pay her friend's fare and hotel expenses; but she accepted the responsibility with a graceful condescension that evoked a fresh gush of admiration from Tiny.

'We will go up tomorrow morning,' she announced. 'I do not want to find that despicable Hudson there.'

Nor did she want to pay for a first-class sleeper for Tiny. They could travel up third by day.

So next morning at nine o'clock Enid and Tiny were sitting opposite to one another when the Diurnal Scot went puffing majestically out of King's Cross northward bound.

At twenty minutes to ten that night Enid and Tiny alighted from the green omnibus and entered the portals of the Glenmore Hydro.

'You have rooms reserved for Miss Madison and Miss Houldsworth?' Enid inquired at the desk. She had booked the rooms in her maiden name in order to avoid the humiliating gossip of her fellow-guests when the exposure of Arthur came.

'Yes, madam. Numbers 46 and 47. Macintosh and Macgillivray.'

'No, Madison and Houldsworth,' said Enid. 'Miss Madison and Miss Houldsworth.'

The reception clerk smiled languidly.

'The hotel rooms are all named after the different clans,' she explained. 'Will you register, please?'

Enid was just going to study the visitors' book with a palpitating interest when a familiar voice was heard from some adjacent room.

'The exports of Mendacia are many. Not the least important industry is the cultivation of the pyrethrum which is the principal source of supply for insect powders all over the world.'

Then the voice abruptly stopped.

Enid and Tiny stared at one another.

'Arthur holding forth as usual about Mendacia,' exclaimed his wife bitterly. She hurried to the room whence the voice had come. She saw about half a dozen guests in various attitudes of drowsiness. She saw a melancholy oval-faced man walking across the room to an armchair. She did not see Arthur.

'The coward!' she whispered to Tiny. 'He hadn't the courage to face me. He must have caught sight of us in the hall and bolted out. The coward!'

'Well, he can't leave here tonight,' said Tiny. 'And if I were you I'd wait and confront him in the morning.'

At this point it is necessary to follow the old-fashioned custom of leaving readers in suspense while the chronicler retraces his steps and relates what had been happening in the Glenmore Hydro since Doggett left it on the previous Saturday morning. It was now Thursday evening, exactly a week after Blenkinsop had travelled northward in the Nocturnal Scot.

Chapter 16

THE KILTED FORM

WHEN Blenkinsop from the siesta-lounge watched Doggett exhausted by tipping catch the green motor-bus at half past eight on Saturday morning, watched the glutted field-marshals and the admirals obviously determined to squeeze out of him the last few miserable half-crowns he had left, he smiled, for he did not suspect that the pillaging of Doggett would ultimately be paid for by himself, with the profit of Pinches and Pinches added.

'Dirty little brute, serve him right,' he muttered savagely, as he turned away from the dark November landscape and followed a lively scent of eggs and bacon into the dining-room.

After breakfast Blenkinsop retired to the supplementary smoking-room and tried to think out his talk on Mendacia for the B.B.C.

'Mendacia! How many of my listeners know even where Mendacia is?'

Half an hour's concentrated meditation had just dragged this opening sentence from the depths of Blenkinsop's being, and he was on the point of trying the *viva voce* effect of it on some carven images of the early Celtic saints on the mantelpiece when he began to fancy that he was being stealthily watched. He rose, walked rapidly to the door, and flung it wide open.

Outside in attitudes unmistakably surreptitious stood the Misses Macadam.

'Can I do anything for you ladies?' Blenkinsop asked with simple dignity.

The faded pink of an elderly blush stained the cheeks of the two sisters. They murmured some excuse about wanting to see Lady Glenmore's oratory and not wishing to disturb anybody.

Blenkinsop threw a contemptuous glance at them, went back into the smoking-room, gathered together his papers, and without vouchsafing a word to the two spies retired with a roundabout deliberation of movement to his own bedroom. Through the keyhole of that even they would hardly venture to peep.

'*Mendacia! How many of my listeners know even where Mendacia is?*'

In the seclusion of his room Blenkinsop rehearsed the effect of this opening sentence aloud. It did not sound effective. His voice seemed to be struggling like a fly in the red and yellow cobweb of the Macmillan tartan. Renata was spending the day at Drumroy with MacAdam, and he was not even to have the pleasure of dining with her at the end of it. Blenkinsop compelled himself to stop thinking about Renata and MacAdam and concentrate upon his talk. *From the earliest times the hardy Mendacian mountaineers* ... there was at any rate some satisfaction in writing mountaineers instead of Highlanders. He wondered whether it was too early to go along to Renata's sitting-room and ask her opinion of what he had written so far about her native land. It was only just after half past ten. She was probably not dressed yet. However, there would be no harm in knocking. Blenkinsop felt he could stand no more of the Macmillan red and yellow. He began to crave the rainbow hues of clan Buchanan.

On leaving his room he threw a quick glance to right and left of him, and to his annoyance saw to right of him at one end of the corridor Miss Caroline Macadam, to left of him at the other end Miss Flora, and with her that vile West Highland terrier which yapped at him as if he were trying to enter its mistress's bedroom instead of coming out of his own. Blenkinsop retreated hurriedly into his own room again. Life was going to be difficult for the next few days unless he could find some way of shaking off these two females. Where on earth was he going to interview the King if these two Caledonian maniacs intended to shadow him like this? That interview was a vital necessity now, if only to test the bona fides of this mysterious Heisswasser. Blenkinsop put aside the talk on Mendacia and addressed himself to the task of writing a long letter to N. He must have some further information about Heisswasser. A nice thing if Heisswasser turned out to be none other than Katzenschlosser himself. Heaven help Heisswasser if he had a large chin! He would not get off with it as he had got off with it in the Palm Court of the Plonplon Hotel. But where to meet the King? Blenkinsop gazed despairingly at the walls of his bedroom, and presently his attention was caught by the framed tariff of the hotel's hydrotherapy. TURKISH BATH. By gad, that was the place! The Turkish bath! Those miserable hags could not follow him down there. He sprang up rejuvenated by his inspiration and set out to reconnoitre the possibilities of the Turkish bath. Looking back he observed with satisfaction the sisters Macadam recoil baffled as he passed through the portico, above which was painted with the finality of the warning above the gates of Hell, GENTLEMEN'S TURKISH BATH. Let them champ their dentures without. Here, at any rate, he was safe from female agents of the Mendacian Republic.

Within the precincts of the Turkish bath the prevailing Gothic and Celtic in the decorations gave way to a lavish orientalism. Instead of tartan the walls were arabesques; heraldic draperies were replaced by Eastern hangings, Glastonbury chairs by divans, old pewter pots by trays of Benares brass.

The shampooer, a sleek bald-headed man clad in nothing but a Turkish towel, came hurrying soundlessly across the tiles.

'Good morning, sir. Bath this morning, sir?' he inquired hopefully.

'I was just looking round,' Blenkinsop explained.

'Very handsome bath, sir,' said the shampooer.

'When is it likely to be empty?' Blenkinsop asked.

'It's empty now, sir, if you were thinking ...'

'Is it usually empty?'

'Well, sir, to be frank, it is usually empty about now. The season's on the dead side. And there are so many other baths in the Hydro people seem to forget the good old Turkish. This is the cooling-room, sir. Very comfortable couches. And if you were feeling a little languid after the bath you could have a nice chop down here and a nap to follow.'

While Bunting, the shampooer, was talking Blenkinsop had cast an eye round the interior. He noted with satisfaction the strategic position of the very hot room. In there the gravest secrets would be safe. Those walls were thick as a dungeon's. And by gad! Yes, by gad, no disguise could stand against such heat. If Heisswasser's chin were false it would melt like butter in an oven.

'I'm not going to have a bath today,' said Blenkinsop. 'But if you could reserve the bath for myself and a couple of friends one day early next week . . .'

'That can easily be arranged, sir. Thank you very much. Good morning, sir.'

When Blenkinsop emerged from the portico that gave ingress to the Turkish bath he looked round for the female agents. They had vanished in discouragement.

The more closely he considered the rendezvous he had chosen for the King and Heisswasser, the more suitable did it seem. The only objection he could see to it was the possibility that the King himself might object to discussing the date of his restoration clad only in a towel. Would he think such a costume too light for royal dignity? It might be as well to get his suggestion approved at The Elms. Then there could be no mistake.

Blenkinsop went back to his room and finished his letter to N. Not wishing to have a letter addressed to the D.E.I. at the War Office noted by any of the hotel staff, some of whom had probably been bribed by Doggett, he hired a car and drove to Fort Wade, the local metropolis which was about twenty miles away in the other direction from Drumroy. The occasional glimpses he caught of the scenery through the driving mist made him long for Renata's company, that they might enjoy it side by side. He came back to the hotel in a gloomy mood which was made melancholic by a note from Renata saying she was going to spend the week-end at Drumroy, but should be back on Monday in the hope of hearing some news.

'Damned indiscreet! Damned indiscreet,' Blenkinsop muttered to himself.

Sunday was an intolerable day. If he succeeded in escaping from the curiosity of the Misses Macadam he ran into the suspicious questions of Mr Lobbins of Covent Garden. And when he managed to fly from Mr Lobbins he was buttonholed by a melancholy oval-faced bore from Nigeria who wearied him with tales about his experiences in Ireland with Sinn Fein. He tried listening to the wireless in the drawing-room in the hope of getting some tips for his talk; but whenever it was tuned in Bach was being performed somewhere, and a few minutes later one of the guests would ask if anybody was particularly anxious to listen to highbrow music. As nobody was it was turned off for the sound of knitting-needles to click and tick upon the air of the heavy Sabbath afternoon.

Monday was hardly less tolerable than Sunday. To be sure, Blenkinsop dined again with Renata in her room, but the evening was spoilt by his resentment over her having gone over to Drumroy for the week-end. She seemed incapable of comprehending the indiscretion of her behaviour, and actually told him that he was sulky because he was jealous of MacAdam.

'And let me tell you, *cher ami*,' she said, 'that I cannot accept your right to treat me like a schoolgirl.'

'I shouldn't dream of treating you like a schoolgirl. But you must remember how vitally important it is that the British Government should not be compromised in any way by this Mendacian business, and for you to go off to Drumroy for the week-end is just the way to do so.'

'I find you altogether too absurd, Arthur,' said Renata petulantly. 'Is it not known that I am going to Drumroy for lunch, for dinner? Am I not driving with MacAdam all the time?'

'You certainly are,' said Blenkinsop savagely. 'But that doesn't make it any better.'

'Bah! bah! bah!' she jeered. 'Let me hear now what you have written to talk.'

'I haven't finished it yet. You can't write a wireless talk in five minutes.'

'But, my dear friend, you have had many many five minutes to write it.'

'Well, I can't finish it until I receive further instructions from London. I hope to get these tomorrow. Don't forget that I must then see Mr Johnson and his friend. I've been thinking a lot about that meeting. What about seeing him in the Turkish bath?'

'In a Turkish bath? What a droll place!'

'It's the only safe place in this confounded hotel. You don't seem to realize that it's buzzing with spies. I know that a Turkish bath isn't the usual place to interview a monarch, but necessity knows no laws, and all that sort of thing.'

'Yes, I think it can be arranged,' Renata decided after a brief hesitation.

'I don't know if MacAdam would like to be at this meeting. It might look more natural if he brought his guests over to have a Turkish bath than if Mr Johnson and his friend came over alone.'

'I shall tell to MacAdam that he must come.'

'And I've no doubt he'll obey you,' observed Blenkinsop sarcastically.

'Oh, chut!'

It was not a happy evening.

'Well,' said Blenkinsop at the end of it, 'I don't want to bore you any longer, so I'll say "good night". Shall we settle Wednesday morning at twelve for the Turkish bath?'

'*Bien.*'

'I'll reserve it for myself and some friends,' said Blenkinsop. 'If MacAdam drives over Mr Johnson and his friend they could go straight in. I'll be there an hour beforehand.'

'*Très bien.*'

'Good night, Renata. Forgive my boorishness. It's the inaction that is killing me. Have no fear I shall fail when the moment comes for action. I'm like that.'

She offered him a lilywhite hand in token of reconciliation and confidence. He bent over and kissed it. There was a lump in his throat as he walked to the door. There was a still bigger lump when he found that the door was slightly ajar.

'By gad, Renata,' he explained, 'somebody has been trying to listen to what we have been saying. I told you this hotel was alive with republican agents.'

'*Mais non, mais non*, be tranquil, my poor Arthur. It is some impudent *femme de chambre* who has wished to peep upon our lovemaking.'

She laughed with a light, a mocking but a heart-rendingly delicious tinkle of mirth.

'Yes, you may well laugh,' said Blenkinsop sombrely, as he left her, a figurine of ivory and ebony whose grace and beauty not even the Buchanan tartan could mar.

But it was not some impudent chambermaid who had striven to find out the relations between Renata and Blenkinsop. It was Miss Flora Macadam who for the sake of her country had risked her reputation by eavesdropping.

'Caroline, Caroline,' she exclaimed when she burst into her sister's bedroom, papered as it should have been with the tartan of her own clan. 'Caroline, there's a plot to assassinate our grand old chief on Wednesday in the Turkish bath. You said that villainous Sasunnach was up to no good when he went sneaking in there on Saturday. You were right. I believe you have the second sight.'

'I have,' said Miss Caroline positively, 'I have, Flora.'

She rose from her chair and gazed into space, a Sibyl with viewless eyes in dark green taffeta.

'I see a kilted form,' she began.

'MacAdam,' Miss Flora exclaimed emotionally.

'Don't interrupt, Flora,' said the Sibyl crossly. 'How can I see anything at all if you keep interrupting? I see a kilted form who will interpose himself between MacAdam and the assassin's knife.'

Miss Flora, whose heart was still palpitating from the nervous strain of opening the door of a room and listening to what was going on inside, was impressed by her sister's vision, but insufficiently impressed not to wish to do something at once about the plot to foil the rising.

'Nonsense, Flora,' said Miss Caroline severely, 'there's nothing we can do tonight at any rate. We have till Wednesday according to what you heard. The best thing you can do is to go to bed and drink a glass of dear St Ninian's water. That will calm your nerves.'

Miss Flora retired a little huffily. She did not think that her sister quite appreciated what she had done this evening. Back in her own bedroom, which was dedicated to the red and black of Macgregor, she felt like flinging open the window and shrieking 'Claymore!' until the sound echoed in wild Ben

Uaine's farthest corries and rang from crag to crag of noble
Ben Buidhe. However, she undressed, and after sipping a
tumbler of St Ninian's water and reading several pages of Fiona
Macleod, she went off to sleep in a dense Celtic fog, through
which she fancied white-gowned Ossianic bards beckoned at
her to save Alba.

It was not astonishing that when a kilted form did alight the
next morning from the hotel omnibus Miss Caroline Macadam
should hastily conclude he was the chosen vessel to save her
chief from obliteration in a Turkish bath.

'But, Caroline,' the younger sister objected, 'he's wearing the
Mackillop tartan. He's one of the hereditary enemies of our
clan.'

'Have you forgotten the prophecy of the Glenmore seer?'
Miss Caroline asked. '*When a Mackillop shall clasp the hand of
a daughter of MacAdam with his right hand and the hand of a
daughter of MacAdam with his left hand there shall be peace
in Alba.*'

'But I do remember that, Caroline.'

'There can be no peace in Scotland until we have Home Rule,
can there?' Miss Caroline asked.

'Certainly not.'

'Very well then, we must bring about the fulfilment of the
seer's prophecy,' said Miss Caroline firmly. 'We must greet him.
I will shake him by the right hand and you must shake his left
hand at the same time.'

Perhaps it was some lingering thought of Worthing's etiquette which made Miss Flora hesitate. She had to remind herself how she had hung head downward over St Ninian's Well to
drink from the original source, and how she had dared to open
the door of Señora Miranda's sitting room and listen to the
conversation between her and the English enemy, before she
could brace herself to commit the apparent solecism of shaking
an utter stranger by the hand.

'I am ready, Caroline,' she declared, setting her denture to
face the task before her.

The kilted form of Miss Caroline's vision last night had just
registered as Miss Caroline herself stepped forward.

'You are a Mackillop,' she said.

The kilted form jumped visibly.

'I am a Macadam,' Miss Caroline continued. 'How d'ye do?'

Instinctively the kilted form put out his right hand, and when it was cordially grasped by this remarkable female he found his left hand being grasped with equal cordiality by another remarkable female.

'You are a Scottish Nationalist?' the right-handed female was asking.

'And perhaps a volunteer?' the left-handed female was whispering.

Mackillop realized at once that by one of those prizes of good fortune which are sometimes awarded to the keen Intelligence officer he had within a few minutes of his arrival at Glenmore plunged into the very heart of the mystery he had been dispatched to solve.

'That's why I'm up here,' he whispered.

'*Am bheil Gàidhlig agaibh?*' asked Miss Flora eagerly, hoping for a spout of her ancestral language to gush forth from this weather-beaten hero.

'They haven't given me the password yet,' Mackillop explained.

'You haven't the Gaelic?'

'No, no, I was born in Broughty Ferry,' Mackillop explained.

'Never mind, for still the heart is Highland,' Miss Caroline quoted graciously.

'Aye, I served in the Blue Watch during the war.'

'For the rights of small nations,' Miss Caroline commented bitterly. 'No matter, this morning the Macadams and the Mackillops have ended a feud which has lasted for over six hundred years. Little did my sister and I think when we searched for the spot where in 1410 MacAdam thrust his brogue into the mouth of the dying Mackillop that we should be the humble instruments of peace.'

Mackillop was a hard-bitten Intelligence Officer who had made his mark as early as the Boer War. 'What Mackillop doesn't know about hush-hush work isn't worth knowing,' was a favourite dictum of P's. At Number Two he was regarded as the man for any investigation that required courage, experience, and acumen When at rare intervals during his Intelligence work in the Great War he had donned uniform, his tunic displayed a double line of ribbons, the unusual pea-greens and magentas in which made ex-military attachés wonder if something had gone wrong with their eyes, for orders like the Lily of Laguna and the White Hippopotamus of Bong did not come even their way.

Mackillop had spent very little of his later life in the land of his birth, and the normal scepticism of the Scot had in his case almost entirely disappeared in the wonder of Intelligence, a long experience of which had taught him to believe in everything except the likelihood of German governesses signalling to Zeppelins with a lamp and a bedroom blind. As a native of Broughty Ferry Mackillop might have thought the possibility of a Sinn Fein rising in the West of Scotland too remote to be treated seriously. As an Intelligence Officer attached to the S.R.D. Mackillop knew that he would never have been sent to investigate matters round about Glenmore unless there was good reason to suppose that such a rising was imminent. This chance meeting with the Misses Macadam showed him how right he had been not to allow the prejudices acquired in Broughty Ferry to interfere with his view of dark Glenmore.

Well within the half-hour that Major Grimshaw had so enthusiastically prophesied Mackillop had gralloched the situation. He did not of course believe his informants when they accused 'Hudson' of being an English agent. He knew instinctively that 'Hudson' was probably an agent of Moscow engaged in fomenting a Sinn Fein rebellion in Scotland. He did not believe that 'Hudson' had the slightest intention of assassinating MacAdam in the Turkish bath. He knew instinctively that 'Hudson' was using the Turkish bath as a convenient cover for meeting the leaders of the rebellion. Mackillop was too old a hand at this sort of job to let the two elderly ladies, who were obviously not in the confidence of the heads, know that he had spotted 'Hudson's' real game. So long as they showed by their obvious suspicion of 'Hudson' that they believed him to be an English agent, 'Hudson' would believe himself safe. He encouraged them, therefore, to keep an eye on 'Hudson' and asked them to report to him in the evening when he returned to the Hydro the movements of 'Hudson' during the day. He himself, he told them, was off to Drumroy to receive his instructions.

'And you will warn MacAdam to keep away from the Turkish bath?' Miss Flora asked anxiously.

'I shall take steps to see that MacAdam comes to no harm. Leave it all to me. And keep your eyes on Hudson.'

'But before you go do drink a glass of St Ninian's water,' Miss Caroline begged. 'You must celebrate the healing of this six hundred years' feud between our two clans, and you must wish for the triumph of our arms.'

Lightly Mackillop humoured these two cracked mugs of his. The waiter was summoned. Three glasses of water were placed upon a table before them.

'*Alba gu brath*,' Miss Caroline intoned in an impressive contralto as she raised her glass.

'*Gu brath, gu brath!*' cried Miss Flora on a higher note.

'Wha's like us?' inquired Mackillop, all Broughty Ferry in that velvet glove of a voice which hid the iron hand of Angus.

For a moment or two, as the taste of bad eggs and old bicycle tyres permeated his being, Mackillop thought that the elderly ladies having seen through his disguise had ruthlessly poisoned him, that he, an Intelligence officer of well over thirty years' experience, had been tricked at last. He was wondering if in his last agony he should have the strength to pierce with his *sgian dubh* the homespun tweed that enfolded his murderesses, when looking round the siesta-lounge he perceived that other guests were sipping from tumblers a fluid that seemed by the expressions on their faces to nauseate them equally. Hope returned.

'That water was a bit of a shock,' said Mackillop.

'I'm afraid most people find it a little strong at first,' Miss Caroline admitted. 'But my sister and I were determined to enjoy it from the first.'

Mackillop rose to make arrangements for being conveyed by car to a suitable stop for reconnoitring Drumroy.

'You haven't drained your glass,' Miss Flora reminded him.

'That's the word! Drains! I was trying to remember what it was like,' said Mackillop. 'Well, I think you'll have to let me off the rest, or this clan feud we've healed so pleasantly this morning may break out all over again. But I mustn't stay joking here with you two ladies,' he added quickly, for he saw that his criticism of St Ninian's water was likely to cast a doubt upon the sincerity of his rebellious nationalism. 'Scots wha hae, and all that.'

With this Mackillop hurried away from the siesta-lounge.

'It's sad how quickly even the best Highlander gets corrupted by Lowland surroundings,' Miss Caroline observed to her sister. She could not approve Mackillop's insensitiveness to the poetry of St Ninian's water.

'But we can forgive anything to a volunteer,' Miss Flora urged rapturously.

'That is true,' Miss Caroline replied. 'And now we must see what that slinking Hudson is doing.'

Blenkinsop, however, was up in his bedroom out of their reach. The ordeal of that broadcast was drawing horribly near, and the form of his talk had not yet materialized from a chaos of statistics. He was worried too by not receiving any further instructions from N. He had told Renata that he was bound to have some news for the King today. Presumably N had thought it was too risky to write and was relying on him to use his own judgement. That looked as if Heisswasser was genuine. If N thought he was Katzenschlosser he would surely have warned him now. Could his letter to N have been intercepted? Could Doggett have bribed the postal officials at Fort Wade? A hundred gloomy contingencies haunted Blenkinsop's brain. He longed to consult Renata, and from her enchanting confidence regain his own. At noon he ventured to go along and tap at the door of her room.

'*Entrez.*'

If Blenkinsop had been an imaginative man he might have fancied that St Peter opening for him the doors of Heaven would speak in exactly that tone of voice.

'There's no news from London, Renata,' he told her. 'Were you going over to lunch at Drumroy today?'

'Why, yes, because it is today that I must tell our friends for tomorrow.'

'Yes, but suppose we have got to postpone it? Couldn't you wait and go over this afternoon? There may be a letter by the afternoon post.'

'I find your English ways *très nonchalant*,' declared Renata crossly.

'Well, we can't all of us be Scotch even in London.'

'I find you a small bit ridiculous when you make yourself so much English, my friend.'

'Yes, but look here, Renata, if you go rushing over to Drumroy and I get some news from London I'm stymied.'

'What is stymied?'

'Why, I can't go over to Drumroy myself without arousing suspicion. You can explain the difficulty to MacAdam when he calls for you.'

'MacAdam does not come today, He will send his auto.'

'That's all right. You can send him a message to say that you'll drive over later in one of the hotel cars.'

'But how can I pay for such things?' she expostulated. 'You speak without a think.'

'We'll pay for the car.'

And so it was arranged. Renata, however, was petulant over her lost lunch at Drumroy, and took it out of Blenkinsop by saying that she had a migraine and could only eat a little nothing in solitude.

The post arrived about five o'clock, but there was no letter from The Elms, and Blenkinsop was just going to ascend disconsolately to Renata's room and communicate the absence of news when a drenched hiker staggered into the hotel and sank down exhausted upon one of the elaborately carved Gothic settles in the entrance-hall.

Overwhelmed by his own worries, Blenkinsop was on the point of passing by like the Levite when to his surprise he heard his name gasped out, or rather the name under which he was passing. He turned round nervously, but there was apparently nobody in the hall at this moment.

'You look very done in,' he said aloud for the benefit of any concealed listener, and sat down beside the panting hiker.

'It's me, sir. It's Sergeant Flack. I've got important papers for you. Oh lord, sir, I thought I never *would* get here.' The messenger fumbled inside his sports coat for the sealed envelope.

'Be careful, Sergeant. This hotel has eyes everywhere,' Blenkinsop muttered. He had just caught sight of those two accursed Caledonian hags bobbing about behind a glass show-case of local industries. 'You're looking very tired. Have you walked far?' he asked loudly. 'You want a drink. Can you walk a few more steps?'

'Yes, sir. I think so, sir.'

Blenkinsop led the way to the library.

'Quick! Give me the envelope,' he hissed, as they entered.

Blenkinsop transferred the dispatches to his own pocket, and rang the bell.

'One large whisky, one small, and a split soda,' he said to the waiter incisively.

By this time Sergeant Flack had collapsed into a deep leather armchair stamped all over with gilded basilisks. Blenkinsop took a seat near him among griffins.

'I'll go upstairs in a minute and read through these dispatches, Sergeant.'

'Yes, sir. Thank you, sir.'

'Did you walk from Glenmore Station?'

'No, sir. Acting on instructions I alighted this morning at the station before Glenmore, and I really have been walking ever since.'

'But why on earth did you do that? You'd have been here by half past eleven this morning with the hotel bus.'

'Yes, sir. I know, sir. But I'm a hiker, and Colonel N made a particular point I was to get out at the station before Glenmore and act up to it. He reckoned it would be about ten miles to the Hydro, but it's close on thirty.'

'Never mind. Drink up this whisky, and have a bit of a rest. Are you going back to London tonight?'

'Tonight, sir? Oh, I don't think I really could. Colonel N said I was to put myself at your disposal, sir.'

'Well, I'll go and read what he says,' Blenkinsop decided.

'Thank you, sir. I started off all right, sir, but it's such a country for hills. Up and down. Up and down. What we used to call a seesaw when I was a nipper. And then I had a bit of trouble with my shorts, sir. They didn't allow properly for my development at the back, sir. You see, sir, you get very musclified instructing in physical drill. So I didn't like to step out as I should have done, in case I stepped out of 'em for good and all.'

The whisky was making Sergeant Flack voluble. Blenkinsop thought it as well to warn him against the ears of foreign agents.

'Are there really, sir? In this hotel? Fancy. Well, it only goes to show they're everywhere nowadays. Youbequietus as Major H. H. said in my hearing once. It's this communism does it. Well, I often say to my missus we didn't know how lucky we was before the good old war. And that's a fact. Well, believe it or not, sir, but when my missus and me was first walking out, and which we did for several years before there was a chance of quarters on the strength, suffragettes were as near to what you might call anything really violent as . . .'

'Quite, quite,' Blenkinsop interrupted. 'I'll see you again presently, Mr Flack. By the way, be careful to avoid any allusion to your military rank up here.'

'I will, sir,' said Sergeant Flack, springing to attention as Blenkinsop left the library.

'And don't on any account salute me like that,' Blenkinsop turned round to add.

Up in his bedroom he read carefully through N's letter and congratulated himself on having anticipated so many of his chief's instructions. He was glad, too, to receive the draft of his broadcast talk, which though it looked extraordinarily dull, would relieve him of any responsibility. The synthetic description of Katzenschlosser, so laboriously built up by Hunter-Hunt from the information about him in the files, was less satisfactory.

ABRAHAM LINCOLN KATZENSCHLOSSER,
b. Milwaukee 1880

HEIGHT: Medium.

(One usually reliable agent describes him as exceptionally tall and another very reliable agent notes him as a short fat man.)

EYES: Blue.

(According to most descriptions, but brown, hazel, and grey are given by reliable agents.)

FOREHEAD: Medium.

(Every agent agrees about this.)

NOSE: Medium.

(Large and small also given, but noses are easily altered for purposes of disguise.)

MOUTH: Medium.

(Some agents give him a moustache. This of course may be false; or it may not.)

CHIN: Medium.

(Sometimes with a beard, sometimes not. N.B. – It is always easy to alter the shape of the chin.)

HAIR: Brown.

(Too much attention should not be paid to this. Red, flaxen, black, dark brown, and grey appear in reliable agents' reports.)

COMPLEXION: Fair.

(One agent usually reliable describes him as very dark indeed. Two or three others as dark.)

Distinguishing Characteristic and Marks:

There is no lack of these according to reliable agents' descriptions, but many of them having probably been assumed by a master of disguise too much attention should not be paid to them. Moles and scars are noted on different parts of the face, but this may be discounted. This applies equally to the limp with which some agents credit him. The characteristic which *all* agents are agreed upon is the expression of stealth which no disguise seems able to conceal. One very reliable agent refers to his 'look of almost supernatural cunning', and another reliable agent says that to sit near him in a restaurant is to fancy oneself eating with a wolf. This may seem a little highly coloured, but it is quoted to illustrate the effect that this remarkable man produces on the minds of agents with long experience. 'Snakelike' and 'foxy' are other epithets which occur.

Blenkinsop shook his head. He saw no prospect of deciding if Heisswasser really was Katzenschlosser from such a farrago of contradictory information. The very hot room of the Turkish bath must be the test. If the features of Heisswasser began to dissolve gradually as he sat there, why, then it might be assumed that he was Katzenschlosser; but if Heisswasser emerged from the very hot room still recognizable as the man who had entered it his authenticity might reasonably be presumed. Even N, always so cautious, was evidently inclined to believe that this really was Heisswasser.

Blenkinsop went along to Renata's room to give her the good news from London, by which she was so much delighted that all her resentment at missing lunch at Drumroy vanished in a moment.

'Oh, my dear friend, you have contrived quite excessively well. Be sure, I shall say to my beloved King . . .'

'Mr Johnson, Mr Johnson!'

'*Comme vous voulez,* but I shall tell to him that when he has chased away these abominable republicans from our glorious Mendacia he must quite surely give to you the Order of the Sacred Source.'

'But that used to be the highest Mendàcian Order,' said Blenkinsop in awe. He could hardly believe that what had been withheld even from the general who presided over the Mendacian Boundary Commission should be granted to him.

'And you merit our greatest Order,' Renata assured him, 'for you can be sure we recognize what you have done.'

Blenkinsop would have liked to bask in this sort of thing for a while longer, but he resisted the temptation to indulge himself and spoke of the urgency of carrying the news from London to Drumroy.

'Don't forget the date of departure must be settled by tomorrow so that I can announce it on Thursday night over the wireless, and I suppose you will want to telegraph to your friends warning them to listen in.'

'Ah, that has been done long ago. They are listening for the news day and night,' said Renata.

'To the wireless from London?' Blenkinsop exclaimed.

'Surely.'

'By gad, I do call that heroic,' he declared warmly. 'Well, if you're ready, I'll go and order a car for you.'

'But I do not think that I can drive alone to Drumroy,' she demurred.

'You can't?'

'No, no. I am frightened in this darkness and rain. You will drive with me, I think, yes?'

Blenkinsop started. The temptation to assent to what she asked was overpowering. He was overpowered.

'It's horribly indiscreet,' he muttered, 'but . . . but if I just left you at the door of the Castle and sat well back in the car and didn't show myself . . .'

'Why, of course you will come, Arthur. Suppose I can be attacked by republicans on the road, what would I do?'

'Oh, yes, that settles it,' Blenkinsop said firmly. 'I shall escort you to Drumroy. I'll go right away and have the car round for you in ten minutes.'

Flack was still in the library when he went downstairs. The voluble stage of the whisky had been succeeded by drowsiness. He was lying back in the armchair, snoring gently while the firelight flickered over his bare knees and wide-open mouth, and the steam rose from his drenched clothes.

Blenkinsop roused him.

'Look here, Flack, you'd better see about getting yourself a room.'

'Yes, sir,' the Sergeant-Instructor yawned. 'Beg pardon, sir, but this Scotch air's gone to my head a bit. Oh, and I was forgetting, Colonel N instructed me to send him a telegram in code advising him that you had duly received his envelope. This is the message, sir.'

Blenkinsop decided that 'arrived safe writing Joe' would compromise nothing if telephoned along to the post-office from the hotel.

'I authorize you to dispatch that telegram from here,' he said. 'I am going out now on an important mission. You had better get yourself some tea and change your clothes.'

'Beg pardon, sir, I haven't got any clothes, only these I'm wearing. Bar a change of shirt and vest of course. My missus created a bit when she found I wasn't going to take any trousers, but Colonel N made such a particular point of me being in shorts, especially when I shied at wearing kilts, that I didn't like to mention trousers to him. He seemed to regularly have his knife into trousers yesterday when he sent me off.'

'You'll look so odd walking about the hotel like that,' Blenkinsop commented distastefully.

'Yes, sir, my missus passed the remark before I came away that I looked like a boy scout who'd been left in a cucumber-frame and swelled up in the sun.'

'Well, of course, Colonel N would know exactly the way hikers do behave,' said Blenkinsop. 'So, no doubt it's all right. By the way, keep clear of two elderly sisters in this hotel called Macadam. They're foreign agents. And there's a man called Lobbins you ought to avoid, and another man called Woodburn. In fact, you'd better avoid everybody.'

'Yes, sir, make a general rule. I should feel safer that way.'

'*I* know!' Blenkinsop exclaimed. 'You can tell people that you're one of the clerks in Hudson's taking his annual holiday.'

'Yes, sir. Would that be Hudson's Soap, sir?'

'No, no, Hudson Brothers the banana importers of King Street, Covent Garden. I'm a member of the firm.'

'Yes, sir. I've got that quite clear. Would it help at all if I was to go about the hotel eating bananas? Because as it happens I've got half a dozen in what they call this rocksack. I hung on to them in case I had to go on hiking all night.'

'No, you don't want to overdo it,' said Blenkinsop. 'Don't forget you're on holiday. You'd want to get away from bananas. Well, I shall be back by dinner-time I expect. I'll give you any further orders later. But you'll be able to get off to bed early. You'd better try to get those shorts of yours dried when you've sent the telegram. I see the name is "Smith". You'd better register in the hotel book as "Smith".'

'Yes, sir.'

'And of course I shall call you Smith.'

'Yes, sir. I won't forget, sir. I once had a godfather called Smith who was supposed to be very wealthy, but he didn't leave a bean when he died. Some said his housekeeper got it all out of him. So it's only fair I should use his name.'

'You'd better not drink any more whisky tonight, Smith,' were Blenkinsop's last words of advice. 'I'll mention to the management that you're one of our clerks, and then you won't have any difficulty about getting a room.'

A few minutes after this conversation Blenkinsop was seated beside Renata in one of the hotel cars, bound as he fondly hoped for Drumroy with twenty blissful miles before them of darkness and rain. He was just tucking the rug round her with the loving care of one who expects to use a rug as something more than a shelter from the stormy blast when another car came glaring and blaring up to the hotel, out of which leapt the kilted form of MacAdam.

'Ah, they have sent for me,' exclaimed Renata. 'Ah, that is good. Now you will not have to be so indiscreet, my dear friend.'

The loving care which Blenkinsop had expended upon the rug was undone in an instant by her to whose comfort it had been dedicated.

'MacAdam! MacAdam! I was just starting with Monsieur Hudson,' she announced.

'Oh, I'm so glad I got here in time, dear lady,' said the Highland chieftain. 'Come along, we've been looking for you all day. Good evening, Hudson. Lucky I arrived in time to save you a long wet drive, eh?'

The feeling Edward the First entertained towards William Wallace was cordial and generous compared with what Blenkinsop felt for MacAdam of MacAdam at this moment. Yet he was never more completely Blenkinsop of the Welch Bays than he was then. He did not show by so much as a flustered movement that he was suffering perhaps the sharpest disappointment of his life since he was passed over for a Brevet-Majority in favour of a brother officer who simply did not deserve it.

'Ah, good evening, MacAdam,' he said in a voice as calm as the Serpentine on a summer's morning. 'Let me hand over to you.'

Then he tipped the chauffeur of the hired car, and with a gallant wave of the hand that masked the chagrin gnawing at his heart, he turned back into the hotel and with steadfast step mounted the staircase to bury his disappointment in the solitude of the Macmillan room.

Let us leave him there to study the broadcast talk prepared for him by Major Hunter-Hunt and the united brains of the South-East Europe Section of M.Q. 99 (E). The epilogue of this day may be read in a report of his activities written out by Mackillop for P.

Tuesday, 25 November

Dear P:

I arrived here this morning and have spent a full and, I hope, fruitful day. I discovered almost immediately that your suspicions of a projected rising were well founded. Your suggestion that I should disguise myself as a Scottish Nationalist was of course admirable. Everything played into our hands straightway. Two elderly female enthusiasts called Macadam let the cat out of the bag within ten minutes. They are not in the confidence of the leaders, but I was able to extract from them the information I wanted to put me on to the leader. This is MacAdam of MacAdam, chief of the clan, and the owner of Drumroy Castle. I decided to see what I could find out there. I found out a good deal.

Drumroy Castle, which is about twenty miles from Glenmore, is an ancient place situated at the head of Loch Roy, a sea-loch winding in between mountains from the Atlantic. Some three miles seaward from the Castle a large steam yacht (not less than 800 ton) is lying at anchor. She was flying neither ensign nor burgee, which is in itself suspicious. I discovered through a shepherd with whom I was able to get a quiet talk that she is a foreigner and arrived here about a week ago. Later on some of the crew came ashore and I was able to overhear their talk. Russians! Now I had already fixed on a fellow staying in the Hydro as a possible Moscow agent, and this discovery made me feel pretty sure I was on the right track.

My next job was to try and get into the Castle. This turned out to be quite easy, thanks to the kilt, and I found the place full of various fellows in kilts, but also a lot of fellows in foreign uniforms, Russians also, though the uniform was unfamiliar. I caught a snatch of conversation here and there in French, and the whole talk was of the day when the attempt would be made. I could not however ascertain how near this is or where the actual attempt will be made. But I hope to manage this tomorrow, of which more presently. Well, to cut my story short, I got back to the Hydro about six just in time to see 'Hudson', that's the suspected Moscow agent, alight from one car and hand over a so-called 'Señora Miranda' to the care of MacAdam who drove off with her in another car. 'Hudson' then went up to his room, and I heard him walking up and down in an agitated way and talking to himself. He seemed to be learning some kind of proclamation.

I made careful inquiries about him in the hotel and discovered (I) that his name is not 'Hudson'. This I learnt from a man in the hotel called Lobbins who knows the Hudson firm well. I ought to have explained that he is supposed to be a banana importer. It looks to me as if under the cover of bananas a lot of dirty work is going on. (II) That 'Hudson' had a confidential meeting with a 'hiker' shortly before the meeting with MacAdam. Now it is noteworthy that this morning this 'hiker' left the train at the station before Glenmore, and apparently arrived here on foot. I'm inclined to think that he is one of the volunteers of whom I gather there are a number lurking in the neighbourhood. (III) That 'Hudson' has been in close confabulation late at night with this 'Señora Miranda' who is a handsome little woman, obviously foreign, but certainly not a Spaniard from the Canary Islands as she pretends, and only interested in bananas as a means of propaganda and gun-running. (IV) That 'Hudson' has arranged a meeting with MacAdam and two other leaders of the rising in the Turkish bath tomorrow morning. I have bribed the shampooer to let me take his place. It was a difficult matter at first. He seemed to be afraid of his professional reputation, so I told him I had been in the Sultan's own Turkish bath and his favourite masseur. After this, with a tenner to help, he made no further opposition. Much will depend on the meeting in the Turkish bath, and after that is over I shall hope to be in a position to send you some more positive information.

What a chance Canonbury has missed over this business! It will be a bold man who says to him after this 'have a banana!'

Yours,
Mac

Chapter 17

THE TURKISH BATH

ON Wednesday morning Blenkinsop with a critical day before him was up betimes and watching with pleasure the departure of the inquisitive Mr Lobbins by the green hotel omnibus. He had grown extremely tired of suspicious questions about his connection with the fruit trade. Nor were the other hotel guests sorry to see the last of Mr Lobbins by the green hotel omnibus. Those who were not taking the cure themselves had no interest in the progress his inside was making under the influence of St Ninian's water and those who were taking the cure wanted to talk about their own insides, for all valetudinarians are egotists and only listen to the tale of other people's symptoms in order to gain an opportunity to discuss their own. And Mr Lobbins himself after Mr Woodburn's record-breaking advance to eight glasses a day could no longer sustain the position he had won as the most conspicuous example of St Ninian's healing influence. His name was not even writ in water. He observed a little bitterly at dinner on the night before he left the Hydro that he doubted if in the long run Glenmore could hold its own with Harrogate or Buxton.

By returning to his business in Covent Garden Mr Lobbins did not have the gratification of seeing the effect of the letter of warning he had written to his friend Hudson. Mr Lobbins was nearer to London by a couple of hours seated in the Diurnal Scot when Hudson and his wife in the Nocturnal Scot were within half an hour of Glenmore. Busybodies who make trouble by writing letters do not deserve to enjoy the spectacle of the misery they cause, and few will regret that Mr Lobbins himself was not present in the siesta-lounge when the usually immobile countenance of Blenkinsop, who was just thinking it would soon be time to go down to the Turkish bath and see that all was in order for the important conference, showed every sign of acute mental distress as the green omnibus reached the hotel on the return journey from the station and from it there alighted to the sound of the piper's welcome Mr and Mrs Hudson.

Blenkinsop had been overtaken by one of those emergencies which are never far away in the life of a Secret Service officer. Forced by the necessity to do some rapid thinking he did not flinch from what for a man of his cautious temperament was an ordeal. It was vital to see Hudson alone, and that immediately. He could not risk being greeted by him as Blenkinsop in front of various members of the hotel staff. He could not risk Hudson's making inquiries when he saw his own address and the more important half of his own name in the visitors' book. Blenkinsop went across to a table and wrote the following note:

Dear Hudson:

Will you come along at once with the bearer of this. I must see you urgently before you register. And do not mention my name to the waiter or say anything to your wife. This is very important.

Yours,

A. B.

The waiter, on hearing the bell from the siesta-lounge, had tried to anticipate intelligently the usual requests from there at this time of the day by arriving with a large beaker of St Ninian's water, which he set down on a small table at Blenkinsop's elbow.

'Your water, sir,' said the waiter tenderly. 'Will you sip it over here, sir, or shall I set it for you nearer the sunlight?'

'I want you to take this note and hand it to the gentleman who has just arrived in the hotel bus. Bring him straight in to me here as quickly as possible,' said Blenkinsop.

'Very good, sir. What name, sir?'

'His name doesn't matter. He's the only gentleman that arrived in the bus just now.'

'And your water, sir?' the waiter inquired.

'Never mind about water. Do what I ask, please at once. It's extremely urgent and important.'

Presently he came back with a rather bewildered-looking

Hudson and followed to Blenkinsop's disgust by the Misses Macadam.

'Why, hullo, Major, who'd have thought of running into you up here,' Hudson exclaimed with an imbecile absence of comprehension.

Blenkinsop made an appalling grimace which was intended to check Hudson's tongue, but which was mistaken by the waiter for the effect of St Ninian's water.

'Shall I get you some peppermint, sir?' he asked solicitously.

'Peppermint? What the devil should I want peppermint for?' Blenkinsop snapped irritably.

'It takes away the taste quicker than anything else, sir.'

'Go away at once,' Blenkinsop commanded. 'If you bring me any more of that water I'll make you drink it yourself.'

The waiter did not stop to be warned twice.

'I'm sorry to separate you from Mrs Hudson like this,' said Blenkinsop in a low voice to the real banana importer who not knowing anything about St Ninian's water was beginning to fear for his friend's reason.

'That's all right, Major.'

'Don't call me "Major".' Blenkinsop hissed. His next words were measured. 'Your coming up here has created what in Montmartre – what in Montmartre I say – is called a contre-temps.'

Hudson put on the gravity with which one hopes to lull a madman into supposing that he is being taken seriously.

'What's up, old man?' he asked. 'You look regularly rattled.'

Blenkinsop of the Welch Bays pulled himself together at this.

'The fact is, Hudson,' he said, 'that I – ah – found it necessary to add – yes, to add a touch of – ah – realism to the banana business by – ah – registering in this hotel under your name – at least under your surname and my own first name.'

'Oh, you did? So you were the fellow Lobbins warned me about. Well, I'm jiggered! But what for? Surely he wasn't right in thinking you were trying on the confidence trick?'

'Of course not,' said Blenkinsop crossly. 'That man Lobbins was an ass. He spent his time drinking water and asking me questions about the whole vegetable system of the world. His brain was addled by this water, which I may warn you is addled itself. I had a little affair of – ah – well, you know the sort of little affairs you have yourself? We've discussed this topic before.'

'That's all right, old man. I'm no spoil sport. But I think you might have left my name out of it. You only saw my old lady in one of her very pleasant moods. You don't realize what she can be like. I've been away from home myself for a week, and if she finds my name and address written down in the visitors' book here she'll never believe me again. As a matter of fact, I thought it would be a good game to come up here incog., so as to catch out this fellow who was taking my name. So I told the wife we'd stay here as Mr and Mrs Yorke Lankester. She was quite tickled by the notion, but if she finds that I've been here already under my own name Trouble will be the next name I shall go under.'

Blenkinsop on hearing that Hudson himself had himself anticipated exactly what he was going to suggest he should do warmed towards him.

'Well, if you're here as Yorke Lankester,' he said, 'that will make it perfectly all right.'

'For you perhaps,' Hudson retorted, with a hint of indignation in his voice. 'But what about me?'

'You told your wife, didn't you, that you were in the Secret Service?'

'Yes.'

'And that I was the head of the Secret Service?'

'Yes.'

'Then what's your difficulty, Lankester? You can tell Mrs Hudson that I am up here on a delicate investigation, and that you've come up to help me. As a matter of fact I have to go down to London tomorrow, and you can tell her it's on business connected with the Secret Service.'

'I'm going back to London myself tomorrow,' said Hudson. 'My new book is coming out this week and I want to be in town so as to sign a few copies for friends and enjoy the whole business generally. I was going to leave the wife up here. She wants a change of air. She's looking a bit under the weather.'

Blenkinsop was not too well pleased by this news. He had asked Enid to call upon the Hudsons, and if she found Hudson at home and Mrs Hudson away it was not going to add to the amenities of his return to Jerbury Chambers or help him to explain why he had not sent her a single letter during his absence. However, his domestic difficulties must not be allowed to assume too great an importance. Things might have been worse. Hudson's arrival had not yet compromised his secret mission.

'We'll go down to London together,' he suggested. 'But if I were you, Lankester, I shouldn't let your wife stay up here too long. This St Ninian's water they all drink here is very weakening to the system. And look here, you'd better make the most of this fine day. It's the first we've had since I arrived. If I were you I should drive Mrs Hudson over to Fort Wade. The scenery is really very fine. Oh, and by the way, you see those two old women over there?'

'The ones in tartan tweed?'

'Yes,' Blenkinsop replied with a shudder. 'They're the most objectionable women I ever came across. Don't encourage them. If you do, they'll follow you about everywhere, especially if they hear you're a novelist. And there's a horrible bore from Nigeria called Woodburn. I should avoid him if I were you. But look here, Mrs Lankester will be waiting to know where her room is. I'll see you later. And be sure you impress on your wife to remember that up here I'm Mr A. Hudson. It ought to be easy for you both to remember as it's your own name. And don't let her call me "Major". Remember that all this mystery is going to be very helpful when you go to Montmartre again on secret service.'

Hudson went off to find his wife. He had been a little inclined to resent Blenkinsop's appropriation of his name on top of appropriating his business; but on thinking it over he realized that all this pretended secret business was undoubtedly going to strengthen his position in the eyes of his wife. As he passed the Misses Macadam he noticed they were eyeing him with an obviously intense curiosity. It would be rather a lark to pull their legs if they gave him an opportunity and make them think he really was a secret-service man.

'There's some devilry going on,' Miss Caroline observed to her sister when Hudson passed out of the siesta-lounge. 'I wonder where Mr Mackillop is. I think we ought to warn him.'

'We'd better find out who that man is,' Miss Flora suggested. They were lucky enough to catch Mackillop just as he was going down to the Turkish bath.

'Oh, Mr Mackillop,' said Miss Flora, 'there's a man just arrived in the hotel, and he and that horrible Hudson whom he called "Major" have been sitting in a corner of the lounge and plotting together.'

'Well, you try to shadow them,' said Mackillop. 'I'm off now to see that your friend Mr MacAdam doesn't come to any harm in the Turkish bath.'

'Bravo! Bravo!' exclaimed Miss Caroline. For this resolve she was ready to forgive his putting a 'Mr' in front of MacAdam and ready to perceive through the tartar of Broughty Ferry the teeth of the true Highlandman.

Sergeant-Instructor Flack after a night of unbroken sleep passed by to report to Blenkinsop in the siesta-lounge.

'Any orders, sir?'

'Yes,' said Blenkinsop. 'I want you to stop two women from following me about. I've got an important appointment in the Turkish bath, and I do not want them to see who my visitors are.'

'Very good, sir. What was your idea of the way I ought to proceed, sir?'

Blenkinsop pondered for a moment or two.

'Go and get into conversation with them. They're probably out in the hall now. They're dressed in tartan and have a white West Highland terrier with them. Tell them your mother was a Macadam.'

'Did you say macadam, sir?'

'Yes.'

'What roads are made of, sir?'

'Yes. When you tell them this they may begin to talk to you

in a peculiar language. Simply say that you have no Gaelic, but
you would very much like to.'

'Like to have garlic, sir?' asked Sergeant Flack nervously.
'But suppose they offer me some, sir. Somebody played rather a
nasty practical joke on me with some water, sir, last night, and
it's made me feel a bit ... well, I don't quite know how to say
what I do mean, sir ... but if I had to eat garlic on top of that
water ...'

'Eat garlic? Who's asking you to eat garlic? Gaelic is a
language.'

'Oh, I beg pardon, sir. We were at cross purposes, as they
say.'

'I don't think you understood in the least what I want you to
do,' said Blenkinsop severely.

'No, sir, I don't think I am quite clear yet, sir.'

'I want you to pretend to these two women that your
mother was Scotch, and then they'll be interested.'

'Oh, I see, sir. I didn't get you at first. I see. Macadam is a
Scotch name?'

'Of course it is. It's like Mackintosh. There are people called
Mackintosh.'

'Are there really, sir? Well, sir, I'm glad I haven't got to tell
'em my mother was a Mackintosh, because I might have
smiled, sir, thinking what my poor old mother would have said
if anyone had up and called her a Mackintosh. I reckon he'd
have had the sharp end of her umbrella where he didn't expect
it.'

'Do you mind listening to my instructions and concentrating
on what you have to do?' said Blenkinsop.

'Yes, sir. I beg pardon, sir.'

'The name of these two women is Macadam.'

'Yes, sir. I've got that, sir.'

'And you must ask them all about the Macadams. One of
them put a shoe in somebody's mouth a good many years ago.
There's a monument to it. You can ask them about that. Try to
get them to take you to it. Say you heard the story from your
mother when you were little.'

'Yes, sir.'

'And there's a well here, which they're very interested in. Ask them about that. Say you want to drink at it and wish.'

'Yes, sir.'

'You'll see the way to work it when you start talking to them. The great thing is to keep them out of the way from about half past eleven onwards. I don't want them to see my visitors arrive.'

'I understand, sir.'

'And remember, if they ask you anything about me, that I am up here buying bananas.'

'Yes, sir. And I'm up here taking a rest from selling them?'

'That's right. And you're half Scotch. I wish now Colonel N had insisted on your wearing that kilt.'

'Well, sir, it's not for me to contradict you sir. But it wouldn't have done, sir. It wouldn't really. Don't worry, sir. I shall carry on much better in these shorts. That is if they don't shrink any more. Minus fours, they ought to be called, sir. I think they dried 'em a bit too fast last night, sir. Still, it's not as if I was going to show these ladies how to touch the toes with the fingers, keeping the knees straight, and inclining the top half of the body in a rigid position from the waist upwards. I don't think they'd stand that, sir.'

'That's enough, Smith. I don't want to spend the rest of the morning listening to your anecdotes,' said Blenkinsop sternly.

'No, sir. Nothing further, sir?'

'Nothing.'

Ten minutes later Blenkinsop looking out from the windows of the lounge noted with satisfaction that the Misses Macadam were leading Flack in the direction of St Ninian's Well, and that Fingal was leaping up to lick his bare knees with every appearance of friendliness. He moved cautiously in the direction of the Turkish bath.

Satisfied that nobody had seen him pass through the portico, Blenkinsop was less satisfied when across the cooling-room came pattering on bare feet not the sleek bald-headed shampooer with whom he had arranged to reserve the bath this morning, but a red-haired freckled man whose florid weather-beaten countenance was netted with fine wrinkles and whose chest was tattooed like a willow-pattern dish.

Blenkinsop frowned. He had tipped the shampooer a pound to keep the bath clear of guests this morning, and here was an outsider already, undressed, too, and apparently about to spend the rest of the morning here. He struck a bell upon one of the Oriental tables.

'Bunting is not here this morning, sir,' said the tattooed stranger, speaking with the kindly accent of Dundee, the result of trying to go one better than Broughty Ferry. 'I'm taking his place. Bunting told me you were expecting company for your bath.'

Blenkinsop had had sufficient experience in secret-service work by now to suspect everybody. He cast a penetrating glance at the alleged substitute.

'Have I seen you before?' he asked sharply.

'I couldn't well say, sir. I work here with mud, peat, and seaweed baths, sir, and I don't think I've had the pleasure of packing you so far. Do you ever go to the Hammam, sir, in Jerbury Street?'

'I have been there.'

'I used to work there as an assistant-shampooer. Perhaps I've had the pleasure of massaging you there?'

'But you're a Scotchman, aren't you?'

'From Dundee. Keiler is my name. I've worked a good deal, though, out in the East.'

Blenkinsop decided that his suspicions were groundless.

'Will you undress right away, sir?' he was being asked.

'Yes.'

This answer was not made on the spur of the moment. Blenkinsop had carefully considered his procedure beforehand. The ideal arrangement from the point of view of secrecy would have been for him to be discovered by accident already perspiring profusely in the very hot room. In his anxiety to keep out strangers he had had to take the risk of letting Bunting the shampooer know that he was expecting friends in the bath. At the same time he could not afford to take the risk of meeting King Johannis for the first time when fully dressed.

It would be a physical impossibility to avoid some suggestion of the deference due to royalty. It might amount to no more than standing back respectfully while the King preceded them into the very hot room, but that might be enough to suggest to the shampooer the presence of somebody of exalted rank and so arouse his curiosity. The very hot room reduced everybody temporarily to an equality. Etiquette and perspiration were incompatible.

Blenkinsop had been seated in the outer sudatorium for over an hour when above the solemn heat of the Turkish bath the sound of voices was heard at last. He moved into the inner sudatorium and sank hurriedly into a deck-chair before the heat knocked him prone. The perspiration which in the outer sudatorium had trickled down him in rills now began to pour as over the seared precipices of noble Ben Buidhe pour the cataracts of winter. He hoped the others would not be long in coming in now. The tax upon his powers of endurance was tremendous. He clenched his teeth. 'I must not give way,' he muttered. A new spring had gushed forth blindingly above his left eyelid. The noise of the perspiration pouring down in a steady stream from his chin on to his middle-age spread was audible in the sweltering silence. A torrent which had started at the back of his neck had been dammed where his back was pressed back against the canvas of the chair and was now racing over his shoulders like a burst reservoir. His legs looked like a stubble field in a heavy September dew. Just as Blenkinsop had decided that not even for secrecy could he stand it any longer, three forms filled the arch between the outer and the inner sudatoriums.

'My god,' a voice exclaimed, 'this is bloody hot, MacAdam.'

'Himmel!' ejaculated most inappropriately another voice.

Blenkinsop staggered to his feet, nearly slipped in the pool that surrounded his chair, and through his sodden moustache advised the newcomers to sit down at once.

'It's worse when you stand up,' Blenkinsop gasped as he sank back into his deck-chair.

'But look here,' said the King in the same perfect English as that exclamation he had uttered on first being struck in the archway by the heat of the inner sudatorium. 'Look here, I don't think we can discuss anything in this.' He stopped abruptly. Two streams of perspiration gushing from his cheeks had met in the luxuriant growth of his fair moustache and were striking his underlip with such force that he had to shut his mouth.

Blenkinsop would have proposed a retreat to the outer sudatorium if he had not caught sight of Keiler the substitute shampooer hanging about the entrance.

'I will not detain you in here, sir,' said Blenkinsop to the King, 'while I read the whole of my talk.'

'My god, no,' gasped His Majesty.

'No, it vass too hot,' muttered the international financier, a swarthy shrivelled man with a beaky nose and a head as bald as a vulture's.

MacAdam said nothing; but a kind of whistling sound escaped from his lips, like the noise of a boiling lobster as it begins to turn to the colour he was now turning.

Blenkinsop searched in his towel for the draft of the talk, the sheets of which at once curled over unreadably.

'Hurry up, for god's sake,' gasped the King.

'Make quicks, if you please,' urged Heisswasser, from the centre of whose bald crown a fountain of perspiration was beginning to play.

Blenkinsop while he fumbled with the crackling pages of his typescript had enough of his wits about him to study the international financier narrowly for signs of assumed features. If that nose was false the next gushet of perspiration must carry it away. It remained. It was not Katzenschlosser, he decided.

'Here is the proposed message, sir,' Blenkinsop read.

'Finally I would say to the people of Mendacia that there is no country to which British commercial enterprise may look with greater confidence in the near future, especially if the happy event planned for (whatever date you choose, sir) should receive the welcome it deserves from the people of Mendacia.

'Nothing remains now but to add the date of Your Majesty's arrival.'

234

'If I don't get out of here at once,' said the King, 'I shan't arrive anywhere.'

With this he rose from the deck-chair and walked towards the outer sudatorium where he collapsed into another chair. He was followed by Heisswasser and Blenkinsop. Behind them in the inner sudatorium there was an explosive noise.

'My god,' the King exclaimed, 'MacAdam has burst.'

Blenkinsop might not love his rival; but he was not the man to let that rival stew to death in a sudatorium without making an effort to save him, and without hesitation he fought his way back into that inferno to see the Highland chieftain caught in the intricacy of a folding deck-chair, the canvas of which had split when he had tried to raise himself and caused him to fall through to the concrete floor. He put out a hand to help Mac-Adam to his feet; but the streaming perspiration on their two hands made it impossible to obtain the grip necessary to elevate such a bulky man as MacAdam.

'Call the shampooer,' gasped the chieftain.

'Can't you turn over?' Blenkinsop asked.

'How the devil can I turn over? Can't you see I'm wedged in this blasted chair?'

Fortunately for Blenkinsop, whose own knees were beginning to sag, the chair at that moment released MacAdam. He made a final effort, rose to his feet, and tottered into the outer sudatorium.

'And this is hot enough,' said the King. 'Let's hurry up and settle our business. Read the message again, please, Mr Hudson. I couldn't follow what you said in there.'

Blenkinsop looked nervously towards the marble slab on which the supreme rites of the Turkish bath were performed. He seemed to fancy that Keiler the substitute shampooer was trying to listen. However, he could not bring himself flatly to disobey a king, and he mumbled off the message again.

'I no hear,' said Heisswasser.

'Give it to me,' said the King.

Blenkinsop, a foreboding of disaster clutching at his heart, handed across the crackling typescript stained with sweat, whereupon the King read out the message as if he were delivering a proclamation to his people.

'Dat vass goot,' Heisswasser grunted. 'I think we most say fifteen tays after dat message can be given.'

'Say the fifteenth of December,' the King added. 'That will give us time to hear what the effect was on the country before we finally commit ourselves. Do you agree, MacAdam?'

'I agree, sir.'

'Because the less bloodshed the better,' said the King. 'And we may even reasonably hope that the populace will welcome us with such enthusiasm that there will be no bloodshed at all. Well, Mr Hudson, I am sure that all loyalists feel under a special debt of gratitude to you. I shall hope to give practical expression to that gratitude and mark my personal sense of obligation in due course. Madame Tekta has spoken most warmly of your devotion. I can only regret that circumstances should have made it imprudent for you to visit Drumroy. By the way I hope your wireless will be working tomorrow night, MacAdam.'

'They've been overhauling it today, sir,' said the chieftain. 'But reception in the Highlands is often very poor.'

'Oh well, the main thing is the reception at the other end,' said the King. 'Are you travelling down to London tonight, Mr Hudson?'

'No, sir. I'm leaving by the train tomorrow morning.'

'Isn't that cutting it rather fine?'

'I shall get to the B.B.C. by nine, sir. That gives me three-quarters of an hour's grace.'

'Oh well, you know best, but it will be a blow to our hopes if you do not get that message over the air. All our adherents are anxiously waiting for the signal. Well, MacAdam,' he went on, turning to his host, 'I don't know what you feel, but I feel that I've had enough of this heat.'

'Quite enough, sir. I think the shampooer is waiting if you're ready.'

The King rose and proceeded to the marble slab. If Blenkinsop had not been so much worried by the incautious tones in which the preceding conversation had been held and if he had read Prescott's *Conquest of Mexico*, he might have compared the advance of King Johannis to be lathered and kneaded and rubbed upon that marble slab to the advance of Montezuma to the stone of sacrifice. He was indeed a regal figure as girdled with a towel and glistening with perspiration he trod majestically the particoloured tiles of the shampooing hall.

'A splendid figure of a man, eh, Hudson?' MacAdam observed. 'If ever a king deserved his kingdom he does.'

'Ach, he vass very goot,' Heisswasser agreed in guttural enthusiasm.

'One begins to understand the devotion of our ancestors to the Stuarts,' said MacAdam.

When Mackillop saw the King place himself upon the marble slab he tried to remember what was the first thing a shampooer did. It was some years since he had had a Turkish bath. There was a good deal of kneading, as he remembered, and a good deal of soaping, as he remembered, and a good deal of rubbing, and, oh, yes!

'Turn over, please,' he said.

The King turned over, and Mackillop lifting the towel administered a tremendous slap to the royal behind.

'Good god,' exclaimed His Majesty, flinging himself over and sitting up on the marble slab. 'What the hell are you doing?'

'It's part of the Turkish bath,' Mackillop explained.

He did not know of course that it was a king he was handling in this amateurish way. He thought it was the Duke of Motherwell, one of the leaders of Scottish Nationalism.

'It's not part of any Turkish bath I ever took,' said the King angrily.

MacAdam, Blenkinsop, and Heisswasser on hearing His Majesty cry out had hurried to his rescue.

'Do you know who you have the honour of attending, you fellow?' MacAdam bellowed in wrath.

Blenkinsop in an agony that MacAdam would give away the secret of the King's identity prodded the chieftain so viciously in the ribs that weakened by the sudatorium he overbalanced on the slippery tiles and fell backwards into the plunge bath. As he rose to the surface spluttering and shouting, Blenkinsop, with perhaps an added verve for the memory of that lost motor drive with Renata yesterday evening, leapt into the plunge bath and dragged MacAdam beneath the cold water a second time.

'For heaven's sake be careful,' he spluttered as they both came to the surface. 'Don't you realize the importance of keeping Mr Johnson's identity a secret?'

'But we can't let that shampooer smack him like that again. Damn it, Hudson, he's my guest. It violates the sacred law of Highland hospitality.'

'Well, protest against your guest being treated like that,' Blenkinsop urged. 'But do be cautious.'

However, as MacAdam and Blenkinsop came up the ladder of the plunge bath they saw that the future of the King had been taken out of the hands of the shampooer by Bunting, who in his discreet voice was lecturing the substitute.

'I'm surprised at you,' he was saying. 'I understood you were an experienced shampooer.'

'So I am,' the substitute argued shamelessly. 'The late Sultan of Turkey preferred me to attend him to anybody.'

'Well, we don't like Turkish manners up here,' said Bunting. Then he turned to the King. 'I'm exceedingly sorry, sir, you should have been incommoded like this. Exceedingly sorry, sir. Kindly lie on your back. Is that quite comfortable? Thank you, sir. Say if I am rubbing you too hard, please. The weather has been unpleasantly muggy and wet lately, sir, has it not?'

Bunting kneaded and rubbed and lathered the King, and then at the end he administered the final smack; but though it rang out like a pistol shot the King did not leap in the air, for he had not felt it.

'That,' said Bunting sternly to his substitute, 'is what you were trying to do, I suppose. But it can't be learnt in a jiffy. Now, sir, I'm ready for the next gentleman. The plunge is seven foot at the deep end, sir.'

When after submitting to the ministrations of Bunting Blenkinsop was lying on the couch in the cooling-room and thinking over the incidents of this morning, he began in spite of the pleasant langour that was upon him to ask himself nervously if that substitute shampooer had been a republican agent. Had N been right in suspecting the sex of the Misses Macadam? Was one of them a man? Or both? They might be. There was nothing feminine about such women when contemplated in cool detachment. But no, Flack would not have been silly enough to let either of them escape and gain the Turkish bath in the disguise of a shampooer without warning him. If this fellow Keiler was a republican agent he must be a new one. But if he was a republican agent he must have overheard a good deal of that indiscreet conversation. Blenkinsop rang the bell beside the couch.

Bunting appeared through the curtains that veiled the languor of the bather. He was wrapped in a gown of towelling.

'Did you ring, sir?'

'Yes, I want to know exactly who that man was who slapped one of my friends in that outrageous way.'

Bunting did some thinking as rapid as Blenkinsop's own.

'Well, sir, I'm really exceedingly upset about what happened. This shampooer was handed over to me as competent, and I made the mistake of not testing him out as I should have done. I hope you will overlook the matter, sir. He's quite a decent fellow really, and it might get me the sack and him too if the management was to hear what happened.'

'You know this man well?' Blenkinsop pressed.

'Yes and no, sir. He's employed in another part of the hotel. In those new-fangled baths, sir. Would you like a cup of Turkish coffee, sir?'

'No, thank you,' said Blenkinsop curtly. 'Well, I'll make up my mind later whether I will complain or not to the management.'

'Yes, sir, thank you. I hope I may be allowed to very respectfully and earnestly beg that you won't, sir. It's the first time since this Turkish bath was opened that any unpleasantness has occurred, and I really am exceedingly sorry, sir.'

The mortified Bunting retired obsequiously.

Blenkinsop was by no means content with his explanation; but he decided that a complaint to the management might only make bad worse. Still, it was exasperating to think that all his careful provision for secrecy might have been to no purpose. Partly, it had been the fault of the conspirators. If they had remained in the very hot room and talked matters out there, nothing would have been overheard. Blenkinsop began to drowse off. The strain of the morning had been intense. Presently he was sound asleep.

It was two o'clock when he woke up to find that the others had already left the hotel.

'I didn't know whether you wanted to be called for lunch, sir,' said Bunting. 'I thought you might like a little tasty something down here, before you dressed.'

'I'll have a chop,' said Blenkinsop.

'And anything to drink with it?'

'Half a bottle of champagne. Where's the wine list?'

The shampooer pattered off cheerfully. He could not believe that a client would report him to the management on top of half a bottle of champagne.

When Blenkinsop regained the upper air from the Turkish bath the first person he saw was Sergeant-Instructor Flack in his shirt sitting on one of the Gothic settles in the hall.

'Oh, there you are, Smith. Are you enjoying your holiday? Come along into the library and tell me how you spent your morning.'

'I can't sir.'

'You can't? Why not?'

'Well, sir, if you'd very kindly sit down for a minute beside me on this seat so as I don't have to speak too loud I could tell you what it is, sir.'

'But why can't you get up?'

'Well, sir, that's why I want you to sit down.'

Blenkinsop frowning did as the Sergeant-Instructor requested.

'It's my shorts, sir,' Flack muttered hollowly. 'They've given out. They were a bit tightified yesterday, but this morning it was more like putting on a pair of kid gloves than breeches. It must have been drying 'em so fast, sir.'

'But you told me you could manage all right,' said Blenkinsop.

'So I could have, sir, if it hadn't been for that blessed well.

Following your instructions, sir, I told those two old ladies my mother was a Macadam, and it seemed to act like a regular charm. They couldn't have been more pleasant, sir. And then I asked about this St Ninian's Well, sir, and said according to your instructions I wanted to wish, and they were delighted, sir. They went skipping off with me like a couple of happy kids, "You mustn't tell your wish, Mr Smith," one of them said. And I said, "What do *you* think? Not half, I won't." I tell you, sir, it was really a treat to be out with 'em, and it went quite against my feelings to think they were a couple of spies. When we came to the well, the older of 'em says, "Now, Mr Smith, if you want to drink properly you've got to lean over head downwards and wish as you lean. My sister and me will hang on to your legs," she says, "so as you don't fall in." So I leant over, sir, and one old dear got hold of one leg and the other old dear grabbed the other. It was silly of me, but I'd got sort of worked up over this wishing and never gave another thought to these shorts of mine. Well, sir, not to detain you too long, they went off like a paper bag. They didn't split down the seam. No, sir. The whole seat came away with a rush. The old ladies let out a yell and left go of my legs, and down I went head foremost. It wasn't deep, sir. But oh, my gawd, sir – forgive the rough language – my gawd, sir, the taste of that water! And I must have swallowed a quart before I got myself right side round. The old ladies were hooking it back towards the hotel the same as if a bull was after them. I tucked the bit that had come out into my belt, but it only goes to show what a strain I put on those shorts, because it doesn't cover the half of what it should do. However, I tied my sports coat round my – me, I should say, and then I thought I'd better sit down here, sir, and wait for you. I didn't like to go up to my room and leave word for you to kindly come up there. I thought it might seem a bit peculiar. I'm sorry I haven't been able to carry out your full instructions, sir, but I didn't think the old ladies would try to get at you in the Turkish bath, judging by the way they hooked it when the seat of my shorts came out.'

'In other words,' said Blenkinsop, 'you want me to lend you a pair of trousers.'

'Well, sir, I wouldn't presume so far as that, only if I tele-graph to my missus to send me a pair I'll have to remain in my room until they arrive. That's quite all right, sir, as long as you don't want me to nip around for you.'

'You'd better be available,' said Blenkinsop. 'I'll let you have an extra pair of plus-fours I brought with me.'

'That's very kind of you, sir. I hope it's not putting you to too much inconvenience.'

'I don't wear two pairs of breeches at once,' said Blenkinsop. 'If you come upstairs with me I'll give them to you.'

Five minutes later Sergeant-Instructor Flack paraded in Blen-kinsop's room.

'They look all right,' said the owner of the plus-fours.

'And they feel ... well, sir, you wouldn't believe how comfortable the lower part of my back does feel. Like a kid at the beginning of the holidays. And I borrowed a nice pair of braces from one of the waiters. Any orders, sir? I could go anywhere in these plus-fours.'

'Tomorrow morning I am going down to London and ar-riving back here on Friday morning.'

'Very good, sir.'

'You will report to me on the movements of the female agents, and you will make discreet inquiries about one of the bathing attendants here called Keiler. The best thing you can do is to go and have a mud bath.'

'What another, sir? But what about your plus-fours?'

'You don't take a mud bath in your clothes. It's part of the cure in this Hydro. You sit in hot mud up to your chin.'

'In hot mud up to my chin, sir? Will I be allowed to scrape myself afterwards?'

'Keiler will do that. That's the way you'll establish contact with him. I have reason to suspect he may be a foreign agent. He's a red-haired man with freckles. He was in the Turkish bath this morning.'

'Why, sir, I saw a man answering to that description go along to the Turkish bath in a kilt just before I reported to you this morning.'

'That wasn't a kilt. That was a Turkish towel.'

'I beg pardon, sir, for contradicting you, but this was no towel. He wouldn't have dared to stop and talk to those two old ladies in a towel.'

'Did this man talk to those two Macadam women?'

'Yes, sir.'

'Why on earth didn't you report that to me?' Blenkinsop asked angrily.

'Well, sir. I didn't pay much attention to it.'

'Katzenschlosser!'

'I hope you haven't caught cold after your bath, sir.'

'What a fool I am!'

'Never mind, sir. I'll nip downstairs and see if I can get you some ammoniated quinine.'

'Katzenschlosser, of course. That's why his face was familiar. Katzenschlosser! And I thought Heisswasser might be Katzenschlosser.'

'That's right, sir, try and sneeze it out of the system. 'It's the best way with a cold that's just beginning.'

'Listen to me, Sergeant, I mean Smith. Never mind about shadowing the two old ladies. You must shadow this man in a kilt. He's the most dangerous foreign agent in the world.'

'Good heavens, sir!'

'It's vital that he shouldn't follow me to London tomorrow. But curse it, he knows I'm going now. Look here, you must stop him at all costs.'

'Why not push him into this here mud bath, sir?'

'He's not a bathing attendant. That's merely a disguise. Wait a minute. I must think what's the best thing to do.'

'Yes, sir. I'll keep quiet while you think.'

Blenkinsop paced the floor of the Macmillan room in an attempt to find a way of outwitting the world's ablest agent.

'Eureka!' he cried after five minutes of white-hot thinking.

'I'm doing what, sir?'

'You will get into touch with the man who calls himself Keiler and offer to betray to him for a sum of money the plans of a Sinn Fein rebellion in Scotland. You can tell him that arrangements are being made to rouse the country under the pretence of a talk about Mendacia at the B.B.C. Do you follow me?'

'Not quite so fast as I should like, sir.'

'He must be made to believe that whenever Mendacia is mentioned it means Scotland. We were talking about Mendacia this morning in the Turkish bath.'

'It sounds a bit complicated to me, sir. But I'll do my best.'

'You must tell him that the gentleman he slapped this morning in the Turkish bath is the leader and that MacAdam ...'

'Was my mother's name before she married my dad,' Flack put in quickly. 'I've got that as clear as gin.'

'No, no, MacAdam is the chief ... look here, I'll get this all down on paper.'

'Yes, sir. Perhaps that would be more satisfactory.'

That evening after dinner – a dinner which Blenkinsop had hoped to partake of with Renata, but which in the end he ate with Mr and Mrs Hudson, owing to Renata's failure to return from Drumroy – Sergeant-Instructor Flack found an opportunity to approach Mackillop who was resting in the library after an energetic afternoon and evening of reconnaissance in a car following upon his fruitful morning in the Turkish bath.

Shortly after one o'clock that night the door of Blenkinsop's bedroom opened stealthily, and the Sergeant slipped in.

'Well?' Blenkinsop asked in anxious whisper.

'To rights, sir,' said Flack.

'Not so bad. Are you sure nobody followed you up here?'

'No, sir, I observed all your precautions. I visited two lavatories on the floor below and the lavatory at the end of this floor, and waited five minutes in each. There's not a soul about, I listened at the two doors of the old ladies, and there was a noise like heavy furniture being moved about in both of them. I never heard such snoring.'

'But Keiler?'

'Mackillop alias Keiler went up to his room as soon as he left me, and he's there now.'

'How d'ye know?'

'Well, sir, I've been roaming around every floor of this hotel, and he must be there. Where else could he be?'

Blenkinsop shook his head doubtfully.

'It's all right, sir. It is really. If you'd seen the way he swallowed that story I told him, you wouldn't worry no more about him.'

'How d'ye know he swallowed it?'

'Well, sir, look at what he gave me.'

Sergeant-Instructor Flack put his hand into the pocket of Blenkinsop's plus-fours and pulled out four five-pound notes.

'If that story had have stuck in his throat, he wouldn't have given me these. Twenty pounds, sir. Will you take them over?'

'No, those are your perquisites.'

'Mine, sir? But what will Colonel N say?'

'I shall make that all right, Sergeant, I mean Smith. You've done your work splendidly.'

'Well, sir, I don't want you to think I had any difficulty. It was really too easy. But there's one thing I'm afraid I didn't manage. I offered to take him over to Drumroy tomorrow, and give him a good squint at the Shinners, and what d'ye think he said, sir? He said, "your information, Mr Smith, only confirms what I have discovered by personal observation". In fact he's had some of Drumroy already, sir. "I'm off to London tomorrow," he told me. I didn't like to try and persuade him to stay, for fear he'd get on to it that I was springing it on him.'

'Never mind,' said Blenkinsop. 'You've done your best.'

'Thank you, sir.'

'Did you tell him Mr Yorke Lankester was a more important rebel than I was?'

'Yes, sir, I said Mr Lankester was in the pay of the Irish Republican Army and the Bolsheviks both. I said his main hobby was starting rebellions and revolutions. Oh, I made him out a red-hot terror.'

'There's only one thing to do,' Blenkinsop proclaimed. 'We must drive to London tonight. We must get there in time to warn Colonel N, so that he can nab Katzenschlosser when he arrives at King's Cross.'

'Drive to London tonight, sir?'

'Yes. Go down cautiously and make arrangements with the night porter to have the hotel's most powerful car with two drivers to be round in half an hour's time. We'll get a fresh car and fresh drivers half-way. We ought to make London with two or three hours to spare.'

When Sergeant-Instructor Flack had retired Blenkinsop sat down at the table and wrote:

Glenmore, 1 a.m.
Thursday, 27 Nov.

Dear N:

I'm scrawling this hurried note of warning to let you know that Katzenschlosser arrived here yesterday morning cleverly disguised as a Scottish Nationalist and managed to get into the Turkish bath disguised as a shampooer, thus overhearing the conference between myself, Mr Johnson, and Mr Johnson's friend. Thanks to the clever work of Sergeant F we hope we have persuaded him that the Mendacian business is in reality a Sinn Fein rising up here. He is going to London by the train I intended to take. In order to give you time to get in touch with P and have him shadowed I am driving down in a few minutes by car and have instructed Sergeant F to get into touch with The Elms with this note. Sergeant F must of course not be used to identify Katzenschlosser, because K knows him. I cannot tell you in what disguise K will travel, but if P gets into touch with the railway people they should be able to let him know in which compartment K is travelling. There are not likely to be many passengers from Glenmore. Everything is in order for the broadcast. The message was approved. The day fixed is 15 December. Heisswasser was undoubtedly himself. There is of course much to tell you, but I have no time now to give you more than the absolute essentials. Unless I hear from you I shall proceed immediately back to Glenmore after finishing the broadcast.

Yours,

B

Blenkinsop hastily sealed up this letter, put it in an envelope, enclosed the envelope in another envelope, changed into an ordinary suit of clothes, threw a few things into a suitcase, and went cautiously downstairs. Here he scribbled another note for Hudson, telling him that he was called away urgently, but would be returning to London by the Nocturnal Scot on Thursday night.

A quarter of an hour later Blenkinsop and Flack were driving at a rapid pace along dark Glenmore, southward bound.

Chapter 18

INTELLIGENCE AT WORK

IT was just half past six when Blenkinsop and Flack reached London. Blenkinsop had contemplated going home for an hour or two and letting Enid have a glimpse of him. On reflection, he decided that a long conjugal argument at such a critical moment in the history of Europe would be more than he could stand, and he decided to remain quietly at his club until it was time to go to the B.B.C. They might want to get in touch with him from The Elms, and any kind of mysterious telephoning at the flat would only exacerbate Enid irremediably. Flack, who had been dispatched in search of N with orders to comb London for him if necessary, was lucky to find the Chief of the Secret Service still at The Elms.

The Sergeant-Instructor's legs wilted in those borrowed plus-fours under the gaze of Colonel N's horn-rimmed glasses.

'I thought I gave you definite instructions about your disguise, Sergeant,' said the Chief sternly. 'Hikers never wear plus-fours.'

'No, sir, but I wore out my shorts, sir,' Flack explained apologetically. 'And Major Blenkinsop kindly obliged me with the loan of these plus-fours.'

N grunted critically, and turned to study Blenkinsop's letter, the contents of which soon drove away any lingering inclination to worry about Sergeant Flack's leg-wear.

'Go and see if Major Hunter-Hunt has left yet. If he has, telephone at once to his private address and ask him to come round here at once,' N ordered.

But Hunter-Hunt was still in the throes of reconciling the reports of two agents, one of which asserted that unpleasant incidents on the Balmanian and Rugarian frontier had never been so numerous and so unpleasant, the other of which asserted that tranquillity on that frontier had never been so marked since the Treaty of Versailles. As both agents were very reliable the problem was not an easy one.

'Read that, H. H.,' said N, pushing Blenkinsop's letter across the table.

'My god, Chief,' goggled Hunter-Hunt when he had slowly sucked up Blenkinsop's information through the straw of his intellect. 'We must get on to Katzenschlosser at once.'

'Blenkinsop seems to have acted with remarkable resolution,' N observed.

'Remarkable!' Hunter-Hunt agreed.

'Well,' said N, taking the receiver from his telephone, 'it's up to us to make the most of such resolution.' He spoke gravely into the receiver. 'Put me through to Number Two. Hullo! Hullo! Is that Number Two? Is P still there? Put me through to him at once. This is N speaking personally ... hullo! hullo! Is that you, P? This is N. Look here, we have positive information that Katzenschlosser ... what? Kat-zen-schlosser ... I'm not coughing into the receiver. Katzenschlosser, the American S.S. man ... Of course you've got him on your files ... Well, can't you get hold of one of your people who does know something about him?'

N put his hand over the receiver.

'They really are the most extraordinary people at Number Two,' he said to Hunter-Hunt. 'Poor old P, apparently quite unaware that Katzenschlosser is the most important foreign agent on either side of the Atlantic. Never heard of him!' Hunter-Hunt clicked his tongue in despair. 'P's all right within the rather narrow sphere in which he works,' N continued. 'But put him on to anything a little off the beaten track of routine, and he's ... hullo! hullo! You didn't hear the name before? Well, I said it as clearly as I could. Yes, Katzenschlosser. You know who I mean now? Good! Well, I've just had definite information that he's in the train travelling down from Glenmore and should reach King's Cross – I think it is eight-thirty, but you can check that ... What's he been doing up there? ... I'm afraid I can't tell you. What we want to know is what he's going to do next ... Yes, I realize that's your pigeon. That's why I rang you up. I thought you could send a man to King's Cross and have him followed ... No, I can't. I say I *can't* give you a reliable description ... What? ... well, because the man is a master of disguise ... no, we don't know what name he's travelling under ... we have at least ...' N put his hand over the mouthpiece and turned to Hunter-Hunt.

'How many aliases have we for Katzenschlosser, H. H.?'

'I couldn't say right off, Chief, but certainly over fifty.'

N turned back to the telephone:

'We have well over fifty aliases recorded against him ... quite, quite ... no use at all to pay too much attention to his name ... look here, P, the point is that there aren't likely to be many passengers from Glenmore through to London ... couldn't you get into touch with the railway people and find out how many booked at Glenmore for King's Cross this morning? ... that's the Yard's pigeon in peace time? ... do you mean to say they'd resent your putting through an inquiry direct? ... well, all I've got to say is, the sooner the country's at war again the better ... I never heard of such pettifogging obstruction ... you think you can manage? ... I hope you can ... this is a golden opportunity to get a searchlight on this man's activities ... I know you can't have him arrested. I never supposed you could ... I'd send one of our men, but since the arrangement with the D.E.I. we've made a point of keeping off counter-espionage in this country ... all I ask is that you should let us know the results of any action you may take tonight ... we want it urgently for our files ... I'm not suggesting that we should do anything ... quite, quite ... but I'm not proposing to involve you in a strafe from the Home Office ... Yes, I know the Prime Minister is in America at the moment. We do manage to get a little information here ... no, of course, we don't want any trouble with the American Embassy ... all I want you to do is to send one of your best sleuths to shadow Katzenschlosser this evening ... you'll do that? Thanks very much ... no, I've heard nothing of any interest from Glenmore ... of course, I'll let you know ... goodbye.'

N hung up the receiver and sighed profoundly.

'I hope I didn't sound irritable, H. H., but really dear old P would try the patience of an angel sometimes. He never seems to get right down to essentials.'

'He's not had your experience yet, Chief,' Hunter-Hunt reminded him.

'Worrying about Scotland Yard and complications with the United States. Yet, if we'd sent a fellow to shadow Katzenschlosser without notifying P there'd have been almost a civil war. You'd have thought we were dealing with the Admiralty to hear P humming and hawing at the other end of the line. However, we must be patient and exercise tact.'

'That's the only thing,' Hunter-Hunt agreed soothingly.

'And in the end when it *has* penetrated, P usually manages something. He was very quizzy about Glenmore. But it wouldn't have done to let him have an inkling of this Mendacian business. P himself is perfectly discreet, but some of the fellows they've got at Number Two are walking gramophones.'

'I know, I know,' Hunter-Hunt said sorrowfully.

'And I didn't think it right to run any risk after what the P.U.S. said about the European situation.'

'Oh, it would have been unthinkable, Chief.'

'I didn't even mention where we got our information about Katzenschlosser. There's no point in telling P about Blenkinsop.'

'None at all.'

'I don't think we need see Blenkinsop himself. I was pleased that he did not come round here. I thought that showed capital judgement on his part,' said N. 'He'll go back tonight immediately after the broadcast. Flack had better stay. We may want to communicate with Blenkinsop if – I say *if* P's sleuths find out anything about Katzenschlosser. Flack seems a useful fellow as a confidential messenger, though he ought to realize that when we send him to a place disguised as a hiker he should provide himself with a spare pair of shorts. He turned up here, as I expect you noticed, in a pair of plus-fours.'

'Yes, that was very bad,' said Hunter-Hunt.

'I don't suppose it's done any harm on this occasion, but you never know, H. H., you never know.'

'Quite,' Hunter-Hunt agreed with a sapient waggle of his globular head.

While this conversation was going on at The Elms, over at

Number Two P was discussing with Major Grimshaw his telephonic conversation with N.

'They're getting extraordinarily irresponsible at The Elms,' he sighed.

'They always were,' said Major Grimshaw, shaking his button head.

'N will not understand that we can't go about arresting people at sight. He doesn't seem able to grasp the delicacy of our relations with Scotland Yard. He *will* think that conditions in this country are the same as in some petty Balkan state. However, I managed to convince him at last that we couldn't arrest an American subject merely to swell his card-index. And his German accent is really ludicrous. It took me about five minutes to realize he was talking about Katzenschlosser at all. It's amusing, though, isn't it, that poor old N has no more notion what's going on in the West of Scotland than poor old Canonbury?'

'Devilish amusing,' said Major Grimshaw, plucking at his moustache contemptuously.

'Of course, I didn't say a word about Mackillop being up there. I should imagine he would be on to this fellow Katzenschlosser already, though he might not have identified him. Anyway, he wouldn't have telegraphed he was coming down from Glenmore tonight unless he had some pretty hot stuff to deliver.'

'I take it you'll send somebody to King's Cross?' Grimshaw asked.

'Oh yes, Mackillop will want to get along here and report to me as soon as he arrives, and if we send along say Eccles he can look after Katzenschlosser, and Mackillop should be able to point him out. Is Eccles in the house?'

'Yes, he came in about twenty minutes ago with a report on the place he was investigating in Stepney. It was dope as you thought, not military information.'

'Did you let Canonbury know?'

'Yes.'

'Was he grateful?'

'Not a bit.'

'He wouldn't be. The police always hate to be taught their own job by us. You might send Eccles along to me, and I'll give him his instructions for this Katzenschlosser business.'

Major Grimshaw retired, and presently a weazened dark little man in a suit of seedy blue serge came in.

'I want you to go along to King's Cross, Eccles, and do a bit of work for us,' said P. 'Captain Mackillop will be arriving by the train from Glenmore at eight-thirty, and by the same train there is likely to be a foreign agent in whom we are interested. Get hold of Captain Mackillop and tell him you're on the look-out for a foreign agent reported at Glenmore. He'll tell you if there's anybody likely on the train. Follow him home or anywhere he goes and telephone as soon as you think he has gone to earth. Then we'll send somebody to relieve you at once, and you can take on again in the morning. Is that clear?'

'Absolutely.'

'Good. You might tell Captain Mackillop that I am waiting here for him and ask him to come along as quickly as possible.'

'Nothing more?'

P shook his head, and the weazened little man withdrew.

The Director of the S.R.D. then picked up the telephone.

'Put me through to Major Grimshaw ... oh, look here, Grim, I'll go out now and get some dinner. I'll be back by a quarter to nine. If Mackillop arrives before me, will you keep him here?'

P was not the man to linger over his dinner when there was imminent danger of a rising in Scotland. He was back at Number Two soon after half past eight, a good quarter of an hour before Mackillop arrived.

Mackillop had not made the mistake of travelling down from Glenmore in a kilt. When he sat down in P's room on this November evening he looked what he was, a man hard bitten by worldly experience dressed in an inconspicuous dark grey suit.

'Did Eccles get on to this foreign agent of whom we were warned?' P asked.

'Yes. There was only one fellow it could have been. A fellow calling himself Yorke Lankester, which sounds like an alias. Eccles was on to him like a hawk. But how did you know he was up at Glenmore?'

'They telephoned from The Elms that they had reason to suppose Katzenschlosser was arriving by that train.'

Mackillop whistled.

'Katzenschlosser, eh? But how did they hear anything at The Elms?' he went on jealously.

'I don't know how they got on to Katzenschlosser, but they don't know anything about this rising.'

'That's a good job,' said Mackillop. 'We don't want the whole business messed up by M.Q. 99 (E). Well, I'd better let you know all I found out. You got the letter I wrote you?'

'I received it this morning.'

'Well, that Turkish bath business went off fine yesterday. In fact it couldn't have gone better. This fellow Hudson I told you about tried to keep them quiet. But I managed to find out that the date of the rising is 15 December. What's more this fellow Hudson is going to broadcast a talk at the B.B.C. tonight at 9.45, in which at the end he will announce the date and so give the signal to concentrate the forces.'

'Good god!' P exclaimed. 'But do you think the B.B.C. are in on this? Of course I always knew they were a set of un-patriotic pacifists and socialists, but I never suspected them of this sort of thing.'

Mackillop shook his head.

'No, I don't think they're actually in on it. The talk is sup-posed to be about Mendacia. It's a dam' clever notion. I had a bit of luck after I got on to the beginning of the business in the Turkish bath. One of the volunteers who'd been right in the thick of it got a bad attack of conscience or nerves and gave the whole show away to me when I crackled a few fivers just to help him along. There's Russian money behind it, and they're getting arms from Ireland.'

'We had that reported some time ago, but Canonbury muffed the investigation.'

'He would. Trust the police! I didn't think of America. But if Katzenschlosser was up there, that means there's American money in it too somewhere. Of course this volunteer who's called Smith . . .'

'Smith?'

'Yes, but his mother was a Macadam, and he was worked upon by his Scottish relations. These West Highlanders will do anything if they get a bit excited; but the body of the country is sound. It's not like Ireland. Well, as I was saying, this fellow Smith didn't realize at all that Yorke Lankester was Katzenschlosser, though he knew Lankester was an important man. There was another Russian in the Turkish bath, but I didn't have time to find out who he was. The other two were MacAdam of MacAdam and the Duke of Motherwell!'

'The Duke of Motherwell? Fantastic!'

'It is fantastic, isn't it? But I gave the ducal bottom a rousing wallop when I was massaging him, and I thought "Ay, you're a fine bloody duke, stirring up the country to disorder."'

'Wasn't that a bit risky?'

'It may have been, but these damned Home Rulers make me angry, and I couldn't resist the chance he gave me. Well, to continue, I think this man Hudson smelt a rat. Anyway, he hired a car in the middle of the night, and what's more made this volunteer Smith go with him. I hope the poor beggar wasn't murdered on the way, but I expect he was. I thought the only thing for me was to take the train and try to get here in time for you to stop this talk.'

'I'll get through to them right away.'

P took up the telephone.

'Put me through to the B.B.C. ... Hullo! Hullo! Is this the B.B.C.? I understand there is to be a talk this evening ... what? You're putting me through to "inquiries". Who are you then? What? Hullo! Hul-lo! Oh, this is "inquiries"! I understand that there is to be a talk this evening on Mendacia by a Mr Hudson. Can you confirm that? There is? What time? ... At 9.45. Well, put me through, please, to whoever's in charge. In charge of what? In charge of the B.B.C., of course ... What's that? Sir John Who? Sir John Reith isn't there? Well, somebody must be there. Do I want the talks department? Yes, if they can give me a sensible answer to a sensible question. I'll hold on ...'

'The usual muddle,' P observed to Mackillop, with his hand over the mouthpiece. 'Why is it that Number Two is the only competent ... Hullo! Is that the talks department? You have a talk on Mendacia this evening at 9.45, being given by a Mr Hudson. I want to know who's responsible for arranging that talk. Who? Mr Lionel Feilden, you believe. Ask him to speak to me at once. He's not in the building? Well, who *is* in the building that has any authority? Who am I? I am speaking for the War Office ... Yes, the War Office. Oh, you think you can find somebody in authority? ... well, please do so. This is a very grave matter. Yes, I'll hold on ...'

'That scared them a bit, Mackillop,' observed P. 'Confounded fellow talking at me from the back of his throat as if he were a ... hullo! I am speaking for General Sir William Westmacott, the Director of Extraordinary Intelligence, of the Imperial General Staff. You have arranged a talk on Mendacia this evening by a Mr Hudson. This talk must not take place for reasons of state which I am not at liberty to divulge ... What? ... Oh, it's impossible for the B.B.C. to pay any attention to this kind of communication, is it? Do you realize that the consequences may be extremely grave? ... What's that? *What's* that? This talk was arranged through Sir William Westmacott? You must be mistaken ... You have a letter from him? ... well, it's very extraordinary. What guarantee have you that this is the talk arranged through General Westmacott? ... The talk was submitted to you beforehand? Yes, but suppose this Mr Hudson gives an entirely different talk? ... I see ... well, who is the announcer? ... You'll find out? Thank you. Yes, I'll hold on ...'

'This is most mysterious,' P observed to Mackillop. 'These fellows are cleverer than we thought. They've apparently got round the D.E.I. ... hullo! Captain Hubert Chancellor is the announcer? That's not by any chance the Captain Chancellor who wrote a novel called *The Foreign Agent*? ... well, could I speak to him? ... He's reading the what? ... the Second News Bulletin? ... How long does that go on? ... very well, I'll ring up again in a quarter of an hour.'

P replaced the receiver on the telephone.

'You know Chancellor, Mackillop?' he said.

'The fellow in M.Q. 99 (E)?'

'Yes. You remember the trouble about his novel? He had to resign, and apparently he's been taken on as an announcer at the B.B.C. Surely after the warning he received he couldn't have been mad enough to ... but no, it's ridiculous. He was quite a decent fellow, though too indiscreet of course for the job he was in. I think I'll tell him who it is speaking. I don't see how we can stop the talk now, but I'll have a shot. I expect he'll welcome an opportunity to put himself right with us after that novel of his.'

A quarter of an hour later P rang up the B.B.C. again.

'Hullo! Is that Captain Hubert Chancellor? Look here, Chancellor, this is P speaking ... yes. I understand you're announcing the talk on Mendacia at 9.45. Do you think there's any possible way of getting it stopped? ... I see ... but surely you could give listeners something else ... Christopher Stone? Who's he? ... well, it doesn't matter ... if he's not in reach he can't put on gramophone records. I shouldn't have thought it required any special talents to put on gramophone records, but I suppose being a semi-government department the B.B.C. thinks it does ... however, the point is that Westy has somehow or other made a bloomer. I can't find out tonight what's happened, but there's something wrong. Do you know anything about this fellow Hudson? ... nor do we, but of course it may not be his real name ... we know, however, that he's in close touch with Katzenschlosser. You remember him? ... not at all, get that idea right out of your head ... he's no myth. One of our people is chasing him round London at this very moment ... well, to return to Hudson, I hope you'll take care that the talk approved by the B.B.C. and Westy is the talk he gives ... this is a matter of really tremendous gravity. I can't explain why, but it's a matter of political importance ... look here, I'll tell you what you can do ... I've reason to believe he will add some message or other at the end of the talk ... will you look out for this and cut him off if that's the right term before he reads this message? ... yes, well, we shall rely on you ... and look here, Chancellor, I know of course all about the trouble you had over your novel, and it struck me that if you cared to help us over this matter I could probably move in the right quarter so that if you wanted to get back ... I can't speak for N of course ... you know how much upset he was, but we might take you on at Number Two. I can't make any promises ... well, what I would like you to do is to follow this man Hudson when he leaves the B.B.C. He'll probably go up to the Glenmore Hydro from King's Cross ... oh, but we'll pay all expenses ... you've got to say good night to everybody? ... I don't understand. Surely you can leave the B.B.C. for once without saying good night to everybody ... I see ... that means you wouldn't get away till eleven ... well, this is pretty serious ... what's that? your wife is in the building ... but would she do that? ... that would be capital. She was with N, was she? Oh, that's splendid ... if she would find out where Hudson goes tonight and stick on to him, that would help ... all expenses paid, and tell her to do herself well ... she'd better take another name ... is she there with you now? ... you'll ask her to speak to me? ... yes, I'll hold on ...'

'This is capital, Mackillop,' said P. 'I was wondering who the devil I could send ... hullo!'

'Oh, is that you, Mrs Chancellor? This is P speaking. Will you be kind enough to do this job of work for us? ... you will? that's splendid ... what name will you take? Can't hear. Spell it. B-l-e-n-k-i-n-s-o-p. But isn't there a fellow called Blenkinsop who's just joined N's show at The Elms? ... Oh well, it doesn't matter. This isn't their pigeon ... all right, then, will you telegraph to me "Arrived safe" and the place you've arrived at and sign it "Blenkinsop" ... stick to Hudson and keep me informed by telegram ...? I'll send up a relief at once ... this is just to get us round a corner ... thanks very much ... good-bye.'

'Well, that's fixed up very satisfactorily,' P said to Mackillop. 'Mrs Chancellor sounds an intelligent woman. I think she'll give this Hudson man a run for his money.'

'I don't like using women in our work,' said Mackillop. 'They always make trouble.'

'You're feeling tired. You'd better go and get some rest. We can't do anything more till we hear from Eccles about Katzenschlosser. We'll have a conference tomorrow morning at eleven and decide on the action to be taken. Of course, what one would like to do is to put the leaders in the Tower. The Duke of Motherwell, MacAdam, and the rest. But the Press nowadays seems to think that the Tower is a kind of Madame Tussaud's. Probably in the end the Government will decide to hush the whole business up. These politicians have no guts. Always thinking of the votes at the next Election. It'll probably end in our warning the Duke and the rest of them that we know what they're up to, and that'll be an end of it.'

'Ay, and the next thing is there'll be Home Rule,' said Mackillop gloomily.

At this moment the telephone buzzed.

'Hullo! Oh, is that you speaking, Eccles? Yes. The man you followed has gone to 5 The Avenue, Norbiton? And you've ascertained that this is the house of a certain William Hudson, of Hudson Brothers, whose business address is 210 King Street, Covent Garden? ... I see ... we'll send a couple of people at once, and then you can hand over ... evidently this is the centre of a big show ... most interesting ... I'll get two other men on to King Street as well ... no, of course not, you want to get back at once to the Avenue.'

P hung up the receiver.

'I believe we're on a pretty big thing, Mackillop. As you thought, these two brothers Hudson are evidently importing something else besides bananas. You might ask Grimshaw to come along to me for a minute. And you get off and take a good rest. Eleven o'clock tomorrow morning for a conference.'

Mackillop went off, and a minute or two later his place was taken by the button-headed Major Grimshaw.

'Grim, my boy,' said the Director of the Safety of the Realm Division, 'we're in clover. This Scotch rising has put us in the way of smashing up the work of Katzenschlosser's organization.'

'Oh good shooting,' said Major Grimshaw.

'The whole business is being worked with bananas. We never suspected bananas before, eh?'

'No, we had a spot of trouble with Dutch carrots last year,

but I don't think we've got anything in our files against bananas. In fact I'm sure we haven't,' said Major Grimshaw.

P told his second-in-command the information about them he had gathered.

'Do you think we can snaffle the whole lot up at Glenmore? Probably all these rifles were landed as bananas,' said Grimshaw.

'I doubt it,' said P. 'And in fact I don't think we want to. It'll be much better to let these people go on thinking that they're working their show under the cover of bananas, and then when war breaks out we can get an Order in Council and seize every banana in the country. In that way we ought to break up any hostile organization at once.'

'But this Scotch business? What are you proposing to do about that?'

'I haven't quite decided. I think we'll put that up to Westy. An English regiment sent up to Fort Wade would nip that in the bud.'

'Quite.'

'I'm not really worrying any longer about this Scotch business. This banana organization seems to me much more important. So I want you to get a couple of fellows on to Covent Garden right away and another couple out to Norbiton to relieve Eccles.'

'Are you doing anything more about the B.B.C.?' Grimshaw asked.

'Oh, didn't I tell you? Yes, I've arranged to have Hudson followed so that we know where he is. But to my mind the centre of interest has shifted to Covent Garden and Norbiton. I'm a little worried about N, though. The Elms people will be fussing to have information about Katzenschlosser for their confounded card-index. I could tell from the way N spoke over the telephone that he rather resented having to call us in. However, it seems to me absolutely clear that Katzenschlosser is definitely our pigeon.'

'Oh rather, every time!' declared Grimshaw.

The telephone buzzed again.

'Hullo? Oh, is that you, Eccles? Yes, P speaking. Yorke

Lankester has just come out and taken a taxi to King's Cross?
... Yes, certainly ... it's the only thing to do ... yes, you'd
better follow him if he goes up to Scotland ... or, wait a
minute, we'll send Hawkins along to meet you at King's Cross
... and he can follow him ... for god's sake don't lose him ...
he's getting more important every moment.'

P hung up the receiver.

'Katzenschlosser has got away from Eccles, but I hope it will
be all right. Eccles is held up waiting for another taxi. That's
the trouble.'

'We ought to have sent him in a car at first,' said Grimshaw.

'I know. But it was one dam' thing after another this evening. The B.B.C., and bananas, and N muddling up everything
over the phone, and this rising in Scotland, and old Westy
hashing matters over this talk. However, if Katzenschlosser
did suspect Eccles was sleuthing him he probably said "King's
Cross", thinking Eccles would suppose he was really going to
Euston or St Pancras. And if he didn't spot Eccles, why it's the
same thing. I think he'll be at King's Cross all right. He probably wants to give Hudson some last instructions after he
leaves the B.B.C. That's my view of the situation.'

'Well, you're usually right, P,' said his second-in-command.

'Oh, it's just horse sense,' P modestly disclaimed. 'By the
way, I haven't told you my new scheme for making things a
little more watertight. I was working it out when all that
business started this evening. Put shortly, I want to arrange to
have the letters of every subaltern in the Army secretly read
by us.'

'That's what I've been thinking was necessary for a long
time,' said Grimshaw.

'I did suggest it once tentatively to Westy, but he raised a
lot of rather foolish objections. However, I think after this
bloomer he's made over the B.B.C. he'll be more inclined to see
our point of view. What I say in our work is "look after the
pennies and the pounds will take care of themselves".'

'Oh, every time!' agreed the second-in-command.

'The argument that the average subaltern doesn't know anything that foreign agents want to know is beside the point. Can

you remember any agent who ever obtained any information worth having?'

'Never,' said Grimshaw positively.

'Well, I intend to press for these powers,' said P. 'It seems to me important that in times of peace we should get as much of our work as we can on to a sound war footing. You may be sure that when war *does* break out we shan't want to be wasting time thinking what measures we ought to have adopted long before the war came. It was disgraceful that those confounded politicians should have been allowed to go yapping round the country about "Safety First". They brought the phrase into disrepute.'

P was away now on a crusade to which he had dedicated his life since relinquishing aviation. His voice took on the solemn bell-like tones of a best-selling novelist talking about his next book.

Chapter 19

ON THE AIR

WHAT a contrast on that November evening the publicity of Broadcasting House offered to the secrecy of The Elms and the safety of Number Two! Commissionaires in resplendent uniforms directed novices of the microphone to the right lift. Pageboys in less resplendent uniforms guided them to the right studio. Enthusiastic listeners up from the country stood in eager groups on the mosaic floor of the entrance hall and gazed in awe at the convolutions of the modern sculpture that proclaimed to the civilized world how the B.B.C. was keeping up with the times. Experienced broadcasters hurried in with hardly a minute to spare. Golden-mouthed announcers in immaculate evening-dress hurried along the corridors from studio to studio. Red and green and white lights flickered over doorways designed in the purest Germanic taste. The air was odorous with balmy antiseptics. Nation was speaking peace unto nation.

Did they pause to think, these hundreds who hurried hither and thither about this great concrete hive, some talking in standard English, some not, that between them and the bombs of hostile aeroplanes out to sever the country's vocal cords stood nothing except a few unknown patriots with dark horn-rimmed spectacles, silent resolute men whose lives were consecrated to secrecy and safety? Not they. For them the illuminated disks of SILENCE merely meant that one individual was doing all the talking, that vaudeville was soothing the mind of the tired business man, or that a couple of debating highbrows were inspiring listeners all over the country to write acidulous letters to the *Radio Times*.

Captain Hubert Chancellor was still very evidently the junior among the angelic company of announcers, though by actual years he was probably the senior. He did not yet venture to arrive in the studio just as the hand of the clock leapt forward to the fatal minute. Consequently he did not allow himself as much time as he would have liked to discuss with his wife the suggestion that she should follow the giver of the Mendacian talk even up to Scotland if necessary.

'Oh, darling,' she had said to him. 'I really must do this. It's such an opportunity to score off Colonel Nutting.'

'My dear Phyllis, do be careful what you're saying,' her husband protested.

Captain Chancellor did not believe that N's name was a secret preserved as perfectly as a fly in amber, but he did not want to be prosecuted under the Official Secrets Act. Since this good-looking man of close on forty had donned the evening-dress of an announcer to present to the ears of millions of talkers on every subject from the origin of the universe to the best way of skimming grease from consommé, he had exchanged secrecy for suavity.

'I'm sure there's some glorious muddle going on between The Elms and Number Two over this talk,' his wife said. 'And I've arranged with P to call myself Mrs Blenkinsop. I think Phyllis Blenkinsop is such a marvellous name.'

'You've not arranged to call yourself Blenkinsop?' Chancellor exclaimed. 'I say, Phyllis, you can't do that.'

'I've done it already, darling. Can't you imagine what that loathsome Glidden woman will say when she hears?'

'Yes, but think of N and Claudie H. H. and . . .'

'But, dearest Bertie, what are you worrying about? I'm doing something for P. *I'm* not to know and *you're* not to know that probably this wretched man Hudson is one of N's plumbers. Now, darling, don't be obstructive, please. Run along and do your announcing like a good boy.'

'But you've got no luggage. You've got no money.'

'I'll get some money at my club, and I'll have plenty of time to go back and pack a few pretties.'

'You're not seriously going up to this Glenmore place as Mrs Blenkinsop?'

'If the mysterious Hudson, goes, I shall go. If he doesn't turn up at King's Cross I shall come back like a good little wife and telephone P in the morning that I lost him in Limehouse. Think of the copy for your next book, Bertie, and do admit that I'm a model wife for a novelist.'

'Yes, but the governors of the B.B.C. might cut up rough . . .'

'The hush-hush work undertaken by an announcer's wife for motives of patriotism cannot reflect upon her husband. Now don't be a military gentleman. I'm going. And I'll love you too marvellously when I get back.' With this Mrs Chancellor cut short the argument by hurrying off.

At twenty minutes to ten Blenkinsop, who had arrived at Broadcasting House three-quarters of an hour before his talk was scheduled to begin, was ushered up to the studio in which he was to perform. Little did he think that the announcer who showed him so pleasantly how to sit at the table, who warned him so pleasantly against making extraneous noises into the microphone, and who explained so pleasantly the system of signalling was his predecessor at The Elms. And little did Hubert Chancellor think as he bent over the table, watching the clock preparatory to announcing the talk of Mr A. Hudson that he was sponsoring his successor.

'I'm rather specially interested in this talk of yours, Mr Hudson,' he said, just before the minute hand of the clock leapt forward to 9.45 precisely. 'I know something about Mendacia myself. Quiet now, and don't crackle the paper.'

Blenkinsop's nerves were in a state of acute tension. He had gone through a great deal during the last week. Even if nothing had been at stake and if he had trained quietly for this talk with sedative drugs he would still have felt horribly alarmed by the ordeal before him. As it was, he had an impression that when the red light flickered to warn him that from one end of Europe to the other his voice was on the air he was attacked by a mixture of apoplexy, epilepsy, angina pectoris, general paralysis, noises in the head, dull pains at the base of the loins, debility, lassitude, coma, black vomit, and death. The microphone grinned at him like a skull. The hand that held the first sheet began to drum faintly on the table. His tongue turned into blotting-paper, from blotting-paper into cork, from cork into cotton-wool, from cotton-wool into a nutmeg-grater, and from a nutmeg-grater into a warm flat-iron. Something that felt like a shuttlecock squeezed itself out of his mouth and fell limply upon the battledore of the microphone. Apparently this was his voice.

The last remark of the announcer before this hideous physical process began returned to him, and while his voice was being squeezed out in a series of shuttlecocks there flashed upon Blenkinsop's consciousness the fearful thought that the announcer might be a Mendacian agent. If Katzenschlosser had been able to disguise himself as a shampooer, was it impossible that he might be in the studio at this moment, disguised as an announcer? The ghastly fancy fled, vanquished by a blessed glimmer of common sense as spectres are vanquished by the dawn. Gradually Blenkinsop regained control over his voice and buoyed up by the thought that away in the North Renata was listening to him he began to handle the prose of the South-East Section of M.Q. 99 (E) less in the manner of somebody with weak eyes who is trying to read aloud without glasses a page of Bradshaw's Railway Guide.

Hubert Chancellor, sitting back on a couch in the corner of the studio and following the talk, was seized with a fancy that in the past he had heard the whole of this talk already. He did not, like a too rash philosopher, accept this as a proof of reincarnation. He made an effort to recollect where he had heard it already, and before long he came to a sentence which he distinctly remembered to have written himself two or three months ago when he was in charge of the Mendacian subsection at The Elms. In fact, as Blenkinsop read on, Chancellor realized that nearly every word of what he was saying had originally been written by himself. It did not take Chancellor long to make up his mind that the talk tonight could only have emanated from M.Q. 99 (E). No wonder General Westmacott had acted as godfather. Chancellor began to puzzle over the imbroglio of which the telephonic conversation with P had been the herald. This was certainly another glorious muddle of cross purposes. Chancellor smiled to himself. He was recalling several other glorious muddles. His mind had ceased to follow the talk in his preoccupation with the currents and cross-currents of Intelligence, when suddenly he heard Blenkinsop's voice ring out as if he were giving an order on parade to the squadron, Chancellor turned hastily to the typescript to find where he was.

'Finally, I would say to the people of Mendacia that there is no country to which British commercial enterprise may look with greater confidence in the near future, especially if the happy event planned for the fifteenth of December should receive the welcome it deserves from the people of Mendacia.'

Chancellor saw Blenkinsop fling his last sheet on the floor. He sprang up to cut the talker off from the world before he turned round to ask if that had been all right.

'By gad, that's the worst quarter of an hour I ever spent,' Blenkinsop declared. 'You must find this life a fearful strain. But I suppose they give you plenty of leave?'

'That last bit you read,' said Chancellor, 'Is it in the typescript we had? It sounded unfamiliar ... I mean to say I couldn't find it in my copy.'

Blenkinsop looked at the announcer sharply. Was he trying to pump him?

'No, it's not in the typescript,' he admitted, 'but I felt the thing wanted a good note to end on.'

'You'll get me into trouble if any listeners write in to complain,' said Chancellor. 'I ought to have cut you off. Look here, we may as well be clear about this. You're in touch with The Elms aren't you?'

Blenkinsop staggered back.

'I don't know what you're talking about.'

'Well, I ought to tell you who I am. My name's Chancellor – Hubert Chancellor. I used to be with the M.Q. 99 (E) people.'

'You're Chancellor?' Blenkinsop repeated. 'Then you wrote that novel?'

'Yes. *The Foreign Agent.* There was rather a fuss about it. All rot, of course; but dear old N let Claudie Hunter-Hunt work him up over it, and it ended in my leaving. But, I say, there's going to be another fuss about tonight. P rang through about nine to try and get your talk stopped altogether.'

'You're sure it wasn't N?' Blenkinsop asked apprehensively.

'No, no. I thought of ringing up The Elms to ask what was

the matter; but you know what they're like if anybody rings them up except on the private line. However, I expect N will tell you what it's all about. Funny thing, I spotted you were from The Elms when you were reading your talk. As a matter of fact most of it comes from a report I wrote for them on Mendacia about a couple of months ago. My god!'

'What is it?' Blenkinsop exclaimed. 'Didn't you cut us off? Don't tell me that what we've been talking about has been blared out on every loud-speaker in the country.'

'No, no, that's all right. But I was just wondering if you were Blenkinsop by any chance.'

Blenkinsop thought rapidly. It would hardly be gentlemanly to tell a lie to the man he had superseded.

'Yes,' he said simply. 'I'm Blenkinsop.'

It was now Chancellor's turn to think rapidly. He could hardly reveal to the man who had taken his place at The Elms that at the prompting of N's rival he had allowed his wife to shadow his successor under the successor's own name. As in a dream he heard Blenkinsop say he ought to be getting along.

'I suppose you're in contact with the famous Madame Tekta now?' he asked.

Blenkinsop looked at him in astonishment. Then he remembered.

'Oh, of course, you were in negotiation with her before . . .'

'Missing Madame Tekta was my chief regret when I left The Elms. Is she as attractive as legend says?'

'She's attractive, yes.'

'I wonder if there's any chance of King Johannis getting back?'

'Look here, I really must be getting along, Chancellor.'

'You're going back to Glenmore, eh?'

'Well, I'm going to Glenmore, yes,' Blenkinsop admitted unwillingly. He could not help thinking that Chancellor's inquisitiveness in the circumstances trembled upon the verge of bad form.

Chancellor resolved to say nothing that might precipitate a strafe between M.Q. 99 (E) and the S.R.D. He knew the horrors of departmental warfare; other people's pigeons lying mangled

WATER ON THE BRAIN

in the gutters of Whitehall ... red ink and red tape everywhere. Oh yes, departmental peace at any price!

As soon as Blenkinsop had left Broadcasting House Chancellor rang up his wife's club. She had been there, but had already left. He rang up their flat. There was no answer. He decided to make an effort to intercept her at the railway-station, and with this intention endeavoured to find another announcer, and persuade him to say 'Good night, everybody, good night' before the dance music came on. It could not be managed. He was the only announcer left in the building by now. He wondered what would happen if nobody said 'Good night, everybody, good night.' It could not be done. It might mean the death of broadcasting.

Little does the listener who jeers at the golden tones of the announcer reck of what may be going on inside the announcer. Little does the listener who accepts as his due that honey-sweet 'good night' think that the announcer's own inside may be gall and wormwood. *Vesti la giubba!* Put on your immaculate evening-dress, *Pagliaccio*. What does the listener care that your heart may be breaking, so long as you do not cough into the microphone?

Hardly had the leader of the dance band had time to announce that the next number would be a fox-trot entitled *Your eyes may be blue but I'm through with you*, than Chancellor after bidding everybody good night was telling a taxi-driver to go as fast as he could to Euston.

'The Glenmore train, which platform?' Chancellor asked in agitation.

'It's King's Cross you want, sir,' said a porter, '11.12 I think it is. But you'll be too late, I'm afraid.'

The porter was right. The Nocturnal Scot had left when Chancellor got to King's Cross, cursing his silly mistake. There seemed only one step to take in the circumstances, and that was to send a telegram to Phyllis at Glenmore warning her what had happened. And this would have to be addressed to Mrs Blenkinsop:

Beg you to return home immediately Blenkinsop known to be at Glenmore will square matters with P   Bertie

And then Chancellor on arriving home found his wife puffing calmly away at a cigarette.

'Bertie, I made such an ass of myself,' she told him, 'I completely forgot I didn't know this man Hudson by sight. And as I didn't want to go up to Scotland unless he was really going too I gave up.'

'A jolly good thing you did,' said Chancellor fervidly. 'I found out it was Blenkinsop himself.'

'Oh, I wish I'd gone now. *What* a game it would have been!'

Blenkinsop himself had reached King's Cross in ample time, and as he paced the platform waiting for the Nocturnal Scot to appear he felt a grand emotion of relief. Apart from the inevitable reckoning with Enid he had little now to worry over. The message, the all-important message to the people of Mendacia, had gone forth. He had baffled Katzenschlosser. He had outwitted the agents of the Mendacian Republic. He had earned the Order of the Sacred Source. He should be standing high in the estimation of Renata. His own chief would be congratulating himself on his subordinate's ability. General Westmacott would be doing the same. And no doubt the Permanent Under-Secretary would make inquiries. That would not mean reward or honour, but it would mean that quiet approval in high circles which is all that the Secret Service officer looks for. Then N had said something about probably sending him out to Mendacia. A delightful prospect. Renata, no doubt, would be too much occupied to give him much of her time or attention. Still he might see her occasionally. And then there was the possibility of opening the Hotel Multum again. He would speak to his brother John about that well as soon as he was back in town. Life was beginning to look good – yes, apart from Enid, distinctly good – apart from the immediate problem of Enid, the difficulty in fact of explaining away his uncommunicative week. He was contemplating a little ruefully his conjugal position when he heard himself hailed as Major and looking round saw Hudson coming along the platform, his face beaming.

'My book will be out on Monday, Major. I found a few advance copies waiting for me at home, and I want you to be so good if you will as to take one up to the wife, and accept another for yourself.'

Blenkinsop assented at once. After that message put over the air in spite of all that foreign agents could do to stop it he was feeling magnanimous. He could not help being a little amused by the importance which Hudson was attaching to the publication of his novel, and he smiled to think how much abashed the little man would be if he only knew to whom he was so naïvely entrusting his book.

Blenkinsop and the author chatted for a while on the platform by the Glenmore coach, and then Hudson said he would be off as he wanted to be down at his publisher's early tomorrow morning.

'Well, good-bye, Lankester,' said Blenkinsop.

'Good-bye, Hudson,' said the author.

The pair of them laughed.

'Naughty, naughty,' the author added. 'Well, tootle-oo!'

Blenkinsop, enjoying the temporary relaxation from responsibility to which his successful broadcast entitled him, did not notice a dark weazened little man point out Hudson to a man who looked like something seen outside the stage-door of a small provincial theatre, nor did he notice the theatrical figure set out furtively along the platform in pursuit of Hudson. He went along to his sleeper, undressed, and got into bed where presently he dozed off for two or three hours. Then he woke up. Finding that sleep had deserted him, he switched on the reading light at his head and untied the string round the presentation copy of Hudson's new book. A chapter or two of that might coax him back into somnolence.

When Blenkinsop read the title the sleeping-car seemed to go dark, and he switched on the roof-lamp. Or rather he intended to switch on the roof-lamp. What he actually switched on was the electric fan, and perhaps this accident prevented his swooning under the horror of that title. Twice already the sudden shocks administered to Blenkinsop in railway-trains have been recorded. This shock was so much more violent than the others that a catalogue of the physical manifestations which attend extreme horror would be of no avail to suggest Blenkinsop's mental anguish. A simple statement of the title of the book will be more effective. It was called:

THE SECRET OF POMONA LODGE

and it was described by the publishers on the jacket as follows:

Mr Yorke Lankester, whose thrilling romance *The Green-Eyed Spy* was one of the outstanding successes of spring fiction, has once again proved himself to be a master of mystery.

This is a tale of how Ralph Grandison, of the British Secret Service, strove to preserve the secret of Pomona Lodge against the wiles of Isaac Schneberger, the head of the Black Cats, that sinister organization of international revolutionaries whose ramifications were world wide. Pomona Lodge was the headquarters of the British Secret Service, and Mr Yorke Lankester, whose knowledge of the underworld of diplomacy recalls that of the late William le Queux, has woven a brilliant and breathtaking narrative. A charming love story adds greatly to the reader's pleasure, and we confidently expect that 'The Secret of Pomona Lodge' will establish Mr Yorke Lankester in the front rank of contemporary novelists, combining as he does a meticulous inside knowledge of his subject with a rare distinction of style.

By the Same Author

THE GREEN-EYED SPY

A ... romance ... often marvellous ...
Dimes Literary Supplement.

The Nocturnal Scot roared through some echoing station. The electric fan whirred on. Blenkinsop lay prone, his eyes fixed glassily upon the Deuteronomical warnings about misbehaviour with the communication cord.

At last he reached a decision, and as he leapt out of bed he realized that the interior of the sleeper was extremely cold. He switched off the fan, switched on the roof-lamp, and dressed. Then he rang for the attendant.

'When do we reach Grantham?' he asked.

'We've passed Grantham some time back, sir. The next stop is York. We should be there in another three-quarters of an hour.'

'I'm getting out there,' said Blenkinsop. 'I've left something behind in London.'

'You're not going on north with us, sir?'

'No, I must get a train back to London.'

'I'm sorry, sir,' said the attendant, 'I'll put your suitcase out for you, sir.'

The Nocturnal Scot swept on northward, leaving Blenkinsop to wander about the dark and draughty immensities of York Station until he could get a train back to London.

'How in the name of all that's incredible did he think of such a title?' Blenkinsop kept moaning to himself; and the raw wind whistling about the bare platforms echoed his moaning.

Chapter 20

ENID INVESTIGATES

THE prospect before Blenkinsop in London was wretched, but at any rate he was spared the shock of meeting Enid on his arrival at Glenmore.

On Thursday night, after Enid had been persuaded by her friend Tiny Houldsworth to reserve her strength for the morrow, she had retired to bed ravaged by the thought that somewhere in the hotel her husband was ignominiously hiding from her.

'Darling, if it will bring you any peace of mind,' her devoted friend had declared, 'I'm perfectly willing to make inquiries about him. But I do beg you to stay quietly resting tonight. Your nerves are not in a fit state for any scene at present. And you want to look your best. If I see Arthur I shall merely tell him that you have not yet made up your mind what action you will take. Now do let me dig around on my own. I'll order some sandwiches to be sent up to your room.'

Half an hour or so later Tiny returned to the room papered with the red of Dress Mackintosh and curtained with the green of Hunting Mackintosh in which Enid wrapped in a rose du barri velvet jacket was sitting up in bed and angrily manicuring her nails.

'The hotel people have evidently been bribed by Arthur to say that he has left,' she announced. 'According to them he left in a motor-car last night, or rather this morning about half past one, accompanied by a hiker called Smith.'

'Accompanied by a hiker called Smith?' Enid exclaimed. 'I never heard such a preposterous tale! Arthur hated hikers. One of the things on which we prided ourselves most at Parvo was that there were no hikers there.'

'Well, Enid, dear, that's what they say.'

'Did you ask them to explain how it was we heard his voice just now when we first arrived?'

273

'They said we must have been mistaken, and then – keep a firm hold on yourself, my precious – they said that there was a friend of Mr Hudson's in the hotel, a Mrs Yorke Lankester, who would confirm this information, and – Enid, be brave – I feel sure that this Mrs Yorke Lankester is none other than Mrs Hudson herself. She was sitting in the drawing-room. An immense woman. Good-looking in that hard way which some people still admire.'

'Of course it's Mrs Hudson,' said Enid. 'Yorke Lankester is the name her despicable husband uses, with which he writes vulgar shockers. I know that. But why did Arthur call himself Hudson when she was coming here as Mrs Lankester?'

'I didn't speak to her,' said Tiny. 'I dreaded precipitating matters. I could not have spoken to her civilly with the thought of what she had made my best friend suffer. But, Enid, this is not the worst. I'm afraid Arthur has another woman up here.'

'Another?' Enid gasped.

'Yes, Pinches was right about Señora Miranda. She's a Spaniard from the Canary Islands. But they say she's not staying in the hotel tonight. She's apparently coming back tomorrow, and, I can't help feeling Arthur may be with her.'

Enid pondered this theory for a moment.

'I believe,' she said, 'Mrs Hudson has heard about this Spanish horror, and that she has come up here under her husband's writing name to lure Arthur back to her. And yet ... and yet why was Arthur bellowing away like that about insect powders when we arrived?'

'It is most bewildering,' Tiny agreed. 'But we shall know all presently, because according to the hotel people Arthur is expected back tomorrow morning.'

'Is he? I doubt it,' said Enid.

'Enid, I don't want you to excite yourself unduly tonight. Arthur's behaviour is wrapped in mystery; but we cannot unravel the mystery tonight, and in the morning it may be clearer. I've brought you up some of the water for which this Hydro is famous. Everybody to whom I talked downstairs begged me to persevere with it and said it worked miracles. I took a sip or two, and though the taste is not too pleasant, I thought if we drank it together . . .'

The management of the Glenmore Hydro was familiar with the spectacle of stout guests. It had assumed that Miss Tiny Houldsworth's reason for visiting Glenmore was the reduction of her figure. It had lost no time in recommending her to the benevolence of St Ninian. Other guests seeing her recoil from the beaker put before her by the waiter had hastened to encourage her to persevere. They were too tactful to suggest that a course of water would make her thinner; they merely urged it would make her better. They spoke of its power to soothe nerves and vanquish headaches. So Tiny had ordered a couple of large glasses of the water to be sent up to her room. These she had now brought with her, intent upon serving her friend at this crisis of her life.

'Are you sure this water is quite fresh?' Enid asked after her first sip.

'That's what I wondered at first,' Tiny admitted. 'But everybody else assured me it always tasted like that. It certainly isn't a nice taste.'

'A nice taste? I never tasted anything so filthy in my life except once when I was hunting as a kid and was thrown into a clump of mangolds which had rotted in the frost. Good gracious, how time flies!' Enid sighed. 'That must be quite ten years ago now.'

'I'm beginning to get a little used to it,' Tiny declared bravely after three or four sips.

'I'm not,' said Enid.

'But do persevere, darling. I know it will do you good.'

They sipped away in silence for a while.

'I find it gets more and more unpleasant,' said Enid. 'It reminds me of something else now.'

'Stale fish?' Tiny suggested.

'No, dead lizard. Once in Italy when I was with my dear old dad – thank heaven he's not alive, Tiny, to see what Arthur had brought me to – what was I saying? Oh yes, I drank some of the water from the tap in my hotel bedroom and I thought it tasted very strange. So I asked my dear old dad to try it and he raised Cain in the hotel, and do you know they found a lizard had died in the pipe.'

'I'm sure, Enid, you would never find anything like that at Alassio,' said her friend eagerly. 'They go out of their way there to make English people comfortable. They know how particular we are.'

Enid and Tiny sipped on gloomily till the silence was broken again by Tiny.

'Did you ever drink the water in your hot-water bottle?' she asked her friend.

'Certainly not,' said Enid. 'Who would? I never heard of such a disgusting habit.'

'Oh, it wasn't a habit,' said Tiny hastily. 'Only, I remember that once after my brother Charles had a tooth out with gas he wanted to play at being a dentist, and he was giving me gas from my mother's rubber hot-water bottle, and I think the maid hadn't emptied it properly, because I got my mouth full of water.'

'How like a brother!' Enid commented with the sternness of an only child.

Then as if she was suddenly reminded that she was all that was left of the old fighting Madison stock she swallowed the rest of the water without removing her lips from the glass.

The next morning Enid went downstairs in a temper that suggested an undue reputation for the sedative qualities of St Ninian's water. In fact, the behaviour of his patients in general was a reflection upon the water, which, however beneficial to the stomach, seemed to exercise a most deleterious influence upon the brain. Yes, notwithstanding the discomfort of that arrival at York in the wind and rain of a November dawn, Blenkinsop was better off than he might have been had he arrived at Glenmore that Friday morning. The bad temper which Enid was in already was turned to rage when Tiny brought her a telegram addressed to Mrs Blenkinsop.

'I saw this stuck up in the hall,' said Tiny. 'Arthur has evidently escaped.'

'The coward!' Enid exclaimed as she tore open the envelope.

'"Beg you to return home immediately,"' she read out,

' "Blenkinsop known to be at Glenmore. Will square matter with P. Bertie." Why, he's got a regular harem, Tiny. Oh, this is too much! I've married a Bluebeard.'

'But who is Bertie?' Tiny asked.

'Who is Bertie? Why, another despicable husband presumably,' Enid replied.

'And who is P?'

'Who else would it be except that impostor of an inquiry agent you introduced me to? I suppose I shall receive another bill of forty-six pounds eleven shillings and fivepence-half-penny for this Mrs Blenkinsop.'

'And Connie Butterwick said Pinches was so reliable,' Tiny sighed.

'Please leave Connie Butterwick out of it,' Enid asked sharply. 'It ought not to be difficult. The woman's a nonentity. I think I'm beginning to reconstruct Arthur's behaviour.'

'Darling, if anybody can you will,' Tiny assured her.

'I believe Arthur was having an intrigue with that blonde giantess Mrs Hudson, and that he came up here under the name of Hudson in order to – well – I needn't go into details.'

'No, Enid, I can guess what you mean.'

'On the way up in the train, you remember, Doggett reported Arthur had a mysterious interview with somebody in his sleeper dressed like a man?'

'Yes, perfectly.'

'And that Doggett was inclined to think at first that this was Mrs Hudson?'

'Yes, I remember well.'

'But that this mysterious individual vanished from the train during the night?'

'Yes, yes.'

'Well, my theory is that this mysterious individual is the hiker, and that the hiker is none other than the creature called Mrs Blenkinsop in this telegram, Bertie of course being her contemptible husband.'

'But what about the Spanish woman?'

'Why, she must have been another of Arthur's mistresses who followed him up here and, we may hope, put him to a good deal of inconvenience by doing so. Then when we arrived unexpectedly on top of Mrs Hudson Arthur lost his head and bolted with this female hiker.'

'But why does her husband wire to her as Mrs Blenkinsop?'

'Because your friend Pinches...'

'Darling, please don't call him that,' Tiny protested.

'Because that ruffian Pinches has seen an opportunity to extract money from her feeble husband, and told him that his wife was staying here as Mrs Blenkinsop, and has offered for a consideration to say nothing to me.'

Armed with her theory Enid set out to find facts to fit it. The first thing she discovered was that Arthur had not been in the hotel last night. This she discovered by overhearing a conversation in the siesta-lounge between Mr Woodburn and the Misses Macadam.

'You didn't hear our standoffish friend Hudson's talk over the wireless last night?' he was asking.

'My sister and I never listen to anything except the Scottish Regional, and it's so difficult to hear that in Scotland without a lot of Germans breaking in all the time,' Miss Caroline replied, 'We once persuaded a Lowland friend of ours to listen to a Gaelic *ceilidh* and he couldn't distinguish between Hitler making a speech and one of our bards telling a Gaelic story.'

'I know you won't believe it, Mr Woodburn,' Miss Flora interposed, 'but we shall put all that sort of thing right as soon as we get Home Rule. What was that unpleasant Mr Hudson talking about?'

'Insect powders,' said Mr Woodburn.

'A suitable topic,' observed Miss Caroline. 'Ten shillings a year to listen to people like that holding forth on insect powders!'

'To do him justice, I don't expect he talked about insect powders all the time. The talk was on conditions in Mendacia, but I cut him off.'

'Indeed, I think you were very wise,' said Miss Caroline.

'By Jove, eleven o'clock already,' exclaimed Mr Woodburn,

looking at his watch. 'Time for my third glass. I always like to get through my first four by noon.'

With this he strolled off in pursuit of his cure.

Enid did not approve of entering lightly into conversation with fellow-guests in a hotel, but the hostility with which these two old freaks had spoken of Arthur led her to suppose that they probably disapproved of his morals and might be able to give her some useful information.

'Excuse me,' she said. 'But I could not help hearing your conversation, and as I know Mr Hudson I wondered if you could tell me when he is expected back.' Seeing the beginning of a disapproving frown on Miss Caroline's forehead, Enid went on hastily to lighten her reputation from the shadow cast by Arthur's. 'My friend Miss Houldsworth and I are staying here together, and as we met Mr Hudson once in Mendacia we were interested to hear he had been here.'

'I'm afraid I can give you no information about Mr Hudson's movements ... er? ...' Miss Caroline hesitated.

'Miss Madison.'

'No information, Miss Madison, beyond the fact that he left here about two o'clock yesterday morning with a man who was not what he seemed,' Miss Caroline went on.

'What made you think he was not what he seemed?' Enid pressed eagerly.

'My sister and I have our reasons,' said Miss Caroline.

'Did anything happen by any chance to show you that this man was a woman?' Enid asked point-blank.

Miss Caroline rose from her chair.

'We are neither of us married, Miss Madison. And I am surprised by your question, surprised and, if I may say so, not a little disgusted. Come, Flora, Fingal will be pining for his walk, poor little man.'

And as she and Miss Flora retreated with dignity from the lounge, Enid heard her observe:

'When we get Home Rule, Flora, we may hope that English-women of that type will give Scotland a wide berth.'

Enid's annoyance with these two tweedbound old frumps was forgotten in the pleasure of finding that her theory about the hiker's sex had been correct. She asked herself if it was likely to cost more to divorce Arthur with three co-respondents than with one. It would certainly cost Arthur more both in money and anxiety, and it might prevent his marrying any one of them. Solicitors, however, were a greedy race. It might be wise to give her solicitors no chance of profiteering over three co-respondents. In that case it would be as well to decide on which of the three she would concentrate. On Mrs Hudson? Where was Mrs Hudson, by the way? Enid made inquiries and found that Mrs Yorke Lankester had left by the morning train for London. Evidently she was again in pursuit of Arthur and his female hiker. If Mahomet would not come to the mountain the mountain must go to Mahomet. No, she would not make Mrs Hudson a co-respondent, for if she did she would do exactly what her husband was wanting, and no doubt he would make it financially worth her while. The Spanish horror? She had a bill against her for forty-six pounds eleven shillings and fivepence-halfpenny. But what was the evidence? A conversation about bananas, and an alarum clock. Let the Spanish horror go back to Spain. And the co-respondent should be this female hiker whose contemptible husband was so anxious to have her back on any terms that he would obviously never divorce her. The co-respondent should be this female hiker who had dared to call herself Mrs Blenkinsop.

Any lingering doubt that Enid had felt about the rightness of her decision was presently to vanish. About twelve o'clock she saw a car drive up to the hotel and from it alight a dark well-dressed woman accompanied by a tall man in a kilt. She went out into the hall and heard the hotel manager say in a voice of profound respect:

'Good morning, MacAdam.'

'Is Mr Hudson in?' the chieftain asked.

'No, MacAdam, Mr Hudson did not return this morning,' the manager replied. 'And we have not yet heard when he is coming back, though some of his luggage is still here.'

'I'm afraid you won't see him now, Renata. We shall have to be on board tonight,' said the chieftain.

'It does not matter nothing,' said Madame Tekta. 'He was

useful to us for a little, but I can write him a small note. You will exspeed it, please for me, to Mr Hudson's address, if he does not come presently?' she asked the manager.

'With pleasure, Señora,' he promised with obsequious soapless handwashing.

'And now, my good MacAdam, I must make my packings. You can drink yourself a whiskysoda while you must wait.'

Madame Tekta passed along to the lift, casting as she went an indifferent glance at Enid who an hour later saw her drive away for ever from Glenmore with the Highland chief.

'Well,' said Enid to Tiny Houldsworth at lunch, 'you may talk about private inquiry agents, but I have found out more this morning than your friend Pinches could have found out in a week and for little more than a quarter as much as he charged me for completely misleading information about Señora Miranda. I have yet to find out exactly what Arthur did do for her, but in due course I shall. I knew when that worm Doggett said she was dark that Arthur was not guilty over her. He has never looked at a dark woman in his life, and I don't suppose he ever will. We'll go back to London tonight.'

Chapter 21

WHOSE PIGEON?

BY the time Blenkinsop was half-way back to London from York he had added as much again to the depression which already weighed him down by the reflection that in his anxiety to prevent the publication of Hudson's book he had disobeyed N's express instructions to return to Glenmore and report on the movements of King Johannis. By the time he reached King's Cross his military mind had decided that his commanding officer would hold that nothing could justify such a neglect of his duty. He decided, in that state of miserable uncertainty which is created by arriving in London in the twilight of a raw November morning and knowing that there is no chance of getting as much as a cup of tea for at least half an hour, to telegraph discreetly to Hudson and return to Glenmore by the Diurnal Scot. After all, the book was not to be published till Monday, and it was still only Friday. He could ascertain from Renata when the yacht was to sail and if Hudson showed himself refractory perhaps he could travel down to London on Saturday night and wrestle with him on Sunday.

Hudson Personal 210 King Street Covent Garden
Have discovered several serious libels in your book stop strongly urge you to postpone publication until I can talk matters over with you stop please telegraph to Hudson Glenmore Hydro that you intend to take my advice which is given entirely in your interest stop consider the publication of book as it stands must involve you in very heavy damages.

Blenkinsop

It is pleasant to be able to record that Blenkinsop's journey to the north was unmarred by any incident and that, after reading *The Secret of Pomona Lodge* and finding all the damage was in the title, he was granted three or four hours of merciful sleep. It is pleasant to be able to record that Enid and her friend Tiny Houldsworth were already well on their way back to London when Blenkinsop reached Glenmore. It is less pleasant

to record that the telegram he found waiting for him at twenty
minutes to ten that Friday night was not an eager message
from Hudson to thank him for his kind advice and to tell him
that the publication of his book was postponed.

Hudson Glenmore Hydro
    Following from D.E.I.
  Major Arthur Blenkinsop must report to me at the War Office at
twelve noon on Saturday 29 November stop
    Following from N
  Do not come near Elms stop do nothing about Juno or Mr
Johnson

Blenkinsop's heart did not sink when he read this telegram. It
dived. And while it was still diving the manager presented him
with this note:

                                               Vendredi
Mon cher ami:
    It is triste that I do not see you again to make a little adieu. Be
sure that S.M. will not forget what you have done and that Renata
will not forget. We make our sailing tonight. Wish for us good
fortune.

                                      Bien à vous,
                                        R. T.

The eye of Blenkinsop's mind enjoyed a brief but lovely
vision of Renata in a blur of Buchanan tartan before he turned
to the manager.

'I want your best car and two drivers. I have to make
London by twelve o'clock tomorrow morning.'

'I do not think you can do it, Mr Hudson.'

'I must do it,' Blenkinsop insisted through clenched teeth.
'My cases will be ready in a quarter of an hour.'

With Renata's note his heart had touched bottom. It remained there; but he steeled himself to face the future like a
gentleman and a dragoon.

We will leave Blenkinsop to that wild drive southward, the
second he had made within three days, and take advantage of the
faster pen to reach London a whole day before he left Glenmore.

At eight o'clock on that fatal Friday morning, just when

Blenkinsop had sent off his telegram to Hudson and was wandering about King's Cross waiting for the Diurnal Scot to back into the platform, the telephone bell of N's flat in X— Street rang.

'I'm sorry to disturb you, sir, half an hour before your usual time,' said his man, 'but Major H. H. is on the phone and wishes to speak to you urgently.'

The Chief of the Secret Service leapt out of bed and slipping into a velvet dressing-gown went to the telephone.

'N speaking ... I can't hear you, H. H. ... what? ... what's the matter with your voice? ... it's the shock? what shock? ... no, I haven't seen any papers this morning ... what? ... everything given away? ... Yes, I'll get dressed at once and come round to The Elms ... too dangerous? ... what on earth are you talking about, H. H., ... no, I realize you can't say anything more over the telephone ... better to meet you at Number Two? ... yes, of course I'll look at the papers ... You'd better ring up Number Two and tell them to warn P that we'll be coming round at ten o'clock.'

N hung up the receiver and called for his papers. There was nothing in *The Dimes* to shed a light on the cause for Hunter-Hunt's almost inarticulate gasps. However, on opening *The Daily Tale* the first thing he read in large capital letters was:

THE SECRET OF POMONA LODGE

A THRILLING ROMANCE OF THE SECRET SERVICE

BY

YORKE LANKESTER

DO YOU WANT TO BE TAKEN BEHIND THE
SCENES OF THE UNDERWORLD OF DIPLOMACY?

IF SO READ

THE SECRET OF POMONA LODGE

A STORY OF BRITISH INTELLIGENCE
AS IT REALLY IS

Ready on Monday   *At All Booksellers and Libraries*

LOGGING AND ROLLS

7/6 net

And when with trembling hands N opened *The Daily Compress* the same shattering piece of publicity leapt at him from the printed page. He rushed to the telephone and rang up Hunter-Hunt again.

'Hullo! Hullo! Is that you, H. H.? This is N speaking. Look here, I've just seen the *Tale* and the *Compress*. I understand now what you were so upset over ... ghastly? ... I should think it was ghastly ... we may all be out of a job before the day is over ... look here, you'd better ring up all the section chiefs and warn them to keep away from The Elms ... yes, and meanwhile I'll ring up The Elms and give Garnett instructions for dealing with the staff ... I'll see you at Number Two.'

N now rang up Pomona Lodge.

'Hullo! is that The Elms? This is the head plumber speaking! Tell Sergeant-Major Garnett to speak to me ... Hullo! is that Sergeant-Major Garnett? Have you seen the papers this morning ... well, you won't have much appetite left for your breakfast when you do, Sergeant-Major ... listen to me now ... you will give orders to every member of the staff as soon as he or she arrives that they are to go home immediately ... listen, please ... and to choose the most circuitous route ... circuitous! ... roundabout! ... yes ... Tell them to exercise particular care against being followed, and if necessary to expend money on taxis ... not to spare any expense in fact ... precisely ... you will then lock up and maintain a strict watch all day, arranging for the night watch to be doubled ... members of your staff leaving this evening must take every precaution ... on no account allow anybody to enter The Elms without a paper signed by me ... the grounds should be carefully searched for infernal machines ... no, no, no, no, not bicycles ... bombs ... bombs ... b for blight o for omelette m for mud b for bacteria s for silly ... yes ... well, if you find any bombs put them in the fountain ... now, is all that perfectly clear? ... right ... yes, if you want to communicate with me ring through to Number Two after ten o'clock.'

Few people who had seen the Chief of the Secret Service walk with elastic step into the Poor Aliens Bureau that morning would have supposed that anxiety was gnawing at his vitals

more fiercely than the eagle at those of Prometheus, or that
upon his shoulders lay a weight of responsibility beside which
the burdens of Atlas, Sisyphus, and Christian were mere blad-
ders. On the other hand, those who had seen Major Hunter-
Hunt enter the portals of the Society for the Protection of
Indigent Gentlewomen would not have hesitated to suppose
that he had seduced at least half a dozen of them in the most
heartless way and was now faced with a nasty scandal in
consequence. A minute or two later when by secret doors from
Number One and Number Three both of them gained the
seclusion of Number Two the contrast between the two officers
was equally striking.

'My dear old Chief,' Hunter-Hunt gasped emotionally. 'Thank
God, you've reached here safely. I've been on tenterhooks in
every taxi I took. And by Jove, I thought I was nearly done for
once. There was a fearful explosion just as I was half-way
between the Zoo and Great Portland Street in my third taxi, but
apparently it was a burst tyre.'

'Steady, H. H., steady,' said his Chief. 'Don't let P see that
you're too much upset. Don't forget we've got the future of
M.Q. 99 (E) to consider, and that whatever happens I will not
agree to any scheme which gives the S.R.D. people any more
say than they have already in our organization. I'm going to
take a strong offensive from the very start and assume that
the S.R.D. staff-work is entirely to blame for this ghastly business.'

And it was under the influence of this resolve that, as soon as
N was inside the door of P's room and saw P himself surrounded by Grimshaw and half a dozen other S.R.D. officers, he
greeted him with these words uttered in tones that cut like
ice:

'Well, P, a nice futile mess you people seem to have made of
the safety of the realm.'

P and his officers were for the moment so much taken aback
by this offensive that they allowed both N and H. H. to arm
their noses with dark horn-rimmed spectacles before one of
them had the presence of mind even to take his own pair out
of his pocket. This tactical advantage was brief. Even without

their spectacles the S.R.D. people were soon able to assert their superiority.

'Look here, N, I'm awfully sorry about this business,' said P, 'and I can quite understand that you're feeling a bit rattled. I'm afraid, however, that the *whole* of the fault lies with your people.'

'Indeed?' N asked tensely, for there was in P's manner a hint of that compassion which seemed to argue a disquieting confidence in the S.R.D. case.

'This man calling himself Yorke Lankester is in reality William Hudson, a banana importer of King Street, Covent Garden. Last night he was in communication at King's Cross with one of your officers, Major Arthur Blenkinsop, to whom he handed two books which we have reason to suppose were copies of *The Secret of Pomona Lodge*. Major Blenkinsop under the name of Arthur Hudson gave last night at the B.B.C. what I believe is called a talk on conditions in Mendacia, and admitted to Captain Chancellor, with whom I have been in communication, that he was in fact Major Blenkinsop. Naturally I'm sorry for M.Q. 99 (E). I realize what you must all be feeling, but if ever there was a clear case for taking proceedings against a fellow under the Official Secrets Act you will allow that this is one.'

'But we don't want ... we can hardly let this case get into the police court,' N objected.

By now P had got his own dark horn-rimmed glasses firmly fixed. He leaned across the table and turned them full on his colleague. The others watched as a crowd of helpless spectators might watch the headlights of two powerful cars rushing towards each other on a narrow road.

'You seem to forget,' P flashed, 'that a case like this can always be heard in camera.'

They were N's glasses that swerved. It was N himself who was ditched by P's ruthless logic.

'What does General Westmacott say?' he called up weakly from the ditch.

'I've not been in touch with him yet; but I propose to get into touch with him now, and I anticipate he will instruct you to telegraph recalling Major Blenkinsop immediately from Glenmore. I do not know yet for certain the object of his mission; but, to be perfectly frank, N, there are indications that M.Q. 99 (E) were interfering up in Scotland with what was not their pigeon.'

This was too much for N. He was not prepared to imperil the European situation by revealing to P and half a dozen of his chatterbox subordinates the object of Blenkinsop's mission to Glenmore; but he was certainly not going to allow him to suggest that M.Q. 99 (E) were poaching on the dovecotes of the S.R.D.

'I've had a rather longer experience of hush-hush work than you, P,' he said with dignity. 'And I think I can claim to know by now what is and what is not my pigeon. If you have any doubts, I suggest you should communicate with the Foreign Office.'

'I have no liaison officer with the Foreign Office,' said P, with a touch of resentment in his tone that tasted to N like ambrosia.

'You can always communicate with the F.O. through the D.E.I.,' N reminded him. 'And though I agree with you that Blenkinsop must be recalled I am not prepared to condemn one of my officers unheard merely on evidence provided by the S.R.D.'

P grunted.

'I assume you have no objection to my inviting this man Hudson to explain how he came to publish a book which proclaims in its very title the whereabouts of your headquarters? I take it you will agree with me that, pending the arrival of Major Blenkinsop at any rate, Hudson is my pigeon.'

'You can do what you like,' said N, 'so long as you don't assume without hearing what he has to say that one of my officers is guilty of betraying the Secret Service. Meanwhile, until it is established definitely whether or not this has been one of Katzenschlosser's coups I am keeping The Elms in a state of suspension. I'll draft a telegram now to Blenkinsop. Will you be good enough to have it sent along to the D.E.I. by a confidential messenger?'

A few moments later N, having reached Number Two by 'Pab', left it by 'Spig', just as Hunter-Hunt who had reached it by 'Spig' emerged from 'Pab'. They passed one another without a sign of recognition, walking in different directions along Z— Terrace, to meet again as if by accident in the Lion House at the Zoo, which they reached by a circuitous route.

'Hullo, I haven't seen you for years, Hunter-Hunt,' N exclaimed.

'Hullo, Churchill, this is a very jolly surprise,' Hunter-Hunt cordially responded.

'What are you doing here?' N inquired.

'Oh, I'm very interested in animals,' said Hunter-Hunt.

'So am I. Have you been round the parrot-house lately?'

'No, I've not.'

'Well, let's go and have a look at them,' N suggested. 'We shan't be overheard in there,' he added in a hoarse whisper.

Amid the shrieking of parrots, parroquets, cockatoos, and macaws N discussed the situation with Hunter-Hunt.

'It's all very well for P to pretend he knew all about Glenmore, H. H. But who put him on to Katzenschlosser?'

'We did.'

'Exactly, and all the thanks we get is to suggest we were trying to poach. All the same, I'm worried. It looks to me as if Blenkinsop has been, to say the least, grossly indiscreet. And yet I wonder. You heard P say he had been in communication with Chancellor?'

'I did indeed.'

'Either Chancellor deliberately made trouble or ...'

N paused while Hunter-Hunt waited anxiously for the alternative to reach him through the demoniac shrieks of the parrot-house.

'Or,' N went on, 'P got on to our Mendacian stunt and muddled it up with one of his monthly revolutions in Scotland. Look here, H. H., if we go carefully I believe we shall be able to stymie P all right. I think so. I'll have a talk with Chancellor myself.'

'You won't forget he's married to that woman now?'

'No, no. I'll work it discreetly. Anyway, there's one thing certain. Whatever happens we shall have to give up The Elms, H. H.'

'Absolutely!'

'I think we'll look for a house in . . .'

But as they found the very house they wanted just where N proposed to look for one and as they may be in that house at this very moment, let the name of the locality be drowned in the screaming of a great blue and yellow macaw just behind the Chief of the Secret Service.

'We'll go and have a look round now, H. H.,' N went on. 'We want something to take our minds off this business until Blenkinsop arrives.'

On this quest the two of them may be discreetly left.

At Number Two P was making an attempt to get hold of Hudson. Hudson, however, was far too pleasantly occupied with the preliminaries of publication to spare the time for telephone calls. He had spent a considerable sum of money on those advertisements, which he had arranged to repeat in all the Sunday papers, and in a dream of the future he was sitting in his den at 5 The Avenue, Norbiton, reading those advertisements over and over again, and occasionally selecting from the fifty or sixty bound copies of *The Secret of Pomona Lodge* one in which he would inscribe the name of a friend. As every time he did this he would not be able to resist reading through a large portion of his fascinating romance the day went by in complete self-absorption. It was useless for P to telephone to King Street, Covent Garden. Mr Hudson had not arrived yet, and the staff of his office were unable to get into touch with him. Nor was P more successful with his publishers, Messrs Logging and Rolls, though in their case he had at least the satisfaction of being able to feel that he had put the wind up them. He did not know what an easy feat that was. He did not know that publishers from a long and bitter experience of authors' indiscretions were as susceptible to the effect of wind as a child's balloon. As for communicating directly with Hudson at his own house that seemed impenetrable except to a search warrant, and, profound though his concept for Inspector Canonbury was, P dreaded Inspector Canonbury's claim to a much wider legal knowledge than himself.

It was not until eight o'clock on that Friday evening that the lust of an amateur novelist was sufficiently sated to allow Hudson to recognize the existence of a world outside the magical world of his own creation.

'There's a gentleman has called nine times now, sir,' his parlour-maid informed him, 'and he doesn't seem to like to go away. Do you think you could see him, sir, for a minute? He keeps anyone on the hop so.'

Hudson emerged from his den and went out into the hall to behold the button-head of Major Grimshaw. Mackillop and Eccles had both contended for the glory of unmasking Hudson; but P with that superb nose of his had already sensed that the Mendacian business was some stunt of M.Q. 99 (E), and he knew that if he were to commit himself either over the Scottish rising or over Katzenschlosser he might easily lose at a stroke the advantage he now held over his colleague and rival. The main objective was to abase the pride of M.Q. 99 (E), and on that he concentrated.

Therefore Grimshaw's orders were to devote himself to the implication of Blenkinsop.

'I understand, sir,' Grimshaw began, 'that a novel of yours has been announced for publication on Monday?'

'That's right,' Hudson exclaimed gleefully. Here was the first tangible evidence of a response to the publicity which had run him well into a couple of hundred pounds already. 'That's right, have a drink? So you read about it, eh?'

'I saw the announcement, yes,' Major Grimshaw admitted stiffly.

'It was pretty striking, I think,' said Hudson. 'Well, when we all ran that combined advertisement "EAT MORE FRUIT" I saw by the extra demand for bananas that advertising does pay, and I promised myself to give my little book a chance. You haven't read it yet, of course?' Hudson's voice suddenly took on a note of childlike awe. 'Or are you a reviewer?'

(How often had he dreamed of a moment like this, dreamed of some grave scholarly form approaching him . . .

'Have I the honour of addressing the author of *The Secret of Pomona Lodge*?

'Yes, I am Yorke Lankester.'

'I am proud to meet you, Mr Lankester. I am Gerald Gould, and I want to say to you that of the several hundred thousand novels I have read since I embarked upon the arduous task of reviewing none has given me quite such a thrill as *The Secret of Pomona Lodge*. It is magnificent, Mr Lankester, really magnificent. I have devoted two columns to my review of it . . .')

'No, I am Major Grimshaw, and I represent the War Office. A copy of your book was obtained from your publishers and read by the War Office.'

Hudson was staggered. He had dreamed of unsolicited testimonials from star reviewers; but in his wildest flights of fantasy he had never dared to dream that his work would win recognition from the War Office. Could this be a preliminary to an invitation to assume the headship of the Secret Service? He waited reverently.

'And I am instructed to ask you, Mr Hudson, where you obtained the information which you have used in writing this book?'

'I worked it out for myself,' said the author modestly. 'Look here, you really must have a drink.'

'No, thanks,' Major Grimshaw replied coldly. 'I'm afraid your reply is rather vague. You say you worked it out? Could you amplify that statement?'

'Well, I write in my spare time, and I've always been interested in good spy yarns, so I thought I'd try my hand at one. I wrote *The Green-Eyed Spy*. Did you read that?'

'That is not the book under discussion. We want to know something about *The Secret of Pomona Lodge*.'

'Well, I just thought of it.'

'You had no communication with anybody you had reason to suppose was employed by the War Office on work of a highly confidential nature?'

'No, I wish I had! I say, are you a secret service man yourself? Look here, you really must have a drink. You know, I'm potty on the Secret Service. Well, I mean to say – what a life, eh?'

'You adhere to that statement, Mr Hudson? You know nobody connected with the War Office?'

'Not a soul. That's telling you straight.'

At this moment the front door opened, and Mrs Hudson, large, blonde, classically emotional, plunged into the tense scene between the button-headed S.R.D. Major and the author of the book which had imperilled the whole future of British Intelligence.

'Azzie!' exclaimed her husband. 'Good lord, where did you spring from?'

'Well, I couldn't stand it up there another hour,' she burst out. 'Well, I mean to say, nobody could. They couldn't really. I knew when you went in for all this secret service bad would come of it. Oh, I had a dreadful time at the Hydro. There were two old Scotch sisters kept poking about wherever I went, and one of them looked through the keyhole, and I heard her say to her sister I was an English spy and ought to be shot. I never spent such a night in my life as last night, and I think they tried to poison me. If they didn't, somebody else did. Only luckily I spat it out. I lay there in bed shaking all over, and I never slept a wink. Well, I mean to say, I didn't dare put out the light, and that awful Scotch tartan or whatever they call it on the walls of my bedroom seemed to be full of Bolsheviks grinning at me. You never ought to have left me like that, Will, when that Major Blenkinsop was up there doing his secret service. He may be your chief, but he's no business to ask you to expose your wife like that. So I took the first train this morning, and here I am.'

'This is Major Grimshaw, Azzie,' Hudson said, trying to wink at her a warning to be discreet.

She was impervious.

'Will, dear, I don't like them coming here. I don't really. I know you'll get the house blown up by Bolsheviks.' She turned to the visitor. 'I don't mean to be inhospitable, but if you're married, Major, you'll know what a wife feels about all this spying.'

Hudson had not been too faithful a husband, but he had never yet positively regretted his marriage. Now, as he saw himself cheated out of a confidential appointment in the Secret Service through the indiscretion of a wife, he did.

Grimshaw, who had obtained the information he wanted about Blenkinsop, at once hurried away to communicate it to P.

'Azubah,' said her husband reproachfully when he was gone, 'you've robbed me of a life's ambition this evening. If you hadn't come charging in like that talking a lot of silly nonsense about Glenmore I might have been appointed Chief of the Secret Service by the War Office. Damn bananas!'

'Will!''

'Damn bananas, I say,' he swore bitterly. 'What's the whole of my life been? Bananas. What was the guv'nor's life before mine? Bananas. What was his guv'nor's life before that? Bananas. Damn bananas, I say.'

'How much did you make out of your first book?' his wife asked.

'I didn't make any money. Nobody makes money out of their first books. It's a well-known fact.'

'How much will you make out of this new book?' she pressed.

'I might make a fortune. I've spent a couple of hundred pounds advertising it in advance. And that's the way to sell a book.'

'Where did you get the two hundred pounds from to spend?'

'From my own pocket.'

'From bananas, Will, and you know it. You think I'm just a silly woman because all this secret service business of yours upsets me. I may be. But I'm wise enough to know that other women don't want to read stories about spies. You write a nice wholesome love story and give up the Secret Service, and then you *may* make a bit of money out of writing. But you'll never make so much out of writing books as you will out of bananas. Do you suppose any of these novelists would write books if they had a good family business in bananas established over seventy years. Not they. Why, even my dear father would never have been a minister if he had come into a business like yours. The Secret of Pomona Lodge is all very well, but the secret of 210 King Street, Covent Garden and the secret of 5 The Avenue, Norbiton is much better worth keeping.'

'And what would my life be without romance?' the novelist demanded.

'What would your life be without bananas?' his wife retorted.

And the answer to this question Mrs Hudson left her husband to think out while she busied herself with the superintendence of supper.

Chapter 22

THE FATE OF POMONA LODGE

BIG BEN was striking the hour of noon as Blenkinsop drove up to the War Office in the taxi he had taken after reaching London from Glenmore in time to obey the summons of the Director of Extraordinary Intelligence. On this occasion there was no smoke-screen of orderlies to preserve his mystery, no furtive little Civil Assistant to conduct him meticulously to Sir William Westmacott's room. He came back to the building he had left not yet a month ago, full of hope, imbued with secrecy, turgid with responsibility, as a secret service officer who had failed to keep his secrecy, than which there is no more pitiable object of frustration. Blenkinsop was one with the barren queen, the sterile racehorse, the unacted playwright, the trumper of his partner's ace.

In the room of the Director of Extraordinary Intelligence were General Westmacott himself and Blenkinsop's chief. Not even for the pleasure of watching the dying agonies of an M.Q. 99 (E) officer would P endanger his anonymity by visiting the War Office in person.

'Well, Major Blenkinsop,' the D.M.I. began, 'have you anything to say?'

'You are referring, sir, to this unfortunate book advertised in the papers?' Blenkinsop asked.

'Precisely. We should welcome any explanation you can possibly offer,' replied the D.E.I. in a tone that was far from encouraging to any supposition Blenkinsop might have retained that his explanation would be of the least avail.

'Well, sir, the publication of this book came as a terrible shock to me. I have not yet had an opportunity of talking to the author about it, but I can only imagine that his choice of the title was an unfortunate accident. If I may say so, there is nothing in the book itself, a copy of which was presented to me by the author on Thursday night, which seems to have the faintest relation to the Secret Service as it really is.'

During that wild drive southward Blenkinsop had rehearsed his speech over and over again. He had muttered it to every landmark in turn between Glenmore and London. It had the quality of an apologia from the scaffold.

'What about this organization called the Black Cats?' N put in. 'Do you see no connection there with Katzenschlosser?'

'I don't think so, N. I'm sure that was equally accidental.'

'But, Major Blenkinsop,' the D.E.I. went on gravely, 'are you not asking us to stretch the long arm of coincidence a little far?'

'I admit, sir, that superficially the suspicion of my having been grossly indiscreet is strong, but I can only assure you on my word of honour that so far as I was aware Mr Hudson had no notion at all that I was in the Secret Service.'

That was another rehearsed speech.

'Wait a moment, Major Blenkinsop,' said the D.E.I. 'We have positive information from an officer of the Safety of the Realm Division that Mr Hudson's wife knew through her husband that you were in the Secret Service. In fact, she went so far as to say that you were the head of the Secret Service. What is your reply to that?'

'I believe it is true, sir, that Mr Hudson for domestic reasons did tell his wife this; but Mr Hudson himself had no idea that in telling his wife I was head of the Secret Service he was telling her what was partially true. He let this out to me as rather a good joke. Perhaps I had better explain the whole circumstances, sir?'

'Perhaps you had, Major Blenkinsop,' the D.E.I. agreed severely.

Blenkinsop thereupon related in detail the facts of his association with Hudson from the beginning, in the course of which he did not hesitate to admit the quandary into which his own domestic problems had plunged him.

'I may conclude,' he said, turning to the Chief of the Secret Service, 'by informing you that last night His Majesty the King of Mendacia accompanied by his Staff, his friend MacAdam, Herr Heisswasser, and Madame Tekta sailed from Loch Roy to make an attempt to regain the throne of Mendacia.'

The Chief of the Secret Service pondered for a while in silence the tale of the shifts and subterfuges forced upon his subordinate by the difficulties of married life.

'I am inclined, General, to accept Major Blenkinsop's explanation,' N said at last, for he had already interviewed Chancellor and from further inquiries had discovered all about the supposed Scottish rising. He had had much too wide an experience of Intelligence work really to believe Blenkinsop's explanation; but that very experience made him realize that for the sake of the future of M.Q. 99 (E) it was wiser to avoid a prosecution of Blenkinsop under the Official Secrets Act, which would only rebound to the credit of the S.R.D., and to use his knowledge of the Scottish rising as a lurking threat to the ambition of P to control all Intelligence.

'Well, if you accept it, N, I am not prepared to press the case against Major Blenkinsop,' said the D.E.I., who was remembering that he himself had originally recommended Blenkinsop for employment by M.Q. 99 (E) and who was as little anxious as N was to give P a conspicuous triumph.

'At the same time,' N continued, 'I do not see how we can possibly continue to use Major Blenkinsop's services.'

'No, I agree with you that would certainly be out of the question,' said the D.E.I.

'The expense of changing our headquarters will be considerable,' said N, 'but Hunter-Hunt and I found yesterday what looks like proving a most suitable new house, and as I understand the Government intends to create an asylum for civil servants whose minds have given way under the strain of their responsibilities, I think that if you, General, would press the suitability of Pomona Lodge in the right quarter we should then have no difficulty in securing our new house. Perhaps when Major Blenkinsop leaves us we could discuss the matter further?'

'Certainly, N, certainly,' said the D.E.I. 'Your project sounds most interesting. But what about this miserable book? Are we to make no attempt to suppress it?'

'I do not think that suppression is feasible, General, unless we proceed against Blenkinsop under the Official Secrets Act, and even then, in the lamentable state of public opinion at present, we might only end by giving the book an advertisement. Moreover, the damage is done. I think our wisest plan is to persuade the Government to start this lunatic asylum in Pomona Lodge as soon as possible. It is within the bounds of possibility that the precautions which are taken to keep the unfortunate patients secluded from the public eye will lead foreign agents to suppose that Pomona Lodge is still the headquarters of the Secret Service.'

'Yes, I like that idea,' said the D.E.I. 'That's distinctly cunning, I think. Well, now if you want to discuss the matter with me in more detail, N, I don't think we need keep Major Blenkinsop any longer. I have several letters and reports to sign, and we shall have lunchtime on us before we know where we are.'

'I'm sorry about all this, Blenkinsop,' said his late chief, 'but I'm sure you realize that it's unimaginable for you to go on working for us.'

'There are my expenses ...' Blenkinsop began.

'If you are out of pocket, I'm sure the D.E.I. will agree to make a reasonable award,' N interrupted quickly.

'But I have a good deal left out of that £250,' Blenkinsop explained.

'Send the balance to me,' said General Westmacott. 'We shall not query your expenses.'

'I had to hire several cars ...' Blenkinsop began.

'Of course! Of course! Cars exist to be hired,' said the D.E.I. 'That is perfectly understood. Well, good-bye, Blenkinsop. On the whole, I dare say we can congratulate ourselves that it wasn't worse.'

Blenkinsop retired from the War Office. He had now to face his wife at home. By the time he reached Trafalgar Square he had decided that the only thing to do was to tell Enid the whole truth, suppressing nothing except the news that he had fallen a victim like so many others to Renata's fatal charm.

Enid was fortunately alone in the service flat when the wanderer returned. Her visit to Glenmore with Tiny Houldsworth had left her with the impression that Tiny was inclined to sponge upon her friends. Moreover, that odd halfpenny in the bill of Pinches and Pinches was still rankling. She had just informed Tiny over the telephone that she had no desire to discuss Alassio with her.

'You probably think the worst of my behaviour, Enid, since that morning nearly a month ago when I told you about the bananas,' Blenkinsop opened.

'I do,' said his wife.

Nevertheless she listened in silence to his long explanation.

'I do not believe you, Arthur,' she said at the end of it. 'I do not believe you, and I shall never never trust you again, but I am willing to forgive you, and when I tell you what I have been through you will realize that in forgiving you I am making a tremendous sacrifice of my pride.'

Whereupon Enid told the story of her sufferings, culminating in that glass of St Ninian's water at Glenmore.

'You drank a whole glass of that infernal water?' he exclaimed. 'Enid, dear, I really am sorry about all this misunderstanding.'

Enid decided that this was the moment to produce Pinches' bill for forty-six pounds eleven shillings and fivepence-halfpenny.

Blenkinsop studied it for some time intently.

'I believe I could charge this to the Secret Service,' he said at last. 'They can't deny that it *is* an incidental expense. Yes, by Jove, I'll write a cheque and send them the bill receipted. After all, it's a proof that my explanation was true.'

Enid looked at him with what is called a wan smile.

'I don't believe and I never shall believe that all you say is true, Arthur,' she murmured in the gentle voice of one who has suffered too profoundly to display any more rancour, 'but if it's any satisfaction to you I will tell you that I do believe you never took the slightest interest in this Señora Miranda or Tekta.'

'I'm awfully glad you feel like that about Madame Tekta, Enid. You see, my idea was that if King Johannis pulls it off we might start again on Parvo. There's a well of most disgusting water on the island if you remember, and after your experience at Glenmore you'll appreciate what might be made of it medically.'

'Yes, Bunny,' she sighed.

Blenkinsop had never realized before the wealth of emotional significance in that inappropriate epithet. He felt that he might again embrace his wife protectively.

'I thought of tackling John about opening the hotel again if the news on the fifteenth of December were good,' he said.

And the news was good; but that is European history, and the intelligent interest which the public takes in foreign affairs makes any account of the restoration of King Johannis superfluous.

Blenkinsop was not forgotten in the loyal rejoicings. He was made a Commander of the Sacred Source, and the ribbon of *eau-de-Nil* watered silk adorns his collar at every ceremony of importance in Mendacia, where the Hotel Multum, much helped by the hospitality it was able to offer to the P.E.N. Club on one of its annual European cloudbursts, now flourishes again, the water of the Parvo well having been discovered to possess that indispensable quality of clarifying the stomach and obfuscating at the same time the brains of its devotees.

Enid was never jealous of Renata, for shortly after his recovery of the throne King Johannis made her his Queen, and a woman like Enid of sound conservative principles and impeccable military connections is never jealous of queens.

MORE ABOUT PENGUINS
AND PELICANS

Penguinews, which appears every month, contains details of all the new books issued by Penguins as they are published. From time to time it is supplemented by *Penguins in Print*, which is our complete list of almost 5,000 titles.

A specimen copy of *Penguinews* will be sent to you free on request. Please write to Dept EP, Penguin Books Ltd, Harmondsworth, Middlesex, for your copy.

In the U.S.A.: For a complete list of books available from Penguins in the United States write to Dept CS, Penguin Books, 625 Madison Avenue, New York, New York 10022.

In Canada: For a complete list of books available from Penguins in Canada write to Penguin Books Canada Ltd, 2801 John Street, Markham, Ontario L3R 1B4.